SINS

AND

BARBECUE

Keeping crime in hand...

...with huge tracks of land

The SparkleTits Chronicles

SINS

AND

BARBECUE

VERONICA R. CALISTO

This is a work of fiction. All the characters, organizations, and events within this book are products of the author's imagination and are used fictitiously. Any resemblance to business establishments, actual persons, or events is entirely coincidental. The publisher does not have any control over and does not assume any responsibility for author or third-party websites or their content.

Fickle Fox Books
Centennial, CO

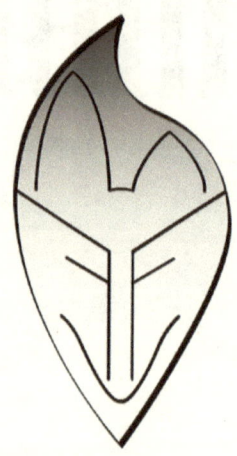

Printed in the United States of America Published by Fickle Fox Books.

DEDICATION

To everyone who's fallen under the sway of the power of hypnoboob.

1 – UPPER CRUSTY

SPENCER FIT INTO the Cherry Halls Country Club better than any criminal had the right to. The unspoken dress code of ALL THINGS BLAND AND BEIGE wasn't the half of it. He cut through the crowd with ease, whole manner molded to the environment. Touching a shoulder here. Speaking words of greeting to a couple of people there. All warmth and smiles and charm. Polite and non-intrusive.

Polar opposite to the man who'd had me kidnapped to pay for my ex's debt.

Right angle to the man I found staring at me when we worked to repair his truck. The truck I'd dropped a woman on top of. Her attempt to enslave a crowd of bystanders dispelled most of my guilt for letting her go. Most of it. Most of the time.

Guilt for damaging Spencer's truck made me show up again and again to help him repair it.

Regardless, I shouldn't have let the promise of a free meal draw me into coming with him to a fancy charity barbeque at an exclusive country club. Nor should I have kept sneaking peeks at him in his country-club costume.

Stepford chic looked good on him.

Danger, Greer Ianto. Danger.

This could not end well for me. "Do you have a minimum length of time we need to stay? Because I've got some job hunting to do." Plausible excuse.

Spencer gave me a sly, foxy grin. Like he read my mind. Or felt me watching him a little too closely.

He shook his head. "Just long enough to make the rounds, grab a little grub, and be noticed. The people auction is at the end of the event."

"The one you get to avoid with me on your arm?"

"Right."

"Even though I don't fit the dress code?" I loved my bright-orange blouse and gray skirt, but my interview best didn't feel up to snuff with these people.

Spencer's eyes bore into me and I couldn't read anything beyond the honey-brown sheen.

Couldn't read it. Felt it, though. Right down to my— "Spencer, if you tell people I'm your girlfriend or your date, you will owe me so much more than you already do. So much."

He laughed in deep delight. "Understood."

Nope. He sure didn't, but I would make certain he did when the time came. Until then, I trailed behind the man and his fine, khaki-covered rump.

A beautiful smell tickled my nose, seducing me like a scent trail in a cartoon. Smoke and meat and fat and spice. Spencer needed to move faster. Telling him would bring more focus to me than I wanted. We had another half-hour before the hunger moved into hanger territory. I'd give him the standard fifteen-minute warning.

"And who is this lovely creature cowering behind you?" someone on Spencer's other side asked.

Cowering? Creature? Oooo, I didn't like whoever this was before I swung around and found myself face to face with a large, lightly-sweating man.

"Greer, this is Preacher Edwin. He presides over at the Shepherd's House." Spencer gestured between us. "Preacher Edwin, this is my friend Greer."

Ah. Large and lightly-sweating preacher. I should not have been surprised that the head of the Shepherd's House would be intermixed with Denver's hoity-toity peoples. He sure didn't look like he hurt for money. With the number of parishioners he swindled on a weekly basis, he probably had a king's ransom stashed away. No wonder he wore a suit worth more than my car. Before it exploded.

"Nice to meet you, Preacher Edwin." I thanked everything good and unholy that Spencer didn't share my last name. It left me on a first name basis with the preacher but kept him from tracking me down.

I nodded to the woman beside him. "Who is this with you?"

She seemed to inflate when notice shifted to her. Cowed Christian

Woman. Something told me she cut though a Sunday church crowd like a shortfin mako. Not as imposing as the great white or the bull, but swifter to her prey. When she wasn't subject to the preacher's watchful eye.

"This is my wife Regina." Preacher Edwin dipped his chin in an almost gracious way.

"Hello." I waved rather than shaking their hands. They could think what they liked. I didn't want to touch either of them.

"It is good to see both of you young people out today supporting such a worthy cause." The preacher threw his shoulders back and nodded several times to us. Kind of twitchy, like we'd asked him the things rolling through my head. The preacher finished up with a thorough blotting of his sweaty forehead.

I gave a bland smile. When we got a moment, I needed to ask Spencer what charity this barbecue was for. Not sure I could support a charity that would have these two as guests.

"Absolutely," Spencer gave the preacher his fake smile, the one that crinkled skin around his eyes without sinking in. "I wouldn't miss it."

Lie. Lying to a preacher. My lips curled a bit more. This, I could watch more of.

"Glad to hear it." Preacher Edwin painted on his own fake smile. Kind of gross. A soggy, cold French fry grease oozing down my back, kind of feeling. "Well, I see some elders of the church I need to speak to, but I will see you at the auction?"

Spencer shrugged in an easy motion. "Not this year, I'm afraid."

I patted his shoulder because it seemed the thing to do.

The preacher fake frowned. This, at least, felt tongue-in-cheek. He even slumped his shoulders over. "That is unfortunate to hear. You brought in quite the pretty penny last year."

His act on the pulpit had to be better than this to syphon so much money out of his stadium-sized congregation. Even as the two men bantered back and forth, I couldn't quite find what drew people to this sweaty, slime-ish man.

"Well," Preacher Edwin finally said, ribbon of sweat careening down the bridge of his nose, "I really must go speak to my man. Big things coming up Sunday. Will I see you there?"

Spencer shook his head. "I am not a Zion, Preacher, you know that. I prefer quieter worship with a little more ritual."

Worship. Huh. I thought criminals only worshipped the mean, mean, mean-green, all-mighty dollar.

"The unshakable Catholic." He patted Spencer's shoulder on the opposite side from me, then shifted his gaze to me. "And you?"

"Baruch atah Adonai." Usurping Hebrew solely for my own benefit, terrible. But people tended to let faithful Jews be.

Good people did.

In America.

Nowadays, at least.

"Jesus watches over you as well. Okay. The church elder is waving me over, so I really must go. It was nice to see you, to meet you, and I hope to welcome you both on Sunday." He dipped his chin in a way he probably thought was magnanimous.

It came across as superior and a little insulting. If he hadn't started on his way, I might have dressed him down like he deserved.

Guh.

"Church elder," Spencer scoffed when Preacher Edwin had moved out of earshot. "Right."

I geared Spencer in the direction of the food again. "What's that supposed to mean?"

Spencer rubbed the side of his nose and gave me a knowing look.

Only I didn't know what he meant. "Huh?"

"Booger sugar."

Ding! There we went. "Drugs would explain all the sweating."

"Notice that, did you?" Some sort of sly thought narrowed his eyes before he looked away to navigate through some half-occupied tables. "Jewish, huh?"

"Nope. Most people don't try to *save* Jews." Since he asked, though, I could too. "Catholic, huh?"

"Lapsed, but yes."

Odd. Of all religions, Catholicism should have convinced him to ride the straight and narrow. Unless he was in the mafia. Hmm. Something to contemplate over my plate of charred meats.

"So glad you made it, son." A voice I recognized spoke before he stepped in our path to the promised land of burger and chicken. Senator Marcus.

Balls.

The valet had called Spencer, Mr. Marcus. I should have connected the dots. But it was a common enough name. Spencer and the man who acted a fool at the reading of a last will didn't have to be related. Didn't have to be father and son.

But of course they were. Because Murphy's Law and reasons.

His father continued with, "And only a half hour late."

Condescending little shit.

"Rearranging my schedule fell into place easier than I'd allotted for," Spencer took his father's jab with more grace than I would have.

Of course, I had a strong distaste for the man, so my reaction might have been a little skewed. Petty? Me? Never. "Hello, Senator Marcus."

The senator's jerking cringe, lip snarl, then forced smile made this whole thing worth it. Ruining his day made mine.

"Miss Greer Ianto. How lovely to see you again."

His "lovely" sounded anything but. Win for me, but my name on his lips struck like a slap on a sunburn. A draw, then. I nodded to him, hoping against hope that this barbeque was not a fundraiser for him. I would flat-out refuse to eat. Even if, as the guest of his son, I didn't pay a dime.

Senator Marcus tried to stare me down, like Jack trying to stare down the beanstalk. Despite what he seemed to think, he could not intimidate me into conversing more with him. I kept my lip zipped.

"Okay, Dad, well, we're going to hit the food line and mingle around a bit before we go."

"Go?" That pulled the senator's focus back to his son. "The auction doesn't start until 2:00."

Spencer shrugged. "I told you I couldn't be on the block. I'm not exactly in a position to accept dates from other women."

The senator looked like giant slugs would ooze out of his mouth.

Delicious.

"I will go remove your name, then. Unless the both of you will offer yourselves up." He widened his eyes. "It *is* for battered women."

Ah. That's what we were here for, though I hated that term. Battered women. Shell shocked would be a better term. Abused and riddled with

PTSD.

Survivors.

"I'll drive up some of the silent auction items to make up for it."

Senator Marcus nodded. "Very good. Will I see you tonight, son?"

Spencer looked at me.

Not certain of what he wanted me to say, I blinked and tilted my head slightly off kilter.

When Spencer turned back toward his father, he answered, "We'll see."

The senator retreated. I wished it was back into the stinking depths from whence he came, but he just sauntered his way toward a pavilion of official-looking tables.

Spencer waited until my plate was half full to ask how I knew his father. Smart man. I paused a moment, using a nod to the man serving macaroni to give myself time to figure out how to say it without offense. Best to investigate first.

"How much do you like your father?" I murmured it to him, just in case. Hungry ears lived everywhere.

"He is the most conniving, manipulative, cold-hearted, back-stabbing, slimy, out for himself and only himself, person I've ever met." He whispered the words, though the last bits came out in snake-like hisses. Sir Hiss in the flesh.

Considering how Spencer and I met, I could have mentioned something about the acorn not bouncing too far from the oak, but it would be a lie. While I didn't know much about Spencer's dealings, there was a kind of honesty to them. Service or something offered for a price. Terrible price, but a definite give and take. The honor of piracy compared to the backhanded dealings of the constabulary.

Spencer, The Pirate King.

"Okay," I moved to the mashed potatoes. "Your father balked at the five thousand dollars Gabe left him in his will."

"Gabe?"

Right. Most people didn't call my old friend and mentor by anything other than his full name. "Gabriel Jones."

Gears turned behind Spencer's calm expression. "Dad said he didn't get anything. That some trumped-up strumpet swooped in and cashed in...that was you."

Strumpet? Wow.

I almost wanted a shirt with the word. "Yes and no to all of that. Gabe had a clause that denied your father his portion when he complained about the sum." I couldn't help my smile at that. Gabe. Poking at people from beyond the grave. That man. "The 5k went to Gabe's favorite charity."

Spencer lifted a suggestive eyebrow as he guided us toward the tables. "As far as the strumpet part of his story?"

Kind of annoying. Completely insulting. "Because a man and a woman can't possibly be non-benefit friends unless one or both of them was gay?" I sniffed, rolled my eyes, and headed toward a mostly empty table.

Two women on the far side. One in a divine red dress. After all the beige, my eyes needed the beauty even if the women were too locked in conversation to notice us. Especially if they didn't notice. I'd already had my fill of the people here. Almost. Spencer's unbroken surveillance was pushing me to the edge with him as well.

He waited for me to get situated to ask, "Well?"

"What?" But, no. He'd asked me a question. Funny how quick I forgot questions I didn't want to answer. "I've known Gabe since I was a teenager. He helped me through some things."

"Like what kind of things?"

Nope. I forced my eyes down so Spencer didn't see my knee-jerk anger. "Don't want to talk about it." Least of all with him.

Heavy, weighted silence. His gaze, a torch on my face though I hadn't looked up to confirm. The chicken in me wanted to keep watching my plate, in case of accidents or something. I hated how often the chicken wore my skin.

I forced my gaze up to his surprisingly open one. Granted, the man had control over his expression that a statue would envy, but this felt genuine. I couldn't pinpoint exactly what the difference was. Extra sheen to the honey of his eyes or a wider pupil. Maybe both. Whatever it was, the man had let his walls slip the tiniest bit.

"Why don't you want to talk about it?"

Not the least because he kept pressing to know more about me while I repeatedly refused learn more about him. And telling him that would shatter the relatively easy rapport we had. Despite his criminal entanglements, I kind of liked Spencer. Shit.

So, I strove for answers he wouldn't interpret as attacks. "I'd like to keep my appetite."

My answer set off the Deep Thought analysis in the back of his eyes. Perhaps I'd given more away by not talking. Perhaps he was a superhero who'd slipped though the union's notice and had begun sifting through all my deepest, darkest secrets. Perhaps I needed to leave before anything like that happened.

"Greer?" The red-clad woman across the table asked.

I thanked the gods and leprechauns for the distraction. "Yes?"

Wait

I knew the woman.

Her face had creased a bit over the years, and her hair had salted more than a little, but Fiona Appleby sat across the table from me. A bright spot plucked right out of the memories I wouldn't share with Spencer.

"That *is* you." She stood and came around the table.

I set my fork down and stood to meet her.

Because she knew everything—everything—about my past, she waited for me to hug her. Giving me the choice. One of the reasons people like me could open up to her.

Fiona wasn't a rich man's wife who decided to take up a cause to fill her days. She survived her own battle with her husband. When she got out, she took up the fight to help all women get out of their unsafe situations and build new lives on solid ground.

She still smelled the same, despite the expensive-looking dress. Touch of pine cleaner under laundry detergent.

"How have you been?" she asked. Standard question with more than the standard weight.

Her, I could answer.

I tipped my head back and forth. "A little wobbly since Gabe's passing." And my car exploding in my face. And the zombies who weren't zombies because starfish-people existed and had those kinds of powers. What was next? Magic kittens who combined to form a giant robot kitten?

Yeah, no, I might have been a lot wobbly. But I couldn't speak those things in public.

Fiona nodded. "Understandable. He was a good friend."

He was.

"Well," she straightened her shoulders. "I don't want to take up all of your time. I just wanted to say hello."

I nodded back, then an idea struck me. "Hey, Fiona. The things with Gabe's estate don't settle until the end of the month. If I went for something at the silent auction, would I be able to wait until then to pay?" Because I would contribute some ridiculous sum to this fundraiser now that I knew the driving force behind it.

A surprised grin lit her face up. "You don't have to buy anything, of course, but I will certainly let them know of your circumstances."

Good. "Excellent."

Fiona bustled away with all the energy I remembered from decades ago. The other woman at the table looked like she got sucked into Fiona's wake. Since Fiona probably had seventeen thousand things to do, this woman would need to learn to swim quick or drown.

I sat back down in a bit of a fog. Fiona had that effect. I shoved food in my face with a lighter heart.

Spencer dragged me back down with, "Do you know everyone here?"

I shook my head without looking his way.

"So, just the most important ones?"

As I hadn't paid much attention to other people, outside the three conversations, I couldn't answer him. So, I didn't.

"You really don't want to tell me anything about you, do you?"

That jerked my head to him. "Seriously? You know things about me that are officially classified because they pertain to the other classified events you should also know nothing about and you are throwing a hissy fit because I won't tell you about one thing?"

"Two things."

"One thing. Now, leave it the fuck alone." I dropped my fork on the table and stood up. All that lovely food and I'd lost my appetite. Balls. "I'm going to check on the silent auction."

2 – REVERSE HUT

WALKING AWAY PISSED me off more than Spencer's probing. Undoubtedly, the escape gave more away than I intended. Balls. To keep from killing him in front of so many influential witnesses, though, I needed breathing room. Another distraction wouldn't hurt.

The pavilion with the tables that Senator Marcus had hurried to only had information for auctioning off people. One of the women asked if I wished to add myself to the list. The sourpuss reactions from the blue hairs on either side of her nearly convinced me to accept, just to spite them. Volunteering to be auctioned off in any capacity stuck in my craw. Too much like a slave auction.

With a polite decline, the three were more than happy to usher me toward the silent auction in the clubhouse itself. Granted, the blue hairs curled their lips in smug satisfaction as they did. Like they simply *knew* I wouldn't be able to afford a thing there. In that, I could spite them.

A double horseshoe of tables sat in the center of the entry way. Few of the tables had anything more than cards with framed pictures standing behind them.

The yacht and powerboat combo in the first picture and crown-jewel worthy earrings in the second, told me what I needed to know about this group of items. All of it was crap I didn't need. Beautiful and nearly priceless crap, but crap.

I thanked my stars when I saw the arrow to another room with more items up for purchase. Spencer strolled past the sign on his way to me.

His shoulders remained straight and his stride easy, but his lips pinched flat as he studied me.

Cautious, but not a beaten dog.

I set my feet in a wide stance. Just in case. Still, I waited for him to get close enough for our conversation to be a private one.

"Spencer, I left the table to give myself cool-off time."

He splayed his fingers, palms up and toward me. "I hear you. As soon as you left, a swarm of people surrounded me."

Maybe he deserved to be stung repeatedly. I folded my arms.

"Yeah, you're probably right." He looked to either side of us under the guise of stretching his neck. No one in a twenty-foot radius of us. "If I keep my mouth shut will you let me follow close enough to scare the vultures away?"

I scoffed. "Scare them away? How exactly would I do that?"

"Between your, um," he fake-coughed, "statuesque form and your directness, no one wants to mess with you. Someone spread a rumor about you telling my father off in public, forcing him to back down."

Spencer smiled a little at that. He probably wished he could have been there to see it.

"I can confirm that rumor is true."

That brought the smile into full bloom. "Do you mind if I ask why?"

Asking permission rather than demanding. That, I could deal with. And it wasn't my big button issue. "Hours after complaining his way out of the money he would have inherited from Gabe, because it wasn't enough, he asked me to come to his fundraiser and contribute to his campaign. Asked me at the funeral reception."

Spencer's smile shriveled into a snarl. "I'm not surprised."

"The rumor left out some details, didn't it?"

He nodded.

Color me not-surprised. The ass. "Okay, Spencer. If you stuff it, you can come on, but remember: I don't care how any of these people see me, or you."

Analysis face took over. Spencer caught exactly what I intended.

I headed to the other room, him dragging silently behind me.

This smaller room had more tables packed in. Some of the items sitting on the display tables, under the watchful eye of a security guard seated near the door.

Smaller pieces of jewelry. Pilot lessons. Resort Spa packages. Skiing and sailing and snorkeling adventures. Oh my! Everything sounded good. I raised the bids by twenty dollars on most of the things as I passed by.

Several new cars and very old cars were also on the block. Bidding wars had sprung up on the Shelby something-or-other and the nineteen-something-something GTO. Not my bag, though they were pretty. I upped the bid on both by the same two thousand the other bidders had, hoping to heavens everyone out bid me.

The Tesla, however, with all its bells and whistles. That car, I could drive. The bids so far hadn't stretched past the car's commercial price point. It was past noon, and the barbeque was only supposed to last until three. If I did this right, no one would care to bid against me before the auction closed.

Eyes closed, I took a deep breath, filtered through the figures the lawyers and accountants had rolled past me. More than I'd ever expected to have. More than enough for several lifetimes. I opened my eyes and bumped the bid by thirty thousand.

An impressed grunt puffed out of Spencer.

I didn't want to know, not really, but my gaze shifted to him with his furrowed brow and otherwise unmoved face. "What?"

"The others were play." He jerked his chin toward the list of specs on the Tesla. "You want that one."

"I'd like that one, yes. If I don't get it, I'd like it to sell for as high a price as possible." Infuriating man. I wished he didn't see me so clearly. I crossed my arms to keep myself from poking him in the chest. "This does not get you out of taking me car shopping."

He blinked, finally knocked a little off-kilter. "When did we decide I'm taking you car shopping?"

"You owe me for coming here with you, if you remember. You know about cars. My car died an untimely, explode-y death." I shrugged like it had already been decided. Because it had.

"We could fix yours."

"When I say it explode-y, I mean just that. Like bomb go boom-boom." In my face, but he didn't need to know that. I expanded my hands outward in the event my words didn't sink in this time.

"Right, right." He nodded, but his attention had already shifted to something behind me.

What? I wasn't important enough to pay attention to? After he practically begged me to save him by pretending to be his girl? I would never be his imaginary girlfriend again.

"Ms. Appleby," Spencer nodded. "Hello again."

I turned around to face her as she answered.

"Hello, Mr. Marcus."

Weird hearing Spencer called by the same name as his father. None of Spencer's minions called him by last name. I wondered if they knew who he was in the light of day, but I filed that away for later. Fiona looked awful.

Pale. Slightly green. Trembling. Beads of sweat forming across the whole width of her forehead. What could have happened to her in the last half hour, I couldn't hazard a guess. Something extreme-ish.

I stepped toward her, hands out and non-threatening. We knew each other well enough not to fear one another, but wounded-animal reflexes were always unpredictable. "Are you okay, Fiona?"

Of course I asked the most asinine question. The answer was clear, but I would not intrude uninvited.

She started to shake her head and stopped to set her feet a tad wider. I knew that move. The scary kind of dizziness where any movement, especially of the head, made it worse. Dizziness or nausea.

Either way, less movement was more.

"Spencer, go grab that chair from the guard."

He darted across the room without a question, which allowed me to focus on Fiona. "Okay. So, we're going to get you a seat, then maybe a little water to cool your brow down. Okay?"

"O—" Her body clenched with her mouth open and let loose.

Chunky splatter all down the front of me. From nipple height down, as Fiona bent over with the force of it. I froze. Locked between disgust and anger and shock and worry. Disangshory.

Fiona dropped to her knees, arms wrapped around her middle and moaned. I wanted to reach out and comfort her. I couldn't figure a way to move without making things worse.

When she sunk down to lie on her side, my situation didn't matter.

I missed her next plume of puke by happenstance. I'd walked around to support her head from the top while she heaved. I knelt in the safer zone near the top of her head.

A chair dropped to its side somewhere near me. I turned my head in time to see Spencer running the other way. Coward.

The guard near the door stood dumbfounded.

Useless piece of— "Hey you! Dial 911!"

He blinked out of his stupor and pulled his phone off from his belt. With him in productive motion, I dismissed him from my focus.

Fiona needed to be moved into the recovery position, but her arms were clutched too tightly around her stomach. I lifted her head from the ground to something vaguely level. I didn't know how long I could hold her this way, but I would do my damnedest.

Footsteps stamped toward me. I looked up.

Spencer. Not a coward after all. He had a huge first aid kit in one hand, an AED in the other, and his shoulder pinching his phone to his ear. "Hold on, here's the woman tending to her." He set the bags down near Fiona's back and pressed the phone against my ear.

"Who am I speaking to?" the woman on the other end asked.

I told Spencer to grab something to clean up Fiona before cradling the phone in the crook of my neck and giving the dispatcher the run down. "How long have we got until an ambulance arrives?"

"The first should be there within the next two minutes. The closest of the rest are at least five-to-seven minutes behind."

I knew richer people of this world held privileges the rest of us only dreamed of, and all, but multiple trucks for one sick woman was overkill. "How many are coming?"

"From the gathered information, of the twenty-odd people affected so far, Fiona Appleby is the worst off, so she'll be treated first."

Twenty people. Shit. This was beginning to feel a little familiar.

Except I knew the woman who'd caused the ruckus the at Lex's art show was dead.

Possibly still walking around, but dead.

Fiona's head jerked out of my grasp. Her whole body convulsed. I scooped Spencer's phone up and over my shoulder with my chin before lunging to grab a tighter hold of Fiona's head. I couldn't let her get whiplash or bang her head against something nearby. At the same time, I yelled what was going on in the hopes Spencer's phone hadn't died when it hit the floor behind me.

I didn't get a good hold of Fiona's head until she jerked to a stop.

A bottle of clear booze sank down into my field of view.

"I have water, too, but thought this might be more effective," Spencer said, and gestured to Fiona with the bottle. "More sterile."

Not a bad thought.

"Could you clean up around her mouth and see if she's still breathing?"

Spencer knelt beside me and poured the booze in a clear stream across Fiona's lips. A not-quite-gentle couple of swipes with a napkin did the trick. Then he held the flat side of the bottle a short space in front of her nose and mouth.

Looking at him from this close was a little disconcerting. At least the mess down the front of me would keep him from trying to move a little closer. "What are you doing?"

"I don't have a mirror." He shrugged without looking at me. His eyes stayed steady on the surface of the bottle. The shiny surface that remained shiny without periodic fogging from exhalation. "Greer."

I knew. I saw it too. "Help me flip her onto her back."

Spencer swept the first aid kit and AED out of the way. I swung the other way, around Fiona's front. The cooling goo sucked around my knees. No matter. I was already a mess.

We eased her onto her back. She looked worse. More flushed, now, instead of the pale and green that had first alarmed me, but she wasn't breathing.

I tipped my head up toward Spencer. "Pumping or breaths?"

He looked at the mess down the front of Fiona's dress and to her relatively clean mouth. I took the position and started pumping. I'd made it to pump twelve when EMTs burst into the room. Spencer looked as relieved as I felt. I happily scooted out of the way for more expert hands.

They didn't balk at kneeling in the mess.

I settled with my back against the nearest wall and breathed while the men tried to resuscitate Fiona. Pushing my eyes closed didn't shut out the sounds of them fighting a losing battle. Tracheotomy. Steroids and fluids. Lifting her onto the cart then using the defibrillator.

Their exit with her felt too rushed and like nowhere near enough.

New EMT's came in, replacing the first couple. These two made a bee line for us. Me on the floor and Spencer leaning against the wall next to me.

"Do you need assistance?"

"I'm fine," I waved them away. "Just covered in Fiona's cooling puke."

They kept coming, so I used the wall to edge my way back up before they made it to me. I held my tongue as the woman flashed my eyes with the light and checked my pulse. When she grabbed for another tool, I spoke up.

"Seriously. Other people need your services more." I kept my hands to myself. It was all I could manage.

The EMT blinked at me a couple times, but she nodded. "You stay right here and someone will be back to check on you."

I saluted my agreement. The EMTs headed out. I stared at the over turned chair a body length away from the mess that Fiona had made. As much as I wanted to sink down into it, the chair deserved more than to be soaked with vomit. So, I stood and waited for other EMTs to tell me I could leave.

New uniforms came in to talk to us. Police officers this time. Their carefully pleasant expressions slipped some when their noses twitched.

They'd caught a whiff of what I'd stopped smelling a while ago. If I didn't look down and I ignored the stickiness of my clothes to me, I could pretend nothing happened.

"Hello, I'm Officer McKinney this is Officer Matuschek." The brown-eyed, blond officer indicated the blue-eyed blond with a tilt of his head. "May I get your names?"

Spencer gave his without any tension while I tried to work my brain through the officers' politeness. Not demanding, but rather asking for information. Must be the country club effect.

I shook my head and answered. "Greer Ianto."

"Very well, Mr. Marcus, Ms. Ianto, did you know the deceased?"

My skin constricted all over me.

"Fiona died?" I knew she might be going that way, but...

The officer's nod crushed the hope that they might save her. I closed my eyes to let it sink in. "Shit."

"I know this may be a hard time, but I need to ask you how you knew the...Ms. Appleby."

So much for not having to talk about this today. I forced my head up and my eyes open. "Case file 98AR558290."

Officer McKinney's lips turned down the barest bit. Considering he was supposed to have his cop face on, his full reaction was probably much larger. "Can you give me a little more detail?"

"Let me get this straight, McKinney." I pushed myself from the wall to stand on my own two feet. I hoped my movement gave him a big whiff of what I was covered in. "You are well aware of the work that Fiona does, as her organization works with the all of Denver metro area's police departments, but you want me to relive the thing that brought

Fiona and I into contact because you don't want to look up the case file?"

His mouth puckered as I spoke. Probably didn't appreciate my tone. For his lack of professionalism, he could suck it the fuck up. It wouldn't surprise me if police and lawyers in Colorado studied my case. My situation hadn't been a quiet one.

Officer Matuschek took up the conversation before McKinney could stick his foot in his mouth again. "That is fine, Ms. Ianto. We will certainly look that up if we have any questions. Can you tell me what happened this afternoon?"

That, I would tell them.

Fiona wasn't a friend, exactly. With all she'd done for me, though, she deserved to have people investigate what happened. Perhaps it was just my up-close-and-personal view of Fiona in the end, but that kind of violent, rapid death didn't feel natural. Not like Oak Express.

McKinney took Spencer to the side to question him. I would have felt more insulted, if the division wasn't standard practice. We weren't married, so we needed to be split up and questioned to look for inconsistencies.

Officer Matuschek frowned the whole way through my story. Not increasingly, just the kind of good, solid frown a girl could count on.

When he had everything out of me, he clipped his pin to his clipboard. A digital recorder would have been more efficient. But they cost more money than pen and paper. Easier to skip ahead on paper too, no matter that it made questioning take so much longer.

"Okay, Ms. Ianto," Matuschek finally nodded to me. "I'm going to have a forensics team come and collect samples from your hands, knees, and anywhere else you may have touched her. They will also collect all of your clothes and take samples from the skin underneath."

I let out a slow breath. "That's going to be a bit of a problem for me. The whole naked thing."

The officer smiled at me like it might smooth things over. "Don't you worry. I'll make sure the forensics people who tend to you are women. They will give you some of our standard issue sweats to wear home."

If only a simple fear of exposing myself to strange men fueled my rejection.

I needed to call Magus.

3 – PHONE A FRIEND

TOO MUCH OF Fiona's puke covered my hands to reach into the top of my blouse for my phone. I wanted to keep as much of me free of the goop as humanly possible. "Officer Matuschek, I'm going to need to make a phone call about that."

He gave me a long blink. "You cannot refuse to give physical evidence."

I wasn't so sure about that, but not the time to argue. "Giving the evidence is not the problem."

"Then what is?"

I pressed my lips together as I considered how to answer. "I'm not sure how much you're allowed to know about that."

Furrowed forehead. Officer Matuschek really didn't like that answer. I supposed asking him to grab my phone and make the call would be too much. I turned toward Spencer. "Hey, Spencer, I have a big favor to ask of you."

He sauntered back over, hands in his pockets and big smile on his face. "Something to make us even?"

"I have vomit all over me and you think a quick favor could make us even?" I squinted at him and jutted my head forward a bit.

"You're right." He held his hands up. "Completely right."

Damned straight, I was. "You owe me so big for this."

Something in him changed. Cold, stillness settled over his face. Like he'd shifted suddenly from bright oranges and reds to a dark, midnight blue. This was the man I'd met when his goons kidnapped me. This was a good part of the reason I would not invite him deeper into my life or secrets, despite his interest.

Dropping the affable veil to reveal the criminal underneath in front of the policemen was not the smartest thing. But it wasn't my life.

"How much?" He asked, cool and collected. Another deal with another business associate.

Knowing Spencer liked me allowed me to blaze on without reacting to the darkness of him. "No, no, no. This is not something money can fix. You're already taking me car shopping."

"Right." Slight thaw.

"I think you're going to need to teach me how to drive a stick. Maybe something else as well, but I can't think of anything right now."

He blinked in surprise, the chill in him crumbling around the edges.

I pointed my finger at—not in—his face before he could respond.

"And if you say anything suggestive about *your* stick I'm going to remind you of how sexy this is." I Vanna White-d the front of my ruined clothes.

The cops watched us without a word. They most certainly were taking mental notes. I hoped their impression of Spencer's attitude shift was not admissible in any kind of court system.

"You win." When Spencer said it, none of his chill remained.

I won and I lost at the same time. Dwelling on it did me no good. "Now that that's settled, I need you to grab my phone and call Magus."

Spencer frowned. "What?"

After flashing my still filthy hands, I let them hang at my sides. "My phone's still clean and I want to keep it that way."

"Makes sense. Where's your phone?"

I pointed to the left cup of my bra.

He laughed and shook his head. "You're shitting me, right?"

I wished. "Don't make this worse than it already is. My collar is too high to get the phone from the top, so you'll need to go through the sleeve hole."

Two women headed our way from the doorway while Spencer froze like a deer in the road. Time to handle this politely was slipping through his hesitating fingers.

"Hurry it up, before I give you a big hug and we both need the strip search treatment."

Spencer watched my face the whole time the fingers of his right hand slipped under my short sleeve. Right hand meant I got the nails rather than the finger pads. Good choice on his part. It meant no accidental grabs. It didn't take him long to make contact with the phone. He tugged too gently to dislodge it.

I sighed. His care to keep from offending me was wasting precious time. "Take a good hold of the phone and pull. Neither one of us will break."

Eye contact of a saint—or sociopath—Spencer pulled the phone free. He smiled as he unlocked the screen. Apparently, he remembered the code from the first time I'd given it to him. When he had me kidnapped.

The man was observant. And remembered way too much about me.

I didn't like his expression, though. I waited until he set the ringing phone against my ear to ask, "What's that smile for?"

"Nothing."

I lifted a brow in question.

"The phone's pretty warm." Shark-tooth smile, like an old cartoon. Unabashed. He wasn't just drawn that way. He actually was bad.

Boobs were warm. Things pressed against them warmed up too. Why did that surprise people? I opened my mouth and Spencer's smile sharpened. Did I want to poke that sleeping dragon? Magus picked up the other line, saving me.

"Greer."

"Hi, Magus. Sorry if I'm interrupting something, but Fiona Appleby threw up on me at her fundraiser, then died so the police want to take my clothes into evidence, but I have that, you know, situation."

Three beats of silence. Then, "Where are you?"

He hadn't dismissed me out of hand. Huzzah for me. Especially since the officers muttered back and forth with the crime scene chicks. Thought bubbles and angry letters practically brewed above them.

"I'm in the Cherry Halls Country Club. Like in the actual clubhouse.

There's a big shindig here today, but the silent auction was inside, which is where I was—the room to the side, not the one where someone is selling a yacht—when Fiona came in and exploded. Not literally, but gastrically. I'm going to shut up now."

Shit. What was wrong with me? Perhaps the smell and watching a person die in agony affected me more than I knew.

"I am not surprised you're in the thick of things again. Hold on a moment."

The line went quiet, save for the three low beeps periodically letting me know I hadn't been abandoned. I lifted my gaze up to Spencer who was, shockingly, analyzing my expression. If I told him to take a picture he'd take it as an invitation

When he lifted his left eyebrow, I shrugged.

I didn't know if Magus would help me. I had to believe that, though I wasn't a part of the union, I was helpful enough a commodity to keep my powers semi-secret.

Magus', "Greer," brought my attention back.

"Yes?"

"Bolt is on his way to forestall the police."

Ugh. Bolt. Not my favorite person, nor my favorite superhero. "This can't be handled by me handing the phone to one of the officers?" I hoped, even though I knew Magus wouldn't send one of his men out for no reason.

"The evidence must be collected by someone trained and certified in its collection. Kai is on the way as well, but Bolt will be there quick enough to keep the police from pressuring you."

The mention of Kai shifted my discomforts some. I loved him, I did, but a few nights of sex had left our relationship in an odd place. My day long, post-climax coma weirded Kai out more each time.

The day I'd woken to find him completely under sway of my hypnoboob hadn't helped.

He knew the blanket slipping down to my waist and freezing him for hours was not my fault. He'd pissed himself at some point. I apologized, but it didn't fix things. And I got it. Having hours of his life stolen, even on accident. I'd have backed away from me too.

Perhaps it was for the best. I hadn't wanted that kind of relationship with him in the first place. Just a way to let off steam. Now, I had double the frustration and some officers consulting with crime scene chicks about what to do with me. I almost wished the group of them would try something.

Fighting could be a fun outlet too.

The lights in the room flickered a few seconds before Bolt made his entrance. Neet effect. Kind of.

"Here's Bolt now," I told Magus, rather than insult the man who'd come to my rescue.

"Very good. If that's all—"

"Just a quick thing," I blurted, trying my best to catch him before he hung up.

"Yes."

"First, thank you. Second, not that I want to keep calling in the big guns all the time, but if things like this keep happening, it might be easier for you if I got the number for the hotline, so I don't have to call you directly."

Silence on the other end again. Long enough for me to think I'd lost him, but he answered just as Bolt made it to the group of us. "I will consider it."

My phone signaled the end of the call. Oh well. I'd tried.

I nodded to Spencer before turning my head toward the new arrival. "Hey, Bolt."

Two of the four law enforcement people, one officer and one crime scene chick, turned to confirm Bolt had, indeed, joined us. Almost like they'd decided who would look away when a distraction came to the door.

McKinney straightened as he greeted the superhero amongst us. "Hello, Bolt." He probably hadn't believed I'd actually called Magus. He could suck it.

"Officer. Officer." Bolt nodded to both and gave the crime scene specialists nods as well. Spencer seemed to be a non-entity in Bolt's mind. I doubted Spencer cared about the lack of attention. The more someone marked him the easier they could narc on him.

Bolt took me in with a quick, assessing glance and asked, "What seems to be the trouble?"

Was that a smile?

Was that rat-bastard smiling at what was cooling and crusting on me?

"Ms. Ianto's refusing to turn over the evidence in her possession."

In my possession aka: all over me. They had a way with false words. "Nope. They can take samples from my hands and knees. They can have the shoes too. But they can't be the ones to take the clothes off me, or watch me as I do."

He dipped his chin a couple of times. Then, "How much control?"

Vague McVaguerson, but that kind of thing was the only way to keep my secrets close to my chest. He probably had practice in that sort of thing. Getting better at it wouldn't be the worst idea for me.

Still, it made it hard to answer. He already knew the power of my hypnoboob over him had been complete. I took a stab at answering the other probable question. "Me? None."

He nodded like I'd only confirmed suspicions. Which was fine. I knew some of his secrets. He could know one of mine.

Bolt turned toward the four law enforcement personnel. "Please feel free to take as many samples from hands and knees, as she said. The front of her dress would also work well. We have our own investigator coming to facilitate the removal of clothing, which he will pass on to you, if that is your wish."

The officers didn't look thrilled to have another agency stepping on their toes. They could deal. A person wouldn't remain in crusting clothes without an important reason.

Thankfully, the officers took Bolt at his word.

Swipes and swabs later, my hands felt a little less disgusting. Of course, cleaning the mess rehydrated the goop and brought forth a wave of sour stench I hadn't been ready for. The chemicals they used made it worse. I turned my face away and practiced shallow breathing so I didn't add to the samples they needed to collect.

By the time they'd finished with my knees, a familiar voice called my name.

"In here, Kai!" Just follow the wave of funk and nausea.

His nostrils flared when he hit the event horizon, but he didn't stop dragging his waist-high case toward us. "Are you the only...victim?" He gestured up and down the front of him, then did the same to me.

"Me and my dignity." I mumbled.

Not quite softly enough. Spencer burst out laughing.

I jabbed a finger toward him. "Do you want a hug right now? Because I feel like sharing."

Eyes glistening, he held up his hands, my phone still in his right.

Kai cast a quick dismissive glare Spencer's way as he tipped his case back to vertical.

Eyes darting between Kai and I, Spencer's expression sobered quite a bit. Slight amusement still frosted his lips, but he'd grown more watchful. Of course, it was too much to ask that Spencer miss Kai's reaction. He paid way too much attention to people.

Just what I needed.

"I am going to set up three stations for you." Kai popped the clasps on his case open. "Similar to a hazmat clean up, but not as extreme."

Such was my life. "Whatever you say."

I would have protested more if he'd told me from the get-go that the "stations" on the ends relied on someone holding up a rubber tarp to protect the rest of the room from me.

Behind curtain number one, a shallow silicone disk basin for me to peel my things into and some damp wipes to get the crunchy bits off. Station number two looked like a wide brimmed cauldron for me to climb into and scrub under a manpowered faucet. A circlet of shower curtain hid this process from the rest of the room. The last rubber tarp hid an absorbent towel and new, clean clothes to cover me.

Kai voluntold Bolt to hold the first tarp. I believed he wouldn't peek. Spencer, on the other hand, could go either way. But Kai had to man the pump for the cauldron faucet.

Whatever. If Spencer looked, I would replace his memory of seeing me with something unpleasant.

"Not sure I like that face," Spencer said just before I ducked behind the tarp Bolt held.

"Good."

Undressing in this way felt worse than posing for Lex. I finally understood a little of what he meant by the difference between naked and nude.

I didn't like nakedness.

Whatever. The faster I moved, the faster this would be over.

"Did it occur to you…"

Bolt's voice halted me with my shoe halfway off. A few panicked looks around the perimeter showed no little bits of him sticking out, save his fingers holding the thing steady.

"What?" I grumbled at him.

"You could have told the women to collect the samples as usual and remember nothing odd about the experience."

My shoe dropped from my fingers. Balls. That was a good idea. Much easier than all of this rigmarole. "No. It hadn't." I unzipped my skirt and shinnied it carefully down my legs. If I did it right, it wouldn't stick to me or roll inside-out and smear me with more goop.

Bolt's smug, "Thought not," stopped me mid-motion again.

"Oh, and I'm sure you had a perfect handle on all your lightning in the first month you were electrified." Shifting my weight to one hip proved difficult with the skirt halfway down. "No black outs or forest fires?"

Blessed silence on the other side of the tarp.

As I'd thought.

I undressed the rest of the way before Bolt spoke up again.

"I apologize. It's been a while since I was green. I sometimes forget."

I checked the edges of the tarp again, just in case. All clear, so I took up the first of the damp towels. "Yeah, well. Now that you've sparked the idea, I could help you forget lots of things." I let a little teasing enter my tone. We didn't have to be enemies.

"Do and I'll fry you so quick." His voice came out flat enough I couldn't tell if he was joking or warning me away.

Either way. "For what? You wouldn't remember that you wanted to."

"Hurry up getting naked. I have places to be."

That almost sounded like a joke. Enough so that I leaned far enough to the side for my eyes to be exposed, but not my nostrils. Sideways Kilroy fun time.

A rueful smile curled Bolt's lips. I whistled until he looked my way.

"If you're going to places without naked women, you're doing something wrong."

He narrowed his eyes, but his smile reigned supreme. He leaned his face as close to mine as he could without moving the tarp. When I raised a questioning brow, he said, "Get in the tub, SparkleTits."

4 – FRAGILE

I DIDN'T FEEL completely clean when I slipped on the robe, long and thick enough to make a nun proud. Hot water and plenty of it was required. I couldn't wait to get home.

To that end, I stepped into the foam flip-flop things that came as part of Kai's hazmat kit and out from behind the tarp.

"All clean," Spencer smiled. Probably because I couldn't spread loveliness with a hug anymore.

"Not in the least. And don't think I won't trip you into the pool of it."

Spencer's smile shrunk. Mine grew. Kai scowled at his equipment as he collected the water I'd washed with into sealed containers. I wanted to wring his neck, just a little. Just long enough for him to tell me what was going on in that thick head. He'd pulled back, which I understood. And supported. But I needed to know if our dip into more than friends was officially over.

Right then, I had more important cookies to crumble. "Do you need anything else from me, Kai? I need to go home and take a real shower."

"We still need you to complete your written statement." McKinney answered.

Yes, they did. Couldn't possibly skip that after I'd already told them everything. I took one of the forms and headed to the low table furthest from the mess.

"Be sure to include what you ate in your statement." McKinney had followed me across the room without me noticing.

I chose to believe he traversed the room for the same reason I did, and not that he found me untrustworthy. Surely, if the superheroes trusted me, the police could too. Unless they didn't trust one another. How did the inter-division politics work?

"Any particular reason why you want what I ate?" I asked without looking up from scribbling.

He sniffed. "Do you need to know a reason?"

There he went again, being all judgmental and condescending.

"Oh, I don't know." I straightened from my crouch and whirled the butt of the pen. "Perhaps to give me a time frame to consider and perhaps think on if anything tasted funny?"

His lips tightened like he hadn't expected me to give him a sensible answer. "Just what you had here. Several people had to be rushed to the hospital and the food will be tested, but you might be able to narrow things down for us."

See? A nice civil answer. I would return in kind. "Oh, well, I'll write it down, but I don't know how much I'll help. I only ate a couple bites."

His gaze intensified on me and his nose twitched. "Is that so?"

What, did he think I would poison Fiona only to allow her to vomit on me so no one suspected me? I'd have to be pretty hateful, and more than a little committed, to do that before calling superheroes to be sure the evidence was collected properly.

McKinney wasn't rolling on all four tires.

Rather than professing my innocence—because even I knew how guilty it would look—I told the truth. "Yeah. I had a full plate but only took a few bites before Spencer pissed me off and killed my appetite."

"*You* lost your appetite?" Kai yelled from the other side of the room.

The conversation hadn't been secret, but I did not appreciate the peanut gallery. Except when it supported my point. I leaned to the side to meet Kai's eye. "Right?"

"Must have been something big." The voice came out all impressed, but the face was all hungry questions. He wanted to know what Spencer did to set me off my even-ish keel.

I wagged a finger. "And that's where you're going to drop this conversation."

"Greer."

"Nope." I shifted myself back around so McKinney stood between us and focused on completing my statement.

Until the shouting started. Kai and Spencer. Bolt's additions to the fray sounded like mumbles in comparison. Reasonable mumblings, but nothing to compete with the other two. No fists had been thrown. They stood too far away to land anything. From their postures, they were ready to rumblllllllllle. Both waiting for the other to make the first wrong move. Or a bell to ding.

I gritted my teeth though the last two sentences of the report and handed it to the officer. "Do you need anything else from me?"

"Not at the moment." He looked as happy about the shouting as I felt, though he had kept his vigil on me. He found me the greater threat.

Ass.

Most days, he wasn't wrong even if he didn't know why. "Call me if you need me, Officer."

He bore his teeth in the approximation of a smile and headed toward the shouting men. I had a couple solutions for this situation. I went with the ubiquitous.

Voice just this side of shrill, I yelled. "Spencer, I'm leaving." The control hurt my throat.

But it worked like a record scratch

Both men stood panting and not willing to look away from the other, but the room fell blessedly silent. So, in a normal voice I added, "It's up to you whether you take me home or I call for a ride."

Spencer came to me without a backward glance.

Kai, for his part, deflated. "Greer?"

Fragile little egos, men sometimes had. "You're still working and I need a shower."

He pressed his lips together, hard, but pulled back the sadness that had seeped in. "Right. When will I see you again?"

"Not sure. This killed me for the rest of the day and money's getting tight." It would never be tight again after the end of the month. I just had to make it to then. The puppy dog in Kai's golden eyes wouldn't let me leave it at that. "Maybe a movie or something. Mike said Well of Souls was good."

Disgust twisted his mouth. "I hate scary movies." There was my Kai. Reasonable. Rational. And not yelling.

His disgust won a giggle out of me. All the fluids he collected off me, and the idea of a horror movie turned his lip. "I know you do."

Leaving the silent auction room felt like victory. Touchdown. Grand slam. Strike twelve after eleven more. I shook my head like I had Rapunzel hair trailing down my back despite my Mohawk being locked back into a vicious pony tail.

Spencer didn't say anything until we'd made it to his car. "What was with that guy, huh?"

He wanted me to commiserate on how terrible Kai was. Two problems with his plan. "Before you dig in too deep, Kai is my friend. Has been for years. Also, I ignored the argument the two of you had. That's between y'all. Don't want to participate. I have enough shit storms to navigate."

From the shifting expressions, Spencer revised what he meant to say several times before he came with. "He certainly has a high opinion of you."

Neutral. Good. Spoken without an attitude. Even better. I took the olive branch. "He sure does. He should." I helped the superheroes with the last big hubbub in the city. Still hadn't received a check.

The last big hubbub I knew about, anyway. Five could have passed by while I struggled to find a job and a little normalcy. I shouldn't have felt annoyed to be left out, but there it was. If I had something to do with myself I might not feel so stuck in the ground.

Spencer pulled into a parking spot in my lot rather than pulling up near the stairway up to my third-floor apartment. I shook my head. "You don't have to walk me up."

"I know, but I thought I'd buy you late lunch, early dinner, or whatever you want to call it."

Him coming up to my place was a barrier we hadn't breached. Unless he'd been a part of the group who trashed the place after my ex dumped me.

I didn't want to think about that right now. It distracted me from the here and now.

My stomach growled, reminding me that I'd barely eaten at the fundraiser. Spencer smiled at my stomach's outburst, but did not push any further. No coercion. No pressure. He'd learned a thing or two today.

And I could use the free food more now than earlier. "Fine."

Stomach won again. I got out of the car without forbidding Spencer to follow.

He followed.

I paused at the bottom step, foot poised to take me higher, then set my foot back down. "You head up first. Head all the way to the top."

He crossed his arms. "Why?"

"This robe billows out like the love child of a hot-air balloon and the four winds." My description won a chuckle, until I added. "I'd rather not have you below me while the robe does its interpretive dance."

"I wouldn't look." His gaze held steady on mine.

Fragile ego again. How to soothe this one over? I was too tired to care. If he left, he left. "Oedipus Rex, Spencer. Help a girl out and head up in front of me, would ya?"

He headed up.

Mayhap I needed to use the soft command more often.

At the top of the stairs, he let me take the lead again. I liked the way he followed orders without me needing to take my top off.

I stretched my hand out to pluck the note off my door before the its content stopped me. Classic magazine letters cut out to spell a vaguely threatening message: YOUR NEXT BITCH.

I frowned at the note a bit longer than I probably should have, trying to figure out what it meant. My next bitch didn't make much sense.

"What's that?" Spencer asked over my shoulder.

I looked at him and back at the note. "It looks like someone who never passed high school English."

"What?"

The note made more sense as a threat. "Nothing, Spencer. It's fine."

"That is the opposite of fine. Now, I'm twice as glad I walked you to your door." His arm snaked forward to snatch the note.

I bumped him gently out of the way. "I want the note clean of any goobers from me or you. Just in case I need it to explain things to police officers."

My door opened smooth like tires sliding on black ice.

"You're just going to leave it here?" Spencer hadn't followed me across the threshold.

I considered calling him a vampire. Instead, I went for my tongs. On my way back to the door, I clapped them a couple of times like Zoidberg. Spencer frowned, but did not disagree. He waited until after I plucked the prize from the door to come inside.

"You probably shouldn't be left alone tonight."

There it was. Subtle, and partially fueled by what we found on my door, but still.

"No, no, no. I'll be fine. Whoever seems to think they can take me down will have to deal with my...sparkling...personality."

He crossed his arms and leaned against the closed door. Non-threatening, but the motion effectively trapped me in the apartment.

"What if the person gets you before you can...shine?"

Fists on my hips, I cocked my head to the side. "I've been shot, repeatedly, and my car exploded in my face. I'm a little harder to kill than your average clam."

"You're not invincible."

"True, but one extra person staying here won't save me from a person who knows I'm harder to kill than the average bear."

Spencer shrugged, all sugar and spice. "You staying elsewhere would be easier than putting a slew of guards on you."

I didn't buy the innocence one bit. If I wouldn't let him stay here, he might as well invite me to his place. "Yep, but I'm not going anywhere other than the shower." I swung around and headed toward the bathroom.

"I thought you were hungry."

If he wasn't here, I'd have stripped the robe off on route. Spencer in the house less than five minutes and already cramping my style.

"Gross trumps hunger." I called back to him. "Give me a thirty-minute lead, then call the Asian restaurant. Menu on the fridge. Chicken curry, medium. Chicken drunken noodle, medium. Beef fried rice. Beef with broccoli. A couple orders of egg rolls. Plus, whatever you want."

Pre-incident-at-Rust Greer would have freaked at the thought of showering with a man like Spencer in my apartment. Of course, that me wouldn't have interested Spencer as more than a play thing. Hard to be flippant about being kidnapped when your skin wasn't bullet resistant.

"You know I could come right in, right?" his voice came loud and clear through the bathroom door I'd left unlocked.

"It would be a mistake you never made again."

Kai made a similar one and steered clear of my bathroom time thereafter.

Spencer's laugh moved away from the door. He either thought I was joking or loved that he didn't intimidate me even whilst naked. Hard to tell with him.

Blessed hot water and soap.

I even shaved to stay under the spray longer. Long enough for the hot water to cool to lukewarm. I wrapped myself in two towels to head to the bedroom. The hall smelled like soy and fat. Beautiful. I hustled my way to my bedroom without looking back toward the kitchen.

"Looking good," Spencer called after me.

Rather than address that directly, I went a different route. My favorite pair of sweats had too many holes for public consumption, but the second favorite only resembled Swiss cheese around the ankles. All of my sleep shirts revealed enough to knock people comatose, so I grabbed my baggiest, hole-less t-shirt. I put a wire-free sports bra on as well.

After enough coconut oil to keep the scalp from drying, I French-braided the hair before it had ideas of rebelling. I sauntered out to the kitchen finishing the last few inches of braid. The scent of warm rice and noodles welcomed me with open arms.

Spencer's mouth twitched in a slight pucker as he handed a plate to me. I wanted to know, but I wouldn't ask. Food became an excuse to not engage.

Was there nothing it couldn't do?

Balls. Spencer waited for me to join him before he filled his plate. It made this feel more intimate than it should be. To keep things casual, I chose the stools at my kitchen bar rather than the dining room table. It left the rest of the feast in close enough proximity to grab without standing.

Spencer dimmed the lights. If I rose to his non-verbal poking, I would have to say the "d" word. Mentioning again that we weren't dating felt like protesting too much.

Still. "Could you turn that back up?"

"I wanted to save some electricity." His lips curled and his eyes crinkled a little in the corners.

A lying, Cheshire smile if I ever did see one. He wanted me to say the word. He would not win this round.

"I don't like the way my skin looks in dimmer light."

"You have a lovely glow." Less Cheshire, more genuine. So, not a complete lie.

Nonetheless, I shook my head. "Exactly."

He relented. Halfway. He rolled the light back up to a level that my glow was almost indistinguishable. At least it killed the romantic vibe.

5 – FURTHER DOWN THE RABBIT HOLE

I PLOWED THROUGH my first place in the blessed silence of utensils, plates, and unhurried chewing. Spencer made a sound as I reached for the two closer cartons. I knew I'd regret it. But I had to. "What's that supposed to mean?"

"Nothing."

I gave him a solid minute of side eye before turning back to refilling my plate. "You don't think that actually suffices as an answer, do you?"

"I suppose not." His lips curled again, like he'd won exactly what he'd intended. Perhaps he had. "I was just thinking about how most women don't eat around people they don't know—men especially—and how you have stomped all over that cliché."

"Yeah, well. Those women are usually trying to impress people—men especially." I hoped I got his inflection correct. "I don't really care if I impress you."

"You already have."

No smile. No joking crinkle in the corners of his eye. Just solid, deep eye contact.

Danger, danger, danger. I needed to say something to break his mood lickity-now. "And I've been ravenous since the bright whatever fell out of the sky and into my chest. I eat like this, and I'm losing weight."

"It's probably this." He drew the tips of his fingers across the back of my hand. "The glow probably takes quite a bit of fuel to maintain."

I did my best to focus on the words and not the fact that I could still feel where he'd touched me. Damn't. I didn't need the complication of Spencer in my life and liking him. I already had a cornucopia of complications.

Eyes locked on the food I was still piling on my plate, I tried to stay on topic. "That's actually not a bad explanation." It was a good theory. I needed to test it. Figure out my output and adjust my intake to balance things out.

Numbers and facts.

That was the ticket to not focusing on the dribble of soy sauce on the nearest corner of his lip.

"Are you sleeping with that guy, Kai?"

And there went all the fuzzy, warm feelings. Virtual ice water in my face and down the front of me. Looking at him without mixed emotions became easy, despite the intense focus Spencer laid on me.

Veronica R. Calisto

"Right now, I'm eating Chinese food."

He set his fork on his plate. Serious time. No hint of other distractions. "You know what I mean. Are you and Kai in a relationship?"

No distractions for him. I, on the other hand, reached out for a third container to dump onto my plate. "Kai's my friend."

"Are you having sex with him?"

I pointed again to the food.

He forced an annoyed breath out. "Have you had sex with him?"

"Yes."

"Do you plan on having sex with him again?"

"I don't know. I hadn't really planned on it the first time." Or the next few. But, once the mouse gets a cookie...

There were two egg rolls left in the wax-paper bag. I'd eaten all but the one that lay half consumed on Spencer's plate. Still, it was wrong to assume without asking, so I tipped the bag toward him. "Did you want one of these?"

"I need you to focus, Greer."

I was. Just not on the thing he wanted me to, but I was focused. For that response, I dumped both rolls onto my plate before I answered. "Let's ignore the whole 'I got puked on because you took me to a place I would not have otherwise been' thing. I missed a meal because you fucking pissed me off and I'm a fucking LightBright burning my way through my breakfast, which was hours ago. What the fuck do you want from me?"

"You know what I want from you."

I did. I didn't know if he wanted it only because I hadn't simpered and fawned at his feet. I didn't know if he would still want me after he'd had me. I didn't know a lot about him. But I knew what he wanted. So, I nodded.

"Do you want me?"

My eyes sunk closed, and I shook my head. "I don't know."

"You don't know." Flat tone. Almost disbelief, but not quite.

I peeked through my eye lashes. He'd narrowed his eyes and leaned quite a bit toward me, like halving the distance would help him to better understand my expression. "No. I don't."

"Is there anything I can do to help you make the right decision?"

Right decision. Right. Whichever I chose would be the correct one for me, regardless of how he felt. But his question left the ball in my court.

I wasn't the kind of girl in need of high romance or grand gestures. Especially in that moment. I just needed him to, "Shut up about it and let me finish my dinner."

A sly smile crept onto his face. I mistrusted it immediately.

He snatched one of the egg rolls off my plate. While his hand was full, I grabbed the half he'd left on his plate and bit down.

"Next time," I told him, wagging the finger-length piece at him. "It won't be an egg roll."

Spencer let out one of his full, rumbling laughs. When he recovered, he saluted me with his pilfered roll. "Tease."

Hardly. But whatever got him through rejections.

I contemplated the tub of cookie dough I had in my fridge. If I baked some now, he would see it as invitation to stay longer. I needed head space. He needed to leave, but he'd looked so pleased at my resistance to his insistence on washing my dishes, that I finally gave in. I didn't want to feed into his mind games any more than I already had.

I would wash the dishes again when I got around to it. I was that girl.

He kept stealing glances at me while he took his sweet-ass time to wash the six items we'd used and the few others I'd had in my sink. I would not be the one to speak up this time. I would not.

My phone had a text from Lex checking up on me and one from Magus. I let Lex know we were go for launch for tomorrow's shooting session. He could wait until then for any details on how my slow descent into madness was progressing. Magus had sent me a phone number without explanation. I got it. He decided giving me the number for the hotline was a good idea after all.

"Why don't you flip on the TV?" Spencer rinsed a plate off in steaming water. "I'm almost done."

Implying he could join me on the couch and we could snuggle our way through some ridiculous sitcom. Hashtag sorrynotsorry to burst his bubble. I shrugged, "I don't have a TV."

His brow furrowed. "Really?"

"Not anymore."

"What happened to it?"

I glared at him like he argued that the sun and everything else revolved around the earth. Arrogant, self-centered, and completely oblivious to cause and effect.

When it clicked, he had the grace to look embarrassed at least. "Right."

Right.

He shut the faucet off. "I'll replace that."

A dinner, some cleaned dishes, and a television wasn't enough to endear him to me. He should know that much. To forestall any further thinking in that vein, I nipped it in the bud. "No, thank you."

"It's no trouble."

But it was complicated. Accepting that kind of gift from him like he was some kind of sugar daddy. Like a free trial that required a credit card to activate. "Chad took one of them. Your goons destroyed the second. Both are mostly Chad's fault."

"He wouldn't have—"

"He did, though. Made that decision. Asshole." I stared at the empty space on top of the TV stand because the anger was easier to feel than the worthlessness that trailed close behind it. "The lease is up in a couple of months. Not sure I'll want to stay here and buying something to move two months later feels silly."

Spencer came around the counter, finally done stringing out the simple task, and sat back down on the stool next to me. He sat with his back to the bar counter. Probably so his face hung in my periphery. "Where would you go?"

I shook my head. "The inheritance means I can go anywhere, really."

After a few beats, Spencer encouraged with, "Uh-huh. And where do you want to go?"

"Home." Such a pretty word.

"Where is that?"

"I don't know anymore." Between Chad leaving and Gabe's death, my life felt unmoored. This was just a place to lay my stuff and now even the memories of that had tarnished.

Gods. I was a short countdown from dissolving into a weepy mess. I thought I'd gotten past this. "You should probably go." Before I really lost it.

"What if the person who made the note on your door decides to make good on his threat tonight?"

The note had completely slipped my mind. My life had sunk to a point of throwing dirt on dirt. Someone would need to toss me something completely different for me to take notice. Maybe someone could throw me a bone. Or a rose with enough thorns to make me feel something above the rest of the din.

I turned to Spencer. "Let them fucking try."

He pressed his lips as he studied me. His laid-back posture put him closer to me than I had realized. Watching him watch me from so close unnerved me a little. What did he see?

Honey-brown eyes bore into mine as he spoke. "I don't think you should be alone tonight."

That was just what I wanted, though. What I needed. Space and silence to crumble into a pile of ash where no one could see me or sweep me away. "You can't stay."

I needed breathing room, but he had halved the distance between us again. "Yes. I can."

Spencer moved slowly, eyes on mine as he crossed the distance. Asking for permission. Indecision locked me in place until his lips made contact with mine. I kissed him back, tasting the saltiness of our dinner redoubled in his mouth. He smiled against me, slipping a hand behind my neck and the other at my hips.

The unhurried need felt so good. I could have let myself float on the wave as it crashed over both of us. And deal with the backlash when he too realized what my chest could do to him.

I pushed him back. Gently, but I pushed.

He got the message, though he only allowed a couple of inches between us. The look in his eyes had a little more of the coldness that had peeked out in front of the policemen, only it wasn't coldness. More like a feral cat. Wildness barely contained within the bounds of a solid human form.

"Greer," he ground out in a tone that vibrated my vertebrae. Then, with a touch of detachment, he added, "You're glowing."

"I'm always glowing." My voice only slightly resembled porn-star huskiness.

"No, I mean I can see it now. In this light."

I dropped my gaze down to my hand pressed against his chest and, sure as shit, I'd increased my wattage. "Oedipus Rex and his pecs."

He furrowed his brow. "Huh?" Confused as he seemed to be, he let me slink off the barstool and away from him without chasing me down with grabby hands.

Arms crossed over my chest, I reiterated. "You should really go."

"Just like that? No explanation?" He straightened on the barstool, but made no motion toward standing and leaving. Nor standing and coming after me. "I deserve an explanation at the very least."

I wasn't certain that was true. I got the impression he wouldn't leave without one unless I got really ugly. He hadn't done anything to deserve the medusa side of me this time.

"I have some things to do tomorrow." Lame. It was a lame excuse for an explanation.

He crossed his ankles easy as you please, like this was poker and he had a couple aces up his sleeve. "I'm just asking for the night."

He was and he wasn't. We both knew that. But I knew something he didn't.

I couldn't see a way around telling him. Not if I really wanted him to leave.

"This," I rotated my hand to show him the back of my arm. The glow had dimmed a bit once I stepped away from him, but not enough, "is why you need to leave."

"Not getting it."

Of course not. I hadn't explained it well enough. Beating around the bush did me no favors. "Since the incident that turned me into a glow worm, I kind of, um, supernova when I orgasm. Bright, bright light. Blinding. Then I crash for at least a day."

Spencer stared at me in silence for a little too long.

His, "Are you making that up?" kind of pissed me off.

"You kissed me, I started glowing brighter." In what world would that be the first story someone comes up with? The self-centered ass. "You don't think I wouldn't love to get my rocks off without losing a day? A whole fucking day?"

He grinned at me.

After setting me off like that, questioning my answer, he was all smiles. "What the fuck are you grinning at?"

He lifted an easy shoulder. "You want me."

"I told you I didn't know."

"No denying it." He waggled a finger at me, stepped down from the stool, and stalked into my personal space in one graceful, predatory movement. "You kissed me back and you're glowing. Not quite a, like you said, supernova, but you've brightened."

His eyes practically sparkled with pleasure.

I'd had about enough. "Can you go now?"

He laughed at me in a way I had begun to hate. With the smug, knowing smile. Bastard thought he'd won. Maybe he had. Maybe I was so high strung that any kind of intimate contact revved me up. Giving Spencer the alternate explanation would only give him more fuel.

I stepped around him and headed for the front door. By the luck of all that was good and holy, he followed me without another word.

No other words until I reached for the front door and he set his hand against it. "Kiss me, again and I'll go."

"That sounds like a quid pro quo kind of extortion." I fought the urge to cross my arms over myself again. "I don't play that way."

He nodded and removed his hand from the door. "You are correct. My apologies. May I kiss you again before I go?"

Damn. He looked so focused and earnest. And his lips looked positively flushed. I wasn't the only one who'd enjoyed our first kiss.

First kiss. First. Crap. I was going to do it again.

I touched the bottom of his chin with two fingertips. This time he waited for me to close the distance. After I had, he pulled me against him. In the event I had any question about my effect on him, I had none any more. Nor about the size of what he brought to the table. Neither helped in my resolve to not press my lips to his.

He stopped himself this time, right about when I'd started to pull back. He probably felt the shift in me. It didn't stop him from grinning with pride at the night-light he'd made of me. I had enough of a glow that he had a faint shadow against the door.

Spencer didn't resist my opening the door for him this time. Just slid his large hands into his pockets with the same kind of smile that had gotten me into this whole thing.

"I will call you."

I believed him.

"Lose the scruff." I nearly smacked myself on the side of the head. I didn't need him knowing I cared that much about how he looked, or the state of my chin the next time we met. Stupid. Stupid. Stupid. There was no retrieving that back from the world.

"I always do before a date." He winked at me before he turned to leave.

There it was. He had me.

I tried to figure where I went wrong. Gabe would have known what I should do.

Without any pretense of baking any of the cookie dough, I attacked the tub with a spoon. The first bite grounded me enough to think clearly.

I was an idiot, that much was clear. Also, I should have worked harder at distancing myself from Spencer. What I *should* do was also clear. End it now before roots grew. But his car was still a mess. One I'd caused. And he owed me for the funky decoration I'd received this afternoon. That couldn't slide without payback.

All of my payback scenarios involved him parading around in increasingly skimpy clothes.

He would win again, somehow.

I needed a safer line of thinking. Like the threatening note from my door I'd slid into a quart-sized freezer bag and tucked in my purse.

With the timing, the note had to be about Fiona's death this afternoon. Someone at the fundraiser had something against me. Knew where I lived, as well. Not the hardest thing to find out once a person knew my name, but who would bother?

Senator Marcus probably wouldn't dirty his hands with threatening me. I still had money he desired. His kind of personality never believed he couldn't eventually convince me to contribute to him. Which meant he would either keep trying to ingratiate himself with me, or find some dirt on me to expose to the world. I only had the two major secrets.

Exposing one would violate some of the secrecy policies of the Gold 4. I hoped. My chest situation had to be too close to superheroes' secrets for the senator to be able to freely share the knowledge.

As far as my other secret, reminding the world of what I'd gone through would put the public squarely on my side. If he did know, he couldn't risk a character debate with me along those lines.

Regardless of the unlikelihood, I'd keep the senator in my suspect list. Sometimes people snapped. And, who knew? He might have as many shady connections as his son.

Spencer wanted to get into my pants too much to threaten to kill me for other reasons. He watched me closely enough to know the threat would not make me bend to him.

Other than Fiona, that concluded the list of people I'd known at the fundraiser. The Preacher's face had been familiar, but only from the local channel Sunday broadcasts. If he'd ever seen me before, he hadn't made himself known to me.

Still, I couldn't put him out of the running, even if I couldn't explain why he might threaten me. He didn't know me enough to hate me.

Chad did. I hadn't heard from my ex since he told Spencer to kidnap me so I could pay back the money Chad owed him. The asshat.

I'd asked Spencer not to kill Chad. Didn't know if he listened to me. Killing my ex would put a damper on whatever was happening between the two of us, though. Spencer was smart enough to know this.

I wanted to ask him about it. In the crudest, most accusatory manner that I could manage. It might discourage him from continuing to pursue me.

Something had to.

There I was, thinking about Spencer again.

Three strikes and I was out. I stuck the tub of cookie dough back in the fridge and gave up on consciousness for the day.

A tinkling smash pulled me out of a dream that felt familiar. Adrenaline washed the remnants away. Someone was in my apartment.

6 – BOOBY CALL

WHOEVER IT WAS had crashed in through the sliding door on balcony, not through the front. The unmistakable sound of shattering glass set me on edge.

I scrambled for the side of the bed where I kept a bat with nails protruding from it. Crude, but I didn't have any barbed wire on hand.

The bedroom door blew open and the light switched on.

"Stop that," the man in the doorway said. "Drop it. Hands where I can see them."

Two inches too far away to grab. I needed to get a weapon I felt safe sleeping in the same bed with.

I lifted both hands, though my right arm was half buried beneath me.

"Roll over so I can see both hands are empty."

I knew that voice, from somewhere.

My skin crawled.

I rolled over nice and easy, sitting up as I did. Partially to get a better look at the voice that set my teeth against each other, but mostly because I remembered. I did have weapons I slept with, two of them. And I rarely wore clothes to bed.

The man's face went slack and I knew him. Not his real name, just his superhero name. Gale Force. The asshole I'd kneed in the crotch moments before I became the world's most enchanting sparkler.

Whatever he'd planned to do, he hadn't anticipated a naked me nor the force of my...charm. Drool dribbled from the corner of his lip and it hadn't been a minute. With him under my spell, I could do so many things. There were bigger issues. If anyone else heard my door shatter, they might call the cops. The whole policeman-versus-rogue-superhero-versus-hypnoboob situation didn't end well in my head. I needed the Gold 4.

Here I went again, calling in the cavalry. Twice in one day. Damn. At least I had the hotline number this time.

Too many rings passed before someone picked up. A whole two minutes. If this had been a life or death emergency, someone would have died in that time. What kind of show were they running over there?

"Greer." Magus. In that same tone he used to answer his cell.

"Gale Force is here."

"He's there?"

I didn't like the lack of shock in his tone. I really didn't. "He busted into my apartment and I have him accidentally in custody. Why don't you sound surprised?"

"We caught wind—"

"Terrible pun."

Magus forged on ahead almost like he hadn't heard me. "Information came to us that Gale Force had been spotted around Cherry Halls before the event opened. They asked him to leave after he blew a pavilion down, yelling nonsense about feministas uniting against him. We think he wrecked things to divert attention from what he added to the food."

Well, that was great. A superhero gone off the deep end. Neet.

"I have him well under control, I'd say, so you don't need to rush to get over here or anything."

"Bolt is on the way already."

I didn't have much time then. "Could you tell him to knock on the front door when he gets here? We'll need to figure out a way for Bolt to collect Gale Force without me collecting Bolt."

"Good plan. I'll let him know. See you when you get here."

He'd hung up before I'd recovered from his complement.

I checked the time on my alarm. 2:27am. Balls. There went the majority of my sleep.

Bolt took longer than I expected. A lot longer, until it occurred to me that he might not have travelled by lightning. Since I didn't need to be completely naked to keep control of Gale Force, I took advantage of the lee time.

I slipped out of bed under the drooling, watchful eye of Gale Force. He might have been excited to know that he'd gotten a little action from me, or at least more than he ever would with his stilted "flirting" techniques. He got the whole view, which I would be certain to wipe from his memory banks at the first opportunity.

Making sure to keep my chest aimed at him the whole time, I dressed my lower half, shoes and all.

Then, I sat on the bed to wait. Topless except the purse strapped over my shoulder. Dear, Penthouse...

The door knock came maybe two minutes later.

Now I just needed to get there without touching Gale Force or him losing eye contact with me. I yelled, "Coming, Bolt," then shifted focus back to my problem.

"Okay, Gale Force, you are going to walk backward into the hallway, a step for every one I take, until I tell you to stop."

We walked almost in a dance with the eight feet between us. When we came into the living room I made him stop and turn with me as I swung myself around to the door. I leaned up against it. "Hey, Bolt you still there?"

"Yes."

"Good. Okay, so the boobs are out in full force. Bolt and only Bolt, which means you, Gale Force should ignore my next instructions until I say Neuschwanstein." A safe word should work. If my hypnoboobs worked as well as I thought they did.

"What's all that?" Bolt asked from the other side of the door. "I didn't catch the last bit."

Probably because muffled German names didn't translate well through wood. "Nothing for you. So, Bolt, when I open the door, I want you to close and cover your eyes with one hand. When I touch your elbow or wrist or whatever, you should be clear to open the eyes, but I would take it as a kindness if you didn't stare at me."

"Got it."

That was it? No teasing or threats? Phoenyx would have tried it. Of course, we had rapport; Bolt and I didn't.

Before I wasted more time over-analyzing, I opened the door and stepped far enough forward for Bolt to enter. He had taken me at my word and done just ask I asked. Kind of a weird feeling. Not that *no one* had ever taken my word. Bolt wasn't just anyone and he didn't like me. He trusted me this far, though. That kind of trust demanded returned faith.

I set my hand high on his shoulder to give him plenty freedom of movement in his arm. He uncovered his eyes, in hesitant jerks until he was sure he would be fine. Then he took a good look at my drooling statue, Gale Force.

"Wow," he said with a quick glance at my face and only my face. "You're taking 'I am woman, hear me roar' a little to the extreme don't you think."

A joke out of Bolt. Who knew. If he could joke, I could too. A little. "Boobs don't make sound."

"They do if you play them right." He smirked. He didn't look at me, but he smirked.

Nowhere to go from there but down. "Okay. How are we going to handle him?"

"I'm going to shock him, like a Taser, but with enough juice to knock him out for a bit. You need to not be touching me when I do, or you'll get a little backlash jolt. Which will be...unpleasant."

I could have guessed the last. Perhaps this was his way of keeping me safe around his power like I'd done to keep him safe from mine. Mutual respect. I could dig it. "How far from you do I need to be?"

"More than three inches away is safe from accidental discharge, unless you're holding a lightning rod."

Terrible jokes sprung to mind. For later.

When Bolt let loose, I would need to jump back from him. Probably also cover myself. I'd wait for Gale Force to be incapacitated to do the last bit.

The two of us walked toward Gale Force in marching unison until I stopped a couple feet short. Just close enough for my hand to reach Bolt without me crowding up on him. The distance made me feel more certain that this crazy thing might work and not end up hurting me.

"On three," Bolt said. "Not before or after, you'll let me go. Understood?"

I nodded. "Understood."

Three came. I jumped back and retracted my arm. Brief, electric lightshow and boom. Gale Force went down like a sack of rotten potatoes. I cheered by grabbing my throw blanket from the nearby couch and wrapping it around myself.

The yin and yang of sparkling boobs. Such as it was with most things, sometimes the boobs that saved your life also got in the way of life. If Lao Tzu didn't say something to that effect, Socrates certainly had a word or two on the subject.

7 – SHIVER ME TIMBERS

THE FAINT SCENT of singed hair floated up my nostrils as I stood even with Bolt and gazed at the prone, smoking Gale Force. This was the second time I'd seen him knocked out and smoking. I couldn't quite find it in my heart to smile about my life echoing itself.

We needed to wrap up before something else fell from the sky and I lost my sparkling slippers.

"You wouldn't happen to have brought a way to haul him outta here, would you?" I asked it without real conviction.

He jerked his thumb toward the door. "I left the dolly, some bungies, and some straps just outside."

"Really? Sweet." I went to go collect them.

The two of us straightened and rolled Gale Force onto the metal frame of the dolly.

"Straps around the thighs, shins, shoulders, waist, neck." He pointed to the body regions as he listed them. "Bungies between and lock them tighter than you think they should be."

I wanted to ask Bolt if the restraints kept Gale Force from using his superpowers, but not enough to know if it wasn't possible.

Bolt didn't object to the speed nor the tightness to which I strapped Gale Force in. He didn't use such jerking force, but he didn't have as much reason to. I started to help him lift Gale toward vertical. Bolt shook his head at me and handed me some keys. "Get the doors."

That I could do.

The neighbor across the hall hadn't opened his door to peek while Bolt wheeled the unconscious man from my apartment. It made me grateful this happened in the middle of the night. Fewer people awake meant fewer potential witnesses. Especially good as we thunked our way down the stairs.

Pressing the key fob flashed the lights on a van parked in the handicapped space. I nearly chided Bolt—not even superheroes were above the law—but the van had proper plates.

"Handicapped, huh?" I opened both back doors.

Bolt tapped his foot against an extendible ramp I hadn't noticed and moved out of its direct path. While I unhinged the clips that held it in place, he answered. "From the time that any kind of aberration was considered retardation of a mental or physical manner."

Straightening, I tucked the blanket more closely around me, wondering why the hell I hadn't grabbed a shirt before we left. "How does that work? I can see you can control lightning, so you must be crazy?"

"More like, 'You are not what we have decided God defined as normal so you belong in an institution where no one else can see you.'" He rolled Gale force up the ramp like a pro. "They had similar reaction to women at the time. 'You don't want to do what a man says? Hysteria. Lobotomy.'"

"Burning at the stake."

"That too." He nodded as he secured the dolly to the side of the van. Vertical and facing the skinny bench along the other side.

I stepped out of his way as he hopped down out of the van. "What about other things, like vampires and shapeshifters and witches."

He shook his head. "You read too many weird books."

"Except, we've seen zombies, so…" I shrugged.

His nostrils flared. "There is no record of anything like that or they would have made laws to regulate them."

"That, I believe."

"Exactly, and since the old laws we do have grant us prime parking when we need it, we don't try to change it. One of the union benefits."

Made sense. I wondered if I could take advantage of the parking permit situation. Of course, it would mean I needed to be a part of the union. The mandatory union which only had male members because only men had superpowers.

Until me.

Perhaps I should look more into the union before volunteering part of my life away.

I wriggled the ramp back into its hole. As in all things, taking it out was a whole lot easier than putting it away. Like dealing with glitter or men. My mind flashed to what happened with Spencer earlier. Yup. My life loved its echoes.

Bolt stepped out of the van and straightened. Cast a quick glance back inside then back at me. "I think it might be safer if you ride in the back."

"In the back with the man who wants to kill me?" I stepped in even as I complained. While I agreed with the practicality, I didn't have to skip-to-my-loo about being stuck in a windowless space with the man.

Actually, there was one window. A two-by-two-inch little opening that connected with the driver's compartment. It had a slider to close it off, which I would do if I needed to whip the girls out again.

"Do you know he wanted to kill you?" Bolt shut one side of the back doors and held onto the other. "As far as we know he was ranting about putting people, women, in their place."

"Fiona Appleby dies practically in my lap and I get a threatening note on my door saying I'm next." I shrugged, not because I wasn't certain but because I was.

He frowned. "There's a note."

"In a baggie in my purse."

"Shit."

"Correct."

"Be ready to play your tits if you need to." With that helpful hint, he closed the door.

The back of the van had no obvious light in it, save my mostly covered arms. I could see perfectly well enough, though, so there had to be some kind of illumination thing going on. Just enough for hidden cameras to catch everything.

I watched Gale Force like a hawk, alternating between his eyes, mouth, and chest. Were his eyes closed and still? Had his mouth moved? Was there any change to his breathing that might indicate him being conscious but playing possum?

The back door opened. I jerked the blanket partially open before realizing what had happened. Jumpy? Who, me?

Another set of eyes meant I didn't need to study Gale Force quite so hard, but I was closer to him. I would be the first one hurt if he lashed out. Better safe than sorry. I kept my eyes on the prize. "What is it?"

"You're here." Phoenyx answered.

Phoenyx, not Bolt. We must have arrived.

I sidestepped my way off the bench, eyes still half on Gale Force until I nearly tripped over a half loop on the floor of the van.

"Whoa, there." Phoenyx held up his hands as if to catch me, though his positioning would have caught me by my boobs.

I reset the blanket about me with a nod. "I'm good,"

"Yes, you are. Here." He dropped one of his hands and offered the other up to me to help me down. "You caught a bad guy. A super bad guy. That's really good."

He said it like I planned and plotted and pursued Gale Force, instead of the other way around.

If I slept with clothes on, things would have ended much differently. Both thoughts sounded like things to not say to Phoenyx, or he would run his mouth. I took the congratulations and his hand with a nod and a smile.

The garage Bolt had parked us in was larger than a residential space.

"Where are we?" I asked both Phoenyx by my side or Bolt hopping in the van to retrieve Gale Force.

"Rust," came from inside the van.

Of course. The same bar in which my peek behind the superhero veil had begun. It made sense, except for a few things. "Aren't you guys afraid someone saw a suspiciously large van pull into a club garage at whatever time of night?"

"Three-thirty in the morning." Phoenyx tugged me toward the doors I recognized now.

The door on our right led into Kai's home, the other into the storage room of the club. Two freezers lived in the storage room. One for food storage and one as a front to the elevator into the nerve center for the Gold 4.

"Magus thought it best to keep the number of access points to Central that you know down to a minimum," Bolt said.

Which made sense, even if it sucked a little. Despite the ways I'd helped them, I wasn't part of the cool kids' club. Just a go-for wagging my tail at any kind of bone they might throw me.

"And," Phoenyx continued, "the people who know this is a club have connection to the Gold 4. So, even if they found the van timing odd, they would recognize it as official business."

"What about the people who don't know it's a club?"

He stopped at the door with his hand on the knob. "They don't notice much of what happens here."

"What do you mean by that?"

And why wasn't he opening the door yet? Instead, he kind of parked himself there and looked past me. I took a gander over my shoulder and realized Bolt wasn't too far behind us. I flattened myself to the side when Phoenyx opened the door.

Right.

Still taking Gale Force in. Securing criminals took precedence.

"There's a mental block," Phoenyx said, after I'd almost forgotten what I'd asked. "The club doesn't register to most people as any different than the office buildings surrounding it."

I trailed after Bolt, leaving Phoenyx to take up the rear. "Like hypnosis?" because the sign outside and the line of people sometimes waiting to get in was a dead giveaway.

"Something like that. Doesn't work after a person has been brought here or the club's been pointed out."

His answer gave me more questions. Some about how that kind of thing even worked. More about how I'd noticed the club in the first place. No one had told me. I'd been alone the first time I finally decided to see what it was all about. But I had seen the place there for years. Before they changed the name to Rust.

Something to discuss at another time.

Bolt came to a halt in front of the freezer. I swung around him and opened the door. Phoenyx blew past me and got the elevator door. Then we all squished into the too small elevator.

It hadn't seemed too small the first time. Gale Force took up a lot of the space and way too much of the air. I nearly cheered when the doors opened. Magus standing in front of the desk waiting for us made me happy I'd held back.

The luscious trees lining the walls of the circular reception room and the grass carpeting the ground—save a flagstone border around the circular desk in the center of the room—didn't seem to matter. Walking in still felt like the principal's office. Perhaps it was the stern, square face of the head of the Gold 4 staring us down as we entered. Just a guess.

"Hello, Magus." I controlled my vocal trembling. Because I was an adult and not in trouble.

He nodded. "Greer."

Happy as ever to see me. Complaining about it didn't make sense. A leader needn't be moved by waves of emotion.

"Report," he said.

I looked to Bolt who had already turned to me. Oh. I wasn't part of the cool kids' club, but they would certainly order me around like I was. Why did it feel like the short end of the stick just poked me in the ass cheek?

"Okay," I turned back toward Magus. "You should probably let me know when you mean me, because I'm not actually a part of your organization."

"Greer. Report." He barked it at me this time, drill-sergeant-like.

I didn't like it one bit, but I hadn't specified how he should let me know. He would probably berate me for wasting his time if I tried to specify now. I took a breath.

And got knocked forward. Down. Reflex kept me from face planting in the grass, but the impact knocked the wind out of me. I gasped for air for half a minute before I had enough to wonder what the fuck just happened.

I pushed myself onto my back in time to see Phoenyx fly across the room, leaves and twigs trailing.

Oh, I got it. Sleeping beauty was up.

Why wasn't Bolt doing anything? Or Magus?

Still heaving, I struggled to sit up. The wind more than six inches off the ground blew fierce. Made breathing hard. My blanket billowed behind me, threatening to take me with it as physics attacked. I clutched at it, trying to reel it in. A sage voice in my head asked me why I bothered. I let it go.

The blanket whipped off into the maelstrom circling the too small space.

Without it, I sat up with much greater ease

The wind stopped. Like someone closed a vault door on a twister. The anger twisting Gale Force's face dissolved into stupor. I much preferred him like this. Perhaps there was a way to freeze him this way, one that didn't involve me living the topless life.

As I stood, I brushed the debris the wind had graced me with. "I guess it's a good thing I'd forgotten to grab a shirt before we left, eh, Bolt?"

No answer. I looked at his crouching form. He had the stupor thing going on too. As did Phoenyx and Magus. Well shit. I headed toward Bolt. At least we had rehearsed this thing once before.

The phone rang. Of all the things.

I guessed crime didn't stop out in the world just because some superhero drama down here. Another ring passed while I tried to figure out what to do. Taking care of Gale Force wouldn't take a lot of time, but probably more than the person on the other end of the line could afford. Since I'd essentially hit pause on this game, I backed my way to the desk and answered the red phone.

"Gold 4. This is Greer." I hadn't known what to say the first time I'd answered the phone. This felt a little better than the first time.

"This is Wallace, Jeffco County Sheriff. The Jefferson County Government Center is on fire. Accelerants in timed releases. We can neither confirm nor deny whether the building is clear."

My mind reeled with the information. I only knew a few buildings in Jefferson county. Only one of them with any ties to any official business. People's lives could be at stake, so I asked. "Which building?"

"The Taj."

The pretty one on the foothill overlooking the area. The building everyone in the Denver metro area knew the Taj Mahal. "Got it. Someone will be with you shortly." I hoped.

They would be if I did this right.

I dropped the phone back on the cradle and stalked back to Gale Force. Still outside of grabbing distance, because caution was better than not.

"Gale Force, you are very tired. You need to go to sleep."

Nothing. His eyes remained open, his mouth still producing an unpleasant amount of drool. It worked so well with him before. Perhaps multiple exposures decreased my effectiveness. Hypnoboob fatigue.

Only one way to find out. "Hey Bolt, would you stand up for me?"

He shot up so quickly he nearly keeled back over again. He was the only other person in the room I'd put the double whammy on before. It seemed to work on him just as well. Better even. It was weird, but he hadn't gotten the full force of it the first time. Touching him earlier could have increased the effect on him.

Wait a second. I'd had to speak him through coming into my

apartment and I'd given Gale Force a word to listen for, so he knew when I addressed him. Perhaps the suggestion lasted within subsequent hypnotic states. Could be inconvenient; might come in handy.

What word was it? Something that wouldn't be brought up in casual conversation. A long word. Blathering blather—no. Something to do with a bird. Swans. Got it.

"Neuschwanstein, Gale Force. Give me thumbs up if you're listening to me."

He did so. With both thumbs. I had to test it. "Just one thumb up. The right one."

His left thumb disappeared into his balled fist. Perfect. Here went nothing. Again. "Excellent. Good job. Now you are tired. Really sleepy. You aren't going to keep your eyes open again when I say that same word from before. Do you remember the word?"

"Neuschwanstein," came out of his mouth with automaton precision. Creepy as hell. No time to worry about the nightmares I would have later.

"Very good. When I say the word, you are going to sleep and you won't wake up until Magus says the word. Can you point to Magus for me?"

With the limited mobility granted to him by the straps at his wrists, he did so.

"Okay. Excellent. Now it's time to go to sleep. Good night."

"Good night." Flat and unaffected as his expression.

A chill shook my whole body. It didn't matter. "Neuschwanstein."

Gale Force's eyes closed, and his head drooped forward. A snore escaped. Might have been a cute snore on someone else.

One thing handled. Now we just needed to take care of a fire.

8 – Breath of Forced Air

I CAST ABOUT for my blanket. Not on the grass anywhere. I looked up and found it dangling from a tree. If the fate of the world depended on my ability to climb a tree, we would all die horribly. Alternatives. I wished I'd worn a skirt. I could have just flipped it up. Dashing from the room would work, but I had info to give. So, option C it was.

"Hey, Bolt. Can I borrow your shirt really quick?" I asked rather than ordered him, but something told me it didn't matter how I said it. The result would be the same. As I walked to him, he stripped his T-shirt up and over his head and held it out to me. I covered my chest.

Magus yelled, "Gale Force." Phoenyx grunted. And Bolt stared at me. His eyes dropped down to where I clutched his shirt against me.

"Do you remember anything of what just happened?" I hoped.

"Gale Force tossed Phoenyx over before he could form a fireball..." He blinked. "And now you have my shirt."

Of course not. Them remembering would have been easy and helpful. Two words that didn't usually happen in my life.

"What just happened?" Magus didn't sound pleased in his confusion.

I couldn't really blame him.

"Okay. First thing's first." I swiveled around to Phoenyx, who was slowly righting himself. "The red phone rang. Sherriff from Jefferson County. Wallace, I think it was. There's a fire at the Taj Mahal in Jeffco. Accelerants and timed explosions. They're not sure the building is empty."

Determination overwrote the confusion on Phoenyx's face. He started for the elevator door.

"Wait," Magus said.

Phoenyx stopped in his tracks and looked at him.

I turned to him as well. "Fire, Magus. Big one." Seriously. What the hell?

He ignored me. "If this is similar to the others, the direct route may be blocked or booby-trapped in anticipation of your arrival. Use the church."

Booby-trapped. His choice of wording couldn't have been a coincidence.

Not the time, though.

"Got it." Phoenyx continued on his way to the elevator. He winked at me as the doors closed.

As far as the rest, I pressed my lips together because I needed to shut up. Not being a cool kid, I was not privy to most of the information going on. For good reason. "I had no right to question you managing your people. I got excited. Sorry about that."

"You are correct," Magus answered, but not in a condescending way. "Now. Would you tell me what just happened?"

Asking the question rather than ordering. Either what happened had rattled him or he appreciated me acknowledging I was wrong. The best way to train good behavior was to reward it without telling people why. "It was almost the same thing that happened at my apartment, so I'll start there, if that works for you."

He nodded.

I gave him the lowdown with as many details as I could remember. He didn't strike me as someone who valued brevity over information. Too many things could get lost in the editing.

He seemed pleased when I handed him the note from my door. More so when I admitted collecting it with my kitchen tongs.

Score two for me.

Both of which I lost when I described what happened when Gale Force had woken up here.

"You hypnotized my people?" he asked, voice even—in the scary way. Still waters, and all that. "You hypnotized me?"

The last might have been the thing that irked him more. The man with the power to control other minds, to wipe the memories from other people, suddenly had it flipped back on himself. It had to be a sharp piece of salty glass to swallow.

"Not on purpose. My blanket flew off. See?" I secured the borrowed shirt across my chest before I pointed up at it. "All I did was sit up."

His lips didn't flatten. He didn't frown. His eyes gave away nothing. His body remained loose. Still, his unhappiness pulsed the air between us. I'd done my best and I'd caught a rogue superhero. Twice. That had to count for something.

"You will tell no one what has transpired here."

Like he thought I just kicked my heels up at broadcasting my frazzled situation.

Anyway, he hadn't disliked my able-titties when I subdued Gale Force. Half hypocritical. Wholly unbalanced. But I nodded. "Absolutely not." He could make my life miserable if he thought I might turn-coat.

Magus eyed me a moment longer, narrowed eyes trying to ascertain how honest my answer had been. Eventually, he turned to Bolt. "Take him to temporary holding cell two, hook him up, then find something for Greer to wear. Something thick."

Bolt tipped Gale Force back and started toward the hallway behind the desk. On the way past me he cast a sly glance my way. "That shirt looks good on you."

I raised my voice before he disappeared completely, "Better than it did on you."

The shirt had barely enough material to cover everything that absolutely needed to be covered. I'd worn bikinis with similar builds, but I couldn't exactly wear the tinier variety. I overwhelmed them with my womanhood, just as I was doing with his shirt.

His laugh echoed back to me. If he'd been closer, I might have gone all oops upside his head. Since Magus was the only person near me, I refrained from deferring to the next customer. Instead, I hugged the shirt around the front of me. "So, what now?"

"Come with me."

Leaving was too much to hope for.

Bolt had moved well out of the hallway before I trailed Magus there. Someone crossed down by the end, past where the bamboo along the walls changed to glass-shelled offices. He didn't look up from whatever paper in his hand he was reading. Had anyone heard what happened in the entryway? Or did their lives buffet them with so much noise that what we'd drummed up hadn't registered?

Whatever the cause, I was glad. Anyone else who came to see what the hubbub was about would have been booby-trapped as well. I could have a whole group of supermen who'd seen my chest but didn't remember. Their subconscious would know, though.

Magus turned left into the bamboo lining the hall. We pushed through a few yards of bamboo and into his book-and-curio-lined office.

Despite the law-library feel, and the jaguar lounging on a tree branch to the left of the entry way, the principal's-office feel reared its head as soon as Magus leaned against the front of his desk. I took my seat on the fainting couch not too far away.

"So," he said then looked up and behind me.

I turned to look at what drew his attention. The jaguar was mid-air and heading toward me.

Fight or flight froze in my veins and stuck me in place. If he'd planned to kill me, I would have died. Fortunately for my neck, the jaguar landed on shockingly soft feet behind me, then climbed up onto the couch to stretch himself across my lap.

"This cat." I shook my head at him, but started petting him before he insisted with paws and teeth.

"Has taken quite a liking to you. And I trust his judgement more than I do my own sometimes."

Bully for me, then, because Magus didn't seem to like me most of the time.

Magus nodded. "He's part of why I haven't followed procedure when it comes to your knowledge of classified information."

Neither of us mentioned that he couldn't hypnotize me to remove my knowledge. No one told me what the alternative to wiping memories might be. Ignorance was probably bliss.

"Still," Magus continued without my input. "Here you are again. In my office. On my radar."

"Not on purpose."

He crossed one leg over the other without shifting his butt on his desk. "It is, and it isn't. The initial cause is outside your control. But when things turn south…"

"I call you."

"You do. Which is much appreciated. The storms that would have happened if you had called the police are…" He took a breath while he considered his words. "Apocalyptic is over stating it. Paradigm shifting, certainly. We superheroes are not in control of much in our lives, Greer, despite the strides made when the unions were formed in this country."

"I know what you mean." I nodded.

His expression soured. "You couldn't possibly." Dismissive tone almost to the point of disgust.

My eyes narrowed as I leaned my neck forward. "Are you trying to make the case that a woman, a black woman, knows nothing of inequality in America?"

His eyebrows shot up and his lips parted in a cartoonish O.

Exactly.

Since he realized his mistake, I nodded and moved past it. "Was there a point to this conversation?"

He pushed himself off the side of the desk to stand. "I am uncertain what to do with you."

That much was clear every time we interacted. "You could give me a job." What the fuck was I saying? I didn't want this. All the unrest and stress. Never knowing what the next day would bring or when my life would be in danger.

Magus shaking his head calmed the rising panic in me.

"You have powers like no one else has seen. I would much rather have them in my toolbox than out there in the world for someone else to pluck, but the law is clear. Not just men. Only males. All males with superpowers are considered men under the law. Regardless of the gender they wish to present in society."

The specificity of his answer kind of impressed me. All the transgender bigotry in the world tossed out the window when it came to oppressing another, more feared group. Huzzah, progress?

"I could have you tested. We already have samples from the last time you were here."

There was something in the way he said it. "Why haven't you already done tests?"

"It would have to be on official record and the anomaly of you would shine a spotlight right on us. The Gold region as a whole; Colorado in particular."

I didn't know what a spotlight on our state would entail. I didn't even know where the spotlight would come from. I didn't like the sound of it either way. "What *do* you have on me, then?"

"One paper file. Basic demographics: name, age, weight, address, and the like. A couple notes in an unattached file of how a civilian consulted with us to identify some pictures. Very little else. The reports of the others who worked with you are just as spare in the details."

That could explain something. "Do you still have the file?"

He nodded. "Because Gale Force worked in the records department, we verified what we had when he snapped and left."

Okay. Gale Force might have made copies of everything pertaining to me, but the information he had didn't mention my chest situation. He didn't know what he would be up against when he came for me. That was definitely to my advantage.

"I'm not sure why you didn't put it all in your files, but thank you. It probably saved my life."

Magus walked over to a chair against one of his walls and brought it over to me. He positioned in such a way that it reminded me of his attempt to hypnotize me. "In return for our silence, and to protect all of us in the future, I am going to need to ask you some questions."

Uncertainty churned in my belly. I didn't want him to know all my secrets. We were all buddy-buddy for the moment, but experience had taught me that kind of thing could shift any minute. I couldn't stop him from asking, I supposed. But he couldn't force me to answer. He probably realized that much as well. This was a trust building exercise, then.

"Okay." I buried my suddenly cold fingers in the warm fur of the jaguar in my lap and nodded. "Shoot."

9 – MUDDY WATERS

MY NERVES SETTLED a bit when I realized Magus didn't care about my early history. He only wanted to know about the things that could potentially affect him.

"How many people have you hypnotized?"

I started counting and realized the number didn't really matter.

"Everyone who's seen me since the thing hit me in the chest at Rust." Wait a second. "No, actually, that's not true. It didn't work on the lady on the roof of the Denver Art Museum. Anterograde."

"And is she the only woman you've exposed your chest to?"

I didn't exactly go around flashing people and charting the effects on the different demographics. Though, it might be a good idea. For science.

"She might have been."

"Perhaps it only works on men."

Not a bad theory, but my sample size was a little skewed. "And a computer."

"What?"

"When Anterograde's video stalled the computer, I flashed a little cleavage to get it going again."

He leaned back in his chair. "I'm not sure what to say to that."

It was a fact. Sensible people didn't argue against facts.

For lack of a better response, I shrugged.

"Is there anything else that I don't know about?"

Probably a lot. Some things probably weren't my stories to tell. Some things were. "I don't think I ever explained how I ended up in the man's truck. The one Anterograde fell onto." Fell onto after I dropped her. Gods.

"Now that you mention it, you did rather glaze over that part of your report. It hadn't seemed important, until we handled the zombie-drone and the one controlling it."

As was my intention, mostly because I didn't understand what happened and wanted to take my own sweet time in figuring it out. The time had passed. I still had nothing. "Anterograde tossed me over the side of the building, something weird happened, and I ended up in that man's office ten minutes away."

"That's not possible."

Except that it happened. He didn't have to believe me. I shrugged again.

"You know that's not possible, right?" He smiled at me like I was a simpleton.

"And going from zero to glowing-skin-that-hypnotizes-people-and-deflects-needles-and-bullets is?"

He tipped his head back against the seat. "You have a fair point."

Of course I did. Why did the head of our state's superhero union question abnormal human things?

With a sigh, he asked, "Is that all?"

All I was willing to tell him. Anyway, he seemed to be full up on how things were working in my life. Since he had other things to worry about, I'd give him the easy out. "Can I go home now?"

"We have some things we need to do in processing Gale Force first." He shook his head, almost a nuzzling the back of the seat. "I don't know how I'm going to word this report."

"Well, you could say I was in bed naked and while he stared at me I beaned him over the head. It's not entirely false." I smiled the smile of the guilty.

His lips parted slightly while he stared at me, eyes wide in shock.

He didn't shock often.

I tried my best to keep a neutral expression. "What?"

"Nothing. That's just a brilliant idea. Doesn't explain everything, but it's a start."

Look at me. Helping to falsify superhero reports at an eighth-grade level. Dad would be so proud.

The superheroes had a lot of things to do before letting me go home. People had to be woken and brought to Magus' office. Stories had to be homogenized to read similar enough to pass outside scrutiny, but not so similar as to be suspicious. Then Phoenyx returned, smelling of fire and some sort of chemical, throwing a wrench in the works.

The fire he'd put out had been set by an arsonist. Sheriff who'd called in already knew that. He didn't know the level of sophistication of the arson. A timer contraption had been planted to start things as well as distribute more fuel at determined intervals.

The arsonist understood how fire worked in a building and with bodies. That throwing accelerant would not help a body burn, because the accelerant burned itself out too quickly. Bodies—and there had been three in the fire—required high heat and a lot of time to burn completely. Even someone looking to burn away evidence needed to find a way to control and feed the fire enough for the body itself to catch. Once the skin burned through to the fat, the fire sustained itself. A phenomenon called wicking.

I learned the coolest things hanging out with superheroes. Cool things that would keep me up nights. If I ever had a whole night to myself to try to sleep. Fat chance of that.

Flaming fat chance.

Phoenyx had shown up in enough time that the wicking process had only just begun on the bodies, though it had been helped along. The arsonist had found a way to get a sticky, flammable substance to adhere to the body in bands and on the clothing. The stuff on the skin, burned hot enough and long enough to sear away the unpainted portion of skin so the fat beneath became a morbid candle. Heinrich Himmler would approve.

Upon arrival, Phoenyx pulled the fire away from everything. The structural damage to the Taj was limited, due again to the use of accelerants. The whole thing looked like the arsonist meant to make a statement of some sort.

Without a note, there was no telling what the message might have been. But, the three victims were women and their teeth were left in. Their purses had long since burned to ashes, as had the pads of their fingers. Preliminary comparison on the dental records had identified them with 80% accuracy. All three of the women were lawyers. Well-off ones at that.

Fiona Appleby, three rich lawyers, and me. What did we all have in common, other than our gender.

"Were they alive when they started burning?" I didn't want to ask it, but I had to know.

"No. They asphyxiated. Only one woman had sufficient skin left for visible examination. She had no obvious ligature marks, so we're still investigating the cause." Phoenyx frowned.

More information than I had asked for, but the answer I'd hoped for.

They died before being roasted. Not great, but better than the alternative. The conversation moved on to more things I didn't want to know. More people. More victims. More deaths, though only a couple more fires. I didn't want to interrupt, but I had another question. "Does anyone know if the three women were members of the Cherry Halls Country Club?"

Three pairs of eyes turned to stare at me. I stared back. "What's the problem?"

"No problem, Greer." Bolt turned back to clicking away on his laptop. "Just something that hadn't occurred to us yet."

Oh. I helped. Yay, me. Did that mean I could leave soon? Or maybe nap in the corner while they figured things out.

"According to the club's records, no." Bolt pushed back from his computer. "None of the women were members. Each had applied at some point, but had been denied for one reason or another."

Balls. A simple association was too much to ask. Everything still felt connected. We just didn't know enough information to figure out what it was. I could be patient, but it came harder when patience meant people dying.

"This was made by Gale Force, all right." Kai came into Magus' office gesturing with a manila folder. "His fingerprints are clear on the tape. No question. And he made the note here. In this facility. He spread the letters he cut out in many magazines, but they all came from here. The fingerprints were harder to isolate on the magazines. Each one of them came from a different office. The pieces fit like a puzzle, though."

That meant one of three possibilities: no one had seen him while he gathered the material, no one had suspected him of any wrongdoing and so they hadn't paid attention to him, or someone else in the Gold 4 knew what he was doing and approved.

All of me hated the idea than any superhero would lash out against me, but one already had and we didn't have any clear reason why. Yes, to put a woman in her place, but why me in particular?

I felt like I could trust the four people in the room right at that moment. I trusted the cat too. The other men...I didn't know. I'd seen some of them, walked past, but I didn't know how they felt about me. These four on my side should protect me from an uprising of sorts. Gale Force had gotten the better of them in the entryway. Some of the other superpowers in the Gold 4 included brute strength and electromagnetism.

My skin crawled.

By six in the morning my nerves were shot and my brain was done. I needed a break. I needed a nap. Despite my clear allies around me, I didn't want to sleep there. Just in case. Sleeping naked in a testosterone-fueled, closed space rubbed me the wrong way. If more than Gale Force saw me as a target, them popping in on me could end badly.

At a lull in the conversation, I stood up. Again, all eyez on me, like Tupac. I needed to ensure a better ending to my story. "I'm going to go."

"Why?" Kai's eyes begged me to stay.

I chose to answer the audio, not the visual. "Because I'm tired."

Bolt jumped in before Kai could continue his two-language conversation. "You're heading back to your apartment?"

The affirmative answer nearly left my tongue before I thought it through. My home was sprinkled with glass from the sliding glass door that Gale Force busted through on the way to get to me. Since I lived on the third floor, the broken door didn't make the apartment an immediate no. I didn't have enough blankets to deal with September-night weather, even with the recent balminess. The sun would be coming up soon to warm things, but not soon enough.

"No." I pulled out my phone to scroll through some numbers. "My bedroom itself is fine, but the living room is another story. I'll have to get someone on it. After the sun comes up."

Once I found the number I wanted, I sent, *You up?*

There was no telling. Lex kept artist hours, which were as consistent as the weather in Colorado. After hitting Send, though, I realized what a bad idea it was. Lex would always take me in because he was that kind of friend. What kind of friend was I if I brought a death threat under his roof? "I know you want to kill me, but you have to go through him first"?

Nope. I didn't like it. And I had another place to go. One that I'd been avoiding for a couple weeks.

It was time to pay the piper. And water some plants. Halfway through a follow up text to ignore me, Lex's reply buzzed.

What are you doing up so early? Or is it late? ;-) DETAILS.

I had to go with something more in depth. *Late, but not for fun. Considered asking to bump up the session, but I'm too tired to be any use. So, never mind. No change. I'll see you later.*

You'd better, SparkleTits. I have paint.

The last bit sounded ominous.

"What's wrong?" Kai asked what the other three men in the room wouldn't.

I shook my head. "Lex has some new ideas. It doesn't matter. Would any of you mind taking me to Gabe's?"

Four pairs of eyes staring at me again. I was getting really good at this. "If you're all busy, I guess I can walk from here." It would be a long walk, possibly shortened by the aid of calling a Luft or an Override.

"Why don't you stay?" Kai again with the questions no one else in the room would ask.

Magus might have said something between an offer and an order. The other two had neither the authority nor a close enough relationship with me to ask. Part of me wished Kai and I didn't have that relationship right then. The awkward, in-between feeling prickled like pins and needles.

I could only think of one way to do this without hurting him.

"I don't want to spend more time than I need to in the same place as

Gale Force. Especially not when I'm sleeping." I shifted my gaze to Magus. "Unless you have a reason for me to stay here."

Magus shook his head. "So long as you keep your phone on, there's no reason for you to remain."

Saints be praised, Magus was on my side. Probably wanted me gone so I stopped distracting his men. Or because he wanted me, and my ability to control him, away from him as soon as possible. Whatever. An endorsement was an endorsement.

"My place," Kai started.

I finished it for him. "Isn't really far enough from Gale Force. Not to my nerves."

Kai frowned at my answer, but it seemed to resonate sense. Exactly what I'd been going for. The distance would be good for both of us. Trouble muddied the water between us. I wouldn't let it explode all over this investigation. Or the next one. Personal life separate from business.

Not that this was my business.

Phoenyx perked up when it seemed the discomfort between Kai and I settled. Chicken. But a smart one. "I don't know exactly where he lives, but I can drop you off."

"As Phoenyx or as Mike?"

He rolled his eyes to Magus, who inclined his chin slightly. Phoenyx nodded to the man and turned back to me. "Phoenyx. Us professional types still have a lot of work to do."

Good. The drive to Gabe's house wasn't too long, but I'd had about enough of the day.

The edge of displeasure danced in the tension of Kai's mouth.

Nope. None of that. Not today. Diversionary tactics in 5...4...3...2...

"Oh, fiddle-dee-dee." I put one hand on my chest and the back of the other against my forehead. "Whatever would this damsel do without you professional types?"

"Expose yourself." Phoenyx smiled.

He had me there. "Balls."

As he got up from the table, he laughed a little smugly. "Come on, SparkleTits. Let's get you home."

Home. Right.

10 – OLD DOG, NEW TRICKS

THE SMELL ROLLED over me as I walked in. Wood and books and leather and sage. Same as it had in Gabe's old house. It usually made me smile. Today, I was grateful Phoenyx hadn't insisted on following me in. He didn't need to see me collapse into a crying mess.

No one did.

As a distraction, I headed to Gabe's greenhouse room.

Watering the plants would give my hands something to do. Something to care for to get me outside my own sadness. Other than a few leaves on the terra cotta tile as I walked the loop, nothing needed my attention. I should have known. Between the drip system and his maid—who I hadn't thought to cancel—everything had been taken care of. Even the hydroponic plantlings looked happy.

Checking on the plants, with the dappled light of the sunrise peeking through the glassed ceiling, got me through the first swell of pain from the gaping emptiness of the house. Exhaustion took over, and a little hunger.

I raided the cookie closet on the way to my old bedroom, grabbing my favorites and Gabe's in one fell swoop. Breakfast of heroes and champions. I claimed neither title, but could use the boost anyway.

Racing up the stairs in twos and threes made me smile. I could see Gabe's grin when he beat me, and how it grew bigger when I bested him. His bedroom door would be open, as always. Welcoming me in whenever I needed an ear or a shoulder. I turned my back to the hallway and ran to the other wing. Why had I even taken that staircase?

Nothing in my old room had changed, other than the bed had been neatly made and the room dusted.

The maid again, I supposed. The glow of morning touched the tips of the mountains in the distance, but not much else. My favorite time to lounge in bed just before dropping off to sleep. Sunrise, I could do without. Sunset set the world on fire and my wall of windows aglow.

I crawled to the middle of the bed and set the cookie bags like staging a perfect bed picnic. I hadn't bothered to turn on any lights as I roamed the house.

Granted, my skin had the faint glow, but it should have been pitch black outside of my radius.

Now that I thought about it, my bedroom should have been too dark to see Gale Force's face. But I had. I saw every detail. I couldn't remember the last time it had been too dark for me to see every detail.

Yes, I did. The night I went home after Gabe had died. The night before the thing hit me in the chest.

Crap, I needed a cookie.

I opened the bag of Gabe's favorite and reached in. Found an envelope instead of a cookie. Scrolled on the front, in his romantic cursive, *I knew you'd find this eventually.*

That cheeky expletive. He would not eat all the cookies just to play one last joke on me, would he?

No. Not this time. Two left. I wouldn't need to pay his grave a visit to yell at him, though he would probably enjoy that reaction. That man. He knew how to tempt me and provoke me better than anyone else.

I hadn't read the letter his lawyer gave me at the reading of his will. It rode in my purse for the time my bravery grew strong enough. The hand in the cookie jar thing. Clever. Made me smile almost enough to dive in. But I'd had three hours of sleep and I knew if I read either letter I might as well give up on sleep for the rest of the day.

After I plowed through the two and twenty cookies I'd brought into my bedroom, I curled up in the middle of the bed and watched the sky light up.

I walked up stairs formed of shadow bricks with light in the seams. Walls rose on either side of me, dark and luminous. They shifted around me as I moved.

A maze of my own making. Brick by brick. Built to keep me safe.

Not just me.

Me and someone else. And something else.

I remembered this place.

I knew these walls. From some time long ago but always with me. I ran for the window open at the top of the stairs.

Beethoven's 5th woke me in all its booming glory. My hands shook as I patted around for my phone. "What is it, Lex?"

He laughed at me.

Morning people were a scourge on the sanity of the world. "Lex."

"I figured you'd gotten a late start because of your early morning, but we have some work to do."

We kind of did, but I did not appreciate all of his cheer and bubbliness. I pulled the phone away from my ear a moment to check. "In what world is ten a late start?"

"The known world, chica. When do you want me to pick you up? Or are you cancelling on me?"

If I cancelled on him I would never hear the end of it. Oh, he'd give me maybe ten minutes because I'd been broken into. He'd give me more if I could tell him that the person was a superhero and he broke in to kill me. But, I couldn't. Magus hadn't said it, but it didn't take a genius to understand where the classified curtain fell.

"I'm good." That was a lie.

"Liar."

Lex knew me too well. "Okay, I'm not good but I'll be ready by the time you get here."

"That's like five minutes from now. Ten, if I take my sweet time in leaving here and catch all the red lights."

"Fifteen. Maybe twenty. I'm at Gabe's." What *had* been Gabe's house. It belonged to me now. How long would it take me to make the mental change-over? Probably longer if I continued living in the apartment through the end of the lease.

"Why are you there?"

Why indeed. "That will cost you breakfast."

"I'm already giving you lunch in two hours."

"I just woke up. You woke me up." I smiled into the phone. "You know how I get."

He forced a breath out. "You're eating it in the car on the way here."

"Fine. Perfect. I'll meet you out front."

One of the benefits of staying here was the couple of outfits I usually left here and a stash of toiletries. Similar provisions had made their way to Lex's right after my apartment had been broken into the first time. I'd popped over to Lex's enough that leaving a few things made more sense than taking them to an apartment that didn't feel like home any longer

I'd scrubbed well enough last night to forgo it this morning. Lex's comment about paint made me cringe. I'd probably be showering again before I left his place. And since I'd be naked—nude—for most of the time, changing before I left had no point.

A quick brushing of teeth, plodding down the stairs, and heading outside still took me longer than it should. Lex rolled up as I locked the door behind me. I glared up at the sky as I walked the few feet to his car. It didn't have to be so bright. The light didn't hurt my eyes, or anything. The brilliance simply didn't match how I felt inside.

I needed some clouds and warm rain.

Lex held a brown paper bag with a red silhouette of Kokopelli on the side. Bless the man.

I opened his car door with a, "Marry me."

He chuckled like a villain and pulled it back from me. "Why are you at Gabe's?"

"Dude broke into my apartment, the sliding glass door this time. Glass everywhere. Classified superhero stuff. They dropped me off here."

His eyes narrowed. "I feel like you're leaving a lot out."

"I am."

He added a frown to the almost-glare.

I couldn't tell him most of what he wanted to know, so I needed a plausible reason why I'd chosen a place to hole up that wasn't his. "Fiona Appleby puked in my lap and died earlier in the day, so I kind of needed a safe place alone to regroup."

"What?"

"What part didn't you understand?"

"How do you even know Fi—" he paused at my pointed glare. "Right. Right. So, why were you near her last night?"

"I'll tell you all about that when you give me the bag." I made the grabby hands in case he had any confusion as to what I wanted.

He passed it over to me like he might toss a steak at a hungry lion: with great caution to keep his fingers attached. Smart, though I could have done without the indulgent eyeroll.

The wonderful aroma of warm green chili blew in my face when I unrolled the top of the bag. Four foil-wrapped beauties sat in the bottom. "Seriously, Lex. Marry me." I lifted my gaze to him so he could feel my sincerity.

"I'm sorry, Honey. I only want you for your body."

Story of my life, of late. Then again, I wasn't exactly in the market to give my heart and soul away to another person. My body was all I had to offer. I dug into my bag of treasures to stop my introspective thinking.

"You have your food, woman." He started down the driveway.

"Talk."

I gave him everything I could, more for myself than because he'd fed me. I needed a person who knew about my issues, for my own sanity. The other people in my life didn't know enough about my new life and I needed someone to lean on. I might need to recruit a superhero to me my new sounding board anyway. Kai...was too complicated right then. Perhaps I could get Mike's number. He knew just about everything and laughed enough to keep me from taking the world too seriously.

Talking to Lex helped set me to rights, except for the person trying to kill me issue. That thought faded into the background as Lex had me paint the front of my torso with thick black paint. I asked him why, beyond the obvious.

Lex started with black as a base, then created a galaxy across me with silver paint stars. Then the play of silver and black fighting for supremacy over the surface of me. All of it using the glow from the unpainted portions of me to light it up.

Certainly nothing he could do with another person, or at least he would need to find another way to coordinate the lighting. He gushed over the beautiful shots. I was just happy to be laying down for the most of it, and with my underwear on, this time.

My phone buzzed under the curve of my back, where I'd tucked it when Lex told me we wouldn't be moving a while. The thing with Gale Force made me too wary to leave it in the other room, as I usually would. I turned the sound off, which didn't matter when the thing vibrated the whole table.

"I'm sorry." Not that I was a professional model, but I hated to cut into his session this way.

"Go ahead." He had the distracted artist tone going on.

Perhaps I hadn't cut into his groove too much. To that end, I arched my back a little and reached for my phone with as little other movement as I could manage.

"Oooo, yesss. Hold that."

I would do my best, but I had to answer. I peeked at the caller. Spencer. Of course. He *would* call when I was in this position. Did I really need to answer?

I swiped the green phone icon, feeling like the popular portrayal of Eve. Weak, weak, weak.

"Greer." Spencer said it low and with a smile I could practically see through the phone.

For just a second, I panicked that he knew what I was doing. That he called right then for that reason. But it couldn't be. Not, unless I'd happened upon a rogue superhero. Gods save me from another one who wanted me for his own designs. "Hi, Spencer."

"How are you doing this fine morning?"

Gods, he sounded like the cat who'd gotten into the cream. And I was the cream.

I needed to focus.

"I'm okay. Kind of a rough night-slash-early morning."

"Couldn't sleep?"

The question sounded like a trap. Luckily, I could divert whatever flirtation he planned to throw my way with the truth. "Someone broke in last night. Kind of hard to sleep through."

Pause. Pause. "What happened?"

There it was. His tone slipped back into its regular lines. Still sexy as hell, but he didn't need to know that. He already had enough working in his favor.

"Basically, what I said. Guy broke in at two-thirty. Ish. I thwarted whatever his plan for me had been by sleeping naked."

He cleared his throat. "Naked?"

Men. Tell them someone broke in, small reaction. Mention being naked, their whole body tuned to you. Time to move it along. "Yes, naked. Which froze him in place until I could call authorities to wrangle him. Statements to the authorities. Didn't get back to sleep until sunrise."

"I didn't wake you, did I?"

Why did he ask that and Lex didn't? Then again, Lex brought me tastiness. "Nope."

"Are you busy right now?"

"Pretty sure I told you I had things to do today." We both knew he didn't forget about it. Men didn't forget the reasons women refused sex with them.

"So, you did."

Gods, I didn't know what to say to that pleased tone.

"Greer, honey," Lex pulled my attention to him.

I willed him to tell me to hang up the phone and save me. "Yeah, Lex."

"Bend your knees, twist them away from me, and keep the shoulders flat." His tone hadn't changed. The phone call hadn't harshed his artist groove. "Push into it with your knees against the table if you can. Good."

My lower back thanked me for the change in position.

"Who was that?" Spencer asked.

Right. I was still on the phone. "Once again, I did say I was busy."

"Yes. And when are you free?"

He'd asked me that already, but I guessed I hadn't answered. The man was persistent. He probably had to be to get anywhere with me.

"Lex, do you have an ETA of when we'll be done?"

It was fifty-fifty of whether I'd get an answer. His camera flashed away rapid fire as he swooped over the surface of my torso toward my head. "The paint's starting to flake a little. Probably another forty-five."

I checked the time and did the math. Lex would finish at noon-thirty. Paint cleaning shower, half hour. Lunch another hour. "I should be free at two."

"The other man said forty-five minutes."

He'd heard that much. Part of me hoped he heard the rest, about the positioning, and he decided I wasn't worth spending the time on. "Clean up and lunch, Spence."

"I could take you to lunch."

"Carbonara with homemade pasta. Sorry." I wasn't really.

"Can't compete with bacon. Dinner, then. You busy?"

He didn't take no, did he. But I hadn't exactly said no. I'd folded and given conditional denials. Too many loopholes he took pleasure in exploiting. "Not at the moment."

"Excellent. I will pick you up at two, then."

"Two? For dinner?"

"You still owe me some work."

I did. Working on his busted vehicle would leave me messy for dinner. He wouldn't be able to take me to a super fancy restaurant, which would be better for me. Less pressure meant less stress. "Okay. I'll text you the address when I'm in a less awkward position."

"You're not at home?"

"Break in. Glass everywhere."

"Right. Awkward position?"

Nope. "Bye, Spence." I hung up before he could pull me into a longer conversation that made me squirm.

"You have a date?"

Why have an awkward talk with Spencer when I could have one with Lex? He didn't even sound distracted anymore. Nope. Eyes wholly focused on my face. I did not need this. "Are we going to finish?"

"Because you have a timeline now?"

There we went.

"Actually, Lex, it's the whole being painted and nude and—"

"Who is it? Is it with that beefcake you brought here the last time? Or Phoenyx? Gods tell me you're dating Phoenyx. The ass on that man." He licked his lips, like Charlie Bucket outside the candy store.

"No. No. He's picking me up from here, so you can meet him, but if you don't get your camera back to clicking I'll end this session myself."

"Touchy, touchy." He reached up and flicked on the blue and red lights.

Pseudo 3D time. Kind of trippy, but at least it meant he'd tuned back into his art brain. Him zoning in let me do the same. Focusing on the shapes my body made when he asked me to move certain ways. It became a kind of meditation, merging of mind with body and nothing else in the room outside Lex's steady voice.

Somehow my whole body trembled when I climbed off the table, the same way it did when we'd had a more active session. The whole layer of paint fractured in glowing lines when I stood and the weight of my chest stretched my skin downward. I frowned at it, but it should all wash away. I texted Spencer the address. Then realized I didn't hear Lex putting his toys away like he usually did.

He stared at me, mouth half open.

Even through the cracks of paint I'd gotten him. Damn me and my chest all to hell.

Frustrated with the world, I reached out for him.

He smacked my hand away. "Don't touch me. Just stand there and let me think through what I want to do with you."

Oh. Hypnoboob hadn't struck again. He'd had a complete artgasm. That, I could handle.

He turned off all of the lights, leaving me as the only source. No effects. No odd angles and zoom lenses. Just me. Portrait. Profile. Bust. Sitting standing. No odd positions to distract me from what he was doing. I hadn't felt this uncomfortable since the first time, when I didn't know what I was doing.

It took another half hour before he was satisfied. I couldn't wait to escape.

The doorbell rang. I grabbed a painting smock and ran for it. It didn't matter who it was. Clutching the smock closed in front, I whipped the door open without checking through the peephole.

Spencer stood on the other side of the door. Cleanly shaven. Bouquet of red and yellow roses in hand. "Greer." His eyes warmed when he spoke my name.

I should have looked through the peephole. "Um." I had nothing.

"I didn't want to wait any longer."

That much was clear. "Um."

"You said that." He offered the roses across the threshold. "Can I come in and wait?"

"Who is it at the door?" Lex called from his studio.

"Um." Eventually my brain would come up with something intelligible.

Spencer laughed his big laugh. The one that tossed his head back, flushed his cheeks, and set his eyes a-sparkle. It didn't help jumpstart my brain.

"It's a simple question." Lex yelled, still out of sight. "Though that sounds like—"

I looked back to explain. He was already coming down the hall.

"Who is this?" Spencer sounded less amused than he had been a few seconds ago.

Yep. When I faced forward he had that crispy-cold quality to him. I could speak to that. Give me scary face any day.

"Lex, this is Spencer Marcus. The man picking me up for a date an hour or so too early." I couldn't deny that this one was a date. He'd shaved like he said he would. Even brought flowers. The awkward meeting at the door like this was senior prom cinched it. "And Spencer, this is my friend Alexander Lexington."

Lex came close enough to flank me and gave Spencer the thorough once over. "Damn, Greer. You are batting a thousand lately. What is your secret? Is it a new shampoo? Can I borrow it?"

"It's the boobs, Lex."

Spencer frowned through the whole exchange, eyes flicking back and forth between the two of us. Then, he shook his head and his eyes fluttered. "The Alexander Lexington? As in the artist who has the show at the Scientific Arts gallery? I wanted to go to your opening but had another commitment."

If I remembered correctly, he'd sent one of his goons to the show. The bouncer outside who had nearly not let me in because I'd been late.

Lex bumped my shoulder with his. "And he even knows me. I like this one."

Maybe Lex should take him, so he would stop throwing me off balance every time he smiled at me. I took the flowers, though, because I was weak and they were beautiful. "I'm going to go find a vase for these." Another escape. I seemed to be doing that a lot lately. Something to work on when I didn't feel like a rabbit.

Lex did the good host thing behind me, inviting Spencer in while the two of them buddied up. That couldn't be good for me. Spencer's eyes kept sliding to me when I wasn't paying attention. He grinned wide when I took a big breath of the flowers. They smelled amazing. He'd chosen well. No denying it.

Time to abandon ship. Again. "Turpentine's in the studio, right?"

"I left a can in the back with some rags for you. Try not to flash the neighbors too much, SparkleTits." Lex didn't even smile when he said it anymore. Like he'd moved on from the joke and decided that was his new nickname for me. At least when other people were present.

I wanted to wring his neck, but it wasn't as if Spencer had never heard the moniker. Still. "That carbonara had better be magical."

11 – DEVIL IN THE DETAILS

SPENCER DRAGGED A finger down the side of my neck. "You missed a bit of paint right there."

I shivered and glared at the fluid still leaking out of his truck's engine. "I probably missed more than that." It wouldn't be the first puddle of fluid on Spencer's garage floor. I could be the next.

"If you need another set of eyes..."

"You'd freeze, Spence. Just like the man who broke into my house." Which would give me the time to put a little breathing room between us. A four-bay garage and he had to lean up against me. Granted, he was showing me how to fix the truck, but he could do so without his hip pressed to mine

He reached between two parts in my hands and twisted something a couple of times. The leak stopped. "I'm also pretty good with my hands."

Silver-tongued devil. I turned to glare at him and his face was right there. An inch away. Smirking his sly smirk. He smelled good too. A spiciness below the engine oil. He'd put on cologne to pick me up, though he knew the date would end up with our hands and shirts smeared with grease.

I narrowed my eyes at him. "You're a dangerous man."

"You've known that since the first day we met."

I did. "Then why am I still here?"

"This." He closed the distance, pressing his mouth to mine and nibbling at my bottom lip.

The soft bites forced shockwaves down through my body. Even without his hands on me, he knew exactly how to send my head reeling.

"Young Mr. Marcus, can I interrupt you for a moment?"

I jerked back from Spencer like a dog caught stealing. My eyes even dropped before I remembered I was an adult and could do anything I wanted with my lips. It said a lot about my feelings on the relationship with Spencer that shame took hold of me first.

Red flag.

Probably needed to heed the warning.

Instead, I turned to see who had stopped my bad decision.

The preacher from the fundraiser, Preacher Edwin I believed, had walked up to Spencer's garage while we'd been distracted. Thank Goddess for the preacher. Strong as my will to tell Spencer no, the libido carried a heavier stick.

Spencer did, too.

"I'm actually kind of busy," he said.

I had no problems with him becoming un-busy with me. No matter how my goose pimples protested.

"The important question, though, Edwin, is how did you even get here?" Happy, flirtatious Spencer had slipped away along the edges.

My guess was that the preacher's arrival probably had something to do with the sweet ride parked on the street in front of Spencer's driveway. Tesla, in all its electronic glory. Not even the cheaper one. It kind of made me sick. A so-called servant of the downtrodden and meek should not have something so needlessly expensive.

"I spoke with your father," Preacher Edwin strolled the rest of the way into the garage like he hadn't a care in the world. "Made sure to let him know of the community service and fundraising possibilities we had discussed at Ms. Appleby's fundraiser, but that I couldn't send you materials because I'd lost your address."

Save the short stint when I'd stormed off, Spencer had spent his time at the barbecue hovering around me. My absence hadn't been long enough for any kind of pitch session.

I didn't like the Preacher's story at all.

He lied, and not about how the congregation needed to give him enough money to buy yacht because God prophesized it must be so. I understood those lies for the simple cause and effect. This struck me different.

Not in the least because the smile Edwin levied on Spencer didn't reach his cold, dead eyes.

Leaving lickity-now would have been the real godsend. I'd already tarried too long. Any further movement would bring the attention in the room where I didn't want it: on me. I knew this drill from way back. Not moving could spare me. Standing still meant the T-Rex could not see me. I took a mental step back and hoped to find something more fascinating to put my mind on.

"Why are you here?"

Apparently, Spencer used his persistent nature for more than annoying me into kissing him. Bully for him.

"Cherish." The preacher said it like it made sense. "She did not show up at the agreed upon time."

Cherish was a person. Okay.

The animation remaining on Spencer's face left. He became the cold, calculating thing I'd first met. Business man and not the kind of business he could flaunt at a charity barbeque. "I am not the person to talk to about that. If you contact my associates—"

"Your associates know nothing. I have spoken to them." That dead fish smile.

Did Preacher Edwin's congregation never see the twisted person beneath the sweet-as-pie preacher thing? They deserved to know who they were pledging their money to.

"So," Preacher Edwin chimed in again after a long slash of quiet. "I come to you."

"And you need to leave."

The preacher shook his head in one slow move, left, then right. "I have paid a considerable amount of money for a long time. I expect to receive what I've paid for."

I didn't like the way the dots were lining up. Money paid. A girl. A man—it didn't matter if he was a preacher or the damned Pope—paid for a girl. Now, he threatened Spencer because the girl didn't show.

Spencer was a pimp. An honest-to-gods seller of women's bodies.

Oedipus Rex.

I fought so hard against knowing about his clandestine activities. I wanted to be the blissful ignorant person and it had nearly backfired on me. He'd almost gotten me, with his sweet talk and hungry lips. It had all been to butter me up. Reeling me in so he could put me in his stable of women.

Again, I thanked Goddess for the preacher showing up at the time he did. I almost allowed myself to do something really stupid. Against my better judgement.

Small, painful blessings.

"Of course, if you refuse, I can always take what I want out of this one." The preacher reached back and pinched my jaw with no warning.

I jerked my chin out of his grasp. "Don't touch me."

I didn't even know he'd been close enough to touch me. Never mind the audacity of someone grabbing another person without permission.

Since frozen bunny hadn't kept me out of this conversation, I moved. Not a retreat. Backing away gave the impression of being some sort of prey cornered. I walked past both of them to the sink. It placed me closer to Spencer. The devil I knew a little better. The one who hadn't grabbed me without permission. Solidarity against a common foe, and all that. But he and I would have some words. The last ones we would ever have.

Walking to the sink had not been an idle move. Part of my overall retreat plan, starting with cleaning the grease from my fingers. Because, smooth as Spencer was, suave did not make up for being a gods-damned pimp.

With a preacher for a customer.

The phone rang. Someone's phone rang. My phone was still, tucked into my bra as usual. And mine didn't have Rhapsody in Blue as the ringer.

"Mr. Marcus," Preacher Edwin said, widening his voice to sound more like the voice of God, or whatever. He spent his time teasing his parishioners out of money so he could spend it on prostitutes. The man knew the power of his own voice. "We are in the middle of a conversation. Hardly the time to take a call."

Spencer's phone, then. Silly me. I'd left mine on vibrate because we were supposed to be on a date.

"This may be the answer you have been waiting for, Preacher Edwin." The preacher's name oozed out of Spencer's lips before he answered the phone, emphasizing that he was supposed to be a man of God, not of the flesh. Spencer knew how to use his voice too.

It was a wonder he hadn't chosen the cloth as well. It seemed the two men shared the highest of moral grounds.

I tried my best to focus on the water and on the sandy soap I rubbed under my finger nails. A hand closed around my right butt cheek and squeezed harder than necessary. A side glance showed me Spencer's hands and attention were all accounted for.

The preacher, then. "I like them feisty."

I rinsed the last of the soap off my hands and turned the water off easy as you please. When I whipped around and thrust the heel of my hand into the preacher's chin, though, I did it with great relish.

His teeth clicked together, hard, and his head tipped back. He took a step back, though. The only part that really mattered. A few feet between us gave me enough room to anticipate his next move. Gave me the time to react.

Edwin grabbed hold of his mouth. "You little bitch." Some blood sputtered out when he said it.

I'd gotten him good. "Such language for a man of the cloth," I smiled. This was fun. Something to vent my frustrations on with no negative repercussions.

"You dirty slut." Blood and saliva dribbled down his chin.

Perhaps I'd knocked a tooth or two loose. Hopefully. It would be a nice reminder to him of what happened when he didn't play nice.

"Spencer, are you going to handle your whore? You see what she did to me."

"She is not an employee."

That was all he said. Not to leave me alone or to not call me anything. Just that I didn't work for him. Swoon, swoon, swoon. I declare. What a man.

"No, no." I stepped between the two before Spencer answered any further. This fool was mine. "You leave him out of this. This is a conversation between you and me in which you touched me, twice, when I told you not to. By my calculations, that means I still owe you one and your nose is currently unbroken."

He narrowed his eyes at me and dipped his chin, as if he finally saw me and not some doxy for him to play with. "I will use every resource in my power to make certain you regret the mistake you just made."

All the brave words and he did not take a single step toward me. He might have learned a thing or two.

"Try me, preacher." I stepped toward him and he took two steps back. Good. I liked that math. "I've already had the worst happen to me and I've had a shitty month to boot. When you come at me, and all the demons in my past come back out into the light, they will bite you in the ass."

Anger flared his perfect, unbloodied nostrils and burned from his eyes. But he kept his mouth shut.

"You need to leave, Preacher." Spencer had stepped out from behind me. His phone was still in his hand, but it hung loose and dark by his side. "And don't ever come knocking on any of my doors again."

He squared his posture as he turned to Spencer, like he might try for intimidating him. Since he'd failed with me. "Cherish—"

"Is dead. Because you took so much effort to find me, I'm going to assume you're not the one who torched her, but if this is the way you treat any woman you come across, you cannot pay enough to spend time with mine. Go."

"I've already paid for the evening."

Spencer lifted his phone, almost in a threatening manner. "And you will pay more to keep that a secret if you don't leave now and never come back. To any of my schedulers. I am done with you and the money you squeeze from your flock."

He glared between Spencer and I, looking for a weak spot between us. There were plenty, including a rift widening as we stood there, but this man could not touch it.

"You two will pay for your sins against Almighty God." He raised his voice to full preaching mode to say the words. Him turning around and stomping to his car shortly thereafter ruined the effect.

Because I still felt a little—yes, feisty—I called after him. "So will you, buddy. Adultery and coveting ring any bells? Pretty sure those hit the top ten list of big no-noes."

He said nothing, just reapplied his glare from before he turned tail to run. It had less effect from the other side of his fancy car.

"You're not him, you know." I yelled it. "You're not God."

Preacher Edwin dropped into his car and sped away. Good riddance.

"Thank you, Greer."

Lips pursed, I rolled my neck around to Spencer. "You don't think we're going to skip over talking about what just happened, do you?"

12 – BEHIND THE CURTAIN

SPENCER'S EYEBROWS ROLLED up on his forehead like he was confused. "I thought it would be better if you handled his handsy-ness yourself. Was that wrong?"

"Not the issue."

"Okay…"

"You sell women's bodies. You're a mother fucking pimp."

Understanding dawned over his expression, but he shook his head. "No, I'm not."

Did he think I was that dense? I balled my hands into fists and shoved them in my pockets so I wouldn't be tempted to use them on his lying, pretty face. "He paid money. He wanted a girl. He came to you.

What part of that is you not being a pimp, you asshole?"

"I am a...madam, for lack of a better word." He stepped toward me, for some reason.

He was smarter than that. He read body language, especially mine, better than that. Usually. And I wasn't being exactly subtle in mine. Feet in a wide stance, a little bit of shifting weight from foot to foot. Hands alternating between clawed and fists, even in my pockets. My lips twitched while I tried to control myself.

On the plus side, he didn't touch me.

"What the fuck is that supposed to mean, Spencer?" Why did I ask that? I didn't want to know. I'd already washed my hands of the grease. All I needed to do was leave and wash my him right out of my hair.

Spencer turned his palms up, empty except for the phone, and stared deep into my eyes. "The women and men set their own prices, with the knowledge I take thirty percent off the top."

"Of course you do." Why not fifty?

I needed to go. I needed to go but I didn't have a car. Spencer had driven me here. Calling for a ride would still leave me stranded with him for much longer than felt comfortable

"For that thirty, they have full medical and dental. Dollar for dollar match to their 401k up to a thousand a month. Taxes are filed promptly. My profit on that business is not the exorbitant rivers of money you're thinking. My auto dealerships bring in more."

I never thought I'd come to the moment that a car dealership was less sleazy. Surprises abounded in my life of late. "That doesn't make exploiting other people, selling *other* people's bodies for profit right. Or legal. Despite what you tell the tax man." I pulled my hands from my pockets and crossed my arms.

He shook his head. "The contracts we have—you can look one over if you want—explicitly outline that sex is not a part of the contract, nor can it be negotiated for, once my people are on site. They choose the people they contract with. My employees, both women and men are escorts, companions, decorations on arms to make the men, or women, look more successful or intelligent. Whatever else they're missing in their life that they cannot find organically or in their timeframe."

"You expect me to believe money is passing hands and there is no sex involved?"

"Of course there's sex." He swiveled himself around to sit his butt against his hoodless truck, just out of arm's length. "I don't regulate their decisions in that. It is always by their choice. Well documented. Not on the clock or on the same evening they're filling a contract. Videotaped to protect them and if they're comfortable and think it will get them more information."

Information meant extortion. It also meant that it was just a means to an end and Spencer was using women's bodies to get it. Even worse.

His phone rang. He snarled soundlessly. "I have to get this."

"Go ahead." It was only thing he was getting, other than a swift kick in the genitals from me.

Spencer put the thing on speaker phone, staring at me as he did. "What?"

"Cherish was the only one headed to the burlesque show who didn't show. We've received calls that Tiffany and Summer are twenty and thirty minutes late for their appointments, a business dinner and a bar opening in river north, but I-25 is backed up from the game."

I didn't want to know anything about his business and Spencer knew that. He also probably knew I couldn't not listen. Something in me wanted him to not be a bad guy, despite all evidence to the contrary. What the hell was wrong with me? The man had a nice face, and body, but he wasn't worth twisting myself around like this. No man was.

"Call them, Brian," Spencer said. "Call them until they answer."

"You should probably see if they had any former contracts with people in common with Cherish." What in the flying fuck? Was I helping Spencer manage his exploitive illegal activities?

His eyes swelled at me like I'd just thrown him a life preserver.

"Who was that?" The person on the other end of the phone call, Brian, asked.

I hadn't bothered to keep my voice low because I hadn't planned on speaking. Shit.

"Check out Cherish's history, Brian. Cross-reference any of her recent jobs with people who have contracts with other girls." Spencer didn't address the other person's question, but he did what I told him to do.

I didn't know how to feel about that.

Spencer continued. "Actually, Wednesdays aren't busy. Call everyone."

There was a pause on the line as someone else's voice mumbled in the background. "Everyone?"

"Cherish was murdered. We need to see if it was an isolated incident or the beginning of a systematic attack on my employees. Don't let anyone go out tomorrow until you've heard back from every single person. Every person, Brian Winchester."

"That'll cause a lot of headaches. Boss."

"Better than corpses. Get it done." He hung up the phone, and his eyes dropped from my face. "I'm supposed to keep them safe. They smile and they charm, listening for anything that might work to my advantage. But they aren't the soldiers."

Spencer had such tight control on how his emotions arranged his features, I didn't know if I could trust the pensive expression and drooped shoulders. With all I'd learned in the last ten minutes, I didn't know that it mattered.

"I'm going to go."

"I wish you wouldn't." He didn't move to intercept me as he said it. Neither did he pull on his polished smile when he spoke. His shoulders didn't straighten. Just stared back at me from that place I couldn't trust.

Without trust in what he was feeling at the very least, I had no reason to stay. "I think it's for the best."

He dipped his chin, but squared his jaw and pushed off from the truck we'd been working on. "I'll get my keys."

Extra length of time alone with him, trapped in his vehicle. While I knew he wouldn't try to take advantage of me, he would use the situation to talk himself out of the hole he'd fallen into. I'd had enough talking for one afternoon. "I'll walk."

"That's not a good idea."

This whole thing hadn't been a good idea. What had I been thinking? Had I been thinking at all or just reacting to his interest in me? Like a moth to a flame, I got burned by the fire. "All the same, I'll walk."

"Greer, listen." He held up his hands. Empty. Non-threatening. No telling what he'd done with those hands that he hadn't told me about.

"Cherish is dead, choked to death somehow they can't identify and her place set on fire. Two others are missing that I know about. I'm sure Preacher Edwin would love to find you walking alone and take advantage of it."

"I can handle the preacher."

"Not if he hits you with his car."

Actually, I might make it out of that alive. It couldn't be any worse than a car exploding in my face.

"Beyond that," Spencer continued, "you've been seen out with me and if this is an attack on me, it puts you in danger."

Another vote for me putting as much distance between us as possible. I pressed my lips together to keep myself for speaking the words. Gods help me, but I didn't want to hurt his feelings. I just wanted out. He had to know how I would receive his words.

He dropped his hands to his sides. "Please, Greer. I don't want to have to worry about you, too."

Him worry. About me. Either he was laying it on thick or he sincerely meant it. I couldn't tell, which was too much of the problem between us.

"Okay, Spencer. I am six-foot-four in my bare feet and not exactly a waif. I've taken enough self-defense to take an attacker down however they try to take me. My skin is damned near bullet proof and if that wasn't enough, my chest can stop a person in their tracks." I set my fists on my hips to pay homage to the Amazons. "I'm not exactly the kind of person you worry over."

"You are exactly the kind of woman I worry over, Greer Ianto." He shrugged, but his eyes never dropped from mine. Cold and calculating and honest. "Night and day."

That expression, without all the civility painted over it. The man of metal and fire. *That* face, I believed. And it sent chills down into my stomach, while my legs trembled. Shit. This was not some passing fancy. He was not playing a game.

"Be that as it may, I need to leave here under my own power."

He dipped his head in a nod. "I will call you."

Not a surprise in the least. "Goodbye, Spencer."

"Will you call me and let me know you made it safe?"

If I refused, he would wait a sufficient period of time before ringing me every ten minutes. I could feel the potential in him. "I'll text."

"Okay."

He waited for me to put some space between us before I heard him take a few steps after me. From the bottom of his driveway, I looked back up at him. He'd stopped at his garage door to watch me go. Tension rode his shoulders, frustration twisted his face, but he made no move to chase me down.

I straightened back around and set my feet to a walking pace I could maintain. When I got to the end of the block, the wind carried an eloquent stream of expletives to my ears. Self-deprecating and world-hating.

I picked up the pace.

My race-walk speed carried me until I'd outpaced even my imagination that I still heard his voice. When I slowed, I tried to focus on anything else.

What to do with my apartment. Nope.

What happened to me that night at Rust that set my skin aglow.

Nope.

Why Gale Force had decided to kill me. Nope.

What to do with Kai. Big nope.

Why Fiona had died. That was too close to my biggest nope of all.

Didn't I have anything in my life that hadn't fallen to shit?

The sun beat down on me, promising good things still lived. The breeze tickled my face and rustled some trees. Crimson and ochre leaves dropped from beautiful old trees, dancing their way down and around me. Some things were still right in the world, even if my corner of it had collected nothing but dust bunnies and doom.

Doom couldn't compete with this sunshine. At least for the moment. I let it and my feet carry me past some of my favorite old houses in Denver. If the exhaust wouldn't have killed me ten times before I made it home, I would have walked along Monaco, admiring the houses the way I did when I drove the street.

For my lungs' sake, I took a side street, admiring beauties I didn't usually get the chance to see.

Massive old houses. Some newly built ones with modern lines in the place of those torn down. I preferred the dignity of the old.

I stepped off the curb. A dog barked at me from somewhere close and I nearly jumped out of my skin. I hadn't been near a fence, but backpedaled my way into the middle of the street to figure out where the deep barks echoed from.

Deep barks. Sounded like a big puppy. The kind the horror master would write about, all slobber and teeth. Not the kind of thing I wanted sneaking up on me. But where was it?

The wrought iron fences had nothing but vines straining against them. The closest wooden fence stood too far away for that volume of barking. It almost echoed. More than the sound bouncing off the houses around would cause.

I looked up, because my life had become just crazy enough that flying dogs weren't outside the realm of possibility. Of course, if a dog with that kind of bark came from the air, I would have died four times over before I finally thought to look up. Still, the lack of air beasts gladdened me. I set my sights a little lower.

I'd swiveled almost the whole way around before I caught sight of the massive paw reaching out from the street-corner storm drain. A mouth matching the bark and the paw threatened anyone senseless enough to dangle a limb in the drain.

Another look reaffirmed that no one had wandered on the street around me. There would be no witnesses if I died a horrible death. I pulled out my phone. No signal. Of course.

Walking up to any of the houses around here would give me nothing. If anyone answered the door I would more than likely be quickly dismissed. I didn't look like the kind of person who belonged in this neighborhood, which was mostly true. While my bank account would set me on equal footing with the owners of the houses at the end of the month, it still put me in new money standing. Not equal. Not the same. Me and Molly Brown.

Monaco was only the one street over. I could wave someone down and have the other person call animal control.

The barking increased as I started away. It didn't exactly stop when I did, but it decreased. Which was odd.

I started toward the dog. The barking continued unabated.

Two feet away, I stopped. Warm breath pulsed out at my shins, or it was just my imagination. The moist warmth at my neck was definitely my own imagination. This was not my smartest idea. The teeth might not pierce my skin, but the jaw could certainly crush my neck.

"Do you need some help?"

The barks gave way to a low, spine-shaking growl.

I clenched the side of my legs to stop my hands from shaking. The growl was an answer. I didn't speak enough dog to know what it meant. Was it a threat, or was the dog answering in the affirmative? Could it be both?

Only one way to do this. "You're scaring me. If you stop that, I will do my best to help you out."

The dog went silent. Its head shifted so the muzzle no longer pointed out the drain. Instead a bright yellow eye stared back at me. Yellow eye set in a massive head I couldn't see the whole of. The head alone wouldn't fit through the drain, let alone the rest of the body. I'd heard of giant sewer lizards, but massive, storm-drain dogs?

"Gods, how did you get in there?"

Barks and growls. Not as loud as the others had been—the dog already had my attention—but the anger shone through. Sizzling in the ferocious noises and burning in the eye watching me. However this dog had gotten to this spot, it had been against its will. Which meant it hadn't been tossed in as a puppy that mutated into a teenaged, crime-fighting beast.

If it had gotten into the sewer, there had to be a way to get it out.

13 — UNDERGROUND SMELL-ROAD

IN MY HEART of hearts, I knew what I had to do. My brain rebelled. A rebel without a plan was not friend to the cause. Without any other option, I had to climb into the drain and lead the dog out of the sewer.

I checked my phone again. No signal. The phone had survived a fall off a several-story building but had no signal when I really needed one. Typical. Story of my life.

Squatting down to survey the opening brought me closer to the teeth and claws of the raving beast. Its eye watched me intently while I figured if my chest would allow me through the drain.

If I sucked it in and crammed the girls every which way, I could do it. Which was a travesty. If my chest had the potential to make it, children could somersault in with ease. Someone needed to fix this. The three bars across the mouth of it did about as much good as a baby spoon shoveling snow.

"Okay, I'm going to squish my way down there with you. Then we will see if we can't get you out of there. Does that sound good to you?"

The growl came out the hole again, the short version. When the paw scraped away and the eye retreated into the darkness of the drain I realize two things. Growling, short bits of growling, meant yes. Also, I'd committed to crawling into the dark unknown. Something in this terrifying, massive dog made me want to free it.

Perhaps something in the dog resonated with me. Maybe it was how it demanded my attention but asked for help. Something this colossal asked me. I fully recognized I'd been chosen by sheer virtue of proximity.

But the dog asked.

Wriggling my shoes into the drain didn't take too long. The reverse-motion, restricted worm took a good deal longer. When I got stuck most of the way in, I would have cut my breasts off. Gladly. I'd gone too far in to crawl back out. Lack of leverage below the waist reaffirmed how bad an idea climbing in had been.

No one knew where I was. The person closest to me...not the one I wanted to contact. Also, the signal thing. I would have to wait for some unfortunate soul to pass by and notice me, just like the dog had.

Finally, one breast popped down, past the scary edge biting into my ribcage, leaving room for the other to come on down. I dropped down the side of the wall. A, "Yipes," fell out of me before my butt found squishy ground.

It stank down here. Not the stench of human waste but of rotting things that had been dampened by rainstorms not big enough to wash the rotting matter away. The decaying soup soaked through my pants and underwear. I nearly chided the dog before I looked up and found it standing over me.

"Hey, big fella."

A long, low growl rolled out of him. The sound was much worse from this seat. Forget my cold, rot-soaked butt. I would die here. In the worst way possible. Good job. Shimmying down into a storm drain couldn't have a better ending.

But he didn't attack me. Just growled and glared at me with those relentless, golden eyes. I might not be on the menu here.

I missed something. What had I done before the growl started?

I'd spoken. I'd said... "Wait, so not big fella. Big gal?"

Silence.

"Okay. Good." I pushed myself to standing and wished I hadn't used the wall to do it. Unspeakable things clung to the back of my shirt in clumps and soaked fabric. I took a pleading glance up at the opening I'd squeezed myself through. High enough that I'd need a running start at the wall and a miracle to make it out of here. No other way to go but further up and further in.

Pulling my shirt away, I peeked at my phone half tucked in my bra. No bars. Yep. The world wanted me to do this thing. Okay. Courage to the sticking place.

The dog had moved closer to me when I stood. Enormous dog. Too big to be real and not a monster from a child's nightmare.

The head came to my chest. Her shoulders were wider than mine. This gal could shit a mastiff and keep on walking. Pale fur—shaggy and caked with things I'd rather not think about—covered most of it. The legs darkened. The feet were so dark they were almost indistinguishable from the shadows near the ground.

What was this prehistoric beast and what did it want from me? Freedom, I gathered. I didn't know if I wanted to be the one to unleash her onto the world. Too late to run the other way.

I couldn't quite smile, but I could pretend the two of us were on equal footing. Respect. Eye contact. I took a breath and a stab at communication. "Why don't you lead the way to where you came from then we can find a way to get both of us out of here?"

She pulled a one-eighty and started toward an opening to the vestibule I'd dropped into. Before she moved, I hadn't noticed much more than the muck and her staring me down.

When she came even with the edge, she turned her head back toward me.

I got the message. Time to go. She moved once I followed.

The tube she led me through teemed with squishy unmentionables down the center. Different friends dangled down from where they clung to the ceiling. My shoes had soaked through by the time I got the correct lurch-crouch combination to save them. It worked until the next section narrowed.

Big Gal hunkered down and managed to slink though without her belly touching. My grace landed me on my hands and knees a couple times before I just accepted crawling.

This was temporary.

I could do this if the dog could.

She'd already managed it at least once, in a fur coat.

Skin rinsed easier than fur.

My four-point mantra repeated as we came to a smaller pipe. This one with a flow of cold stinky water. It couldn't be just water, not with the funk. But I couldn't move forward if I figured out what it really was. So, water. Just water.

Water, water everywhere and it had too much stink.

Big Gal's belly got wet. She had to drag herself though this one, scrapping all sides as she wiggled her way through. It should have meant no disgusting matter left to cling to me.

No dice.

No coins floating in the air or Christmas-colored plumber brothers in the pipe either.

Everyone got painted this go-round, with the bonus of Antarctic temperatures. Fun.

I hated the pipe, the dog, and myself. I should have stayed home today. The home that had been broken into twice. I had no safe place to call my own.

The pipe led to a rough tunnel pointed vaguely upward.

My half-frozen fingers mapped gouges from claws that had dug their way through the hard-packed earth. The rough surface made for decent climbing, though. Even up through the two feet of reinforced concrete. I tried—and failed—not to be alarmed that the dog who weighed more than me could dig through two feet of concrete and rebar.

If she could do that, why would she bother flagging me down?

When I cleared the hole, I rolled out onto my back, closed my eyes, and just breathed a moment. Dirt caked on top of the moist filth on my back as I laid there. The back could match the front, then. Putrid parfait.

Not my favorite. I wanted to tap out.

Going back the way we came would only add another layer to the fun. Rotten-lasagna Greer would be worse than the parfait. No way to go but up.

Not to mention the huge obstacle nudging my foot with her warm snout.

"I know, I know." I told her as I sat up. "I'm coming."

Where I was coming, I had no idea. The room Big Gal brought me to, was a cube roughly ten feet in every direction. It also had deeply scoured, but not dented, metal walls and a door that would have been at home in a bank. No lights to speak of, beyond the light shimmering off my arms and head, which wasn't much. Enough for me to see by. I wondered if I needed any light at all to see.

Not the thing to investigate from inside a vault.

Something as solid as this should have held riches beyond imagining. Instead, it held me and a dog the size of a small, healthy bear.

If it had been me locking this dog away, I might have used this room as well. "The metal walls were a little too much for your claws, were they."

Low growl.

"Well, let's see what we can do, shall we?"

Big Gal paced while I tugged and twisted at the workings of the door from this side. There should have been some sort of fail-safe for a person who'd been accidentally locked in. Unless the thing had been built specifically to lock people in. I didn't like the implication. I needed out of here. And not through the sewers.

When I turned toward the dog, she stopped her pacing to look back at me. On the side of uncanny, but with a head that large, she probably had more brains than the average house pet.

"I have one more thing I'm going to try." And Gods, I hoped it worked. If it didn't, the both of us were out of luck. "But I need you to, like, close your eyes and cover them before I do."

Nothing. She didn't move. She didn't make a noise I could take as affirmation or disagreement. Big Gal just sat and stared at me.

Too much had passed between us for me to believe she didn't understand. She would have given me some indication that I needed to explain what I meant. This stare felt more like judgement. Refusal and judgement.

I wasn't even certain that closing the eyes would be insufficient, but I didn't want to risk it. Making her mad might be the long, painful end of me.

"Listen, Big Gal, I have some tricks up my... um... shirt, but I don't want to put the whammy on you when I try it out. Which means I need your eyes closed and covered." Listen to me. Whole sentences and slang to explain something to a canine.

It worked, though. She whuffed at me. I couldn't tell if it was amusement or annoyance. It might have been a mixture of both. Regardless, her lids closed over her beautiful golden orbs and she settled one of her paws over the upper portion of her face.

If she'd been a person, I would have made sure she kept them covered. I trusted Big Gal to hold this posture. Not to mention, I didn't want to annoy her any more than I probably already had.

There was no reason my idea would work. Still.

Using just my left hand, I spread the neck on my shirt and pulled it down as far as it would go.

White light bloomed across the surface of the door, which hummed under the palm of my right hand. I pushed gently, not straining myself against it as I had before. It gave. Wheels spun, bolts slid back into their hiding places, and the circle of three-feet-thick metal swung out at the touch of my fingertips.

I would hyperventilate about it later. For the moment, I pulled my shirt back up—lest someone came to see what caused the glow—and turned back toward the dog.

"Okay, Big Gal." I lowered my voice because it seemed the thing to do with the door open. Someone bad could overhear us.

She pulled her paw away, looked at the crack visible around the perimeter of the door, and licked the hell out of my face. One swipe of the tongue was all it took to dampen the whole left side.

Her tongue might have been cleaner than anything I'd contacted while I crawled the sewer, but ew ew ew ew ew. Layers of grossness and she'd taken a big taste of it. And me.

I hoped she didn't take a liking.

Big Gal moved from the face lick of legends to heading out the door without skipping a beat. I wanted to rub my face off. Everything on the surface of me was unclean. Halfway through the door, Big Gal turned her head back around to me. I got it. It was time to go again.

Skin rinsed clean.

Memories didn't, but skin rinsed clean.

I took a breath, reminded myself again that skin rinsed clean, then started after her.

14 – Worse Than Her Bite

DESPITE ALL THE money someone had poured into the door and vault, the hallway had the dilapidated feel that could only come from habitual disuse. Peeling wallpaper. Open doors hanging askew while the closed ones gaped around the edges. Smell of dust and dry wood. Shag carpeting. Different kind of gross than what we'd crawled through. The kind of place Mystery, Inc. would be called to investigate.

The shag crunched with age under our feet as we snuck along.

Correction, the carpet crumbled under my feet. Big Gal stalked forward on feet that kissed the ground with barely a rustle. Silent and powerful. Grace in motion. Beautiful. Even under the muck and dirt clinging to her fur. How anyone had ever caught her, I could not imagine.

A glass door loomed ahead of us when we turned a right corner. I stepped back, dropped to a knee and peeked out.

The glass had the barest frosting on it. Enough to obscure details if a person didn't stand up close and personal. Big Gal and I crouched a few paces from the door, far enough to keep mostly in the shadows. No one stood directly on the other side of the glass. Just spiral metal staircase and another door on the far side.

My love of horror movies told me the killer would get me if I went upstairs. Of course, melanin-deficient people had a much higher survival rate than my people.

Damned, either way.

As this wasn't my rodeo, I looked to the girl in charge. I opened my mouth to speak, then thought better of it. Just because things looked abandoned didn't mean they were. The vault had certainly been in working order. Someone had locked her in.

Instead of talking, I made sure her eyes were on me when I pointed up, raised my eyebrows, then pointed straight toward the door and lifted them again. She was smart enough. She should understand what I asked.

Big Gal sniffed and pointed her nose at me.

I knew she didn't mean for us to go back the way we had come.

She sighed, which kind of made me feel like a child.

Eyes locked on the door at the end of the bend, she stalked her way out to the opposite side of the hall. She watched the door close enough that I felt safe to creep over to meet her, though I kept to a deep crouch as I moved.

From this angle, I could see the tip of a bent knee just to the right. Someone sat guard just outside the hallway.

Well, poop.

Also, there was a third doorway in that room, on the right side. Too many options complicated things. More choices would be wrong. None of it mattered until we got out of this hall.

I could probably open the door and catch the dude with the hypnoboob in fairly quick succession. Catching him before he sounded the alarm, however... No guarantee of that. Big Gal and I needed a guarantee.

Feet appeared at the top of my view of the staircase. My heart wanted to run back into the cover of the hallway on the left. Big Gal didn't move, though. The darkness on this side of the glass door wouldn't keep them from seeing her. The filth all over her didn't dim her pale fur enough. I stood and stepped in front of her.

Browns and blues and filth gave better cover. We weren't in the square of light beaming from the door. Provided the two men stayed on the other side of the door, the two of us were good. If they didn't, hypnoboob would save the day.

"When's the last time you checked in on her?"

"Shawn." The guy stood up from the chair. A little taller than the man who just came down, but the new man had more bulk to him. Perhaps someone should let our guard have some steroids. Or a sandwich. "She's behind three feet of titanium and steel. You saw the scratch marks the last time we dosed her. She can't get out."

"And when's the last time you dosed her?"

"Nearly four hours. It'll be at least another two before she wakes enough to eat again."

A vibration started up behind my back. Low. Almost audible.

I reached back to Big Gal and patted whatever I came into contact with on her. Filth and dirt didn't matter when someone needed comfort. Even when the someone was a dog large enough to take down a yeti. Especially when that someone was a dog large enough to take down a yeti.

"If you're sure she's down for the count, you should head upstairs, Justin. Dinner just came and you're not going to have time later."

"I know, I know, Shawn." He waved at the shorter man as he started toward the stairs. "Big show tonight."

"Come on, man. Don't act like you're not excited to see that bitch get what's coming to her."

Justin paused with his foot on the first step. "Which bitch?"

"Does it matter?"

Justin started laughing and Shawn started laughing and they both chuckled their happy asses up the stairs.

I wished I could growl like Big Gal behind me.

"We'll get them." I forced my voice low, so I didn't shout and bring the bastards back down.

Big Gal stepped around me and headed toward the door. I followed close behind. I moved to grab the door. She set her teeth carefully around the doorknob and twisted her head to the right. Apparently, she only needed my help on the big door.

As soon as she pulled it open enough, I slipped through with my fingers ready and hovering near my collar. Just in case. But the tiny room was empty. I didn't even hear footsteps ringing on the staircase anymore. Voices carried down, though. All men, which didn't surprise me after hearing the conversation between the twat waffles.

The door to the right was locked. I motioned for Big Gal to cover her eyes. This time she did without questioning. A measure of trust between us. I flashed the door and turned the knob.

Boobs opened all doors.

The stench of piss and shit and sadness accosted me as soon as the door cracked open. Sad barks and growling broke my heart. This wasn't the exit. This was more important than the two of us getting out of there as fast as possible.

I dodged into the room lined with metal cages and held the door for Big Gal. She slipped in after me. I closed the door after her and she let out a barrage of barks. The whining, the barking, the growling in the room. All dropped to silence. Myself included. I didn't even want to move, lest I piss her off, but we couldn't just stand here.

Someone would come down eventually. And we'd be in heap-big trouble.

The cages I could see had locks on them. Some key locks. Some with number pads attached to them. Those probably would take a master key, if we could find it. On the off chance, I asked Big Gal. "Do you know where the keys are?"

She tapped the door with her back foot.

Not in this room. Probably in the pockets of one of the assholes who just left. Shit. Whatever. I would try my chest at some padlocks.

Big Gal let out a soft woof. High pitched yipping answered her. She took off down the length of the room. I ran after her. Telling her to stop would do no good. I knew what those tiny sounds meant and I knew that kind of desperation.

When I caught up to her, she stood in front of a metal door. The yips came from the other side. Big Gal set her paw against the door, then moved back and covered her eyes. She knew the score.

So did I.

I flashed the door open. "Go on, Big Mama."

She pushed me out of the way and dropped her head into the pile of wriggling, black and white fluff. Black and white fluffs who each had harnesses on them with a blinking green light. I didn't know much about dogs, but these pups felt a little young to have equipment on them. They looked too young to have been weened.

A red spot flashed in the matted fur near Big Mama's shoulders.

Trying not to disturb the reunion, I patted my way toward her neck. A braided belt circled tight around it. She growled as my fingers met the collar. When I looked, she had her eye on me. Bringing her to her babies might not save me from her if I made a wrong move here.

I kept my hands where they were, willing her to trust me. "We won't get far if this thing has a tracker on it."

She dropped her head, out of range of my fingers unless I squatted to follow. Her teeth came out, half threatening and half mother-soft. She slid one of her canines along the edge of the harness on one of her puppies.

"Puppies first?"

She whuffed a warm breath at me.

I made sure the way was clear behind me and plopped down in the thick of them. "Got it, Mama."

It took a little while to figure out how the dang harnesses fastened. Longer than I wanted it to. Once I got the first little puppy free, a girl-pup with fur the film-negative of her mother's, freeing the next didn't take long.

The din in the room slowly increased as I worked. The other dogs cautiously feeling out if they were allowed to sound off again. They shouldn't be here. If I sped things up with the pups, I might be able to free all of them, too. Maybe sic them on their former masters. Except that would be a continuation of the abuses they'd already endured. The dogs didn't deserve those orders. Perhaps Big Mama could find another way to make the men pay.

She'd been smart enough to find me.

The lights on the harnesses in my lap still glowed an ominous green. I wondered at the difference between the puppies' harnesses and what they had around Big Mama's neck. I counted the pile in my lap.

"Thirteen. Wow, Big Mama, is that all?"

Rather than answer me in a way I recognized, she nosed at one of the puppies. The first one I'd freed. The pup with black fur fading to white at the paws.

She was the smallest of them. And didn't seem to be moving much.

"Oh, no you don't, baby girl. We're not losing anyone today. Not after all this." I scooped her up, and Big Mama let me.

Her acquiescence could have been a good or a bad sign. The slight chill in the pup held no ambiguity. She'd been warmer when I first picked her up. It could have been residual from her brothers and sisters. We needed someplace to warm her and a quick escape.

I tucked her inside the top of my shirt.

Big Mama nosed the lump resting on my chest.

"I'll keep her here a moment while I get that thing off you."

She stepped closer to me and lifted her head up, completely

exposing her vulnerable neck to me. Trust, whole and complete. A smarter woman might have picked that up when Big Mama let me see to her puppies. Then again, a genius wouldn't have crawled into the sewer with a gigantic dog.

I raised my arms carefully, so as not to jostle the little one too much. When I got Big Mama free, I might try some vigorous petting to get some blood moving in the little body. Warm the blood and move it around. Sounded good.

Big Mama's collar had some hidden extra fun to it. Choke collar with the spikes woven into the braid of a belt material. Terrible, durable, and stylish. No one ever had to know you hated animals with this pretty, ugly number. Fairly sharp spikes as well. Disgusting. Worse than crawling through the sewer tunnels.

The collar had to be spun counterclockwise to flatten rather than erect the spikes. I spun it three-quarters of the way around before I finally touched the round, black-plastic clasp with the glowing red button.

On such a medieval-looking dog torture device, the red button would be the thing of last resort. No telling what it did. The metal woven throughout the collar in contact with the dog. Sounded a little too electro-shock for me.

Tiny holes perforated the otherwise smooth underside of the clasp. Too tiny to be screw holes. At least, not ones that could hold the palm sized thing together. Twisting the bottom toward me pushed some of the spikes further into Big Mama's neck, but gave me a glimpse down inside the holes. Needles. The dosing the men had been yammering about.

Gods. I hoped the puppies' harnesses had left this bit out. Perhaps this was the difference between the red and the green glowing lights.

I shifted a switch on the side of the plastic piece. One of the needles came out to play and milky liquid squirted out of it before it went back home.

Oedipus Rex. I'd found the manual trigger.

The switch on the side had four notches it could be moved to. I'd moved it from two to three. Three to four got me the same surprise from a different hole. A little bit of pharmaceutical whack-a-needle.

Sweet.

Except, not.

When I pushed the thing a little farther in the same direction, the thing released. I unstrung the thing from around her neck with extreme caution. There could have been another surprise.

Perhaps there had been another way to go about it, but I couldn't figure one.

Forcing all the shots to be given before the thing could be removed. That was evil and efficient in all the worst ways. I'd prefer a purple fool with a gauntlet of infinity stones.

As soon as the last of the collar slipped from Big Mama's neck, something odd happened.

She changed.

Grew larger before my eyes.

Taller, wider, sleeker. Body of a muscular greyhound, the size of a horse with feet that dwarfed my head. The teeth grew to saber-tooth sizes in a mouth large enough to close around them. Claws each the size of my hand.

If that wasn't enough, all the decaying things and dirt matted in her fur burned away. A nearly-invisible wave of heat from her snout to the tip of her tail cleaned her right up. Her fur that I'd thought was pale, burned itself to bright, eye-searing white that faded into the darkest black I'd seen. The light that reflected off the bulk of her didn't seem to reach her feet except the shining black claws.

Her eyes glowed golden light down on me. Kind of the way my skin glowed, but not. Maybe we had different sources. Like I burned gasoline while she burned coal. Both produced energy and light, but with different repercussions.

I stared up at her, feeling the dampness and grime more now that the two of us weren't in it together any longer. "I hate you so much right now."

Her gigantic tongue lolled out at me in a big doggie smile.

"Yep," I stood, still cradling the puppy in my shirt. "I hate you, but right now we need to figure out the quickest way to let the rest of these dogs free, so we can all get out of here."

Usually, I wouldn't risk freeing the whole pack of unfamiliar and mistreated animals. I had faith Big Mama could keep them all in line.

"Freeing the rest of the dogs," a voice came from an impossible place because no one could be behind me, "will not save you from what I do to you for trapping mine."

I whipped around to the man who had materialized out of thin air.

Behind me.

In the little room the puppies had been kept.

The one with only one doorway.

The doorway I half-stood in.

Weren't giant, mutant dogs enough? I didn't need this...

Calling him a man didn't quite seem to cover it. He was certainly male. Broad shoulders. Long legs. Taller than me. Deep auburn hair dripping from a tan face aflame with anger. His eyes glowed like his dogs, only his glowed the deep vibrant green of unearthed emerald and summer grass.

The robe he wore blew in a wind that did not exist. Not in any a way I felt. I smelled it, though, the heavy, sulfurous musk. The tendrils of the dark, gossamer fabric him danced in ways no fabric should. Holes appeared and disappeared. Like black mist or smoke.

He was beautiful, in his fury. An angel I knew from a time my heart happily forgot.

"I'm guessing," I cleared my throat that had gone dry, "that Big Mama is your dog."

15 – DEATH KNELLS

THE ARTIST DREAM of a man stepped toward me. Towered over me by at least six inches. A rare thing. Though, I wouldn't have been surprised if he grew another few inches like his dog.

His eyes shone bright enough to cast shadows across his face. A gorgeous green I wasn't certain actually existed, despite the evidence glaring at me.

"Those words," his voice rumbled, deep, "will be your last without agony riding them."

A tiny little sneeze jerked against my chest.

I pulled my shirt open enough to peak down into it without giving the man looming over me a show. Twin yellow glows peered up at me.

My heart melted a little. I didn't even care when she sneezed again, in my face. "You can sneeze on me all you want to right now, little girl, as long as you live."

"Return that puppy to Scheherazade." The man's voice took on a softer quality. Almost like he still planned to kill me but didn't want to disturb the little one in the process.

When I looked up at him, I got the impression I wasn't far off. If this man could appear out of nowhere, he could probably thwart my silly powers.

Big Mama wuffled her nose in my business again, but she kept it outside my shirt. The puppy yipped a little at the attention. I smiled at the dog who's head now stood at my height. "Is that your name, Big Mama? Pretty name for a pretty dog."

"Hand her over."

Big Mama turned her head toward him and growled. Deep and low. The puppy in my shirt did her best to imitate her mama. She even squirmed a little against me.

"That's right, little girl. Fight with all you have." I scratched the top of her head and ended up being a chew toy. She had no teeth to gnaw me with, nor much strength in her bite, but she moved more than she had. Good sign.

"What in the hell is going on in here?" A new voice broke into the moment.

I pressed my back against the doorway to keep both men in my sights

Big Mama, or Scheherazade, barked at the new intruder the same way she had when she first came into this room. Loud and vicious. All the dogs in the room fell quiet again except for the black-and-white fluff pile playing at their mother's feet.

The man half-behind me said, "I see," before strolling around me and past his eerie dog. His easy pace halved the distance in less time than it should have taken.

The other man's "Who are you? How did you get in here?" peppered out at double speed.

When the two met, the tall man set his hand on the other man's chest.

Agony spilled from his throat in a wail meant for death beds and trauma patients. I couldn't look him in the eyes while he screamed that way. Chicken? Yes. My sanity could only survive so much.

I dodged to the left and halfway down the row of cages. Anything to push what was happening in the room out of my sight.

The sad and abused dogs became the lesser of two evils.

The dog I hid behind looked as worried as I felt. Chihuahuas shook all the time, though. No use projecting my worry onto another animal.

I nearly jumped when the twisted wailing stopped, jarring my world back into relative silence. I was next. Despite everything, there could be no other way. The footsteps came around the row of cages. Confirmation.

Green light, then the rest of the man came around the corner and all the way up to me. Scheherazade strode next to him. He was as beautiful and eerie as she. They were a fine pair.

"I trust the judgement of Scheherazade, at this juncture, that you had nothing to do with the trapping of her and her babies."

The best news I'd heard for at least the past month. Whatever else happened today, I would be able to poop easily. The hard part would be holding it in as I stood here.

He followed up those words with. "However."

So much for relaxing. At this rate, might still lose a hold of my pucker string.

"If what I just did hurt your sensibilities, you may wish to remain in this room whilst I clean the rest of the house."

Locked in this room, with potentially-seasoned fighting dogs and a corpse. Not on my top ten ways to spend my day. Arguing with the man who could draw those terrible sounds from a man at a single touch. Much lower on the list.

So, I nodded. "I can't see that I have much choice."

"Guard the puppies, then. We will return." He whipped around. The way he did made me want to buy a cape for him. "Come, Scheherazade. We have work to do."

We, he said. Between the teeth and whatever he had done, I didn't want to know what the two of them were capable of. Unfortunately for me, they left the door open. I heard screams of "Monster!" and less articulate things. Terror and pain reigned above while the puppies and I stood apart from it all.

I tried my best to not think about how long the two were gone or to imagine what the noises meant. I could not walk down that mental road and come out the same on the other side.

Scheherazade trotted back in the room with her tongue dangling out of her mouth, amused and entertained with what just happened.

Nope. Didn't want to know.

"Very well, Greer Ianto, as soon as you pass over the puppy, you will be free to go."

Back to my life where everything made sense. Ish. "Will the little one make it?" The little squish face. I didn't want to give her up.

"She will be fine." He dipped his head as he said it, as if nothing could naysay him once he had spoken his decree.

"And the rest of the dogs?"

"Hmm." He turned his head to this side then clenched his fist.

Metal rained down from the cages and fell to the floor with satisfying thunks. The locks. From every single cage in the room. No longer on the cages. On the floor in rusted pieces. What the shit?

Then again, hypnoboob.

Who was I to judge normalcy?

The upper level of cages sat too high for most of the dogs in them to hop out on their own. I helped the nearby Chihuahua down.

The man joined me in carefully setting the dogs on the ground. When we finished, he squatted down in the midst of them. They all stared at him, uncannily focused. "You are all welcomed to join me if it is your wish. If you choose a later date to join my pack, that is also acceptable."

His pack. And a dog that defied all logic of natural doggery. Perhaps because Scheherazade was not natural.

I waited for the man to stand and turn his attention back to me before I asked, "What are you?"

"I think you know." The light in his eyes danced to their own music. Music I recognized.

"Tell me your name."

He shook his head. "You tell me my name. Go ahead."

"The devil?"

The man scoffed. "The Devil is a construct. A phantom made by men who feared their deaths because their soul recognized the evil in the deeds they committed."

"But you are the Devil."

He nodded, lips curling ever so slightly. "When it is required of me. Like with those men who would pit animal against animal for no other cause but their own pathetic amusement."

If he only wore the Devil's horns when bad men feared what they'd done in their lives, then he had to be, "Death?"

He bowed. "One in a constellation of others, but yes."

I couldn't begin to fathom the number of questions I needed to ask him.

As if he felt the weight of them, he turned the other way.

A river of dogs proceeded us out and headed up the spiral stair case. Those too small to make their way up under their own power, were carried up by one of the other dogs.

Scheherazade's babies surprised me the most, though perhaps they shouldn't have. Tiny, mewling things and they climbed their way up with little apparent difficulty. I followed them up, the caboose of this wild train, and all the way out to the front of the building.

Despite everything I'd just seen and crawled through, the sun still shone and the beautiful old house we came out of still graced the neighborhood with classic lines. Half of the dogs scattered. The rest of them sat in an orderly group on the lawn and waited for Death to join them.

Weird.

I reached into the top of my shirt and scooped out the little girl. She squirmed in my hand in a promising manner. Scheherazade took her from my cradled hands. Despite the massive, sharp teeth I had no worries for the baby's safety or mine. Pup in tooth, Scheherazade touched her nose to my chin in gratitude, a warm and moist touch that covered my whole chin. She probably would have licked the side of my face again if she wasn't carrying such precious cargo.

"You are absolutely welcome, Big Mama."

She whuffed a breath before she disengaged with my chin. As the left, she gave Death a look I could not interpret. He watched her go a long moment before turning back to me and reaching his hand into the space between us.

I should have been warier about taking hold of the hand of Death.

No one would confuse me with a smart woman.

Death's face remained neutral, leaving me to decide if the offer was a challenge, a threat, or a thanks.

I went with option three and met his hand with my own.

Rather than shake my hand, a wave of heat pulsed over my body. An explosion from my hand outward that felt a little like slipping into a bath on the edge of too hot. Just for the moment. My hand had already cooled before my face passed through the event horizon.

My feet. My feet were dry in dry shoes. I looked down to be certain. They were even clean. My shirt and the front of my pants were. I no longer felt a swamp growing in my nether regions. The joy of being clean and dry after however long made me jerk Death's hand toward me and pull him into a hug.

He froze a moment then curled his arms around me. Just tight enough. I even felt his cheek rest against the top of my head before I pulled back from him.

I needed that more than the dry cleaning. My stance felt stronger and my breath easier.

Death gave great hugs. Who knew?

"Thank you."

He inclined his chin at me before turning toward the congregation of dogs awaiting him.

"I understand the presumption." I spoke expecting him to go on his way, but he stopped and swiveled back toward me. Bits of him still moved in that not-wind. I continued. "And you can refuse, but I wanted to know if I could ask you a question."

His unreadable green eyes bore into mine.

"You don't have to answer, of course." I frowned. "But I guess you already knew that. It's not like I can give you that permission since you already have it."

"Ask your question."

I think the both of us were relieved when he cut off my babbling. One question was a lot of pressure. Inane things and ideas I could never understand passed through my head. But, I let most of it go and went with the simplest thing: "Are you happy?"

A smile ripped across his face, brighter than the sun on mercury. It ramped up the glow of his eyes. They competed with the daylight. "I am today, Greer Ianto. I am happy today."

That was the second time he used my name. I hadn't told him or his dog. Such was the mystery of Death, I supposed. Or at least one of them.

As he stepped into the middle of the oddly quiet pack of dogs, I wished I could say the same as Death. That I was happy. Scheherazade rubbed her head against his chin once he was in range and I could feel my own eyes shine with jade envy.

Maybe one day.

My eyes started watering. Except, the man and his dogs were the only quivering things in my sight. It wasn't me. They disappeared in the ripples on the surface of a clear pool. Just before they all disappeared completely from sight, I heard Death's voice as if his lips pressed against my ear. "There are women inside who need your help, upstairs. If you can stomach it."

16 – Blood Red Head

IF I COULD stomach it. Sounded like a challenge.

Back into the mouth of the beast I went, though I had no fear of people coming out to attack me. The screams that had echoed down into the basement rang in my mind. Death had taken care of all threats. Though with him gone, more people could arrive any minute.

What had the two assholes said? Something about getting in dinner because there wouldn't be time later? They'd not mentioned how soon later was. Couldn't ask them now.

I hustled up the grand staircase, which left me panting. Gods. I needed to work out more if I planned to keep saving people.

The first door at the top of the stairs lay open. One man stared at me from where he'd bent over a desk. Blank stare. Like no actor in a movie could replicate. As I got closer to the room I noticed a few things.

Aside from the desk holding the guy up off the floor and a couple filing cabinets, the room didn't have much to it. No other doors. Not even a window. There was one other man inside, leaned back in an office chair against the wall nearest me, with his torso ripped open. At some point, he'd had a heart and lungs in there. All the organs above his diaphragm had been removed.

The lungs lay on the floor beside him in meaty pieces. The heart was missing in action.

I swallowed hard against the screams in my memory, grateful to the world that Scheherazade had taken a liking to me.

The edge of white bone poked out the back of the other man. Enough for me. The two of them wouldn't cause me any problems. Until I tried to sleep.

The lock on the next door didn't take much effort to coerce. I wished it had. The effort would have given me time to prepare. Women trapped in cages. Little bigger than the ones the men had used for the dogs. The women crouched over and curled into balls. Bloodied and scraped up. Clawed. Bitten.

I finally got the joke the two bastards had thought so funny as they frolicked up the stairs. Bitches fighting bitches. If they hadn't been dead already I would peel back their skin and massage salt in.

For starters.

Anger flared hot and juicy, vibrating along my skin. I needed to keep it together if I was going to get these ladies out of dodge.

I forced a breath and a second one, then stepped into the room.

The woman closest to the door barely saw me. Had to be some kind of drug-induced haze. She didn't look as banged up as the others, but it would probably be hours before she could make any sense.

"Are you here to rough us up too?" Came a voice from just beneath the drugged lady.

I'd forgotten to look down. The cages were stacked two high.

My veins still boiled too hot for me to give a convincing smile, so I didn't even try. "No. I'm the rescue."

She didn't look impressed, but that could have been the puffiness on the left side of her face. Or the blood matting her red hair in clumps.

I squatted down so she didn't have to press against the side of the cage to see me. "Did they drug all of you?"

"Obviously. You think I'd take this over the burlesque with Mr. Holier Than Thou But Can't Keep His Hands To Himself? I'll take the gropes, thanks." Her words slurred a little around the edges, but she seemed with it, otherwise.

"How long have you been here?"

She shook her head, then stopped herself abruptly with a hard blink. "Don't know. Lost some time."

I tilted my head to gaze around the room. The other women trembled and moaned a bit, but none of them had reacted to my entrance. Nor the conversation red-head and I were having. Something felt squiggy about this. "Why aren't you knocked out like the rest of them?"

She took hold of one of the ends of her bloodied locks and shook it at me. "It's the red hair. We don't go down as easily as the rest of you."

I didn't believe her. She could be acting to keep me here while reinforcements gathered outside the house.

"Some sort of genetic co-migration of factors," she waved her hand at me like I knew the rest. "*He* said it's because my ancestors committed atrocities and worshipped false idols. Doesn't stop him from requesting me."

Requesting her for what? But I had a more important question. "Who said that?"

"Preacher Handsy Edwin."

No shit.

He *was* handsy.

If she knew the preacher... "Cherish?"

She narrowed her eyes and dipped her chin down. "How the fuck do you know my name?"

"Because my life is nothing if not complicated." I prayed to the signal gods and pulled out my phone. Full bars. Would have been nice to have before I crawled through the sewer. I couldn't complain too much anymore. Death had cleaned all the goo off me.

"What's that supposed to mean?" Spittle sputtered down Cherish's chin. Her words came out nearly all in sibilance.

"It means your boss will be happy to know you're alive."

I straightened and debated who to call first. No, to the police. Even if I explained everything to them exactly as it happened, they wouldn't believe a word. Probably only had a fifty-fifty shot with the Gold 4. Better than nothing.

Hating myself a little, I navigated to my most recent call and hit send. The bastard answered after the second ring.

"Greer? Good. I was starting to get worried." Spencer sounded relieved and I hadn't said a word.

Balls.

Here went bursting his bubble. "Cherish is alive."

Two beats of silence. "No, she's not. The fire marshal confirmed it."

How did Spencer have a connection with a fire marshal—Nope. I didn't need to know. Time to focus. "I'm not sure who was in that apartment when the place got torched, but I found Cherish."

"Apartment?" Cherish mumbled. "Tracy? Is she okay?"

I squatted back down. "Who's Tracy?"

"My sister." Big, fat tears started down her cheeks and I hadn't told her anything. Much.

I mentioned Spencer being glad she wasn't dead and a torched apartment. Shit. Maybe I had given the whole thing away. Callous as it felt, I walked a little ways away from her. I didn't have time for Cherish's tears.

"What's going on?" Spencer's voice came stripped of emotion. Business time.

"I stumbled on a..." How best to put this? "A modern-day gladiator kind of thing. With dogs and women instead of men and lions."

"What?"

No time to explain things any better. "Later. Anyway, some things happened. Now, all of the men in charge are dead but there are quite a few abused and drugged women here."

"Where are you?"

"It's better if you don't know. I'm about to call the Gold 4 so you need to keep your distance if you don't want your secret exposed." What was I doing? Why was I helping him? Why had I called him first? "If you give me pictures of any other women you're missing, I can let you know if they're here before the cavalry arrives. Okay?"

He had to have pictures somewhere. How else could he sell them to potential renters?

"It's three. Three, I'm missing, now that you found Cherish. I'll send two pictures of each."

He hung up.

While I waited for the photos, I started down the center of the room. I could be a little glad there were fewer cages in this room than there had been in the basement, but I hadn't been into any of the other rooms.

My phone buzzed before I had to follow that yellow brick road. The photos he sent for all three girls were professional shots. One with full on make-up and one without. Each labeled with their names.

The Nubian dark woman was Summer. The Indian woman, Mira. And Japanese woman was named Tanaka. All pretty without a speck of make up on, and goddesses to worship with the full paint job. Spencer was one for diversity in his harem. I might have been more impressed if it was for the sake of it. I had a feeling that his choices were the result of filling his pocket. "Exotics" probably fetched a higher price.

Every inch of flesh I glimpsed as I walked the line showed more pink hues than anything else. It didn't mean we were out of the woods. I had a feeling. That tonight would not be a good, good night.

Rather than delay longer, I called the Gold 4 hotline as I stalked out of the room and flashed my way into the door across the hall. Jackpot, of a sort. Women of all different colors of the spectrum had been chained around the room. Some by the necks, some by the hands. All to display their assets to the best effect.

The body of a man lay splayed in the center of the floor, his chest peeled open. His glazed eyes stared up at the ceiling. Lifeless and heartless.

As he had been in life.

The women around the room stared too. At the corpse, at the ground, and at me. Fear and disgust. A couple of them had greyed a bit. I needed to keep the call short before the women sunk further into shock. If someone at the Gold 4 ever picked up the damned hotline.

One of the women going into shock was Spencer's Summer. The Indian woman half-suspended from the ceiling in the corner could have been his too. Mixed victories. I had to be sure.

My finger was poised to disconnect and call Magus directly when he answered with his customary, "Greer."

I resisted the urge to kick the dead asshole as I stepped around him. If I didn't fear going to jail for tampering, I would have done so. Repeatedly. "I'm in a house near Monaco where the big, pretty houses live. Like with the big trees that tunnel the streets?"

"Yes, I know the area."

"Okay, the people in this house were running a fighting ring, dogs and women. They're all dead now—the bad people, not the women—and I need a little help getting the women out of here."

"Just rescue and medical?" He took it all a little too calmly. But then, as the head of the Gold 4, he probably saw more oddness than most.

I ran what I told him through my head. "Yes, except there may be people coming, soon-ish, who planned on viewing the festivities." My voice escalated a notch or two. Facing people who would allow this kind of thing to go on unnerved me. People who came here for a lark, shook me much deeper.

"Where are you?" Magus kept his voice nice and even.

I did my best to emulate his composure. "I don't have an address. Do you need an address?"

"I will when help gets closer, but right now we're only getting a general direction from your cell phone."

Moments when I was happy technology kept us all on the radar. "Okay, good. Good. I'm going to find something with the address on it."

The room with the first two bodies flashed in my head. A desk. Filing cabinets. Perhaps it was naïve to assume a place like this kept good records, but Hoffa knew everyone had to pay taxes. No matter how fraudulent the rest of the enterprise.

I ran through the hall. The anger that had pumped me up fueled me now. It thrummed through my veins like I really was a superhero.

A minute in the room, frantically opening drawer after empty drawer while the two bodies kept their silent watch and a dirty-copper scent tainted the air, killed the righteous feeling. Grim determination replaced it. I would find something or run back outside when the emergency relief came.

"Greer," Magus' calm voice prodded me. "Did you find the address?"

"Not yet." I glared at the man bent over the desk. "These bastards—"

Something lay half under the man.

"What about them?"

"Hold on."

Most of the man's blood had dripped down his back, though quite a bit had pooled on the desk. The phone still in the man's hand sat above the flow. I leaned a couple different ways to get the light to glare off the screen the right way for me to see the trail his skin oils made.

Just a box for a security code. Ridiculous. But simple enough.

His thumb was still warm and mobile as I moved it out of the way to draw the security code.

Gross.

I pulled up his text messages. Three messages in had an address, the dead man sending to another person. Just to be certain, I looked for another sent address. It took another seven texts, but the same address got sent out to another number.

I gave Magus the address with the caveat that I found it on the phone of a dead man. No way to be sure.

Magus assured me the address came up close to my general location.

"Good." Running outside to find the address didn't sound fun. "One problem solved."

"Do you need me to stay on the line?"

That Magus even asked squared my shoulders. I had support if I needed it. Help was on the way. For the moment, though, only one person could free the women.

"No, thanks. A couple of the women looked to be going into shock. I'll need both hands."

"Very good." He disconnected.

I started around the desk to leave, but some paper beneath the man stopped me. All those empty file cabinets. He'd had his phone and this paper out when Death came for him. I knew, I knew, I *knew* that I needed to leave it alone. That kind of evidence was best left to the experts, of which I was not.

But what if it had the real address in it? Or another, where this kind of thing was going on right now? Or worse.

Reaching over the bloody desk with pincer fingers, I touched the paper. The paper bound into a book of some sort. It wouldn't budge. Not even when I slid my fingers closer to where his body lay on it and pulled. There was no slipping it out easy. I clenched my hand into a fist, set it against the front of his shoulder, and leaned with my body weight.

He moved, as did the edge of the blood. It started toward my prize. I slid my free hand under the book, slid it away, and let him go again. Before I could consider many terrible things to do to him, I swung around on the balls of my feet and walked away.

The address I gave Magus had been scribbled on a sticky note stuck to the inside of the front cover. That convinced me. I pocketed the book and texted Spencer. *Found Mira and Summer. Alive. No Tanaka yet.*

I counted fifteen women chained up when I walked back into that room. I hadn't even checked all the rooms up here. Freeing all of them could take too long to save anyone else who might be hidden in the house.

Bolt's words rang in my head from the day before. Let the chest out and talk the women through what I wanted them to do. Worth a shot.

Except, forcing the women to act without their permission felt wrong. If I asked them, though, they could agree to what I said. If they wanted to. Shit. If I had the time to waffle, I had the time to pull the locks off each and every one of them.

We didn't have that kind of time.

Instead of pulling my collar down, as I had been doing, I pulled the bottom of my shirt up. All the way up my back so I could pull my arms through. Once I had the equivalent of an infinity scarf, I tucked the bulk of the fabric so it hung down my back.

Most of the women glanced my way once I unleashed the shine on the room and got stuck that way. For the last two, I said, "If everyone could turn this way, that would be great."

One-hundred percent attention. Wouldn't mother be proud?

"Police have been called and they're on the way. I am just here to get you free as quickly as possible. So, provided you can reach them, can you please take hold of all the locks or bolts or whatever is keeping the chains tight on you and turn them toward my chest."

The women moved in clockwork unison. Creepy as shit. I couldn't finish this soon enough. I hoped this worked, or I'd feel wretched about this for the rest of my life. I would anyway. I fucking hated this. "Okay, if you would, see if you can pull them open and take your chains off."

Locks clinked open. Wrists and necks pulled free of the metal and leather binding them. With the top halves free, the women leaned down to do the same with their ankle bindings.

"If you're free and someone else can't manage their own bindings, please help them out."

Another command compounding the first two. Nice language and the right reasons didn't matter. My stomach already churned its unease.

My phone vibrated. Spencer. I opened the text.

Thank you. Keep safe.

I'd let myself be safe once I freed the others.

The thanks soothed me some. Like I wasn't the worst person on the planet for what I could do. What I had done. If the women I'd victimized thanked me, I would appreciate it more. Maybe. Not hating me would have been enough.

Once they were all free, they stared at me like robots awaiting their next instructions. Their dead-fish gazes twisted the knife in my gut. Time to end this. "Okay. Some of you looked a little faint before I hypnoboobed you, so I'd like you to be careful. Also, if you want to, please remember what I said and what I did. I don't want to force you to forget anything, so it's up to you."

Superheroes trying to kill me were one thing. Gale Force could forget every time he'd ejaculated, for all I cared. These women deserved more. I pulled the bulk of my shirt around to the front of me and watched the women fall out of my spell.

17 – Behind Door Number Thirteen

Mira looked at her wrists where the leather straps had rubbed them a little raw. "What just happened?"

Shit. I couldn't win.

"Her chest glittered like the full moon and then I couldn't do anything other than what her voice whispered in my head." Summer answered Mira, in a beautifully thick English accent.

The other women spoke up in murmurs, either confirming or denying Summer's explanation. Relief spilled through me that they did, in fact, remember what happened while I put the whammy on them. But we didn't have time for dissention.

It took several claps before the women simmered down, which I was grateful for. It meant they didn't have any lingering need to do what I said.

"Summer's right. Hypnoboob." I pointed at the center of my chest, then at all of them. "Controlled you just long enough to let you open the locks. Sorry to pull that on you, but you're not the only ones here."

The women stared at me, confused. Perhaps a little scared.

"The men who kept you here are dead. Not sure when the others planned to come, but we have police and superheroes on the way. Before they arrive, can I ask you to keep secret how I freed you?"

"That your boobs have magic powers?" The woman nearest me asked, arms crossed over her own. "I'd rather not be locked in the looney bin because of you. Hmm-mmm. No sir."

One vote for keeping my secret. Some of the other women murmured things to that affect. Vaguely blame-y toward me. Which I deserved.

"Good." I cut off the last mumblings. "The room across the way has women in cages. If you can find the keys and free them, I'm sure they'll be grateful. If you want to wait in here until the police arrive, that's fine too." Boobing the cages open would work, but not without hitting the already drugged women too. Anyway, helping others out of the same kind of circumstances was a great way to jumpstart the healing process. I backed my way toward the door to give them room to decide.

"Where are you going?" Mira, again.

"I still have some doors to open, maybe more locked-up people to free. I don't know. The room just before the stairs has two bodies in there. You might want to avoid it."

Not exactly a pep talk, but it felt like the marching band was leaving the field for second half shenanigans. To prevent any accidents, I strung my arms back through the sleeves of my shirt as I headed down the hall.

The next few rooms were empty, save for cheap beds and some lube on the tables near them. In that moment, I would happily give up my power for Phoenyx's. The whole house needed to be burned to ashes.

The last room before a narrow staircase, was not empty.

Tanaka sat on the bed. Her ugly, white robe hanging open to reveal a pretty, black bra. Crimson spots speckled the dingy robe. Dexter would have approved. Tanaka, seemingly unphased by the blood, glared at the prone form of a man on the floor. A man whose heart was also missing. Kind of poetic.

"Tanaka," I said gently, but loud enough that she heard.

She didn't move. It didn't feel like a drug-induced haze. Not like Cherish and the others. Tanaka's whole body sang of tension and panic.

"Tanaka, did he hurt you?"

"Death came, as I'd prayed for." Her voice warbled to the same rhythm of the twitching muscles in her hands. "Death came and ripped his heart through his chest. Death ripped the heart out but did not let him die. He screamed."

I knew those screams. I refused to watch Death's show for just this reason. My life had too many moving parts for me to fall to mush before I things settled.

Telling Tanaka I understood rang shallow. I did and didn't. "Tanaka, are you ready to go now?"

She looked up at me then, eyes nearly as green as Death's. Though, hers didn't glow and they had a slight cloudy film to them. Odd color on a

Japanese woman. "Death smiled at me before he left."

My first instinct, to reach an arm around her and usher her out, felt wrong. Instead, I nodded at her from the doorway. "If he killed the men, and smiled at you, then you are safe from him today, right?"

"Right." She mumbled it without feeling.

I reached a hand out to her. "If Death smiled and left, we should leave too."

"What if Death comes back?"

Lying would hurt her worse. It would certainly shake the trust I tried to build. "He always does, in the end. If we've lived well enough, we can greet him as a friend with a smile."

She frowned at the heartless body. "But that man..."

"Did he hurt you?"

"Not yet."

Good. Progress and logic.

"He spoke of the other women he hurt. How they bled for him."

"And now he's paid back his blood debt." Come on. Believe with me.

Her eyes dropped to my hand, and rose back up to my face. "Do you think so?"

"Nothing else could warrant that," I pointed at the bloody hole that had once been solid chest, "from Death himself."

What the men had done to his dog and her puppies was also a blood debt. They probably owed more than their bodies held, so their hearts also became part of the pot.

Tanaka stood, walked to the body, kicked it hard in the side, then stepped over it. When she looked back up at me, the cloudiness had cleared. One decision and one kick to solidify her resolve seemed to set

Tanaka back to rights.

One less thing to worry about.

"Greer!" A voice from somewhere else in the house bellowed my name.

Five hands clutched at the back of me. I hadn't realized the women from the other room followed me the whole way down the hall.

"It's fine. It's fine." I told the group behind me as I backed us up out of the doorway. "He's calling for me."

The hands released me as I stomped purposefully back down the hall.

"Upstairs." I called back. "You alone?"

"Police and medics."

I almost recognized the voice. Yelling distorted things enough to give me doubt. I had to remind myself that Gale Force wouldn't announce himself upon arrival. He smashed first.

Phoenyx nearly made it to the top of the staircase as I came to it. Four men decked out with more gear than usual for a house call. I'd had enough experience with cops lately that I recognized the difference. They expected a fight of some sort. If Death hadn't taken care of everything. They would have been right.

"Report."

It sounded so much nicer when it came from him than it did from Magus. Perhaps it was the situation. Right then, reporting meant handing the reins to a more qualified person.

"The men are still dead, kind of gruesome, and I freed all of the women from this floor who weren't in cages."

He frowned. Unmistakable despite his mask over the top half of his face. "Cages?"

"Yep."

"Shit."

Yep. "The women have been a little roughed and a lot drugged. So, a lighter touch would be better." My eyes drifted over Phoenyx's shoulder to the SWAT-dressed cops.

The one on the left asked, "Have you cleared the third floor?"

"No, but I'm sure, if men were up there, they're dead now too."

He lifted his visor out of the way. "If you didn't clear the floor, how do you know that?"

Pinching my lips together, I shifted my gaze back to Phoenyx.

I disliked pulling this kind of rank or pitting law enforcement agencies against each other. Joe Schmoe Cop, born and raised in Denver, Colorado, would not believe me. And if my life continued down this path, the police needed to respect what information I did give them. Which meant proving my worth to a higher authority.

"Right." The officer got the message and took the snub like eating moldy sauerkraut. Probably better than his reaction to the truth.

Phoenyx led the sourpuss officer and others the rest of the way up the stairs. As I'd done more than my job, I headed down the stairs. More people streamed in the front door as I came to the bottom step. The medics had over prepared in the good way. I pointed up and behind me. "The show's that-a way."

The clump of them surged up the stairs with energy I simply didn't have. A nap at home would have been ideal, but I hadn't given my official report, just enough to get people here and to prepare people on the scene. Even if I left now and made it to bed, they would find me and break up my beautiful sleep.

I plopped my butt down two steps up from the bottom. My phone vibrated. Just an update from social media, but it reminded me. I texted Spencer. *Tanaka's safe. She's one tough cookie.*

Since I knew he would respond, I waited.

Thank God for you, Greer Ianto.

That, I hadn't expected. Perhaps Spencer wasn't so lapsed a Catholic as I'd imagined. Except for the shady dealings. And willingness to exploit people and extort money. And kill.

Still. That quick of a response left little time for editing. The man was a study in contradictions and I didn't like the way he made my head fight my heart and body. I just needed something to tip me one way or the other so I could be happy with a decision and not this wishy-washy mess.

18 – WRAP IT UP

WATCHING THE EMERGENCY personnel surge up and down the stairs, alternating people and equipment made me happy to not be one of them.

A shadow slipped over me from behind and stayed. I tilted my head back to see the source.

Phoenyx smirked down at me, then sat down next to me. "I wondered where you ran off to."

I hadn't run anywhere after rescue arrived. No energy to even attempt.

"Do you want to tell me what happened here, SparkleTits?"

I kind of did. Of all people, I had the best chance for either him or

Kai believing me. Still, "Is Magus coming, or are you the official person on point?"

"No, he's on his way." Phoenyx turned to face forward rather than look at me. "There have been a few more deaths than usual, without obvious connection, so he was checking things over at another scene."

That made sense. Independent of them, I'd come across deaths myself. I nodded.

"What? Am I not good enough to give the story to?"

I bumped his shoulder with mine. "I hope you stay to hear it directly from me and not a filtered version, but I'd rather not repeat myself."

"Hmm." He stretched himself back up to towering his shadow over me.

Was it possible for a person's to shadow to feel warm? It could have simply been the heat of him blending in my perception.

On the other hand, I'd met Death.

Phoenyx moved out of range before I could test. Later, then.

Magus came in nearly fifteen minutes later. Despite his pristine golden mask, he looked haggard, a little rough around the edges. I'd only ever seen him in calm, cool control. Something big enough to ruffle his feathers stressed me.

I stood as he entered, respect and the knowledge that his presence meant something for me to do. He nodded in greeting to me, and I hoped a little in approval for my show of respect.

"Is there a place where we can speak unobserved?" His voice still came out with the collectedness I'd come to expect from him. Perhaps things weren't as bad as I'd first assumed.

"Actually, you hit the jackpot when it comes to that kind of thing." I turned to call to Phoenyx, but he was already heading down to meet us.

He'd probably been watching for Magus as much as I had.

Once Phoenyx caught up, I started off. Neither hesitated on the metal spiral stair case, though Phoenyx asked. "What's down here?"

"Another body in a filthy kennel through the door on the left. No clue what's in the room behind us, but forward is what we're looking for." I pushed the glassed door and headed down the hall.

The smell of the storm drain had seeped its way into the hall. Bound to happen.

"Are there any lights?" Magus slowed his speed.

I could see perfectly fine. The darkness hadn't bothered me earlier. I didn't have much on me, but I had me. The arm sleeves would only go to my elbows. Kind of annoying, but my pants made up for it. Full thigh-light display. I led the way into the darkness.

When we came to it, neither man seemed keen on stepping into the vault. I couldn't blame them, but I needed it for my explanation. A bit of physical evidence since all the puppies left.

Phoenyx took my story fairly well—with some smirks.

Magus tightened up all over.

Neither reaction mattered. I would not beg them to believe what I knew was true. Lack of energy had moved me past caring.

After several minutes of half glaring at me, Magus' expression cleared. I didn't know why. "Whomever you met has done a great service to the lot of us and to you in particular. I hope that you thanked him properly."

Oh. Magus believed that *I believed* what I told him and had been bamboozled.

Most of what happened could not be refuted. The deaths. Bodies missing hearts. Evidence of dogs. Giant hole in the floor of the vault. Magus didn't need to believe everything until and if it became necessary.

"I certainly did thank him." With a great, big hug. Magus probably didn't need to know that much.

Phoenyx moved enough to step across the threshold into the vault. I lifted my arms higher so he could see. He formed a ball of fire that hovered a half foot above his hands. Not steady light, but brighter than my arms. I could have given him brighter, but he wouldn't have remembered it unless I told him to.

The light of from the flames flickered against the scored walls. He moved to the hole in the floor Scheherazade and I had crawled up out of.

"Whoa." He crouched down and dipped his fingers into one of the gouges in the concrete. His eyes had widened considerably when he looked up at me. A little of his disbelief in my story had fallen away from him, perhaps.

Either way, I shrugged. "Yeah, Big Mama had some pretty wicked claws."

"We will send the police down this way when they are finished with the initial canvasing upstairs."

They should have already come this way. Maybe they had and left when they found no girls or bodies. I didn't need to be party to that. I'd done more than enough. "Do you need me for anything else?" Because my bed was singing me a merry tune.

"I think we are finished for the moment." Magus code that he had my number and knew where to reach me, if and when they needed me.

Which was good by me, as long as I got to leave this pretty hellhole right then.

"Phoenyx," Magus added with a nod.

I hoped that meant he would be getting me home. I headed out of the vault and up the spiral staircase without waiting.

Walking out of the house felt like breaking the surface after a dive. The warmth of the sun and tickle of breeze welcomed me back to the idea of beauty and light. I closed my eyes and focused on that and my own breath.

Phoenyx tapped me on the shoulder. "We're in the way."

We were in the way. I peeked behind us. Magus was not with us. I might have gotten my wish in escorts home. "Can we stop for a drink before you take me home?"

He smiled wide. "That, I can absolutely do. I'm buying, since you managed to save the day again. Come on, SparkleTits."

I started down the steps with Phoenyx in tow, only then noticing the crowd gathered on the other side of the wrought-iron fence. Women huddled in blankets and sweats way too big for them stood closest, with the police surrounding them and blocking off the street.

A few people stood on lawns across the street in expensive looking clothing. I assumed they owned the houses they spied from. If they hadn't seen the mess of dogs disappear from sight, they'd missed most of the story. Perhaps what they did see would make them a little more willing to spy on their neighbors before the police were called.

Unless they already knew what went on in this house.

My fingers tightened into fists. I wanted to interrogate them, but it was not my job. None of this was. I didn't have a job. But, a gaggle of women stood free and alive because of me. No job could give me that kind of self-satisfaction.

Well, one job could.

The women rushed at me when I came even with the first of them. The cops didn't stop them. Neither did Phoenyx, the coward.

Arms circled around me all at once. Thanks. Blessings. Tears. The score of women circled me in a group hug of relief and deliverance.

When the bulk finally broke apart, each of them hugged me. Individually. Thanking me and letting me know I could call on them if I ever needed anything. Anything. Even the women who had been too frightened of me upstairs had changed their tune. The reality of what could have happened must have sunk in.

I kept from dissolving into a blubbering mess by the skin of my teeth. When the last woman let me go, a warm hand settled in the middle of my back.

"We've got to go, SparkleTits."

The man was looking to get killed. Except there were witnesses. So many witnesses. The women would probably side with me—the favor they thought they owed me. The police beyond the pack of women, though. Despite inter-agency rivalries, nothing banded law enforcement like criminals.

I'd get him. Later, maybe. When we were alone. But the damage was already done.

"No, wait," Tanaka patted her borrowed clothing. "Hold on. Take my phone number so I can call you, or you can call me, or something."

She had nothing to write on or with. Her eyes widened in panic as the other women voiced similar sentiments with identical, empty-handed results.

Phoenyx tapped my back, but didn't say anything else. We had no place to go but to a nice, stiff drink, so he had no reason to rush me. He probably knew this would happen if I let the women go on long enough. No way to get out of the hot seat without hurt feelings. No way except to accept the inevitable.

I had no pen on me, but I had my phone. "Here. Just put your name and number in the phone."

I pulled it out from where I'd tucked it and handed it over to Tanaka. The lines of tension cinching her brows toward the center relaxed. Whatever else I did, this felt right. If it made them feel better or more secure in the world that had just shaken them, it was worth it. Even if I deleted every number as soon as I got a moment.

Phoenyx thumped my back. The flat eyes and face half covered by his mask gave me little clue when I turned to see what his problem was. Probably not a good sign. I rolled my lips in and tipped my head their direction.

What did he expect me to do? The ability to do something, anything, had calmed them.

He gave me a double blink, which told me nothing.

The women finished with my phone rapid fire and passed it back to me. Before they could start another round of hugs, I gave Phoenyx a sharp nod. "Let's go."

They parted to let us through, some of them drifting off toward a police van on the corner. If I'd known that would work, I would have tried that before they gobbled me up. Though, the grateful attention might have been the toll I needed to pay to pass the bridge. I felt like a billy goat.

I let Phoenyx lead the way. Since he acted in an official capacity, he would probably fly us out of here. I didn't know what he needed for clearance to take off. With all the things going on, I should have paid attention to that sort of thing.

This time, apparently, it wasn't all based on his needs. A space roughly six-by-six had been marked off with gold ribbon hooked onto four poles.

Phoenyx shook his head as he unhooked a one of the ribbons and stepped to the side for me. "That's not allowed."

"What's not allowed?" I stepped through.

"Giving your personal number to victims, bystanders, or law enforcement personnel outside of Gold 4 is against seven regulations."

He fiddled the ribbon back into place with the kind of care than came from anger, or annoyance, before he came to me.

I shrugged. "Pretty sure that only applies if I'm a part of the Gold 4. As a private citizen..."

He did the double blink again, followed by wide eyes and an off-center smile. "Huh. Jump in three, two..."

We jumped and shot into the air. A little faster than I was accustomed to. More of my focus centered on Phoenyx's disapproval of me. It meant, until I pointed out my independence, he had seen me as part of the team.

"Anyway, I can just erase the numbers and names I don't recognize."

Phoenyx grinned. "They texted themselves with your phone. They have your number, too."

Balls. I hadn't anticipated that, especially with how fast they passed the phone. I had an inkling of what name they texted their phone. "About you calling me *that* name in public. What's the deal?"

He managed to look a tad chagrinned. "Reflex. Sorry about that. Can't use real names in front of the public."

And that was the only other name he could call me that I responded to. It irked me too much to ignore. Also, it wasn't inaccurate. Which the women were well aware of. "Hey, wait a second. You yelled my name when you walked in."

"Whoops." He pressed his lips together.

The only response he felt inclined to give, apparently.

"Nuh-uh, there has to be a reason for that and the switch."

"Land."

I was tuned in enough to understand what he meant and braced feet to hit ground. I'd ridden this cowboy.

Before Phoenyx scurried away, I slid my hands to his arms to hold him in place.

His forehead crinkled above his golden mask.

I crinkled mine right back at him. "Mike." I said it low, since there were regulations, but he knew damned well what I wanted.

"I guess when I saw you were in no need of help—were in fact helping to save other people—it must have switched in my head. Like you were another member of Gold 4."

Confirmed.

"At that moment, when I was busting—pun intended—open the doors to make sure I'd gotten everyone, I kind of felt like a part of something bigger, too." I let his arms go. "Until it all caught up with me and I felt like a wrung-out rag."

"Oh, SparkleTits. That's all part of the fun." He slung an arm around my shoulders and ushered me toward the steps.

The steps up to the Arapahoe County Courthouse and police station. I hadn't noticed where we'd set down.

This was not what we had discussed.

"Hey, I thought we were going to..." Speaking the name of the bar in public while heading into the police station was probably also against regulations. I finished my dangling sentence with a lame, "the place."

He chuckled at me and opened the door. When I came to the other set I opened it for him and poked his side as he passed by. I fell in step behind him, fully prepared to continue my prodding until I got the answer I needed.

"We are going to the place to do the things," he cast an amused glance my way. "But official work, means eyes are watching and could track me."

Someone tracking him without some sort of governmental satellite would have impressed the hell out of me. I couldn't see how someone would do it, but I'd take Phoenyx's word for it. My own glittering skin proved how weird the world could be.

"So, down, through the other place, and back up at the final destination?" I could be vague to keep things secret. More than the friends I had there, I loved the bar. Had since the first time I'd gone in. Felt welcome straight off the bat.

"You got it."

Excellent. So long as I got my beverage for doing such a good job today.

A Sparkle Snack. Sparkle-darkle doooo.

I needed to stop before anyone plucked that thought from me and shared. SparkleTits was enough to deal with.

19 – SILVER-TONGUED

THE AFTER-WORK, HAPPY-HOUR crowd started trickling into Rust fifteen minutes after I claimed my favorite bar stool. The influx made me feel better and worse. I'd appreciated the relative quietness, but I anonymity came better in crowds.

Kai stopped hovering over me with more to do. The grapevine told him a little of what had happened. I felt no inclination to run through it all. Not in the bar where everyone could hear and judge.

Mike sidled up to me, freshly showered and changed out of his leather hero garb. I had a moment's wonder that his hair wasn't still damp. Until the smarter part of me reminded the rest of me that Mike could control fire. Fire meant heat meant he probably didn't need to wait long for anything to dry.

"I see you're about finished nursing that beer." He tipped his chin toward the last bit of my red ale. "How'd you like it?"

"It didn't blow my skirts up, but it's fine."

He narrowed his eyes at me. "Just fine?"

What was his—crap. I got it. "You made this one, didn't you?"

"I did."

Now, I'd hurt his feelings. Men tended to get emotional about the things like beer and sports in a way most women didn't. "I'm not really a beer girl, as I told you, but you know what I would really like, Mike?"

He lifted his nose so he could look down it at me. "Do you really think you've earned it?"

I pointed at myself. "Crawled in storm drain. Met Death. Saved his gargantuan dog, her puppies, and a bunch of women to boot."

"You what?" Kai set down the drink he'd been in the process of making.

Whoops. I'd either been too loud, or Kai'd been focused on every word I said. I could deal with his reaction later. Right now, I had important business to tend to. I flashed Mike my best grin.

Mike scoffed, "Now you're just bragging. I'm not sure I can contribute to the intoxication of a braggart."

"You already have." I slammed the last of the red ale. "See?"

He shrugged to some people across the bar like they were an audience for the play he was putting on. So long as he played his way behind the bar and made me his shot, he could act however he wanted.

His joking slipped away as he pulled the glass down. This drink was serious business.

Instead of trying to watch Mike's hands fly between bottles, this time I watched his face. Complete intent and unabashed focus. The same kind I caught on Spencer on more occasions than I cared to consider. Totally didn't need to think about his laugh when I really amused him. I was not thinking of him.

Mike lighting my shot on fire brought me right into the moment again. He scooted it to me with the reverence it deserved. "Phoenix Breath, for the hero of the day."

"Thank you so much." I pulled it toward me like it could warm every part of me that had ever been chilled.

"I think I might be jealous of that shot," Kai mumbled from further down the bar.

I cast a sidelong glance that direction. He had already turned back to his customer, so I waited for him to look at me. Like I knew he would. "You should be jealous of me."

I threw the shot back in a slow tip of the head. The evolution of the smoky-salt sweetness to the hot, spicy smoke in the last dregs of it. Beautiful. Like the beach at sunset with the little phosphorescent creatures glowing in the waves.

My phone vibrated, because of course it would. I shook my head and ignored it. Just a half minute more to take it in, to allow the heat and smoke to dance on my tongue. When I licked my lips, I caught the salty sweetness again.

Gods, yes. My shoulders dropped and the muscles along my spine released enough to allow me to slouch a bit.

"Good?" Mike asked, smug pride dripping from his voice.

I couldn't even snark at him. Just smile and open my eyes to find him drinking in every bit of my reaction. "Fan-fucking-tastic."

"I'll take two of whatever shot that was." A man had taken up residence next to me where Mike had been.

I hadn't even noticed him. In one sense, that level of inattention was bad. On the other hand, my day of lifequakes hadn't killed my ability to relax. Something I could take pride in, but quietly so life didn't test me again.

For his part, Mike's lips curled in a sly smile. Then he patted me on the top of my head with a, "Good girl," before starting on the two new drinks.

While the shot still had me in its sway, I pulled out my phone to find out what fresh hell had erupted. Spencer. Of course.

Did you make it home okay?

In a bar. Drinking. I'm good. Really good. Mike knew some serious alcohol magic.

You need company?

I had company. Lots of company. Probably not the kind of people Spencer would want to hang out with. But I couldn't tell him that I was in a bar filled with off-duty superheroes and their people. *Bad idea.*

Why?

Crap. He was really good at this.

"You look like you're thinking too hard." Kai and Mike had switched places.

Kai was just the friend I wanted to help me to talk to another friend. Huzzah. Ugh. "Everything is thinking too hard after today." *It's a cop bar.*

"Then maybe you should go to sleep. I can't give you ride until later, but you're always welcome to stay here." He offered without any obvious pressure.

If I stayed, we'd probably end up in bed together which would put him at risk for being booby trapped. While I had no specific plans, I didn't want to lose the day. Or slip into dreaming for a whole day with the current fodder. I shook my head. "Today feels like a day to lock the boobs away from the world for its own safety. You know?"

But I couldn't do it at home because I still hadn't called anyone to repair the sliding glass door or to cover it. Despite all my wins today, I'd lost some, too.

"I hear you," Kai nodded.

I nearly berated him for agreeing with me about my loses before I remembered that I'd only thought it. And Kai couldn't read minds. Which was a good thing, since I'd been having a text conversation with Spencer.

Lex wouldn't mind me staying the night. If I bemoaned my state enough, he might even feed me. It was my turn to buy dinner, but I couldn't cook like him and neither could anyone else. He was an artist in many fields.

I had another message from Spencer when I unlocked my screen. *I'd brave it, if you're brave enough.*

A challenge. Probably because he knew how it would rile my blood. If I'd been in an actual cop bar, he might have convinced me. Even knowing why he said it. Gods, that man.

I switched to my stream of texts with Lex. Something simple. *Mind if I crash tonight? I've got juicy stories.*

Can't dish tonight. Date. But mi casa su casa.

Date? In all the back and forth earlier, he hadn't said a word. Good for him. I would drill him for keeping it from me.

Another Phoenix Breath slid in front of me. I blinked up at Mike, half to tears. "Thank you."

"Yeah, well don't get used to it." He gave me a stern, stern look. "You get too sauced and you'll start stripping off all your clothes and then where will the rest of us be?"

"Right where I want you?"

His face twitched all over as he fought a laugh. He coughed his way back to his composure. "This is your last one."

My chest clenched. "Ever?"

"No. Tonight. I'm going to take you home after. You're going to crash hard after your date with death and two of these."

I didn't feel like I'd ever sleep, but, if he kept the magic shots coming, I would not argue being cut off this evening.

My eyes rolled back as I gave myself over to the second shot. Just as good as the first. Life was beautiful. Birds were singing. Sun was...setting. But it set the few clouds in the sky ablaze with orange and scarlet glory.

Mike waited until I slouched again to get me moving, because he was nice like that.

My skin tingled as I got up. It felt nice. Everything was nice. Kai lifted his head in a nod as Mike twisted me around toward the exit. I smiled and waved.

As Mike maneuvered me through the crowd, I patted my chest. No phone there. Pockets. No phone, but a book of some sort. I quick-twisted away from Mike's light grip on the back of my neck and dodged back to the bar. Kai had my phone in his hand, held out to me with an amused curve to his lips.

"You should put this somewhere safe."

I snatched it from him and tucked it in my bra on the left side. Left cup for quick drawing with the right hand.

His eyes dipped down then climbed back up to my face. "Those are the most dangerous parts of you."

"The head's what you've got to watch out for." I winked at him then darted back to Mike in the middle of the half-empty dance floor.

"Greer," Kai yelled over the ruckus, which died down at his raised voice.

I shouldn't have been surprised he could reach such a volume. He was a bartender. Even here, where Colorado's superheroes came to unwind, friction and alcohol got the better of people. I'd never seen anything that gave away the secret identities of people. But, nothing broke up an argument like a voice that could rattle the bar.

Scuttling away fit my temperament. I turned back around and set my fists on my hips, defying my skittishness.

Since the whole bar had quieted to watch this train wreck, I gave them what they wanted. I tossed my head like my hair had fallen into my eyes and gave a smile I hoped was coquettish instead of completely ridiculous. "What do you want, Kai Ironwood? I have men waiting on me."

A couple of chuckles simmered.

"I was wrong. Your mouth is definitely the scariest part of you."

I let my head tilt like a crow catching sight of something shiny. "Kai, you poor dear. You have no idea of the dark, dangerous things that never make it past my lips." I tapped my temple, pointed at him, then swiveled around on the balls of my feet.

Mike's lips pressed into a hard line beneath his laughing eyes. When

I got within range, Mike murmured. "He's still looking, girl. Everyone is. Keep strutting."

Who was strutting? The only way to move with speed was to throw the hips into it. I appreciated the encouragement, though it could backlash all over him when we stepped off the stage.

20 – PEEL BACK THE RIND

BY THE TIME we climbed into Mike's truck, he'd moved past the laughing stage. He gave me the long blink as he started the car. "You have that man wrapped around your little pinky."

At more than six feet, not much about me could be called little. That wasn't the reason my eyes dropped to my hands. "I'm heading to Lex's tonight. My house is still a mess thanks to your friend Gale Force."

"Not my friend."

"More yours than mine, with the attempted murder and stuff." I flicked my hand to wave it away, then shook my head. "Frankly, so is Kai."

"Don't play that with me. You could have snapped, pointed to your feet, and gotten a spit shine."

"Except, I can get that without snapping. Or asking. Or wanting. That's the problem." My nails were certainly interesting as the silence grew between us. If Mike wanted me to look at him, he could drive me all the way to Lex's.

"Why is that a problem?"

"Because a stray boob can take his will away when I'm not awake. It scares him." I turned to the last glow of the sunset.

"Ah. That would be a problem."

Road rolled out beneath us in a soothing rhythm that I didn't want to let ease my tension. "It kind of scares me, too."

"That's perfectly normal."

That got me to look back at him even though I'd committed to avoiding all eye contact. He helped me, unwittingly, by keeping his eyes forward. "Manipulation of fire is not the easiest cross to bear. Sometimes it controls me as much as I do it. Most of the time it whispers to me about how easily one thing would be to light or the challenge of burning something else."

"I..." What could I say to that? Apologizing felt shallow. "I didn't realize."

"No one outside the Gold 4 does. Few inside. One of those secrets that would shake the confidence of the public so we cannot speak of it." He gave me a smile that looked like a grimace when the light hit it right.

"More regulations." Though, I agreed with this one. People didn't need much provocation to turn against outcasts. The superhero union did a good thing in giving men with abilities a place in society. Giving the "different" people a role helping the "normal" ones, made for a nice, polite system for everybody concerned.

Kind of like slavery.

I didn't know how the thought soured in my head. Something to chew on later. "Mike, how do you cope? I mean, if you don't mind my asking. How do you keep it all together?"

"The image of my brother and sisters' faces the last time I saw them. Every time the fire deafens me to everything else..." His hands tightened on the steering wheel for what looked like a count of ten. "They haunt me."

"Oh," breathed out of me in the barest of a whisper. I realized the fathoms I didn't know about Mike, though I called him friend. Kai and I had the same chasms of ignorance.

Mike must have felt my eyes on him. At the light he took a hesitant glance my way, then frowned.

"No, they're not dead."

Wait, what?

He forced out a hard breath. When the light turned green, he blinked forward. His body got oddly loose for this kind of conversation.

"I was mother's favorite," he started, deathly calm.

Balls. I knew that careful flatness.

My heart tried to drown him out with thumping. I wanted to stop him before he got any further, just to save myself the pain. The things it would bring up in my mind. But I knew more than most what it took and what it cost to tell someone else *that* story of their life. I would neither stop him nor dredge him for information. It needed to be his story at his pace.

"Our special time, she called it. Which is why I couldn't talk to anyone about it. I'm the second oldest, right between my sisters. Was the smallest, if you can believe it, except for Tim who was only three at the time." His voice came out smooth and even. The sound of hundreds and thousands of rehearsals to make it seem like you'd come to accept the trauma, though you never truly did.

I had that voice too, sometimes.

"I just couldn't anymore. Refused. Told her no. Then she threatened to make Tim her favorite. She couldn't do that. I couldn't let her."

Gods.

"It just came out of me, the fire. A column of all the hate and rage and shame she forced me to swallow. I didn't stop it right away. She screamed as she burned. A horrible terrible sound that I relished hearing from her. She deserved years of this if I could keep it going that long. My sisters came in and saw what I was doing. Tim saw mommy on fire. Started to cry. Stopped me before I..."

Shit. He needed a hug. If he let me. We needed to get to Lex's in a hurry.

"They were so shocked. Later, at the hospital, after they'd had time to process, they..." He let an easy breath out. The amount of control to keep his whole body relaxed. Remarkable. And terrible.

Perhaps he could teach me a thing or two.

"I was a monster to them. They shied away even worse when I told them why. How it happened. They could not, would not, believe it happened. Thought they would have known. So, to them, it didn't happen. Their poor injured mother. Injured because I was a freak. She became a saint to them in the time it takes to watch a movie. And if she was the saint..."

"You became the monster."

He nodded. "Bingo." He stopped the car and turned it off.

That explained his unwavering ability to not let the fire in him take over. "Do you want a hug?" Because asking consent saved faces from being punched.

"Yes, I do."

I unbuckled my belt, slid over, and wrapped my arms around him.

Mike didn't hesitate like Death had. He let me hold him as long as he needed. Something else he could teach me.

When he finally pulled away from me, he let me keep a hold of one of his hands.

"I know how this is going to sound." I bit my lip and looked out the window, praying for the gods of whit and discourse to smile upon me so I could do the same.

While my eyes were averted, I recognized where we were. We'd made it to Lex's faster than I thought.

"While I did not have the sexual abuse situation like you, I know how it is with a bad mom." I squeezed his hand with both of mine. "Right now, my body's all tingly and I don't want to fuck with that. Without the tingles, I might not ever make it to sleep. But look up my mother if you wish. Henrietta Carlotta Madison."

I always said the three names, like John Wilkes Booth. Both to emphasize the horror of what she did and to distance myself. Her last name was never my name and my father gave me my first name. "Though, if you remember the name, you don't need to look it up."

"Madison." he frowned in concentration. "I know it sounds familiar."

I rescued one of my hands from around his, so I could put a finger to his mouth. "No. Not tonight. But, on another day, we will discuss this. If you want to. Tonight, I drink-ied, so now I'm going to go sleepy."

"Okay. Raincheck." He nodded, vehement. "And cheer up, I'm sure you can still snag Kai if you try hard enough."

I didn't need or want to be the one trying so hard, not to talk someone out of a fear reflex. Especially when I felt the same way about it as he did. I missed when it was easy. Kai would flirt and I would laugh it away. And my tits didn't sparkle. "Are you going to be safe driving home?"

His whole face contracted toward the middle in his confusion. "Greer, you're the one who drank, not me."

"Telling those stories has more in common with downing in alcohol than most people think." I gave a long blink. "But you know this."

He nodded. "I do. Why don't you go inside and go to bed? Lord knows your beauty rest was cut into. Not to mention the other things."

I didn't mention any of those things. I did give him a kiss on the cheek before I hopped out of the car.

I leaned against the inside of Lex's front door just for a few moments. Eventually, Mike's truck came to life rumbled away. Good enough.

"Greer, if that's you, could you please come in here and help me decide on a tie?"

"Who else would it be, Lex? The ghost of Christmas past?" I pushed off the door and headed up the hallway.

Mundane things wrapped around me and my heart sang out in gratitude. The simple act of teasing Lex about his nerves grounded me. My feet felt more solid on the ground when I had to answer the door because Lex was too flustered and needed another minute to get his head right.

"Hello," I reached my hand out into the twilight to the fine-looking man waiting on the step. Confusion looked good on his thick eyebrows and in his grey-blue eyes.

Despite his confusion, he gave me a solid handshake. "My name is Greer. Lex would have been ready, but I popped in on him in the middle of his routine. So, I get to be the Wal-Mart greeter."

A smile washed his confusion away. "I'm Clinton. Clint. I was worried I had the wrong house."

"That is completely up to you. But if you want to, come in and wait with me in the kitchen." I turned my head to yell the last word over my shoulder.

"Got it." Came from deeper in the house.

Straightening, I nodded to Clint. "He can meet us in there and I can offer you a drink like a good hostess."

"I'd like that, thank you."

Because my day had been such a rough one, I indulged in checking out Clint's butt as I closed the door after he stepped in. Not bad. Not bad at all. His jeans didn't leave much to the imagination in the buttular region. I approved.

I sucked at small talk in the best of times. A couple of drinks in was not the best times, but Clint seemed to know the waters better. Salesman usually did. Even salesmen who didn't know what do with their hands. I did my best to keep my smile to myself until Lex walked in.

He'd collected himself into the smooth artist I remembered at any of his art shows. Clint's hands stilled when he caught sight of him. He kind of froze everywhere. I tried to scuttle away to hide because I grinned like I'd spackled my face with Smilex.

Lex caught my arm as I tried to pass by him. "What is it, Greer?"

I gave him some high-quality side eye. "I don't know why you were complaining earlier. You don't need any magic shampoo or anything from me to catch you a fine specimen of man."

His eyes snapped wide open and his cheeks pinked. Some of his confident, unaffected air burned away in his embarrassment. I couldn't see Clint, but I assumed I hadn't offended him because of the laughter rippling behind me.

"I can't believe you just said that." His tone screamed that he knew he shouldn't be surprised about it.

I shook my finger in his face. "No, no. This one is your fault. I tried to leave." I turned toward Clint whose cheeks had reddened a bit as well. "He stopped me. You saw me try to be good."

Clint lifted both of his wide hands and shrugged. "She did try to leave."

"Jebus." Lex rolled his eyes toward the ceiling. "They're already teamed up against me."

"Maybe next time you'll know better. I'm going to bed and I'll have earplugs in, so don't be shy." I kissed Lex's cheek as it reddened anew.

His hands slipped off my arm absently as I pulled away.

"I like her," followed me out into the hall.

"Everyone does. That's what I'm worried about."

Not everyone liked me. One lovely person had tried to kill me this morning. Then, there was my mother. But I'd drunk enough that I could sink into darkness if I let myself. I'd done enough of that for the day.

So instead, I listened to the murmuring on the other side of the door. The pleasant back and forth of Lex's low and Clint's lower voice. A little shared laughter as the two passed down the hall to leave. The door closed and left me in silence.

I took in a large breath and released it slowly. Happy as I was for Lex to be on a date with the hallmarks of success, I wished he was here. The kerfuffle in my life left me wanting something old and comforting. And I had nothing like that. I had very little of that. I had a letter from Gabe.

It wasn't much, but it was something I could hold onto. I had the letter in my hand and sat down in the middle of the bed before I thought to turn the light on. Perhaps needing lights had become a thing of a past for me. Still. Creature comforts. I pulled my shirt off, lighting the whole room despite my full coverage bra.

On the off chance, I set the letter in my lap and I clapped twice. Nope. My headlights didn't turn off. Oh, well.

The letter smelled like Gabe. Somewhat like his cologne, but more like the man underneath. Indescribable. Like the difference in smell between red and yellow roses, like the one's Spencer had given me. I closed my eyes and just breathed Gabe in for a moment.

Before I blubbered all over the letter, I pulled it away from my face to read.

After so long in the sun, I am grateful to finally lay down in the shade and sleep. I want to thank you for always being the one I could trust and I apologize that I haven't given you the same kind of confidence in word, though I have in action.

I know this is the coward's way out, to leave you this note when I know I won't be there to feel the repercussions. You have taught me better than that, from the first time we met.

I've left you something. Hid it a long time ago, hoping to find my courage, but you've been my courage for so long, I couldn't brave angering or scaring you away. I'm sorry. I suppose it denotes a lack of faith on my part and I'm sorry for that.

I left it in our secret mail box. The key is in the place the day and night always shone through.

I love you and I hope you love me too when you realize the lie I've allowed to curl between us.

Again, I am sorry.

You may always have thought you were my shadow, but you are the light that has shined through me, showing me my own shadow that I feared.

Be better than me. Do better than me. Embrace the shadow in your light because there you will find your power.

Not what I expected. Not what I hoped. Not what I needed, though his voice flowed through my head as I read his beautifully scrolled handwriting. Damn. I should have just taken the slight buzz and tingle and gone to bed.

Now?

I abandoned the bedroom for the kitchen.

Half the grapes. A plate of lasagna. Some roast beef. Pickles. Potato and apple chips. The homemade ice cream finished off my odd meal. The breadth, and volume, of the meal reminded me of when I'd been pregnant. Before my mind followed that white rabbit, I curled up on the couch and turned the television on.

The shadow staircase rose above me again. This time, I didn't hesitate, raced up in steps twos and threes. The window at the top looked out onto nothing. Or something. Thick fog hung in the air obscuring the view.

I reached out into it. Felt the cool dampness and the push against me. With nothing more but ephemeral air, the fog pushed my hand back. I expected it, somehow. Remembered it. From a time long ago. This was how it was supposed to be. I slammed my fist against the wall of fog and it knocked me down with a breath.

Lying on my back, only an inch away from rolling down the long and steep stairs, I laughed. This was right. No amount of forcing would let me in, but I knew the key.

I rose up to my knees, just high enough to set my chin on the edge of the window.

It always managed to be the same height to me. No matter how quickly I grew.

I smiled at the wall and ran my fingers through the edge of it. "Hello, old friend."

"I love you to death," Lex's voice startled me awake. "But if you call me old again, not only will I cut you, I won't let you have any of this bacon I'm cooking."

I shot straight up to vertical. "You wouldn't dare." I whipped around on the couch, to find a shirtless Lex and a disheveled, but smiling, Clint.

Lex shook tongs at me. "I would. You know I would. Happily."

I did. Which meant I also knew that any taunting of Lex while Clint was in earshot would result in the same baconless state. I couldn't have that. "I'll be good."

He twisted his lips to the side. "Calling me old, is not being good."

"I wasn't calling you old," I pushed myself off the couch with a stretch up toward the ceiling. "I was sleeping."

"Mmm-hmm." He clicked the tongs at me, then busied himself flipping the line of bacon on the griddle.

I stalked around the couch, across the living room, and settled my elbows on the stone counter of the kitchen bar right next to Clint. "I was sleeping and you woke me up, but I will accept your apology for such a grievous act in the form of bacony-goodness galore. Hello, Clint."

He smiled a little for me. "Morning, Greer."

"Good morning, Lex," Lex lifted his voice. "Maker of breakfast."

"King of sass before I've woken up enough to take your crown."

He winked at me without looking up from the griddle. "If you want French toast, get to slicing the bread."

I got to slicing.

Lex waited for me to get into the swing of it before he said. "Have a little midnight snack last night, did we?"

"Midnight, nothing. It wasn't that soon after you left."

"Miss me that much?"

He had on his sweet, innocent smile when I looked up to him.

"I know you have bacon, but I have a knife." I circled the tip at him, in case he doubted my resolve.

"Whatever, woman. What prompted the epic grazing?"

Some of the answer could not be bandied about, all willy-nilly. If I looked up at Clint, it would let him know that he was the reason I clammed up. "You know how my life fell spectacularly to shit almost a month ago?"

"The whole lost Gabriel, car, job, boyfriend in a day combo?"

"Shit," Clint mumbled not super quietly.

I pointed the knife his way to emphasize my, "Exactly," before I wiped the thing clean. "So, yesterday was the bad things ruin date, me walking home, meet huge dog, find women locked in cages combo."

Lex shook his head. "Sometimes, I'm jealous of your exciting life."

"But this is not one of those times."

He nodded. "This is not one of those times. At least you were having a nice dream, though. With the speaking to an old friend."

I tipped my head back and forth. "Kind of. Weird. It's a dream I haven't had in...forever and I've had it twice in two days. Twice and you've interrupted me both times."

"You were late for work and then breakfast." He gestured at the griddle, then jerked his thumb at the fridge. "Get the eggs and cream."

He left out the spices for the toast, but I knew what he wanted. He didn't trust me to mix it, but I could get the ingredients. He was right to mistrust my French toast skills. But I made a mean breakfast potato. Since we had a guest, I started grabbing things for that without being asked.

"If an old dream cropped up after years without it, something had to have triggered it." Clint said. "Something from the last time you dreamed it or close enough to it to pull your subconscious back into that state of mind."

I swiveled around on my heels to face Clint. "What are you, some kind of philosopher salesman?"

He shrugged. "My mom is a psychiatrist. Some of it stuck."

"Probably crammed down your throat," Lex added. "Right?"

"When I was younger."

"Huh." I turned back to my preparations and tuned out their conversation.

Something that reminded me of when I used to dream of travelling through shimmering doorways to new worlds with different kinds of people. Saving the daughter of the fire king from the stone pirates. Sailing with lightning men through rivers of molten glass. Helping nightmares escape the unicorn dungeons. And always with the best friend I had through my childhood.

My mother made very certain I knew he was imaginary, the friend of my dreams, but I never had a bad dream. Whenever a dream started to turn that way, I could always whisper his name in my mind. His name and our secret phrase for each other: verum in luce et umbra. Truth in light and shadow.

Hmm.

21 – BEST PART OF WAKING UP

AT SOME POINT in the process of cooking breakfast, Lex and I swapped places without any discussion. We'd done this enough times to know where the other needed to be. This was the kind of comfort I wanted the night before. Instead, I got a letter that shook the solid comfort I had in my memories of my oldest friend.

We laid out the breakfast feast along the bar, rather than shift things off the kitchen table to clear room, including the bouquet of roses from Spencer. I took the barstool closest to the table, though it put me closer to the flowers perfuming me with sweetness and guilt.

Something poked into my hip as I sat up on the stool. I leaned awkwardly toward Lex and stretched the left leg down. It still took some working back and forth to get the thing out of my pocket. Standing would have made it easier. But I didn't want to.

The book I'd taken from what became a crime scene didn't look any worse for the wear, despite sleeping with it in my jeans pocket.

I set my elbow on the counter and set my cheek in my hand, both to give the two of them as much privacy as possible and to shield Lex from seeing what was in the book. Just in case.

The first few pages of the thing were a calendar. Sparsely filled toward the beginning of the year. More activities starting near April. Some of the items in blue, some in red. No key to explain which color meant what. I flipped to September to get a little guidance.

Yesterday, "Dog show," was in blue. Dog show. Bastards. Schadenfreude reared its two-faced head. Not only was I glad they died, the agony of their deaths sweetened my mood. I hoped they got more on the other side. Too bad I couldn't call up Death and put in a request.

The day before their dog show, "Appleby" was written in red.

I got it, mostly. Blue were their sick events. Red were targets or places targets would be. Maybe even people to hit. Hard to tell as Fiona's foundation bore her name.

I didn't like the connectedness of it. Not isolated incidents but a conspiracy. A conspiracy with a superhero as a member.

Possibly more than one.

Another red event was scheduled for Friday, underlined with blue. Circus. I didn't like the sound of that, but Ringling Brother's didn't hit Colorado until October. Of course, Cirque du Luna had set up shop in big tents outside the basketball stadium. Their shows didn't start until next weekend. Though, a secret performance for the wealthier people to attend, without worrying about rubbing elbows with us peons, would not surprise me.

Us peons.

I wouldn't be, at the end of the month. Provided I survived until then. All the situations I let myself get dragged into might have something else to say. The idea of being able to help and turning my back on someone stuck in my craw. Twisted my stomach up. I couldn't let this lie.

Not to mention, a secret Luna show sounded like just the kind of event a person might hire an attractive escort to accompany them.

Setting that aside for the moment, I flipped past the calendar to pages of names. A single name written at the top of each page, in either red, black, or blue ink. Some of the black names had a blue underlining. Some of the red names had a black X scrapped through them. Beneath the names, notes. Occupation. Description to the point of a rough sketch. Likes and dislikes. Secrets to leverage against them.

Whether or not information completely filled the page, the last note on the page had stars. No one had more than five that I could see, though some were filled in and others had only the outlines. A ranking system of some sort. Easily changeable when a person gained in importance.

The book had no kind of order, neither importance nor alphabetical. Though the blue names toward the front tended to have more filled in stars than the later names. Order of inclusion into the group or cropping up on their radar.

I flipped to the back. Quite a few pages still empty. I couldn't quite decide if that was good or bad. Not a large enough movement to take over the world. Buying the book with so many pages showed confidence in their cause.

Whatever the cause might be.

Eventually, I found the last entry. My name. In bold, red letters with one star outlined at the bottom. The lack of faith kind of offended me. Only the one star. I'd already showed them I was worth more. But I'd left no witnesses with memories to tell tales. Except for the score of women I saved. They probably wouldn't share their knowledge with whoever locked them up.

I needed to work on my PR.

If I planned to pursue this kind of thing.

Since I continued flipping through the names in the book, I kind of was continuing this path. Plan or not.

Brian Winchester rang a bell, though I didn't know where from. Boris rang a bell too. Not a super uncommon name, but I'd only ever met one in real life. And It made me realize where I remembered Brian from.

Urge to kill rising, I flipped through the rest of the book only focusing on the names. If I saw Spencer's name I would march my happy butt right over to his house and kill him myself. I really would. Maybe even see if I could recreate what death had done. He wouldn't be able to escape me if I wore gloves while I worked. Plus, the bonus of no fingerprints. If I did it right, no one would even suspect me.

Luckily, for both of us, no Spencer.

No Gale Force either, or not by a name I recognized. I didn't know most of the other superheroes real names. Just Kai, Mike, and Karloff aka Magus. Kai and Magus were certainly not in the book. I'd passed a couple of Michaels, but I doubted he would join something like this. We had enough of the same demons. He wouldn't go that way.

The elimination left too many superheroes in the running to being on the wrong side. My first instinct, to call Magus, died a quick death. The phones were probably recorded and analyzed by people I didn't know I could trust. Also, it would tell him I stole something from a crime scene.

Not something to do until I had something more important to divert his attention.

Lex was busy. He would take me wherever I needed to if I asked, which was exactly why I wouldn't ask. Kai would too, but conflict of interest. And, anyway, I knew a man who already had a leg in this fight.

Making sure to hide the book by my leg, I stood. "I need to make a phone call."

Lex looked down at my plate and looked up at me. "You haven't eaten half of what's there. Are you okay?"

Not in the least. "I didn't say I was finished. I'll be back."

Lex's, "Okay, Arnold," followed me down the hall.

I'd have some kind of quippy retort when I came back. After the phone call whetted my appetite for a few things.

My phone sat on top of the letter that had sparked my binge the night before.

Gabe had wanted me to embrace light and shadow. Some of that meant not shying away from what he had failed to show me. Perhaps I could kill two stones with one bird.

A bird who had texted me last night after I'd stopped looking at the phone. *Be honest. Am I ever going to see you again?*

Today was his lucky day, I guessed, though not necessarily how he hoped. I detached the phone from the charger and dialed, hoping he would not answer and save me from the flaws in this plan.

"Hello, Greer."

Of course, he answered. And of course, the smile in his voice speaking my name made me smile as well. This would be a tricky negotiation. "Hey, Spencer. Are you busy?"

"Not too busy to speak to you. What's up?"

Damn the man. Focus. I needed to focus. "I have an errand I need to run and I have some information that could be useful to you. I was wondering if we could trade favors. Do you have a ladder?" Trade the favors and be done with this thing between us because I didn't like feeling this unsettled.

"Yes, I have a ladder. Am I the first person you called?"

"Yes." What was he getting at?

"And do you think having the balance of a favor owed and a favor given will make this easier for you?"

Son of a sadist, I walked right into that one. Why couldn't he just let this be simple? Simpler? Why did he want to twist me up in knots and smile at the quivering results?

Fine. If he could rip off bandages I would rip off the scabs. "Do you hit them?"

"Hit who?" The warmth of his voice cooled.

Small victories. "The women you own."

He let out a sigh. "I do not own them and I do not hit them. They are all beautiful and I need them to stay that way because men let their guards down around beautiful women and women relax around beautiful men. That is what I need, a lowering of guard so that things slip out and my employees can collect the information for me without force or suspicion. Because the men who hire them don't expect or require intelligence in women, especially not in beautiful women. That is their weakness. *They* are who I exploit. Not my employees. I need them strong and healthy. I need them smart and perceptive. I need them loyal, Greer. Fear steals all of that away from me."

Quite the speech. I wasn't certain if I let him ramble on because I wanted to believe in him or if I was looking for an excuse to hang up. It could have all been a lie. But there were truths. Fear did not foster loyalty and it killed the thinking mind.

His words gave me more than insight on how and why he valued those women. It explained some of why he was after me. My lack of apparent fear, even when he'd had me kidnapped, had sparked his interest from the start. I believed that he didn't force these women to sell their bodies for him. Not forcing them did not mean he was a good person, though.

"Where are you?" Spencer broke into my thoughts. "I can pick you up."

I should hang up the phone and find a new way to do what I needed to. Magus wasn't in the book I stole from the crime scene. If I contacted him and met him in person to discuss things, he might help me weed out the names he recognized.

"I'm at Lex's again." My traitorous mouth.

"I'll be right there."

"Wait don't come right now. We're eating breakfast."

"Bye, Greer." The smile in his voice oozed all over me before he hung up.

We both knew he was on his way over right then. I tried my best, but couldn't help being happy for it. That damned man.

I tossed the book and my phone on the bed, then stomped my way back to the kitchen.

Lex looked up from the conversation he and Clint had been having. "Something wrong, honey?"

Everything and nothing. I nodded my head and pulled another plate from the cabinet. "Spencer's coming over."

Lex's eyes narrowed as I set the plate down and reclaimed my seat. "I can't tell if you're happy about that or not."

"Neither can I."

Clint choked down some laughter. He was lucky Lex sat between us, though I was certain my glare could pass through Lex and cause the death of this salesman. Lex grabbed a couple of pieces of bacon, another slice of French toast, and placed both on my plate.

This man was a keeper. I kissed his cheek and dug in.

The doorbell rang not fifteen minutes later.

"Would you like me to get that?" There Lex was again with his sweet, innocent, sin-ridden smile.

I stood, slowly. "I will hurt you, Lex. I really will." If he hadn't remained seated, we would have seen if I was capable of it or not. The laughter as I sauntered down the hall, that much I could handle.

Spencer looked good in the morning light.

Balls.

Smile on his cleanly shaved face and another bouquet in his hands. Lilies, this time. Stargazer, dark purple, and bright red. Damned Spencer. I hadn't said a word and he somehow managed to bring my favorite.

I took the bouquet and plunged my face into it, peeking up at the man through the petals. Spencer grinned wider. Scowling at him was not effective with my face still buried in flowers he brought me. I didn't have the heart to snarl by the time I pulled them away. Instead, I stepped back to let him in.

He chuckled. "You have pollen all over you. Here. Let me." He kept his hands poised in the air around my cheeks a moment until I nodded my acceptance.

His fingers brushed lightly, probably taking more time than necessary. When he brushed my lips, my knees quaked.

"I hate you so much right now." I kept my voice low and earnest, so he knew I meant it.

He dipped his head toward mine. "Exactly how much?"

I slipped my hand around the back of his neck. He let me pull his lips to mine. He smiled against me before kissing me back soundly.

His eyes glowed triumphant as he pulled back.

I scowled at him, this time from inches away. "Come on. I wasn't joking about breakfast."

The heat of him chased close behind me on the way back to the kitchen.

Lex cast a sly smile my way as I walked back in. I declined to respond. Instead, I picked up the plate I'd grabbed for Spencer. When I turned around, he was right there. Standing two inches away from me.

"Here." I passed the plated over. "Serve yourself while I find another vase for these."

He took the plate with a nod and a curve to his lips that did wicked things to my blood pressure. "Yes, ma'am."

I retreated across the kitchen with my plausible excuse. Lex knew he had a couple in the cabinet below where Spencer spooned eggs onto his plate. He smiled around a forkful when I looked back to him, but he didn't say a word. If not for my plate of food still waiting to be eaten, I would have spent more time arranging the flowers.

My plate of food made me brave enough to wash my hands and sit back down between Lex and Spencer. For a forkful, there was peace. I thought we might have smooth sailing.

Then, "So, Spencer, what brings you over here this fine morning?"

I could have murdered Lex, which would mean Clint had to go as well. Couldn't leave witnesses. Spencer, I could count on to keep his mouth closed.

"The same thing that brought me here, yesterday," Spencer said.

Apparently, I could only count on him to keep his mouth closed if something felonious was afoot. Or if I killed him. I looked at him out of the corner of my left eye. Killing him shouldn't be difficult. He wouldn't even fight me taking my shirt off.

His eyes took in my expression as I contemplated his death and did not balk. "My plans yesterday got interrupted and exploded in my face. Now, I'm making it up to her."

Eating part of my breakfast was making it up to me?

"Exploded in your face? How so?" Lex asked as if I wasn't in the room.

Spencer might have spoken of me in third person, but he looked me in the eyes when he did so.

"A preacher who's a friend of my father showed up while we were working on my truck. Preaching hellfire and brimstone." He set his elbow on the counter and rested his chin on the back of his hand. "Lord knows what brought him over there in the first place. Then, my dealership called. Huge emergency. Someone got injured and was heading to the hospital. A big ol' mess."

He lied so smoothly, intertwining the real and the fake into something plausible without batting an eye. I hated it. I hated that it made me question everything that fell out of his mouth. Because, I wanted to believe him and I hated myself for it.

"A couple questions," Lex said.

Why? Why did he need to ask more things that made me regret inviting Spencer over?

"Go ahead." Spencer was game. Of course, he didn't have any qualms about telling my dearest friends lies upon lies. It wouldn't affect him at all.

"First," Lex started. He even set his fork down. "What kind of dealership and how many?"

"Auto. New and used. I own all of the Auto-Riffic dealerships."

Spencer had gone with something easy to look up and refute. Not the smartest plan if he wanted people to believe him. Unless it was true.

"Wow!" Lex sounded properly impressed, as he was supposed to. "How many dealerships are we talking about?"

I forced a breath out. "Seriously, Lex?"

Spencer answered anyway. "Enough."

"I only ask because my jobless friend could use some security." He smiled at my glaring. "You understand."

"And Lex seems to have forgotten that I'll be more stable than he will, when things finalize at the end of the month."

"So, he's looking for a sugar mama?"

I pinched the bridge of my nose. Lex enjoyed this way too much for me to win playing defense. I could go on the offense, but I didn't know enough about Clint to poke at them. Another tactic, then. "Considering how the last one fucked me over, perhaps you should all be more concerned with what *I'm* looking for."

"And what, exactly, is that?" Lex said it nonchalant, like it didn't matter to him.

He cared and he asked me in Spencer's presence purposefully. To see me squirm and to put Spencer under pressure. The second part felt like him being a good friend to me. I wasn't so sure about the first.

Spencer stilled beside me. Without seeing him in my periphery, I could feel his patience to hear my answer. Chewing and swallowing a mouthful of food didn't give me near enough time to come up with a full and tactful answer. Whatever. Tact was for tacticians. I was more of an ass-nailer.

"Right now, I could use a little loyalty, Lex. People who won't give me up or give up on me at the first sign of trouble. I'd like people to stop breaking into my home. Stop trying to kill me, maybe? Maybe people could stop dying around me for long enough for me to get my bearings again. I realize normal, or what I used to call normal, flew over the cuckoo's nest a few weeks ago, but I want a life that's livable."

I didn't add that I needed someone to stand by me when the world did fall apart and help me put my pieces back together. Admitting it, even in my own head, felt like failure, though I knew all people needed people. Just like Streisand sang.

I stood up from the bar. My plate still had food on it. Frustration in my feet fueled my movement. The short trip to the stovetop didn't calm the twitching, but there were still two unclaimed pieces of toast and six of bacon, a couple spoons of potatoes, one of the eggs. Food could ground me when moving failed.

"That doesn't sound so hard." Clint added as I zeroed in on the food, which saved him from my glare.

"You'd think." Attacking him with the litany of lovely events from the past month felt like over-kill. He didn't deserve it. Since Lex seemed to like him, I would be good.

Spencer cleared his throat. "Can I have one of those strips of bacon, before you finish the rest?"

I turned my head to glare him away from my bacon and found him staring at me with that deep, intense way he had. Despite the question, I don't think he cared at all about the bacon. I lifted the plate and stretched it over to him, while my heart rattled against my ribcage.

The small smile of triumph curled his lips as he took a strip. He knew I knew. Bubble, bubble, I was in trouble.

"Shit," Lex breathed while Clint let out an extended, "Daaaamn."

I refused to blush. Not now when I had to contend with the panic dancing in my bones, too. If one reaction got loose, the rest would trample all over me. Couldn't let that happen. I dropped my eyes to my plate and ate with my butt leaned up against the oven. Far enough that no one could touch me or steal from my plate. Close enough to watch the three men spark up a conversation that had nothing to do with me.

Spencer watched me three quarters of the time.

And Lex watched him watch me.

Dropped my cleaned plate in the sink with relish. At least I could escape this uncomfortable situation.

Spencer stood, with his half-finished plate in hand.

"No," I waved him back down. "I need to shower and change real quick."

"Quick?"

"Yeah, like ten or fifteen minutes?" I looked at my wrist like I still wore a watch. Old tick. "Why? Do you have some time limit I need to keep in mind?"

He shook his head. "The last shower took you almost an hour."

Clint stared hard at his plate, though it didn't hide his smile. Lex fluttered his eyelashes at me. He wanted details when we were alone.

Couldn't let those kinds of assumptions fly free. "And if you remember, Spencer, before I took that shower a woman had puked down the front of me before seizing and dying."

Clint stopped smiling. Lex's lip curled in disgust.

Spencer tipped his head to the side. "True."

I nodded to the three of them and left the room. Chariots of Fire echoed in my head at my one victory.

Just before I rounded the corner into the bathroom, I heard Lex warn Spencer. I paused to eavesdrop, though Lex hadn't dropped his voice.

"I can't kill you, but if you hurt her, I swear to gods, I will find a way to make you wish I had."

I *had* asked for a little loyalty.

Spencer being threatened that way from Lex was almost laughable, except I knew the way Lex's mind worked. He didn't do physical harm. No one knew how to do propaganda like an artist, though. Legal, affective, effective propaganda. And artists' loves and hates lived forever.

22 – OLD AND NEW

SPENCER LEANED FORWARD to look through my window at the pale green house with forest green trim I'd had him park in front of. "So, where are we again?"

Hand on door handle, I took a steadying breath. "This is Gabe's old house."

"Gabriel Jones lived here?" He dipped his head down to get a better view of the second story.

"Yeah. So did I, for a time." I got out of the car before I said any more.

Between Gabe's letter festering in the back of my head and the sight of the old house, my core trembled. Gods, I needed to keep it together until Spencer dropped me back off. If I could do that, I could handle everything else.

Probably.

Spencer scooted around the front of the truck to catch up to my slow walk up to the door. "Should we get the ladder?"

"Not yet." I didn't want to scare the people inside. Introductions needed to happen first. Provided they were home mid-morning on a Thursday.

What was I even doing here?

I knocked on the door, not pausing long enough to talk myself out of it. Spencer settled a hand on the small of my back. My head whipped around to him. He quirked an eyebrow. A challenge.

The door cracked open before I could tell him to let me go, or not.

The woman who opened the door looked less than happy to see a visitor. The spit-up on her shoulder and baby on the opposite hip might have had something to do with it. "Yes?"

"Hi, Ma'am. You don't know me, but Gabe, that's Gabriel Jones, was my close friend, and it seems I kind of own this house now."

Her lips tightened. "Yes?"

Not the best start. I forged on. "So, I thought I'd come by to give you my number if you needed things fixed or whatever and—"

"You're not kicking us out?"

My head jerked back. "Why would I do that?"

"Because we're paying way less than the rent you could be getting in this market, but it's all we can afford right now, and with the kids..."

I waved my hands before she went through the whole thing. "I'm certain Gabe had a good reason why he set things up as he did and I'm not going to mess with it."

Tears had started to well in her eyes. "Really?"

"Really."

"Because I was so worried when we heard of his passing, then we heard nothing and I didn't know what to think and with the rent going up around the city as it has, we would be homeless if we couldn't live here."

She'd really started crying and I couldn't do a thing about it. I wasn't that girl. Not today.

An adorable little girl with dark skin and blonde, kinky hair wrapped her arms around the woman's leg. "Why are you crying, Mama? What's wrong? Who is it?" She levered a stink eye at me that I could learn a thing or two from.

"It's okay, baby girl. This is the lady Mr. Jones gave the house to after he died." She patted her daughter's head.

"What's her name, Mama?"

The woman set her fingers on the screen door. Spencer and I moved back as she pushed it open. "Why don't you ask her yourself?"

The girl hid somewhat behind her mother's leg, but looked all the way up at me. "What's your name?"

My height intimidated some adult people. I squatted down to her level and held my hand out to her. "My name is Greer. What's yours?"

"Grace."

My smile froze on my face a moment as I realized part of why Gabe had rented the house to these people. That had been my daughter's name.

Her shaking my hand pulled me out of my shock.

"That's a good name. And what's your mama's name?"

She giggled. "Mama's name is Mama."

I laughed with her. Of course it was.

The woman apologized as I stood and offered her hand to me. "Ivy. My name is Ivy."

"Greer." I shook, impressed with her grip. "Greer Ianto."

"And this is?" She looked to my left.

I'd almost forgotten Spencer next to me, because I wasn't used to someone being there. He reached his own hand to meet Ivy's. "Spencer Marcus."

Time to go in for the kill before I lost my nerve. "Okay. Part of why I came over was to meet my new-old tenants, but I also came because Gabe let me know that he left something in this house for me."

Concern furrowed her brow. "The place was empty when we moved in, and he didn't drop anything by that I know about. I could ask my husband if he knows anything when he gets home and we can call you back."

"It's not something you would know about. We had a secret hiding place we used as a mailbox back and forth when I lived here."

She blinked. "Oh. That's weird."

Not as weird as my life since Gabe died.

"Would you like to come in?"

"I would, yes. Do you mind if he gets the ladder?" I jerked a thumb at Spencer.

"I...guess not." She shrugged, a little dumbfounded. Like she couldn't believe what was happening today.

I understood, but I didn't have the time for disbelief. Not today. Not most days, anymore.

Spencer kissed my cheek before he turned back down the path to retrieve the ladder. Taking liberties while I was distracted. I would show *him* taking liberties.

Later.

I held the screen and Ivy held the wooden door as Spencer maneuvered the ladder inside. It couldn't be straightened in the front room. Ivy lead the way to the great room in the back of the house without my needing ask. The ladder spoke loud enough, apparently.

Spencer stopped in the doorway of the great room and tipped his head back to take it in.

Five evenly spaced skylights across the ceiling. Windows galore across the opposite wall. Grey-brick, wood-burning fireplace on the left side of the room. Huge, built in bookcases on the right. Home. For a long enough time that the smell of baby wipes and plastic toys didn't diminish the feel of it.

Spencer cast a look back at me over his shoulder. "Where do you want me?"

A grin played in the shine of his eyes. He knew exactly what he said and how it could be taken.

Glaring at him would only tell him he'd won. "Second skylight on the right."

"As you wish, Darling."

There went my chest rattle. My knees, too.

He set up the ladder without looking at me, but I knew, I *knew* he enjoyed his effect on me. The nearness of him, and the knowledge that he was staring at my ass—yup, I checked—as I climbed, distracted me from why I was there until I got to the top. There, auto pilot took over.

I pushed the releases on either side of the skylight and the hidden shelf slid free the first two inches.

The key to our mailbox rested on a vacuum-sealed bag containing the first baby blanket I knitted. The only one I ever wrapped Grace in while she lived. I fisted my hands and counted to ten before opening the shelf far enough to pull the key and the blanket out.

Ivy's, "Well, I'll be a monkey's uncle!" reminded me that I had an audience. An audience who didn't know me well enough to ignore me losing my shit at the top of a ladder in the middle of their home.

Slow, steady breathing as I came down to kept from losing my grip. Literally and figuratively.

"I never would have guessed something was up there," Ivy said as I stepped off.

Since that was kind of the point, I didn't sass her about it. Instead, I gave her a wink, like the sight of the blanket hadn't ripped my heart out. "You ain't seen nothing."

It was supposed to be a secret—I didn't want her to see anything—but I wouldn't store anything in the mailbox anytime soon. If I locked everything before I left, she wouldn't be able to either.

I curved my hand into the top of the fireplace in the center and pushed the button just above the brick. The brick under my knee shifted. I pulled the brick out from its place and retrieved the other key. Long and skinny, like in an old cartoon. Which, I supposed, were modeled on the real thing from an earlier period.

Ivy's surprise when I replaced the brick was priceless.

"What's she doing, Mama?" Grace asked.

This time, instead of making her ask me, she pulled her little one out of my way as I walked across the room. "She's searching for treasure, Gracie."

I certainly was.

The large round knob of the dimmer switch took a little finesse to pull off, but it came. Leaving the key holes bare. I slid the long skinny one in first, chased it with the regular sized one, and turned them opposite directions.

The book case to my left clicked like it always had. Gabe kept it well-greased when we lived there. I was happy it moved easily as I pushed the nearest section in and pulled the next section toward me.

All this for a manila envelope. A manila envelope and my baby's blanket, I supposed, but still. There had to be a better way than making me disturb this woman's day to find two things.

"Is that all?" Ivy sounded disappointed.

I nodded, and I got it. The envelope didn't even feel that thick, but it felt heavy with Gabe's guilt, somehow. "I said it was a mailbox." I pushed the second section back into position, which pulled the other one flush.

She huffed. "Pretty fancy stuff for a mailbox."

Maybe, but Gabe never locked it when I lived with him. It seemed less odd when you pushed the bookcase out of the way daily, sometimes more than once a day, looking for the response to the last note you left. "I'm going to take the keys, because I really don't want to climb back up there to hide them. Do you want me to lock it before I go?"

Offering to leave it open hurt, but it was the right thing to do. She'd let me in without fuss.

Ivy looked down at her daughter. "Yes. I'd hate for her fingers to get caught."

Trying to keep my relief off my face, I smiled. "I understand."

The bookcase clicked like clockwork as I twisted the keys in the full circle and replaced the dimmer knob. "Okay, well. That's all for me. We'll just let you get back to your business, unless you had any questions for me?"

"You said you would leave your number?"

"I did." I clutched the keys, envelope, and blanket. I didn't want to set any of them down.

"Your hands are full, Darling. Let me."

He did it again. Called me "Darling." And it kind of, almost, felt right. He wrote my number down for my new tenant while I clutched my things to my chest like they were ill-gotten.

A number he had memorized, apparently.

He also took her number down for me, then tucked it in my front pocket watching my face as he did it. Gauging my reaction and enjoying the hell out of the tiny intimacy. If I hadn't stuffed the book with the list of names in the breast pocket of my button up, I had no doubts of where he would have tucked the number.

After making absolutely, positively certain the number wouldn't accidentally come popping out of my pocket, Spencer moved away to collect the ladder. He didn't wink when he was ready to go. Just gave me an innocent grin a grandmother wouldn't believe.

Cheeky bastard.

When we got back to his truck, Spencer set the ladder against the side and opened the door for me. He also held out a hand to help me up into the seat. I used my full hands as the excuse to accept the first but refuse the assist. He didn't seem discouraged when he finally climbed in the driver's seat.

He pointed with his chin at the pile I clutched against me. "What's with the blanket?"

Nope. We weren't going down that road. Rather than fly off my top and walk my happy ass home again, I set the blanket in my lap and went for diversion.

I tugged the book out of my breast pocket and took a moment to figure out exactly how I wanted to explain. The smile slipped away from him. As ever, Spencer recognized my mood shift.

"I found this," I wagged the book once, "in the same place I found your women yesterday."

"They're not *my* women, Greer. Like I told you—"

My fingers on his lips stopped him.

I understood his argument. That wasn't the point right now. "I accidentally took this with me out of a crime scene."

"How do you accidentally steal from a crime scene?" He didn't seem to mind my fingers on his mouth.

Neither did I.

Focus.

"I was looking for the address to give to Magus then I ran to free the women that were chained up and forgot about it. Not important. The important thing is I can't give it to the cops right now and I really can't hand it over to the Gold 4."

Spencer kissed the tips of my fingers, then twisted my wrist to the side just enough to move my fingers to his cheek. "Why is that?"

"I know I can trust Magus and a few others. But a superhero tried to kill me and—"

"A superhero tried to kill you?" He stared at me like I'd grown a new head, absolute shock riding belief.

I nodded. "Yesterday. Bashed my windows in. That's why I was over Lex's this morning."

"Greer." His face bent around the corners. Concern touched with a taste of wrath.

"I don't know who else among the superheroes might have known of his...views or might have helped him hide things. I don't know any of their real names." That wasn't completely the truth. I said it because it protected my friends, but it felt wrong. "Scratch that, I know a few real names. But you can't know that I do."

His lips tightened, but he nodded to me, both acceptance and encouragement.

"Anyway. I might have recognized some names in this book, but I only remember a couple first names from your people. I have a feeling you will know more."

"What is it?" His eyes finally dropped down from my face to look at the black, fake-leather cover on the book.

"A calendar. A plan of attack. A roster. Some combination of the three. I think it's safer with me than most other people, so I'll need it back." I made a plate of my hand and held the book out to him. "But you should look through it."

Spencer set his hand on top of the book, then leaned in and gave me a soft kiss.

"What was that for?" I asked, trying to keep my insides from turning to jelly.

He lowered his chin. His eyes dropped to my lips a moment, then lifted back up to my eyes with fire blazing. "I need a reason?"

No. I supposed he didn't.

My non-answer made him smile and kiss me again. Slower. Deeper. With an insistent tug on my lower lip until I let him have it. I opened my mouth to him and pushed against him, taking as much as I wanted of his darkness before I pulled away. He whispered, "Greer," and it shot right down to my nethers.

I shook my head, but had to answer. "Later." I couldn't deny what I wanted, no matter how sensible saying no was.

Spencer stared at me wordlessly for a long moment, the heat still riding the wake of his focus on me. He finally nodded, "Good," before plucking the forgotten book from my slack fingers.

It left me watching him as he flipped through the book. His eyes narrowed much earlier in the calendar than when I looked through it.

This had been the right impulse.

Rather than studying him, I opened the manila envelope. A single letter on thick paper in Gabe's scrolling cursive.

My Little Umbra,

You may think you remember the first day we met, but you'd be wrong. That was our reintroduction after I'd been gone for what moved like decades to me and years for you.

The first time I saw you, you were running as fast as your feet could carry you away from the giant, grey spider giving chase. Giggling the whole way. When she caught you, and nibbled at your face, you squealed in delight. I knew you were a special kind of heart.

I stepped out of the shadows. She hugged you closer to her and took up a defensive pose. Against me. Few people ever find themselves worthy of the devotion of a spider, let alone one so rare. Each leg well over ten feet long. Practically glowing with magick. I thought she might kill me, but you stopped her. You spoke to me without fear or malice, proving me right. You invited me to play with you.

I want to tell you that the beautiful things we saw together, the evils we fought together, were real. Everything you've ever heard of exists in place your heart recognizes. Both light and shadow, bad and good, exist. And you will relearn that they exist along separate axes in the same space.

I also want to tell you why I left the first time. While, yes, I had hoped it would sweeten the discourse between your mother and you, I left to protect you. I left you a gift in the witching pool, one that comes with a burden but something I knew could only come to you. You who giggles with spiders and dances with lightning.

I am sorry and I am proud. I love you and I am ever in your debt.

When the time comes for you to pass Bob on, I wish for you to find someone as worthy as I had the good fortune to.

Lux.

Verum in luce et umbra

Oedipus Rex and his pecs.

Crap on a cracker.

Shirley Temple's pimples.

Gabe was both of the closest friends I'd had in my life. The friend of my childhood dreams and the man who saved me from my adult nightmares.

How in the flying fuck was that possible?

23 – WE ALL FALL DOWN

MY PHONE VIBRATED in my left bra cup. Because, why wouldn't it ring right now when I needed the semblance of silence and peace to figure out what the fuck? I caught sight of the name on the ID before I answered, which was good. Yelling profanities at my nephew was not the way to be. "Hello?"

"Aunt Greer, are you alright?" He panted quite a bit as he asked me, which quickly dissolved into coughing.

The coughing saved me the time asking him why he wasn't in school. If he hadn't sounded panicked, I would have thought he was joking with me just to make his sick day go by a little faster. "Of course, I'm okay. Why wouldn't I be?"

"Dad said the building on the news wasn't yours, but it looks like it. They found some bodies, then a fire started and they had to wait for the firemen to come."

Gods, I didn't like the sound of that. I could call the building manager to verify, but they weren't great at answering my calls.

"Well, I'm perfectly fine so—" My phone beeped that I had another call. "Would you mind holding on, Gannon? That's my other line."

"I mean, I guess. I only called to make sure you hadn't died—"

I only felt bad about cutting off the rant for half a breath. I'd make it up to him. "This is Greer."

"Greer, Gale Force has escaped."

What, now? Magus could not have just told me that. I had to be dreaming. "How is that even possible?"

"We're not entirely certain right now. He was being transferred to a secure facility and there was a breakdown in communication and vehicles."

I couldn't deal with this. Not then. "When did this happen?"

"About twenty minutes ago."

"Uh-huh, and is the burning apartment building my nephew saw on the news mine?"

He paused. "Let me check." Then the sound fell to the waiting silence and periodic beeps that let me know he hadn't hung up.

Spencer settled his hand on my thigh. I looked up at him and his expression opened in question. I didn't have any answers. So, I just stared and hoped that it was a big fucking coincidence and my life was not spiraling down Hell's shitter.

The silence on the other end changed. I turned away from Spencer.

Gannon had to have been wrong.

"That is your building."

"Why wouldn't it be my building?"

"I am sorry, Greer. From the preliminary reports, a tornado spun out of nowhere and took the building down."

Out of nowhere. How about out of the mind of a man who decided I caused whatever fucking problem he seemed to have in life. Poor little bitty, that Gale Force. He had such a hard life.

"The fire doesn't seem to have been started with an accelerant. Perhaps the electrical sparked things when everything ripped apart."

"That doesn't matter. How many people?"

Magus took in a breath. "Greer, you need to be careful with that kind of thinking. This is not your—"

"How many fucking lives did that asshole take because he got a stick up his ass about me needing to bend to his will."

"Oh." Magus sounded surprised.

While I didn't really want to know, I had to ask. "What did you think I meant?"

"That you were going to blame yourself for the lives he's taken trying to kill you."

"Fuck that."

"Indeed." Papers flipped in the background. "The body count isn't clear yet. Three confirmed."

Most people worked during the day. It might have saved their lives, though not their homes and security. At least I didn't need to worry about getting the sliding glass door fixed. No sense in putting any money in to fix things at this point. This was all act of thought-he-was-a-god, insurance claim fun now.

I needed to work on damage control. "You're sure you didn't write down any other addresses for me, right?"

"Correct."

That meant Lex should be safe. As would Gabe's house. I had a place to stay tonight, if nothing else. I just needed a plan of attack and I had an idea. "What's his name?"

"I can't tell you that."

Magus didn't even try to play like he didn't know what I meant. Which was good. I had no time or patience to deal with roundabout shit.

"You are telling me that this shithead has tried to kill me twice, now. Twice. And you don't think I deserve to be on a first name basis with this asshole?"

"There are regulations, Greer, and they exist for a reason."

I wanted to strangle the man. "And what of the regulations if he's not alone in this. He might be the one out and about with his crazy, but what if there are others in the Gold 4 working with him? Others who knew his plans. Others who helped him escape so he could kill at least three people already. Aren't there regulations against aiding and abetting a murderer?"

The waiting silence filled the other end of the line for a few breaths. Then, "I'm sorry, Greer."

"I am, too." I hung up the phone. With everything going on and Gale Force breaking all the rules, I didn't understand how Magus could hold so tight to the regulations.

The phone buzzed at me. My nephew still on the other line. Gods. I needed to maintain a semblance of calm long enough to get off the phone from him. I hit the reconnect button, "Hey, Gannon, are you still there?"

"What if I had hung up, huh?"

"I would have called you right back." As soon as I stopped yelling at the world.

"Did you have nice chat with whoever was more important than me?"

Oh, man, he had strengthened the force of his whining. Bolstered his whine with guilt and attitude, like any teenager worth his salt. I enjoyed it much better when I was not the target. Then again, I had something to counter with.

"Actually, no. That was a friend of mine letting me know that the building you saw on the news was mine."

Dead silence, followed by "I knew it!" and a coughing fit.

I doubted that very seriously. If he had known about any of the shit going on in my life of late, I would owe him sooo many wet willies.

Gannon's "What do I tell Dad?" came out with much less conviction than the rest.

I didn't know. What was someone going to tell me? "Why don't you tell him that that was my apartment, but that I was nowhere near when things went down?"

"Are you sure you're fine?"

Nope. "Peachy. *You* told *me* about my own apartment, remember? I didn't even realize what happened."

"Okay." He didn't sound completely convinced. Only placated for the time being. "Will you come live with us until they fix your apartment?"

"And mess around with you and your cold? No, thank you. You sound gross." A cold on top of everything else would be...just my luck, actually. No reason to help my luck along. "I've got a couple places I could be, actually, so I should be good."

"Are you sure?"

"About avoiding the cold? Absolutely?"

"No, Aunt Greer," Gannon said. "About the rest."

Oh, the lies we tell children to keep their worlds shiny and bright. "I'm really good, Gannon. You can let your dad know that and worry about resting up."

"But it's so boring."

"I know. Would you rather go back to school?"

I could practically see him stiffen up around the words he spit through narrowed lips, "No, ma'am."

I wouldn't have asked if I didn't already know the answer. "Okay, then. Maybe if you're really good, and you're feeling up to it by then, we can have a couch-drive-in night on Saturday."

Staying in with him could be the best for both of us. We both needed the down time to recuperate.

"Okay," his voice brightened. "See you soon, Aunt Greer."

The beginnings of a coughing fit sputtered through the line before he hung up the phone. I took a slow breath in.

"Greer?" Spencer asked, low.

I didn't even turn my head to look to him. "You might want to plug your ears a moment."

His hand pulled away from my thigh.

I let loose. A scream followed by the loudest stream of cursing I'd let out in years. It took longer than usual, double the breaths before I'd spent the burning edge of my frustration and had fallen to panting.

My hands shook. I tried to ball them into fists to stop the trembling. No avail. Hard to stop the hands when the whole rest of me shivered too.

Hands surrounded mine, warming them from the outside. I hadn't realized they were cold.

"Greer, talk to me, Darling. Are you okay?"

"Who the fuck knows?" I swung my gaze up at him.

Concern had his pretty face all bent out of shape.

The 1812 Overture rang out, loud and proud in the car.

"What the fuck is it with all the phone calls right now?" I asked the ray of sun sitting on the dashboard. "Did someone make Poseidon release the kraken?"

"That can wait," Spencer assured me, while he tried to warm me with just his hands on mine.

"Answer your phone, Spence."

"I'll get them back later."

I rotated my head to Spencer and locked his gaze with mine. "I might be dealing with some shit right now, but it will take a lot more than this to break me again, now answer the damned phone."

He jerked it out of his pocket and held it in the space between us. Speaker phone again. He hadn't learned from the speaker phone mishap. "What?"

"Tanaka's refusing to go out tomorrow, Boss."

I knew that name. I'd saved her. And I didn't know the voice on the other end of the line, which made it even better. Hopefully this one wouldn't tell me Tanaka had died when she was really locked up in a cage somewhere.

"What?" Spencer didn't sound mad, just curious.

"She started spouting something about how death was coming for her and would find her if she went." The man answered. "I don't know, Boss. She sounds really wigged out, but the contract has already been signed and paid for."

No surprise there. I assumed a lot of the girls who I'd saved had pre-paid contracts.

I asked, "Where is she?" without waiting for permission to speak. This might have been part of his work, but I'd saved Tanaka. If she needed me to do so again, I would.

"Boss?" The man on the other line asked.

"Answer the question."

"I assume she's at her other job, at the dressmaker's."

"Send me the address. I'll take care of it."

"Yes, Boss."

The call disconnected.

Spencer cursed.

"What?"

"I need to take you back, but if Tanaka's lost her grip, that's more important."

Like I hadn't proved myself capable of finding my way home when I needed to. Even if it came with a detour and a few new furry friends "If Tanaka's having issues with yesterday and Death, I'm probably the best person to speak to her."

"I'll break the contract if I need to. That's no problem."

"Do you want her to go to the thing tomorrow?" Who was I, asking this? I thought I hated this part of him.

"If she wants to." He scrubbed his hands over his face a couple of times, then pulled them back over his hair. "It's in the book you stole, so I might be able to get enough info on what the fuck's going on."

He'd mussed his hair back some. I had to mentally sit on my hands to stop myself from messing it up more. If his eyes had been open I might have tried my luck anyway. "Tomorrow's some sort of exclusive Cirque du Luna show?"

Spencer started the engine as he nodded.

I wondered how one got a ticket to the show. Were they super expensive or was this one of those events by invite only. Either way, this felt like the wrong time to ask.

Spencer's phone crowed. He pulled it out of the cup holder he'd tossed it in and handed it to me. "That's a text. The address, probably. Copy it to my nav app, Journey, will you? The security code is an M."

I could learn so many things by poking around on his phone. Even with navigation running. When he wasn't looking, I could export all of his numbers to the police or worse. All the damage I could do and he handed the phone to me without a second thought. I knew newlyweds who wouldn't do the same.

Gods.

I pulled up the last text, trying to not see the name. The level of trust necessitated a reciprocal respect of privacy.

He was right. The address. I copied it into the Journey and let her guide our way to a dress shop in the Cherry Creek area.

Spencer grumbled his way through the cones and construction diverting us from the most direct route. I recognized well enough the section of street we'd been diverted around.

"Calm down. They're probably still cleaning up from my car

exploding."

He dropped to silent and rocked his head around to me. "What?"

"I'm pretty sure I told you that was what happened to my old car."

"You mean, *exploded* exploded?"

I nodded. "In my face. After it was stolen and found again."

Spencer turned back to focus on the road in front of us, which I was grateful for. No need to test my limits for shits and giggles.

"What exactly to do mean, in your face?"

"Spencer. You are one of the few people I don't sugarcoat my words with."

His lips tightened, but he said nothing.

I had to know. "What?"

"I just don't like the thought of you getting hurt."

Damn. I didn't expect that. And I kind of needed a new mood in the car before I melted into a puddle. "I wasn't, except for the bruising. Like when you shot me."

"You fell out of thin air." He wagged a finger at me.

"Then you shot me."

"Because I thought someone was trying to kill me."

The back and forth between us. Much better. I could breathe a little easier. "Do people often fall out of thin air to try and kill you?"

He cast a look at me without turning his head. "I've had some complicated weeks in my life."

I laughed. I had to. Oh, I knew he was only mirroring my words from the day he had his people "escort" me to his office. But he had no clue. No clue. Criminal shenanigans could shift away from normal Joe Schmoe life, sure. But glowing skin and zombies. Death and his hounds. Who knew what else.

Spencer didn't even wait for me to finish laughing to ask, "What?"

"*Your* life is complicated?" I wiped a tear from my right eye.

He paused a moment to shake his head at me while he twisted around to see where he was parking. "Just because you've shot well past abnormal, doesn't mean my life isn't complicated."

"Cute." I shook my head.

"I'm cute, am I?"

There he went again, and again I couldn't deny my attraction to him. He let the question hang in the air while he pulled all the way back, then straightened his truck. After he put the truck in park he gave me that deeply amused look. We both knew what he waited for and he had the patience to wait me out on this.

I needed to just suck it up.

Because he wanted an answer, I took liberties. My eyes wandered down to take a long survey of him, pausing on the highlights. Large hands. Arms and chest that moved with the ease of hidden strength. Firm hips. Powerful thighs.

By the time I brought my eyes back up to his, Spencer's mouth had split into a wide grin, but his eyes had fallen into that consuming intensity. I smiled a little, too, that I could affect him with one look. What's good for the gander. "Spencer. Cute is not the word I would use to describe you."

I stepped out of the truck an inch or two in front of Spencer's grabby hands.

He practically flew around the car to meet me. "Where the hell do you think you're going after that."

"Tanaka needs help." Curling my arms around my daughter's blanket grounded me a bit.

He invaded my space and I breathed in his musk and the spicy cologne mixing with it. Honey-brown eyes warming. "I need you more."

Shit. I kind of needed him too. But, "Not right now."

"Why not?"

"We're in the middle of the street and we have shit to do. Now come on." I stomped my way up the street because I knew if I didn't, Spencer would find some way to convince me to change course. It wouldn't take much. Or, it wouldn't have until I caught sight of Tanaka through the front window of the shop.

The fragility of her customer service smile was apparent from this far away and her hands shook as she rung something up. Shit. She really needed help. And I thought our conversation yesterday had sewn up her frayed edges.

I slowed my roll and turned my head to the side to speak to Spencer. "I need you to work with me on this."

He nodded. "I'm with you."

"Okay, Spence. Follow my lead."

24 – BESPOKE AND BESOTTED

I SLOWED ENOUGH for the other customer to leave before we came to the door.

The door chimes rang abnormally loud as Spencer caught the door and held it open for me, or maybe that was my own perception. I nodded and thanked him as I passed. Rather than head straight for Tanaka, I moved to the rack in the center of the room.

Close enough for her to recognize me, but not so close as to crowd her space until she was ready. I shifted my blanket to my left arm, holding it a little tighter than I preferred.

"Why didn't you leave that in the car?" Spencer asked, voice low but not so low as to keep Tanaka from hearing.

Good. She could hear us having a normal conversation. "Your car getting stolen then blowing up in your face makes you a might-bit leery of leaving things in the car."

"SparkleTits?"

I whipped around and put a finger to my mouth to shush her. "Don't say that too loud."

Her eyes widened. "I'm sorry. I don't know..." She trailed off, but I got the picture.

She didn't have another name to call me by. Gods damned Phoenyx.

Rather than chide Tanaka for his big mouth, I came toward her with my hand held out. "You can call me Greer. That's what I go by. Most of the time."

She took my hand in both of hers and shook it solidly. She froze when she caught sight of something behind me. I peeked behind me, just to make certain nothing new had cropped up. Nope. Just Spencer.

"Mr. Marcus." Her voice trembled.

I hated the hell out of that.

"Tanaka."

Before proceeding, I took another look back at Spencer to make sure he was behaving himself. His usual demeanor could intimidate someone already on edge. Today, he had his people-meeting face on, the one he wore to the fundraiser. Safe for public consumption. Good man.

To be on the safe side, I smiled at Tanaka when I swung my head back around. "I'm hoping you could help me out with something."

She centered her gaze on me, like Spencer might bite her if she didn't. With her focus on me again, she steadied. "Anything." Her hands pulsed around mine.

Most people didn't mean it when they threw out absolutes. I believed Tanaka would help me with whatever was in her power. The level of fealty in her gaze rubbed me the wrong way. Perhaps, I could find a way for her to repay her debt and help her in the same breath.

"I need a dress for an event tomorrow. Black tie. Right, Spence?" I brought him into the conversation with the twist of my head.

"That's right."

He was going with my story, just like I'd asked him to. Nice. I blazed on. "I usually don't wait until last minute, but, did you hear about that freak tornado that hit the apartment building?"

She nodded. "Terrible."

"Mine."

Her eyes widened. "Oh, that's horrible."

"Yeah, well." I shrugged with nonchalance I didn't feel. "C'est la vie. I need a dress."

After a quick, assessing look of my figure, she tugged me to my left. "It would help me if I knew where you were going."

"Sneak preview of Cirque du Luna." I continued speaking, though she had frozen in place at the mention. "Spence has some sweet connections."

"You're going to du Luna?"

Lying to her like this was wrong. It didn't have to be a lie, though. And if I went, I really would need a dress. "If I can get a dress in time."

Her shoulders straightened and the tension pulling at her lips eased. She patted the hand still in her clutches and pulled me across the floor. "Have no worry about that. We'll get you fitted faster than a fox. Now. What color were you thinking, hmm? Red? Orange would look beautiful on you."

It would. It did. "I didn't want to stick out that much."

"We always do, though, don't we?" She winked at me.

As many ways as I could take it, I chose to steer the conversation in the direction I needed it to go. "We? Are you going to be there too?"

"Yes. I mean, I was." The tiniest bit of uncertainty wormed its way back into her voice.

"What's stopping you? I know you have something fabulous to wear." Smile. See, I was nice and happy and you could be too, if you came with me to the ball.

Her lips pressed together. She leaned toward me, fearful conspiracy dancing in her eyes. I squatted down so she wouldn't need to raise her voice.

"What if he comes back?"

I knew who she meant. But for our run in to be a spontaneous coincidence, I couldn't know. "He who?"

She dropped her voice even lower, so the word barely made it to audible. "Death."

"Did you see his dog around?" I cast my eyes about. As if Scheherazade could hide anywhere in this store.

Tanaka squinted at me like I spoke in Farsi. "Dog?"

"Yeah. The reason Death came yesterday was to collect his dog and her puppies. People had abused the puppies. His dog, the mother, too. That's why he did what he did."

Her pupils shrunk almost down to pen points. "What." More statement than question.

Keeping even with her emotional level, I nodded. "Yeah. Massive beast, around my height. Beautiful. Smarter than normal." Smart enough to collect a person to save her and her puppies.

"I didn't see any dogs," Tanaka didn't sound as deep into her fear as she had been.

I nodded. "He left with them, but mentioned there were women who could use my assistance. Understatement." Death, the king of understatement.

"Maybe he's just seen so much of everything that nothing phases him, you know?" Spencer added from ten or so feet away. Tanaka and I hadn't been speaking in low enough voices to keep it just to ourselves.

No matter. Another voice could be helpful if it was helpful.

"Death, jaded?" An almost smile ghosted Tanaka's lips.

The words sounded like a shot to rival Mike's Phoenix Breath playing with sour and sweet. Hmm.

Tanaka steeled herself. "You're sure you're going to du Luna tomorrow?"

She wouldn't go if I didn't. I'd done this to myself. Next time, I would creep in and out of saving people and not force them to remember. Sure, it meant controlling people's minds without their permission. Not my kind of action, anymore.

"We'll be there." I nodded and cast a look Spence's way, because I meant it and I needed him to know.

His brows furrowed, but he seemed to smell what the rock was cooking.

"Then you need this dress." Tanaka whipped a cherry red number off the rack next to her like a magician with their final trick.

Pleated, deep V-neck. The kind of deep collar I used to love but could not wear anymore. The bell skirt probably hit most women below the knee, but it would certainly hit above mine. Not terribly high, but enough to win me the looks the neckline didn't capture first.

I reached out and fingered the butter-soft fabric. "I can't wear that."

"Yes, you can." Spencer was suddenly right behind me, heat of his body distracting me from my purpose in life.

There could be no arguing with Spencer's vehemence, so I spoke to Tanaka. "You know the glow I saved you with? I can't turn that off."

"Ah," she hung the thing back on the rack, only to have it snatched up again.

"You can wear it inside. On an evening we don't go anywhere." Spencer draped it over my arm. Sensing my resistance, he added, "Try it on for me?"

He could get me to do a lot of things with that intense focus beaming on me. Defeated, I forced a breath out. He grinned.

"Whatever, Spencer." But I was smiling too. "But seriously, I need something that isn't low cut or could be made to be."

Words I never thought I'd say.

Maybe I'd buy the red dress and lounge around Gabe's empty house. My empty house.

Tanaka's face flipped into the consideration and calculation. A blink of Eureka and she stalked through a nearby door. I turned a bemused glance Spencer's way. He still had his eyes on the red dress.

The man enjoyed red. I could use that. I already had a couple of underwear sets I could knock around in, just in case. Hmm.

Tanaka returned before my thoughts could turn graphic. Pity, that.

The flowing fabric on a hanger that she came back with was also red. I wondered if she'd done so on purpose because of past experiences with Spencer. Straps, wide enough for support in the front split in to five skinny straps each on the back. Each of the skinny straps dotted with rhinestones so the back had a network of sparkle that trailed down the back.

The bright red at the top faded in a gradient to the bottom hem of gossamer blackness in the back. The hem in the front stopped at knee-height.

Tanaka smiled at me when I finally looked at her. She knew. She knew her job well, apparently. "Let's get you to the fitting room and see how much work we need to do."

I agreed and trailed behind her like a little puppy.

She pulled back the curtain on a small-ish room with a pedestal in the middle and doors in the other three corners. "All three rooms are free, and this is a far as *you* go."

I turned around to find Tanaka standing between Spencer and I. Amused frustration played on his lips as he tried to side step her. Whatever fear she'd been wallowing earlier, and whatever effect Spencer had on her as her employer, she stood firm. Dancing in sync with him as he tried to wiggle past, almost like they practiced it that way. I had to cover my mouth and laugh at his growing frustration, though he didn't bowl her over.

"You should probably listen to the woman," I stepped up behind her, but not close enough to impede her movements. "She survived Death."

Spencer reached around Tanaka, balled his fist in my shirt, then pulled me to him. I miscalculated the length of his arms, but didn't complain when he devoured my mouth for much too short a time.

He smiled at me, not even half satisfied, when he pulled away. "I'll be waiting."

My eyes followed him as he walked back down the hall. Right before he turned the corner, he looked back to see if I was watching—I was. Of course I was. He'd sent my blood pressure through the roof, then left me all hot and bothered. I mean, perhaps I deserved it after my performance in the car, but I didn't have to like it biting me in the butt. Though, I did. I wouldn't mind him biting me a few choice places.

Spencer smiled, then disappeared around the corner.

"Wow," Tanaka didn't even attempt to lower her voice.

Since Spencer had already disappeared, I dropped my eyes to her. "Wow, what?"

She studied me, then gave a light shake of her head. "Ten years, and I've never seen that."

I swallowed a smile. "Really?"

"Not that we're friends, but I don't know anyone who's seen him out of control like that. Usually, he watches and calculates. Like a machine, acting in his best interest." She pointed to her left. "Why don't you take room one and come on out to the stage when you're ready."

"Stage?"

She pointed to the pedestal. I nodded and ducked into the room.

While Spencer had been handsy with me, he still acted in his best interest. What he thought was his best interest. Lords knew why he wanted me. He hadn't lost control yet, though. I felt him riding the line with me. Pushing to see where I would push back and where I would fold.

My stomach trembled at the idea of Spencer with no walls up.

It took me three tries to hang the dresses up in the room. The video in my head distracted me from the outside world. I needed to focus. "Which should I put on first?"

"Whichever you prefer."

Which *did* I prefer?

Tanaka gave me a knowing smile when I walked out in the solid red number, my shirt draped across the top of me for her protection.

I only half deserved it. I might have leaned this way without Spencer's reaction earlier. There would have been no contest before the incident at Rust left me at full glowworm status. Deep V all the way, though I would have chosen a purple fabric.

Tanaka nodded. "A good start," then started tugging at places and pinning things.

I closed my eyes and let it happen.

"Stay there a moment," she told me after a time, like I would risk moving with all of the sharp metal poised to give me the poking of a lifetime.

Sharp metal, I remembered, which wouldn't be able to pierce my skin.

"Okay," she bustled back into the room and around to the front of me, gorgeous violet square of fabric in her hands. "How much do we have to cover?"

Bless the woman. I hadn't even begun to figure out how to solve my problem and she had it well in hand. Now, if only I knew the answer to her question.

"Not sure, really," I shrugged, because what else could I do. "It's a new situation."

She pressed her lips together and stared at my chest like it would reveal its secrets if she stared hard enough. If it were that easy, several people in my life would have achieved nirvana. Most things didn't work that way.

Trial and error time, SparkleTits edition. "Why don't we do this? You start talking—maybe a speech or something you have memorized—and I'll start lowering the walls of Jericho, so to speak. When you fade out, I'll knew where you need to cover me."

Tanaka shook her head. "This is, by far the weirdest—Let's give it a shot."

"Welcome to my life."

She gave me a sympathetic pat on the shoulder, "But I'm grateful to you and your breasts."

Now, she made it awkward. I couldn't think of a thing to say back to that.

Much to my surprise, she saved me from the moment with, "Half a league half a league, half a league onward. All in the valley of Death rode the six hundred."

Charge of the Light Brigade. While it didn't bode well for the event tomorrow, it rang a little close to home. Except I was the six hundred with the world shooting potshots in my face. Watching her like a hawk, I scooted the edge of my shirt. Half an inch, half an inch, half an inch downward. Until Tanaka's words started to slur.

I shifted it back up until her eyes sharpened again and stopped. "Okay."

The line she had to cover me up to was depressingly modest. No one would bat an eye if I wore something like this in even the most conservative church. What was the point of wearing a beautiful dress that hugged all the curves nice and tight if you couldn't show at least a little dimple of cleavage? "This sucks."

Tanaka laughed at me. I glared enough for her to cover her mouth, but it didn't stop her.

"I am sorry," she managed after too long a time. "You remind me of a rebellious teen girl shopping with a conservative mother."

I kind of felt that way.

"Other than the color, I chose this because it stretches nicely." She demonstrated. "In the event you need to pull it down. If it makes you feel better, I can make it removable. Tiny buttons on the top and one on the bottom where it gathers."

Removeable would help, but having my life back would be better. My life with my lying boyfriend in our so-so relationship, the job I hated, though not enough to quit, and the car that ran most of the time. Hmm. Perhaps not. "Yes, being able to remove it would be nice."

Tanaka set her foot stool down in front of me and had stepped halfway up before she paused in confusion. "How do I do this part without getting hypnotized?"

Giving out the secrets of one's power was a big no-no. Lex knew, because I'd learned on him, accidently. And Kai knew, for reasons. I hadn't told Spencer, yet, but he would know soon. Tanaka was a different situation. I kind of liked her, wanted to trust her, and I needed the dress modified.

I had to tweak the truth. "As long as I'm touching you with both hands, you're fine." Not exactly a lie.

She frowned. "That's the only way."

Damn. I needed something else to tell her. "Not the only way, but you're not Spencer, so..."

Her eyes widened in the understanding I wanted her to have. "Hold on a moment."

I did so again while she slipped into one of the dressing rooms. She came back out in her bra, underwear, and garters. All black and lacy. Sexy, but no. Not what I was shopping for that moment. Perhaps she'd gotten the right understanding but the wrong impression.

"I need your arms as close to straight as possible for the fabric to lay right. So, elbows bent with your hands on my waist and we'll readjust as needed."

Thank gods. I didn't need to figure out a way to let her down without offending her.

Tanaka seemed to work faster without her dress on.

Didn't we all.

With everything pinned, she shooed me back into my dressing room to switch to the other dress. She still hadn't dressed when I came out in the new one. I took to the pedestal in front of her with my lips pressed together.

She laughed at me again. "This is just in case we need to do the same with this dress."

"I hope so. I'm not really in the mood to be seduced." Actually, I was. Just not by her, right then.

Tanaka crooked a finger at me. I leaned down to her, hoping I hadn't misjudged.

"You're pretty and all, but there's no way in hell I'm going to try to steal Mr. Marcus' woman. No way in hell."

I wasn't exactly his woman. Not anything official. Despite all my best efforts, though, it did seem to be going that way. "Can I ask you a question?"

"As long as you stand up straight and don't move."

I did as she asked, while trying to figure a nice way to ask what I wanted to know. Maybe there was no nice way. "Has he ever hit you?"

She laughed—laughed. Even had to stop working to pull herself together. "He's too smart of a man to do that."

"How do you mean?"

"Most of us could destroy his carefully public face if he did."

My lips parted, but I couldn't think of a thing to say to her.

She cast an amused glance up my way. "Everybody plays a fool."

I was no exception to that rule. "But I though you guys were prostitutes and he was—"

Tanaka cut me off with a head shake. "I tried telling him. With his set up, he could be making three times what he is. Easy money."

"I wouldn't call it easy money."

"Compared to eking out a living on the street, with john's who might stiff you and no one verifying they are who they claim and no one verifying you make it home safely. All the drugs and abuse and fear."

Her hands started shaking.

The pupils contracted.

The Tanaka I'd first met bubbled back to the surface. I'd asked all the questions and pulled her right back to that ugly place. Fuck me and my curiosity. I needed to find a way to fix this. "How did you get attached to Spencer and his...outfit."

She forced a hard blink and set her hands to working. "On my way to relapsing, I walked in the wrong door at the wrong time. Saw and heard things I shouldn't have. You know how it goes."

I didn't.

"Anyway. Mr. Marcus offered a way out. Out of the street, the drugs. As for the rest..." She shrugged.

My questions had already dragged her down, which should have been enough to deter me. But, I had to know. "As for the rest?"

"I miss it, sometimes."

"What? Being a prostitute?"

She nodded.

"Why?"

"Getting paid to the thing your best at and that you enjoy," Tanaka smiled a serene kind of smile. "Never worked a day on my back. Escorting is a whole different set of skills."

Huh.

25 – A Taste

SPENCER JUMPED OUT of his chair all eager beaver when I came around the corner. His eyes flicked all over me like it had been weeks or he was checking me for damage. He didn't even divert his attention when Tanaka popped out behind me.

"It shouldn't take more than two hours for me to finish."

He reached for his pocket. Tanaka fluttered her hand at him. "No need."

That pulled his attention from me. "She's not paying for anything."

"Correct. Today is on me."

Most people would have been happy to have people arguing over who would pay for them. It rubbed me the wrong way all over. "Tanaka, I should have the funds at the end of the month, so..."

"Consider this payback and don't think of it again. Now, go. Go on and we'll see you both in a couple hours. Go, go." She hustled us along in the same spirit she had in keeping Spencer from entering the dressing room. Unflappable and unstoppable. She shooed us all the way out the front door.

I half expected her to lock the door behind us.

"Well, we have a couple of hours to kill." I shifted the blanket to one hand, so I didn't need to hug it around the front of me. "What do you want to do?"

Spencer smiled at me, eyes half lost to the heat I'd seen when I left him that way in the truck.

"Sure, two hours for you, but I'm out for at least a day and I break my promise to Tanaka about going to du Luna." A small detail occurred. "You do have ticket's or whatever, to get into it, right?"

"I'm on the list."

"Good." One problem solved.

"When *is* your schedule free enough to...spend the day with me."

He completely glossed over the best part, the night, but I caught his meaning. We were in public, and all. "I'm good tomorrow evening after the hubbub until Thursday."

A slow breath simmered out of him. "That's more than one day."

I was well aware.

Whatever rolled over my eyes made Spencer let out a low chuckle. "Booked. Then, right now, let me feed you, woman. I know you're hungry."

Yes, I was hungry. I had been since fate hit my chest with the glitter stick. Oooo, pretty lights—now I need to eat a cow. "You should probably also stock up your fridge, too."

"I have a separate freezer filled with everything your little heart could desire."

Untrue, but since the conversation had already gotten so derailed from eating, I took that conversational step back. I started down the sidewalk to his truck. "So, where are you taking me?"

"Wrong way." He said, grinning like a school girl when I pulled back around to head toward him. He loved his games or loved seeing me off balance. Knowing him, he probably loved the combination.

I wouldn't mind seeing him off balance.

Spencer walked us to some hole in the wall place that prided itself on European fusion. Whatever. The food was tasty. I hadn't expected Spencer to feed me. From his fork. While his eyes drank in my mouth closing over his fork. After the first forkful he offered me, my mind wandered.

He was a bad influence.

Tomorrow evening couldn't come soon enough.

Tanaka said nothing about the two dresses when we went back to pick them up. She simply handed the black-and-blue stripped bag over to me with a pleasant smile. Her hand didn't shake at all.

I'd done that. I'd settled her nerves about Death. She thanked me as I left. Spencer held the door for me.

If it hadn't been for the destroyed apartment, and shattered view of my two closest friends being the same person, today might have been an okay day.

As I clicked into my seatbelt in the truck, Spencer levered a serious expression on me. Focus, but not the heavy, gonna-kill-everyone kind. He'd slipped on his somewhat-safe-for-public-viewing mask. "I need to...clean a little house this afternoon. With your apartment gone, I'm not sure where to leave you."

"What? Do you think I might disappear?"

He frowned. "More likely you'd get hurt somewhere or kidnapped and I wouldn't know a thing about it."

There he went again, being cute and vaguely annoying at the same time. Considering the way my life had shifted, I couldn't even laugh at the idea. "Then take me with you."

He blinked. "Do you mean that?"

I'd managed to throw *him* off balance for once. Good. "You read me so well. You tell me."

His eyes flicked over my face for a long few seconds before his lips curled. He leaned toward me and I met him halfway, taking as much as he did. The look he gave me as he pulled back rolled through my body and settled in the base of my spine, thrumming and dancing to the rhythm of the truck.

Damn.

Since Spencer had said he needed to clean, I expected him to pull into his driveway at some point, not into the garage half-filled with other cherry-red vehicles. I'd only come here once before. The second time I'd been to Spencer's office, I hadn't exactly planned it and, I didn't know how to recreate the freak teleport thing which dropped me in the corner of his office.

One of the pool tables in the room had a game going on it, though the men abandoned it when Spencer walked in. The men on and around the couches came to attention at the sight of him, even if they didn't stand up for him.

Now, "Clean a little house" took on a different shade of meaning. I wouldn't have been so eager to join him if I'd known what he meant. Too late now. Balking and making him turn around would take away from his authority. I was in it for the long haul, now.

Balls.

No one was in the room when he opened the door. He flicked the lights on and closed the door behind us.

Spencer paused a moment between the two leather chairs facing his desk to toss an amused grin my way.

I had to ask, "What?"

"This is where we met?"

Damned man. Ne needed to focus on the things at hand. I did what I could. I glared back at him. "This is also where you shot me. Repeatedly."

"I'll do the same tomorrow night." He winked, pressed a quick kiss on my lips

I waited until he pulled back to push him away. "This is not what I thought you meant by cleaning your house."

"What did—oh." He frowned. "I could take you somewhere. Maybe Lex's?"

Inconvenience Lex for a few hours because it was convenient for me? Not again. Anyway, "Leaving would cause you more problems which could cause me more problems."

"What do you want to do?"

Seven things that all opposed each other. "I don't want to know the gory details. Can't. I deal with the Gold 4 on what's becoming a regular basis and if I know bad things I'm going to have to tell someone. If you weren't so..." Frustrating. Enticing. Demanding.

He stepped closer to me, fogging up my thoughts with the scent of him. "Yes?"

"I shouldn't be here." Balls. "Where do you want me?"

His nostrils flared, but his voice came out all business. "I was thinking, in the corner, but I don't know."

I leaned to the side to see the corner he meant. The unadorned corner behind his desk also had no direct light aimed at it. "Is beside your desk good enough? I don't want to crowd you or steal your thunder, but I would draw more attention glowing in the corner. And I'd rather not sit with my back to the people you don't trust."

His eyes flicked over the room, calculating. "You sit at my desk. I cannot sit for this."

Fair enough.

I swung around his desk with him hot on my tail. This could be a problem. "But, you're not going to stand over my shoulder the whole time, are you?" It made me look like a Spencer groupie. Dealing with the kind of reaction that gained me would make me stabbier than usual.

Bemused curl to his lips, Spencer set two fingers against the top of my sternum and eased me down into his seat. Nice, curve-hugging leather wrapped around my back side while a plume of musk and spicy cologne rolled up and over me.

Spencer leaned down slowly, moving until his face filled my field of vision and I could taste his breath in mine. "Maybe." He pressed the words against my lips then straightened and moved away from me.

My shirt and pants clung to me in uncomfortable ways. Damn him.

For his part, he moved around to the front of his desk and set his butt—his very nice butt—against the edge on my right. Easy pose, almost comfortable, but I could practically feel the tension in him as he bent down over a small control panel to my right.

When he said, "You may come in," into the microphone, all evidence of warmth or play had left his voice. His face had fallen back into the sharp lines of a freshly whetted blade. There was the man I'd met when he had his goons bring me here, all the more intimidating for the lack of facial hair. I'd been right in that, at least. The scruff had softened him, like a quarterback with a bit of pudge in the middle and a bum knee.

The mean faces of men filed in the door, all taking in the sight of me sitting at the boss's desk and Spencer standing in front in too casual a pose. I didn't like this at all.

The charm and heat let me believe I had a cartoon tiger selling me sugary cereal. Heeeeeee's GREAT!

Spencer was no cartoon. He was a criminal.

As were the eight men who stood at attention in front of him.

How had I gotten here?

It was too late to leave, because I wanted Spencer. Despite everything else I knew about him, I could already feel him peeling off my clothes while I dug my fingers into the muscles of his back.

Shit.

I recognized a couple of the men who came in. The bouncer from Lex's art gallery opening, whom I'd seen again in this very room. Garren, his name was. Just the kind of name an over-muscled asshole would have.

He sneered at me. Ugly. "He said you'd gone soft," he said.

I scoffed.

"What's that, princess?" He lifted a hand to his ear.

Princess? If anything, I was Merlin. If he really thought I was the boss's main squeeze, which was near enough to the truth, he should have been making nice with me. Not half insulting me in front of him.

Spencer kept quiet.

This time I knew why, at least. He would not protect me where it would weaken my position. His silence also gave me leave to say whatever I needed to. So, I spoke my mind.

"You're a fool if you think there's anything soft on that man with regards to me, Garren." I smiled all wide and pretty. "Rock fucking solid, or I'd stand to greet you."

Some of the men laughed, which I kind of expected. Men liked to talk about penises and their sizes—physically and metaphorically—in front of other men. More than a lot of them would admit, for fear of being labeled gay.

They wished.

"Boss, you'd better get your girl before something happens to her and her smart mouth."

A threat, eh. Probably not the best time to poke the sexually frustrated bear. I waited, though. Waited for Spencer to respond however he saw fit.

He tipped his head to the side in invitation. "Go ahead. I know you're just dying to."

The bastard was enjoying this. He kept his tone as cold and flat as it had been since the men had walked in, but the words betrayed him.

United front. That's always what was needed. That the unity still allowed for a little fun, gladdened me.

An ugly little smile warmed my face. "Considering that a superhero has tried twice and failed—again twice—to kill me in the past forty-eight hours, it might be a better idea to deal with this mother fucker right here." I jerked my thumb at Spencer. "Because this does not concern me and you might not want to piss me off."

Garren's eyes fluttered in several blinks while his brows reached toward each other. Probably trying to figure me out. If I was lying, I could have all the gonads. If I was telling the truth, I could be a much bigger threat to him than he first perceived. The two images of me toggled in the expression on his face.

He should probably work on the untouchable criminal expression. I didn't care that his lack of facial control left him an open book, but it probably made him a liability to Spencer.

That was a slippery path to let my mind wander down. It probably would not be the last one, damned Spencer. He could have left me alone and I would have been...sadder. Maybe a little lonelier, too, for the absence of him. It wasn't often that someone read me as well as he did.

Gabe had, from the first. But then, our first meeting hadn't been our first meeting.

I settled back more comfortably in the chair and tried to remember the words in the letter.

Playing chase with a giant grey spider. I couldn't put it past me. I'd had vivid dreams up until the time I'd lost my daughter. Losing her broke that part of me, the imagination and hope that the world could be a beautiful place.

If I closed my eyes, though, and ran the words through my head again and again, pieces came back. The wiry hair all over the spider and how rough it felt against my lips when I kissed the top of her head. The warm, dusty smell of her. The way Lady's segmented mouth parts would wriggle at me when I smiled at her. Lady. That was her name.

She'd been a good friend too. As good as my shining one, with the shadows in his eyes. Gabe, as a boy, who had somehow managed to become an older man in the five years he'd left me alone with my mother. If he had told me when he was alive, I could have asked him so many things.

Now, all I could do was remember him. Remember how we would race to the top of the stairs made of light and shadow. The winner would be the one to open the way through the fog.

I raced to the top like he still ran beside me. At the top, I sank to my knees and set my chin on the base of the window. This much hadn't changed, at least. I smiled at the thick fog and blew a long, slow breath into it.

The grey parted, like in a Charlton Heston movie. In waves that boiled and mounted on top of each other. A path just wide enough for me meandered downward. I stood and stepped over the base of the window onto the fog with no fear of falling. This was my fog. My breath had constructed it, splitting my first tears into a fog thick enough to confound anyone who followed me without permission.

Young Gabe always had my permission, but he always waited for me to come here. As much as this was our place, this was mine. My safe place. My impervious castle. My home. If he left something here, though, he had come one time without me.

The walk down through the fog felt longer than I remembered.

Perhaps it had grown with me. Maybe it had grown with the tears I'd shed recently.

Or, I'd chosen the longer method.

I turned my feet parallel to the path and leaned back. The familiar cool of the fog enrobed my back. It only gave me a little push. That was all it took to send me slaloming down the slope to the dry river bed.

Dry. That wasn't right, but it was true. Cracked, crusty, russet earth spanned my vision as far as I could see. It wasn't possible. The river had flowed blue and crystal clear in a perfect circle as wide as I wanted it to be. When Gabe and I wanted to swim with the fish-tailed horses or the river squid, I could barely see the curve of the ring. The far edge of the river nearly invisible.

When we wanted the garden, the river flowed only as deep as our knees and as wide as the both of us stacked. Enough to splash one another, but not enough to keep us from our destination.

The earth crumbled under my feet as I walked out onto the crust. Dust kicked up as I walked. The garden was nowhere in sight. I dropped to my knees.

Had the love in me really dried up?

Because, that's what flowed in the river like water. Love in its purest form. But I was a loveless husk of the girl I had been. Just like my mother tried to beat into my head.

Worthless. Useless.

26 – BEST LAID PLANS

FUCK THAT NOISE.

My mother was a bitch who wouldn't know love if she soaked in it long enough to prune. I might have been out of practice, but I loved.

I loved my shining friend when I'd been a child. I loved Gabe separately from his younger incarnation, even if I was pissed at him for keeping secrets. And I loved my baby girl with everything in me.

My knees sank into tepid mud. I set my hands in it as well and squeezed. Mud was a far cry from the raging river, but it was a start.

Looking up, I caught the flash of the wavy image in the distance. I squeezed the mud in my hands a little harder, letting the moisture well up around my fingers. It flashed again. Farther away than I'd ever seen it, but I recognized the fan of an emerald palm.

A mother fucking start.

My face stung and I nearly fell out of the chair at the force.

"Did you hear me, bitch? Hands up."

What the fuck?

Garren stood over me, hand poised to hit me again. I blinked at him, then risked a glance around the room.

Three people, other than Spencer, had their hands up and had been lined up next to him. The muscles on Spencer's neck had popped out, but he didn't give much more indication of his displeasure at the change of fortune. His neck smoothed out as I looked past him, as if his anger moment only had to do with Garren smacking me silly.

Beyond Spencer, five people had guns out, pointed this way. Things had changed considerably since I dropped off to sleep.

"That's right, bitch. Rise, and shine."

I really wanted to hit him. But, I needed to play this cool. He didn't know about me, so I had the advantage and a general plan.

Hypnoboob him. Subdue him. Then hit him when he could remember it.

Good. I had a plan.

I edged my hands toward my top button.

Garren shoved a gun up my nose. "No, you don't."

"I assume you want to see my weapons."

He frowned a little, eyes narrowing a bit. After my speech earlier about not pissing me off, he probably wondered what my angle was. Even without that, anyone in my position would be trying for the best way to get out of the bad situation. We both knew that. He simply didn't know to which weapons I referred.

Yeah, he had a gun, but I only had a sprinkle's worth more patience. Also, I knew the gun would probably only bruise me. It would hurt like the dickens, but bruises healed better than death. "Look, you have three options: let me keep the weapons, have me reach my hand in and pull them out, or let me open the shirt to retrieve them."

"You're not keeping them."

The hell I wasn't. Really, his choices came down to the second two. I already knew I would keep my tits. Whipping one boob out could be fun. But maybe not as effective as having both on the team.

"Pull the shirt open. Slowly." He pressed the gun against my forehead. "No kind of funny business."

He was in for a treat. I had nothing but shenanigans for him. Shenanigans that started well before he hit me. Now, he could deal with all of it.

Thank gods for wearing the button up shirt.

I made the effort to risk a little glance at Spencer. He pointedly dropped his eyes to where my hands undid my shirt. When he looked back up at me, his eyebrows danced a moment. A question probably in the vein of asking me what the hell I was doing.

I widened my eyes back at him. He should know the answer.

My buttons took a lot longer to undo than I'd planned for. A lot could have happened in the near minute it took me to unbutton the last one above my waist line. Fortunately, things went as planned to that point.

As for the rest of the plan, I opened my shirt.

Garren's eyes went dull and the pressure of the gun barrel against my face decreased. Good. "Without taking your eye off my chest, I want you to join the people on the other side of the desk."

He pulled back from me. I turned with him, keeping us lined up. When he had moved far enough to the right, I stood and climbed onto the desk. My pants stuck to my knees as I mounted, but I made up without falling or rotating my chest far enough to lose the attention of the men.

Standing at the top felt a little, "Oh Captain, my captain," for my tastes, but I needed to see all the faces, expressions of mute compliance. The high ground called to me.

The whole room of men stared up at me. Some women would have loved this level of adoration, except this was not adoration. More like the unsettling feeling that came from opening the door to find a doll standing just outside.

Watching.

I pulled my shirt completely off and dropped it on the chair behind me. Business time. "Okay, everyone with a gun pointed at Spencer and his loyal people needs to listen to me. Take your fingers off the triggers and point the guns toward the ground."

They all did. Not that I hadn't expected them to, I just wished they moved a little less like marionettes trying to follow my instructions. Though, that's effectively what they were, puppets with my chest acting as Geppetto.

These puppets still had a lot to before they could be real boys.

"Okay, same people I want you to take the clips or magazines or whatever out of your guns. You will then, take the bullets out of the magazine or clip or whatever and toss those bullets over whichever shoulder you so desire. Also, any other bullets, like ones that may already be in the chamber or if you have a revolver, take those out too and throw the bullets over your shoulder as well."

If they had all moved in unison, I might have been a little wigged out. They all moved at whatever speed was their normal, though they all emptied their guns without looking down at them. It spoke of a long familiarity with firearms, which might have been more comforting if they weren't playing for the wrong team. Amateurs tended to have more accidents. I could take an accident aimed my way, but I didn't want anyone here to suffer because I hadn't been more specific.

Each man finished with the festive sound of bullets hitting the back wall at sub-subsonic speeds. We had a party now. I held back from tossing my hand in the air and yelling, "Opa!"

"Now, the five of you with emptied guns in your hands. I want you to set them on the floor and, without the intent to hit anyone with them, kick the guns toward this side of the room."

Metal scraped against terra cotta colored concrete into a herd at Spencer's feet.

What next?

Questions needed to be asked of these men, but I was not the one to ask them. I needed Spencer, or he needed me, but something else occurred to me. "The five of you who acted against Spencer, pull out any other weapon hiding on your person. If you have more guns, unload them the same way you did the first, and kick them across the floor. Any knives or other blades or garrotes or anything else potentially dangerous, also set those down and kick them across the floor without the intent to hit someone else here."

All kinds of things came out. Guns, switchblades, butterfly knives. One of the men had brass knuckles. The pile growing on the floor felt half comical. These people walked around with that kind of artillery on them at all times. What did they think would happen to them? They were the ones committing crimes.

On the less funny side, these people had come in to speak to a boss they'd turned against loaded for bear. They could have come in, guns a-blazing, and left me alone in a graveyard. I thanked the gods for small blessings.

Once the men stood still again, I had nothing else to say to them. But, I had a ringer.

Careful to keep my chest properly aimed, I sat down on the edge of Spencer's desk and scooted off to the ground. Spencer hadn't moved much since I dosed off. I sidled up to him and slipped my right hand into his left.

He jerked. His eyes darted around in alarm, taking everything in. I guessed he noticed the lack of guns first, which I couldn't blame him for. It took him a little while longer for him to realize where everyone else in the room had their eyes trained.

"What the hell?"

I Vanna White-d my shirtless self. In particular, I underlined the part of me glowing the most.

"Yes, that is a pretty bra, and I'd love to see you without it, but I need you to tell me..." his words slowed down as the connections fired in the back of his eyes.

"Hypnoboob," I nodded to confirm.

He dropped his gaze down to my chest, looked over at the men still frozen in my thrall, then came back to my face. "Huh. Those pack quite a wallop, don't they?"

"Boobs tend to, yes."

Amusement tickled his lower lip. "Not usually—why aren't I zonked out as well? Am I immune?"

Wouldn't that be nice? Someone who I didn't need to worry about?

"Sorry, Spence. You missed out on me disarming the bad guys. Badder guys." I lifted our joined hands. "Skin to skin contact."

"And why are your hands muddy?"

I looked at my free hand. A film of red mud dried on my palms. Bending a little forward explained why my knees felt sticky and a little cold. Mud there. Feet, too. Huh. Turning back to Spencer, I had to shrug. How did I explain that the mud had followed me from my dream place that I shared with a younger incarnation of Gabe who just died? "It's complicated."

He tipped his head back and laughed silently but hard enough to shake me where I clung to his hand. I didn't see what was so funny, but I loved seeing the joy bubble out of him like that. He looked good laughing. Head thrown back and not clinging so tightly to his control. Hmmm.

His eyes practically glowed with happiness when he straightened and looked to me. "We need to get you a new word, Darling. That one doesn't quite capture the magnitude of anything in your life."

"You don't appreciate the nuance of the word."

"I'll show you nuance." Spencer moved to stand in front of me, but I strong armed him back and out of the way. He frowned. "What's wrong?"

"Nothing." I jerked my chin toward the group of other men. "I just need to keep the headlights pointed at the deer."

"Ah." Eyes narrowed and mouth wickedly curved, he pulled me toward him, using our clasped hands to slide me in front of him.

I didn't put up much fight. He rewarded my lack of resistance with his lips against my shoulder, my neck. He reached across and pulled my mouth to his, smiling as I fed at his mouth. Warm. Hungry. His hand on the side of my face slipped down to my neck and started creeping down. I pulled my head back. "Stop."

He stopped, but glared at me. "What now?"

"The deer." I pointed to the other men in the room.

"It's fine. They're well and truly out of it." He tipped his head toward mine again.

"Not if your hand dips down any further and covers me up." I waited.

He blinked, understanding dawned. Without taking his eyes from mine, he trailed his fingers back up to the safety of my collarbone. From there, they drew out almost to my shoulder, caressed the lateral side of my right breast, my side, then crept around the front of me. My breathing slowed and deepened. He spread his whole palm against my belly, tips of his fingers dipping under the top of my waistband. "Is this better?"

Gods. A single stroke of his fingers around my interesting parts had my heartrate humming. "Yes and no."

"No?" He dropped his eyelids halfway and split the distance between our lips.

Two could play at that game. I arched my back against him, rubbing my behind against the front of him. I smiled at his tiny groan and the stiffness in his pants.

He set his lips lightly against mine and spoke. "Tell me you want me."

"I want you naked and on top of me, but we have some shit to do first."

Spencer rolled his hips against me and shook his head. "Why is there always an excuse?"

"Obstacles, Spencer. The same obstacles. Actually, the same one with a few hurdles and bumps along the way." I sucked my lower lip against my teeth while I stared at his mouth. If I had a day to kill, this would be a whole different conversation. "Let's get this shit over with so we can get to more important things."

Muscles moved in his mouth while he swallowed that. I watched all the movement and didn't mention that we wouldn't have had sex in the office regardless of the audience I needed to keep entranced. Business spaces and personal spaces were not the same spaces for a reason.

In that vein, I shifted the conversation to the timelier. "I'm fairly certain I've gotten all of the weapons from those men, but you probably need to ask them a few questions. Right?"

"Right."

I moved to step out of his personal space, but his hand held me firm against him. He lifted an eyebrow at me. Same challenge he'd levered on me before, but it wasn't one. I had no problem with the warmth of him pressed up against the back of me. It would be better without his shirt between us. I didn't mention it. One of us needed to focus on some bad people. Stripping any more clothes off would throw Spencer off his game again.

Me too.

As he questioned his men, I focused on the timber of his voice and the way it rumbled against my back rather than the specifics of what he said and the answers. The sounded flowed through me while I tried to figure out how I pulled mud from my dream out into the real world. Shouldn't have been possible.

Neither was Gabe being my childhood dream-friend.

Spencer pinched my side.

I slapped his hand and swung my head around to him. "What the hell?"

"You didn't hear me repeating your name?"

Clearly, I did not. "What did you want?"

His eyes flared warm a moment before he reined the desire back in. Purposeful. "I'm finished asking the questions I would risk asking with you in earshot."

Ah. Time to go.

Spencer shook his head as he passed my shirt back to me. "Damn shame for you to cover up."

"Yeah, well. This isn't exactly the best venue." I gestured to the room of frozen men with my chin.

"Any venue is—"

I pressed my fingertips to his lips to stop him. "No. Not the first time. Now, are you sure you've asked all of the questions you need to?"

"Not in the least, but you'll want to leave for the things that I need to ask and things that I need to do." Despite the way his lips seemed to caress my fingers, he spoke in a flat, pragmatic tone. Not a threat, a simple statement of fact spoken with no kind of remorse.

A smarter woman would have run screaming. I *was* leaving, but I should have ducked out of more than the interrogation.

Still, he hadn't tried to kill me in the past few days, nor was he in cahoots with anyone who had. And he halted his information gathering before it got ugly because I did not want to know. Despite the weirdness shining out of my life, he did not balk.

All of it kept me from retreating completely. The rest—his charm, how well he read me, the way the brown of his eyes warmed when he caught me looking at him—was a bonus.

This couldn't last forever, but while it did, I'd enjoy the hell out of him.

"How long do you think you'll be, Spence?"

I didn't know how long interviewing criminals who had turned coat might take. Silly me. If I stayed, I could learn this completely normal information and sink into Spencer's completely normal life because the world was a wholesome, idyllic little snow globe.

"About an hour." Spencer tipped his head to the side a moment. "Maybe two."

An hour or two of gun-laden, magic rainbows I didn't want to deal with. "I'm gonna go take a walk."

The muscles along his jaw tensed. "I'm not sure that's a good idea."

"Why not?"

"This isn't the best neighborhoods to take a walk in." He traced a line along my side almost idly. Almost.

I closed my hand around his fingers and pulled them away from me so I could think more clearly. "Spence. I'm not the kind of person that people tend to single out."

He leaned toward me, making me catch my breath before he

breathed, "Yes, you are."

"Flatterer." I rolled my eyes, but it totally worked on me. "Text me if you need more or less time."

He frowned. "Greer."

I really didn't like that tone, like he meant to forbid me. "What?" My voice dropped to reflect my displeasure.

Spencer forced a breath out and shook his head. "Be careful."

Much better. For that, I kissed him, long and slow. "I'll try."

He set his forehead against mine without turning me toward him. That much he had learned well enough. "You will be the death of me."

"Come on, now." I slipped my arms though my sleeves without pulling my forehead back from his. "You dredge up enough trouble without me. Are you ready for me to close up?"

"Not hardly."

That meant yes, since he wasn't thinking with his smarter head. His hand creeping around my side confirmed his distraction, so I used it to my advantage. I closed my hand around his fingers and moved them up to the back of my neck, where he started rubbing gentle circles.

Good enough.

I buttoned my shirt up from the bottom, faster than I'd unbuttoned it. As soon as I got to chest level, men started rustling. I pinched the rest closed and dropped my eyes to focus on closing the last few buttons. Some curses and threats flared while I took my sweet time. I was not about to pass through the men until Spencer's people had an unassisted, firm upper hand.

Silence fell again, several tense breaths passed before one of the men called out, "Boss."

"A moment, Trevor." The words came out in that cold voice, though his eyes on me felt anything but. "Greer?"

The question needed no further explanation. Time to go.

"I'll be back in two hours, then."

Spencer nodded, reaching into his pocket as he did so. "If you want to take a nap in my truck while you wait." He held the keys out to me.

I certainly didn't want a nap, but united front was a good plan. Much as I wanted to kiss him goodbye, distraction would do him no favors, so I took his keys without any extra flair and headed toward the door. Quite a few of the men watched me, while confusion reigned supreme on their faces. Couldn't blame them their wariness; tables had turned completely and none of them knew the how or why. Better that they recognize things had gone wonky and I was the X-factor. Perhaps next time they would let me steer completely clear of the danger.

If there was a next time for any of these men.

Better to not think about it either way. Even if they had been good men at one point.

Halfway to the door I stopped, right next to the man who thought smacking women was a good plan in any situation. He and I both deserved the karma from that interaction.

I turned almost completely around to ask. "Hey, Spencer?"

"Yes, Greer."

Rather than flat out ask what I wanted, I darted my eyes toward the man without turning my head. No need to project my intentions. Spencer frowned. He had to understand. He always seemed to.

After a brief pause he inclined his chin. "If it's quick."

That, I could do.

Without further ado, I balled my right hand into a solid fist and socked the man in the jaw with half of my weight behind it. His head whipped to the side and he staggered back a couple steps, but didn't fall. Shame. That would have been a sight.

The dude had the nerve to look hurt and surprised as he righted himself. Someone else in the room grumbled that this kind of thing was why they had switched sides in the first place. Behind me, something hard met meat, followed by pain noises. Letting these things distract me from the man I'd hit was a rookie move. The gun trained on him might not deter a reaction from him.

"You will regret that." He said it in that calm, sure tone where most threats lived. "You will rue the day you met me."

I shook my head, partially wondering where he pulled that from. "When Spencer's done with you, I'd like to see you fucking try something with me." I gave him my sweetest smile before resuming my trip to the door.

My fingertips had barely touched the doorknob when Spencer called my name. What now?

When I turned back to face him, he had my bag of dresses and blanket in his hand. Whoops. "Oh, wow. No, yeah. I meant grab that." Funny how visiting my dream space and people threatening me with guns pushed that right out of my head.

Halfway back to Spencer, Garren muttered, "Stupid fucking bitch deserves what's coming to her," not quite quiet enough.

Mid-step, foot hanging in the air, I froze. If it had been just the two of us, I would have knocked him out. But these were Spencer's men and he needed them to retain their respect of him. They also needed to learn to respect me outside of being arm candy. "Spencer?"

He let the arm holding the bag out to me drop to his side. "Quickly."

Quick meant not savoring things. It also meant not holding back. Especially since he hadn't heeded my warning punch.

An ugly grin splayed on my face as I whipped around to the mouth too big for its own good. The man holding a gun on him stepped out of the way. Smart man. Garren was anything but.

"What do you think you're going to do?"

I faked a punch toward his jaw. He leaned back and lifted his hands to protect his face. Leaving his stomach vulnerable. I threw my whole weight into this punch. He curled over, around my fist, pulling his face into range. I kneed him in the nose with all the flair Richard Simmons could ask for.

The man crumpled to the ground. I didn't think he was dead. I hoped he wasn't. It meant complications for Spencer. And I didn't want to have killed a person so easily. I couldn't check right then. Didn't want to know.

"Crazy bitch," echoed from the far-left corner.

I whipped around. "You want some too?"

"Greer," Spencer said behind me. Did not explain.

Didn't need to.

I retrieved my bad, mumbling, "He deserves—"

"I'm well aware. He deserves all that and more." He nodded. "This is mine. And I will handle it."

If we'd been alone, I would have said something about how he'd better. As was, I snatched the bag from him and strutted out the door. I consoled myself for the missed opportunity by thinking about taking Garren down. Warm fuzziness carried me all the way out to Spencer's truck to drop my bag and out into the warmth of the actual sunshine.

27 – VIOLENT DELIGHTS HAVE VIOLENT ENDS

THERE WERE A few more bail bonds places and warehouses in the area than I would usually have chosen to walk past. Spencer's caution still felt like an overreaction. Whatever. Skipping through after dark might be poking the beast. Right then, the sun shone bright. After checking my phone to make sure I knew when-ish to head back, I started off down the busier street to my left.

Half an hour's walk took me out of the bail bonds area to the land of slightly dingy-looking strip malls. I was headed for a knickknack store when my nose stopped me. Fat and smoke rode the air. I pulled a full three-sixty turn before realizing the space next to the knickknack store was a Mexican restaurant. The place looked rundown and sad from the outside.

I walked into a room filled with Spanish speaking people of all sorts and a smell that I could swim in. The hostess, a little, teen girl who looked barely legal for working, strode up to me in a red shirt, khakis, and an air of confidence I wish I'd had at her age.

Hell, I wished I had it right then.

"How many?"

"Just me."

She grabbed a menu and started back down the way she'd come. I spied other tables as I followed, drooling at every plate.

The table she led me to sat in the middle of the room. Not usually my favorite. She set the menu down in front of the chair that would put my back to the front door. Also not my preference. Didn't matter. I'd eat in the bathroom if the food delivered what the smell promised. I poured over the menu. Wanted everything. Ordered more than normal people would. Didn't care how others might react. The waiter, who didn't look much older than the hostess, said nothing. Even his face remained polite at my quantity.

Score.

At the first smoky, meaty taste of carnitas, I had to close my eyes.

"You smell like the ocean," a man said from too close to my right side.

I opened my eyes. Yep. Old dude was talking to me. From about a foot away. While I tried to come up with the proper response, I flicked my eyes a little past him. The couple at the table just on the other side had their eyes on the two of us. Neither seemed inclined to jumping to my rescue.

"Thank you," because I couldn't think of anything else to say to him that didn't end with the invitation to fucking ease himself on down the road.

He shook his head slightly. "How is that? How do you smell like you just stepped out of the ocean?"

If I knew the answer, I wouldn't tell him. It probably had something to do with pulling things out of my dream space. Damned if I could explain that to myself, let alone to him. I'd just have to console myself that he didn't smell any weaponry from the situation in Spencer's office. He might just, if I didn't hurry him along.

"Sir, I don't mean to be rude or anything, but I'm kind of having a religious experience with this food and you're interrupting." The room had gotten oddly quiet. No telling if it was in response to what I said or happenstance. Whichever reason, I felt the eyes on me.

Dude's nostrils flared, but his eyes contracted in almost the same way Spencer's had the first time we'd met. Like he couldn't quite figure me out.

Someone in the back laughed, then a head poked out of the door the food had come from. Hair as white as daisy petals, the woman looked old enough to be this man's mother. "Hey, Carlo. Let the woman eat in peace."

"She hasn't answered my question."

"She doesn't want to speak to you."

"She's too pretty to eat alone."

Okay. Yep. Done with giving him the benefit of the doubt. I set my elbows on the table and hunched over my plate, mantling like a hawk over her kill. The second bite of carnitas made up for having to deal with Carlo.

He peppered me with a few more things I ignored. It faded into the rest of the din as people started back up on their conversations.

Unadulterated, meaty bliss through half of one of my plates. Then, the front door swung open behind me in a slam.

"Where is that filthy fucking snake that defiled my princess?" An angry woman yelled over the din of the restaurant.

The room dropped to dead silence. Deeper than when the people had been listening in on my convo with Carlo.

Oh good. Drama.

People pushed out of their chairs and slid out of booths around me. I mantled harder and continued shoving food in my face. Not my monkeys or circus.

"Don't you fucking dare try to hide him. We're not leaving without stringing him up." The woman was pissed. And "we" meant she brought a crew with her. Really wishing I'd switched around to the other chair right then. Not that I wanted to be involved. Knowing what I was dealing with might have been nice.

"I'm pretty certain," the white-haired old woman from before popped out the door, wooden spoon in hand, "that I told you what you could do with your whore of a daughter."

Welp. This would get ugly.

"Rules have changed," angry woman behind me ground out in a way that would ruin her voice. "Stella's pregnant. Your snake's the only one who's touched her."

Pin drop silence.

The raise of tension ripped through the air in a palpable wake.

Maybe I could just drop a couple of twenties and leave. I leaned to the side and wiggled my fingers down toward my purse.

Some sort of blade pressed against my cheek. "Not so fast," said a voice. A man's voice. Whoever he was, he walked on the tips of angel wings. I hadn't heard him come at me at all. Even better reason to get the hell out of Dodge.

I shifted my eyes along the arm holding the blade to the square, tan jaw. "I just wanted to grab some money to drop on the table and leave. This feels like a family affair, and I'm not that."

He scooped my purse away from my table with his toe and kicked it into the nearest booth.

Asshole.

My annoyance forced me to push back from the table and turn toward him. He kept the blade pressed against me as I did so, meeting my eyes with an unflinching, bright-green stare. He almost looked bored.

"If you broke my phone, you asshole—"

"You will buy a new one." The flat even tone of someone who expects no guff.

I wasn't one to roll over and accept things like that. Not when I could help it. "The correct answer is 'I'll brake your pretty face,' but good try."

He certainly was pretty. Now that I'd turned, I could see that all of the new, black-leather clad people who'd crowded in were pretty in that southern Latin way. Any of them could lead the festivities at Carnival in Rio. They also looked like that same feisty energy of celebration had been turned to this angrier task.

Behind the woman who seemed to be the center point of people spread through the restaurant, a girl cowered. Not quite cowering. Shoulders rolled in, arms crossed, but she held her head high and glared at the back of the center woman's head. Stella, I presumed.

Center woman stabbed her finger at the white haired one. "You will pay to scrape out the filth your disgusting animal planted in my girl."

The girl in question flinched at the ugly description of abortion. Flinched and wrapped her arms around her stomach. I knew that stance. Enough was enough. "You need to stop."

"Shut up, bitch." The knife pressed harder against my cheek as the man spat the words at me. "If you ain't family, this don't concern you."

There were different kinds of family.

This was sisterhood.

I stood, towering over the pretty man threatening me with the knife. It slipped down my cheek a little, though his expression remained unphased. Good for him, but annoying for me. I could have used his second-guessing himself to my advantage. No matter. I leaned to the side to make it obvious who I was addressing and who I was ignoring. "Do you want to keep the baby?"

Stella's eyes took on that mirror shine as she clutched herself and dipped her chin in a tiny nod.

The woman, Stella's mother, whipped her head around to me. "Doesn't matter what she wants. And who the fuck do you think you are, sticking your nose in where it doesn't belong?"

Most of the time, I didn't know who I was anymore. But now? With this? I was that girl. "It doesn't matter what she wants? Listen to yourself. You sound like Henrietta Carlotta Madison."

Her eyes blazed brightest green and she launched herself at me. I braced rather than dodged. Mid-leap her body rippled and a huge black cat—claws and teeth flashing—knocked me over. Landed on top of me.

My head hit something. Hard. Couldn't focus on it. A jaw built for crushing clamped around my throat. Claws raked my torso.

I would bruise, but I would survive. I pushed. The cat had more muscle than I had bravado. I tried to inhale. My air was cut off. Clawing at the cat's mouth won me nothing. My power made me cocky, arrogant, like nothing could take me down because I could conquer the whole world with impenetrable skin and tits that shined like justice. My sight dimmed like tinted glass.

I bucked, jerking my body as much as I could. Only my legs flailed. She held me still. Hot slobber dribbled down my neck. Less disturbing than the incessant growl singing of my death. Cats were built for hunting. I was not. But I was a survivor.

I reached my hand up, fingers scrabbling for the candy-green eye watching me with hatred and wrath.

A claw hooked my underwire and ripped my bra away from me.

The pupil I could see dilated. I hadn't air to speak, but my hands were free. I pried the jaws open with little resistance.

Breathing hurt. What sweet pain, though. I drank it in for a minute or so before deciding I should probably sit up and figure out what hid in the silence around me.

Mayhem. Mayhem and melee had erupted while the panther that had been a woman nearly killed my arrogant ass.

Tables had been broken and knocked askew. Black cats, spotted cats, and humans—oh my—in all manner of fighting postures. Blood and fur everywhere. Food dashed to the floor. My heart wept at the waste. As for the rest, my mind reeled. Perhaps it was the oxygen-deprivation fun I'd gone through, but people didn't turn into jaguars or leopards or panthers or whatever the hell these people had become. But, neither did skin glow and hypnotize people.

Greer Ianto, this is your life.

In the back of all the aftermath of fighting, with a cut bleeding profusely down his cheek, the boy who'd taken my exorbitant order without a question held Stella close and she clung to him.

Two households, both alike in shapeshifting, in fair Denver.

The Bard rang ever true.

I climbed my way to standing, then on top of the table behind me. Here this went again, except I got to deal with all the dirty work this time.

"Everyone pull away from the person they're fighting with, without injuring them further, and turn back into your human shapes." One of those sentences you never thought you'd say.

People moved and melted back into their bipedal shapes. Clothes appearing as they did. Weird. Were their clothes part of them or was it that the power that shifted them between shapes took that too? If they hadn't been killing each other I could have asked.

"Okay, we're going to talk about all of this but first, you." I pointed to the woman who'd jumped me and set the whole fight into motion. "Because you cannot manage your anger like an adult, I'll do it for you. Every time I say the word Neuschwanstein, you will shift to your other shape and sit for a whole thirty seconds. That only applies to you and only when I speak the word, but don't think I'm above spreading my influence."

I fucking hated this, just not as much as I hated what this woman was about to do to her daughter. "Does everyone understand me?"

Nods all around.

"Good. Now, since you ruined my shirt, you need to give me yours."

She unbuttoned the flannel blouse mechanically. If she'd had nothing on underneath, I might have averred, but she had a prettier bra than my shirt had been before she got to it. She could suck it for so many reasons. Tiny-boobed women always got the pretty clothing.

Her shirt would never fit me. I knew that from the word go. It was big enough to cover my breasts and that's all a girl could ask for in times like these.

I eclipsed my chest without climbing down from the table. People came back to themselves like out of a dream and into a real nightmare. No one immediately attacked anyone else. Bonus. The spectacle of me standing on the table seemed to be distracting enough. That and the confusion of what just happened to them.

"As I was saying, Miss can't stand ugly truths." I sighed. That kind of speaking would get us nowhere. "Ma'am, what is your name?"

Her eyes narrowed at me. "I don't tell witches my name."

"Witches aren't real." And neither are shapeshifters. Shit. I didn't know anymore. "Whatever. Fine. Listen, Bitch Who Tried to Kill Me."

She jumped at me again.

I hopped off the table, over her head with a, "Neuschwanstein." I landed bad. My knees buckled and I rolled into the feet of the man who'd held a knife on me. The roll reminded me that Bitch had clawed the shit out of my torso.

It hurt.

My stomach rumbled.

At least the man hot-footed away from me like I burned him. Eyes wide in fear. The uncertainty I'd wanted earlier.

To everything there is a season.

I stood before Bitch Who Tried to Kill Me could, though she twisted, hissed, and fought against my order. I waited. Waited for her to stand back up. Waited for her to step toward me again. "Neuschwanstein."

The woman plopped her butt down and cursed a blue streak at me. I waited.

We played the game three more times before she stopped trying to attack me and glared.

"Okay," I rolled my shoulders back. "Now that we've established that."

"You have made an enemy today and you will die for it." The fire in her gaze almost made me believe it.

"This is the third time this week someone's tried to kill me. Take a number." There was that cockiness again. I needed to steer clear before it bit my butt again. Time to get to the point. "You can threaten me all you want, but when I tell you that you sound like my mother you can take it as the fucking gospel and die mad about it."

She blinked at me. Anger still burned in her gaze, but that might have been the first thing I said that registered. Progress. Baby steps.

"Now, whatever beef you people have against each other, that is not their beef." I pointed behind me, hoping the couple hadn't left. Couldn't risk looking away from the woman to verify. "Look at them."

"Get your hands off my—"

"Neuschwanstein."

Four-footed, her butt hit the floor.

"You're glowing," a man to my right said in that awed kind of confused tone.

"I know."

"No." He sounded more certain this time. "You're really glowing. Brighter than the lights in here."

I had a little time before the woman could stand up, so I turned my head. "I know."

The man who mentioned me smelling like the ocean, Carlo, stood closer to me than a lot of the others. His eyes roamed over my exposed skin like he was trying to figure out where the glow ended. Nothing sexual inherent in the look. More like he would have paid P. T. Barnum five dollars to goggle at me. Who needed two other rings?

"What are you?"

If I knew the answer to that, I'd have a lot less stress in my life. I shook my head at him. "I don't really know. No one else seems to either." Except the man who died without explaining things. The letter had only touched on the surface.

Before my conversation with Carlo deepened, I turned back to the cat Bitch Who Tried to Kill Me.

Once she could stand, she rippled back into a woman with all the dignity I'd never have. "You cannot govern what I do with my own daughter."

To a point, that was true. "But, how is forcing her to get an abortion, or beating her until she miscarries—"

"I would never." Her voice rumbled in inhuman ways, but she didn't make any aggressive movement my direction.

I shrugged. "I've heard those words before, practically ver batum, coming from my mother. And then you attacked me. Would have killed me if I wasn't whatever the fuck I am. Tell me where I'm wrong."

She opened her mouth and said nothing.

Rather than run over her, I gave her the space to fill the silence. She closed her mouth.

"I ask again. How is forcing an abortion or a miscarriage on her any different than what you're accusing him of doing?"

Hard blinks. At least she was thinking it through this time. "He—"

"They. They had sex. They. Wait." I had to be sure, so I raised my voice, "How old are you two?"

"Seventeen," from the boy.

"Almost eighteen," from the girl.

Good. "And did he force you?"

She said, "I'd like to see him try."

Salty. I liked it. It meant she wasn't cowed by her mother's awfulness nor by the situation. I nodded to the woman. "See? Consenting people on the edge of adulthood."

She shook her head. "He left when he found out she was pregnant. He knew, and he left her to deal with it."

I moved around to position at least one person between me and the woman, so I could glare at him. "Is that fucking true?"

He pulled Stella closer to him. "Nana wouldn't let me come."

"Is that fucking true?" It took some bobbing and weaving to find the white-haired woman.

She had to be Nana.

My kind of arrogance rode her shoulders when our eyes finally met. "She's trash. Her whole family's trash and I won't have my—"

Someone punched her in the jaw.

I saw it coming.

Could have warned her.

Didn't.

If the fighting had broken out again, I might have felt bad. As was, the woman who punched her stepped back into a circle of her own people and no one counter-attacked. Good enough for me. But I still had to ask, "Who are you that you think you're above them?"

She sniffed at me. "I am descended from royalty, as is my family. We cannot dilute our blood."

"So, yay incest?"

Her head jerked back. "How dare you?"

"The only way to keep only royal blood in royal lines is rampant incest. Tell me where I'm wrong."

A woman's laughter rumbled behind me.

Nana glared past me. "Neuschwanstein."

"Nope. Sorry. Only works for me."

More laughter from behind me. Nana took a threatening step this direction, either toward me or the other woman. I held up a finger. "I'm getting hungry. You really don't want to test me right now."

She stopped moving. The strong hate in her eyes did not stop. "Why are you even here?"

Oh, I see. Let me talk up a storm when it looked like I was on her side but now that she was the frog in the frying pan I needed to leave. Typical. "I came for lunch. Stayed for the show." I rolled my fingers around at the scene.

"It's time for you to go."

Maybe it was. I twisted around to the couple. "Are you two planning on leaving?"

They looked at each other in that instinctual way. The two of them probably wouldn't be separating any time soon.

"I don't want to," the girl finally said.

"And do you want the baby?"

"Yes." From both, in unison, smiles on their faces.

That was that. I shifted so I could see both angry matriarchs at once. "Well, then, you people are going to need to find a way to live with them being together."

"Never." Nana shook her head almost violently.

"Fuck no." From black-cat lady.

I swung back to the couple. "If you want to take me to a good restaurant around here, I can get you to a safe place until you can get on your feet."

White haired woman's, "You will die before I let you steal my great-grandson," blended with the other woman's, "The fuck you will."

Consensus between the women at long last. I mean, they were wrong, but they were in accord. "You can't push people away then complain when they leave with someone who won't treat them like shit. Now, you can either sit down with each other and work out the details, or I'm going to support them in whatever they want to do."

Stella's mother scoffed. "Right. What *they* want. You expect me to believe you haven't worked whatever witchery on them?"

Grumblings of agreement rolled through the restaurant.

That hurt. But I saw where she was coming from. Where they all were. "I had everyone in this room under my power and the only thing I did was to keep you from attacking me again or anyone else. If you think I couldn't force the lot of you to strip down and have an orgy in the middle of I-25, you'd be wrong." Probably.

That pin-drop silence fell again. I let it hang.

"How do we know you didn't?" Stella's voice rang out from behind me. "Or that you haven't done something else?"

"Because I fucking hate doing it at all but mother fuckers keep trying to kill me, or kill people I care about, or kill strangers for their own shitty reasons, so I have to keep doing things that make me hate myself the way I hate my mother and I fucking *hate* it." My hands trembled by the time I'd gotten the sentence out. I panted for air.

Everyone around me stared at me like I'd turned into a big cat. Oh wait, no. That was them. But I'd definitely let too much of my own ugliness out. I didn't have enough food in me to rein it back in. My glow had even pulsed a couple notches brighter. Apparently, barely controlled anger could do it too. Who knew?

I rotated my head around, meeting the eyes of every single person in the room until they looked away. All except the soon-to-be new parents and the matriarchs. The kids didn't deserve the stare-down. The matriarchs, I didn't have the time it would take to make them submit. I'd probably have to drop the shirt and do the thing I hated to make it happen. To them, I asked, "Do you really want your kids to end up as fucked up as I am?"

They looked at each other in the same kind of motion the couple had done earlier. Accord. Seeking confirmation between themselves rather than attacking. The enemy of their enemy—

"Um, Ma'am?"

I rotated around to the only person who'd had the gonads to speak in the wake of letting them see the monsters inside me. The boy on the road to being a man. "Yes?"

"Do you want me to bring you something to eat? You didn't exactly get to finish."

Messiah chorus sang through my veins. I could have hugged him. "Yes. Do you remember my order?"

"Yes ma'am," he turned to Stella. "Did you want something?"

"I'll have what she's having."

I giggled a little at the movie reference she didn't know she made. I looked around for anyone else to commiserate with. Carlo had covered his mouth, but his eyes were suspiciously merry. Good enough. I turned back to the couple. "You should probably give her about half of what I ordered."

The boy laughed, kissed Stella's forehead, then shook his head at me as he headed toward the kitchen. "You have a lot to learn about cattus. Especially pregnant ones."

28 – NEW FRIENDS

TURNED OUT, ORION, the waiter and father-to-be, was right. Stella ate with the same kind of hollow-leg gusto as me. Tiny as she was, I wouldn't have guessed. We didn't talk much as we chowed down. I didn't ask about how they changed shape and she didn't ask about the glow peeking out from around the shirt I pinned to the front of me with tight elbows.

Orion hovered nervously nearby, wavering between making extra, *extra*, sure we didn't need anything else and bopping all over to clean up around the other cattus.

He dropped my purse on the bench next to me after he set the second round of food in front of us. I pulled my phone out with a prayer to the gods of wholeness and technology. The screen was not cracked. It turned on like nothing wrong had ever been done to it. Thank the gods. I loved this phone.

I checked the time, then did the math. "Shit."

Stella's eyes widened. "What?"

"Nothing big, I just have five minutes to wolf this down before I need to walk back."

"How far do you need to go?" Orion was Johnny on the spot again, skidding to attention like the Road Runner.

"Only a couple miles, but—"

"I can drive you." He had all the peppy energy of the cartoon.

I wondered if he would make the noise for me. "Sure. That would be nice. Thank you."

He set his hand on Stella's shoulder. Mouth full and eyes on me, she still leaned toward him just the littlest bit. She might not have even realized. Kind of adorable. Was I that cute at that age?

"It's the least I can do," he squeezed Stella's shoulder. "Really."

Passing it off as nothing would dig me into the politeness tennis match that always ended love-love. "That gives me another half-hour or forty-five minutes. Thank you."

"Thank *you*."

By the time I needed to leave, Orion had the restaurant looking almost as it had when I walked in. Neet trick, that. I leaned toward Stella as I scooted out of the booth, "I think he may be a keeper."

She smiled as bright as my cleavage. "I know."

Orion road-runnered next to the table. "Are you ready to leave? Give me like five minutes and I can meet you out front."

Perhaps his eagerness came more out of wanting to leave than desire to wait on my whim. All things considered, I would want to leave as well. Even if the worst of things was over. "Not quite yet. I'll need the check—"

"You're not pay for anything. Not today or ever." Backbone and nostrils flaring.

Oh yes, this boy would be okay. That kind of fervor, I would not argue with.

"Well," I scooched the rest of my way out of the booth. "Before I leave, I'll need a shirt that will actually fit me and I'm going to talk to your matriarchs. If you want to meet me in front in like ten minutes, though, that should be good."

The two of them did that concerned-meeting-of-their-gazes thing when I mentioned speaking to their matriarchs, but Orion nodded to me as I finished. "Not sure what I can do about the shirt, but I'll see."

He loped away with a cat's grace. At least now I knew why.

The two women glared up at me as I approached their table. Not quite united, but I was certainly the enemy. I had no problem playing that roll if it kept the two of them civil.

I snagged a chair from nearby and turned it around, so I could face them and use the back of the chair to hold the shirt against me.

"What do you want now?" Orion's grandmother hissed at me.

"I just have a few questions."

Her forehead rippled displeasure while her lips parted ever so slightly. Stella's mother just stared. Close enough. "How many people know about you, outside of you people? I mean, not *you people*, you people. But, like, cat people, people."

More staring, which I couldn't blame because I could word goodly. "Okay, let me do better. I'm asking if anyone in the Gold 4 knows that you exist so I don't make a faux pas and mention you to people who shouldn't know."

Hackles rose. On both women. I'd heard about that kind of thing, but never seen the hair on the back on someone's head actually rise. Eerie AF on a human.

"How do we know you won't tell the superheroes about us?" Orion's Nana used her words.

I appreciated that. "Equivalent exchange."

Both blinked their confusion.

Uncultured swine. "I tell people about your secret, you tell people about mine."

"But your so-called heroes already know about you." My friend, the Bitch Who Tried to Kill Me, growled at me.

"Yeah, but Joe Schmoe on the street doesn't. And I'd like to keep it that way." I hoped they could hear the sincerity in my voice, but I guessed it didn't really matter. I pointed to Stella's mother. "I'd also like to undo what I did to you, if you'll allow me."

Growling increased.

I lifted my hands. "I get that. If you change your mind, I'll give you my number. Do you have a pen?"

A pencil slid into my peripheral vision on the left. I took it with a "Thanks" and held a hand out to the two women for something to write on. Because trust and two-way streets and things.

Attack McGrowly-Pants pulled a napkin out of the dispenser and slid it over to me, eyes never wavering from mine. Interesting. But, then, she seemed to be a woman of action. I rewarded her faith, nodding to her as I took the napkin then looking down to write the number. If I couldn't trust her enough to take my eyes off her how could I expect her to trust me.

"Good. Now, I just need a shirt and I can get out of your hair."

A scarlet shirt slipped into my side view the same way the pencil had. This time, I turned my head just far enough to see my benefactor. My slightly creepy acquaintance, Carlo, held the shirt out to me in a kind of reverent way. He even kept his eyes down and pointed away from me like I might be the sun or something.

I took the shirt with a thank you and he scuttled away, backward, without turning his back on me. Huh. Here was hoping that he would be the only person to treat me like that. Ever.

The shirt slipped over my head with a little effort, the perpetual problems of the bigheaded. Fortunately, that was only tight spot in the shirt. The rest of the shirt swam around me and the chairback as I strung my arms through. Part of me wanted to be angry at the ridiculously over-sized shirt, but bigger beat smaller.

Standing without taking the chair with me took some doing, but I managed. I slipped the first borrowed shirt out from under the red one and held it out to my attacky friend. Her top lip crinkled in a snarly way. "Keep it."

"It wouldn't fit me." I let it fall from my fingers to the table in front of her.

Before the woman voiced her disgust, I spun on the balls of my feet and headed toward the nearest exit. The people between the front door and me practically sprung out of my way. They did it with grace, though.

I would have tripped all over myself.

Orion waited in his car outside the restaurant, just as he said he would. Stella rode in the back. I climbed in the car before anyone else got the bright idea to come looking for either of them. Still, I wanted to know, "Are the two of you running away after all?"

Stella leaned far enough forward that her head hung between mine and Orion's. "No. I just wanted a few minutes alone." She settled a hand on his shoulder.

After he set the car in motion, Orion took hold of her fingers and kissed the backs. Adorable. Me in the car with them didn't equate with alone. Probably the closest they got, with their big, wacky, kitty families. I did my best to hush up.

Halfway back, it occurred to me that bringing people to Spencer's doorway, even cattus with secrets of their own, was a bad idea.

I directed Orion to a building a block past Spencer's building, and around the corner. The added distance would mean a longer ride back alone for the two of them. Win-win.

Except for the part where I waved my happy ass into a building I didn't belong in and found myself in a lobby filled with lizard people. Actual lizard people, with scaly, serpentine heads coming out of suits. Nicely tailored suits. I didn't know much about fashion, but if the suits weren't bespoke, I'd cannonball into the bog of eternal stench.

The noise of my entrance through the inner pair of doors turned all those scaly heads my direction. Blue tongues flicked out between lipless mouths. Holy, balls. David Icke was right. I had so many questions about Denver International Airport and the hidden tunnels.

Perhaps when I wasn't getting murderous eyes from the lot of well-dressed lizards.

I waved an apologetic hand to the group. "I'm sorry, sirs. If you could give me just a moment for that car to get far enough away, I'll be right out of your...scales."

Shapes crept toward me from either side. I didn't move out of their range. The only options would put me back outside where Orion and Stella would see me or in the face of the sharpest-dressed lizard. A shirt with a looser collar would have been mighty useful right about then. If my charms worked on lizards. It worked on the cattus, but who knew?

"Who are you?" The lizard in navy blue with a yellow tie asked.

The way he asked made me wonder where his mushroom lounge chair and hookah pipe were.

Rather than assume this would go badly, I decided to treat it as a social occasion. I stepped toward him in a confident but non-threatening manner. Smooth three steps. Hand stretched out to meet his.

"My name is Greer Ianto—" probably should have used a fake name "—and you are?"

Auto pilot clicked on, and I had the touch. A palm smoother than it should be pressed against mine while the rough pads of his clawed fingers wrapped around the back of my hand.

"Aldin Davis." The words came out clear, without the hiss I expected. "What are you doing here?"

"Some people I just met just dropped me off and I didn't want them to know where I was actually going." Not smart. Regardless of how well things seemed to be going, telling an unknown man that no one knew my whereabouts was supreme pizza stupid. His frosty-blue eyes widened some, from a slit to a football shape. No way to tell if it was a good or bad thing. My lizard brain said it might be time to make a break for it.

His blue tongue slithered out and flicked up and down a couple of times an inch in front of my face. Not good. When the tongue retracted, the eyes closed back to slits.

Doubleplusungood.

Diversionary tactics needed to aid escape. "Is it true about the miles of tunnels under the airport and the Illuminati and all that stuff about you guys running all of the governments from the shadows?"

Someone laughed a hissing laugh and quickly stifled it. That was something.

"Excuse me?" Aldin did not sound amused. The face didn't move enough for me to really analyze, but the flat tone and stiffening of the hand around mine spoke volumes.

New-ish tactics. "Never mind that. Does the Gold 4 know about you? I feel like things could get particularly interesting with Magus if you guys ever—"

"Take her out back."

I dodged to the side, but Aldin held my hand fast with more strength than I could hope to possess. I didn't make it far. An arm wrapped around my midsection and lifted me off the ground with the same kind of strength.

Kicking backward at things my feet would reach did no good. The goomba lizard still carted me away like I weighed all of three pounds.

"This is a bad idea." I kicked out and managed to hit one of the other men, this one in a charcoal suit with a red tie. Score one for me. "If I disappear, Magus will search for me. He will find you and you'll rue the day."

Rue the day? Who even talked like that—Fucking Garren. Not the person to emulate.

Someone grabbed a hold of my flailing legs and that was the end of that. He even dampened the body-worm wriggling I wanted to do. Dampened, but not stopped. If I kept going, I could work my overlarge shirt up enough to help me out.

The two carried me down the well-lit hallway, past so many dark and empty offices. No one else was in the building. No one but the asshole lizard, who might have remembered to give me a fake name, and his cronies.

The green glow of an exit sign signaled that my trip was about to come to an unfortunate end. After all the shit this week, this would *not* be the way I died.

Dude holding me by the midsection swung us around so he could back through the doorway. I latched onto the doorway as he tried to lead us through. My fingers nearly ripped off, but my grip stopped us dead.

He jerked.

I held tight.

Holding on might not save me, but it could give me the time to figure out what would.

The door to the outside was too dark. No sun hit this alleyway so in the day, which meant the chances of someone seeing us were slim. The shaded alley practically smiled and welcomed me like the opened arms of the grave.

"Enough of this." Charcoal suit pulled out a hand-held, black-plastic thing with two metal teeth poking out from one side.

I recognized it straight away. And the danger. "No. You shouldn't—"

He pressed the stun gun against my ankle. A sharp heatwave blasted through my skin, then I pulsed in one bright, orgasmless supernova.

Lizard lips who tried to stun me flew down the hall in a smoldering arc. My struggle-cuddle buddy and I shot backward.

29 – THIS AGAIN?

Veronica R. Calisto

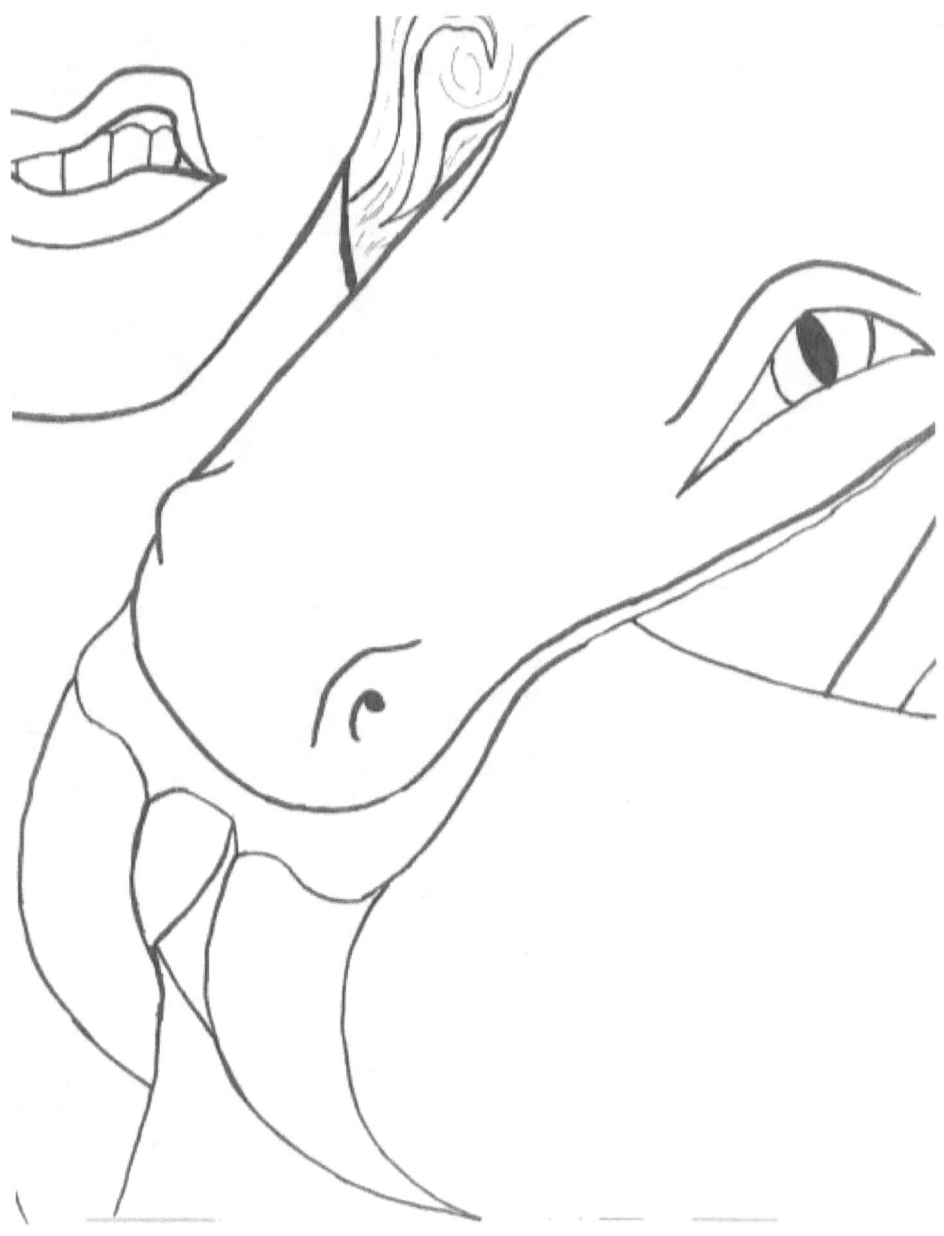

Veronica R. Calisto

Veronica R. Calisto

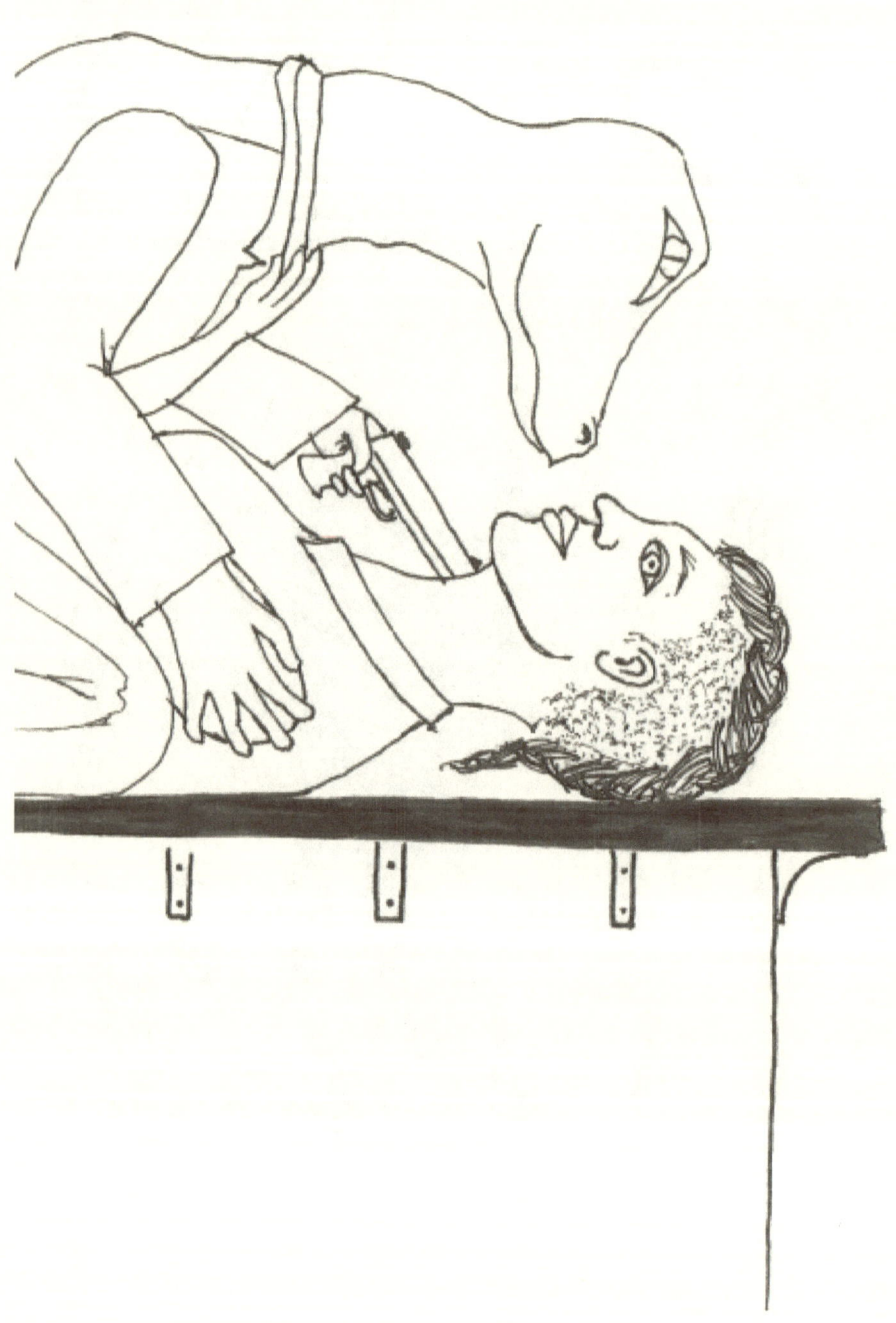

30 – SEE NO EVIL

A COUPLE OF gunshots blasted, another bruised my neck, and I stabbed the lizard man in the eye with his fang. A golden stream oozed out. Three more shots rang out, one in my side, one again in my chest.

Someone yelled, "Don't shoot her."

My "Yes, shoot!" was smothered by the lizard man hissing a demon chorus as he reared back.

He leaned to the side to get away from me. I tangled my legs in his and followed his movement. We rolled off a desk, him pulling the trigger twice more before we landed on the terra cotta concrete floor. Me on top of him, this time. He jerked and wriggled to escape. It felt like riding a prize bull

"No." I tried to sweep the gun aim off my body. "You're going to—"

He jerked the gun up and shot me right under the chin.

That was it.

I stabbed him in the hand, the throat, then the other eye.

His whole body tensed, including his trigger finger. Another bullet hit me in the jaw, then the gun dropped from his hand as his fingers disintegrated into golden sand and pebbles. His head too, falling apart into a pile of gold sand, all except the fang I hadn't broken off. It turned completely transparent save a vein of black through the center to the needle tip. The broken fang in my hand was solid gold. When had that happened?

The body shifted under me, the way a bean bag chair did, my weight on the former lizard's suit adjusting the fill distribution. My stomach rebelled.

"What the fuck?" Someone in the mostly-silent space to my right wheezed the words. Hard flesh hit softer flesh forcing a moan in the same timbre as the voice.

There was no reason to punish him for asking a poignant question. I needed to gather my bearings a little before I could give any kind of answer, reasonable, true, or good enough for people to accept and move on with their lives.

A hand lowered into the space between me and the desk. A bit of rusty brown crusted the cuff. I trailed my eyes up to the owner. Spencer. Of course. Not looking particularly alarmed at my unexplained arrival in his office again, nor at the unknown creature I'd just killed. Just him holding out his hand with cold, focused eyes. Standing in front of his desk, which must have been what the lizard and I first dropped onto.

I reached up to take his hand and stopped when I realized I'd used the hand still holding the broken fang. Before I gave him the other, I scooped up the whole, crystalized fang. He pulled me to standing while I did my best to ignore the way the remains in the suit moved.

Once I was vertical, Spencer dropped his eyes down to my aftermath, then lifted them back to me.

I preempted whatever he might have said with, "Sorry about the mess."

"The back of your shirt is half scorched and half burned completely away."

Curling my back confirmed that the shirt had had it. I sighed. "That shouldn't surprise me. And yet..."

"And yet, that isn't the shirt you left here in."

What could I say to that? "You were right. This is a dangerous neighborhood to take a walk in."

One of his eyes narrowed. Both twitched.

I shrugged. "Things got a little complicated."

He tipped his head back in one of those riotous laughs that did things to my chest and other parts. My skin might have pulsed a watt or two brighter.

I hoped he didn't notice that.

He shifted his grip from my hand to my chin with a look that said he had noticed, naturally, but he didn't act on it. Instead, he tipped my head back and to the side. Either checking for injuries or proving to any observers that there were none. Probably a bit of both.

"Did my men hit you?"

"Couple of times, but, whatever. Better safe than sorry." I shrugged.

"True." He nodded. "I need another fifteen minutes."

Oedipus Rex. "Do whatever you need to. I'll just wait in your truck this time."

I turned to go.

Spencer's hand clapped over my eyes before I'd made the complete 180 toward the door. "You don't want to see this."

Whatever it was, I believed him. Now that he'd covered my eyes, I categorized the things I'd been smelling without realizing it. Shit. Piss. Sweat that stank of fear. The salty-metal tang of blood. Nope. Yep. "Well, get me outta here, then."

Smart man that he was, he kept one hand over my eyes, lest I open them and became pillar of salt. He wrapped the other arm around my half-naked back and cupped my hip. A light pressure and I started moving.

The room felt bigger this way. Much more terrain to cover. Some of it was the slightly zigzagged route he took me on to avoid things. Most of it was the vulnerability of relying on foul smells and the softer sounds of men struggling or in pain to tell me how close I was to my goal. When Spencer halted us, I hoped we might be through, but he kept the hand over my eyes steady.

"Big step here."

Not done, then. "Big as in wide or as in tall."

"Both."

Not good. Not good at all.

Tall at least meant it wasn't a pool of blood. Or not just a pool of blood. Could be a body in a widening pool.

I took the big step. Something—a hand—clamped on my right ankle. I stomped down and the hand clenched tighter. Squeezing my eyes closed hard enough to hurt, I squatted and stabbed the hand with the two fangs still clutched in mine.

He screamed. High-pitched and awful.

I straightened. "Get me out of here."

Spencer's hands regained their place over my eyes and at my hip. We started moving. Two steps later he barked, "Door."

The doorknob squeaked. Cool, stale air swiped my face. A few more steps and the staleness wrapped completely around us.

Thank gods.

Spencer removed his hands from me and I turned toward him.

The door behind hadn't been closed completely, merely cracked enough for the one man near the door to keep an eye on us. Men stood on either side of the door as well. Their faces twitched to the rhythm of the screams from the man I'd stabbed. Spencer twisted his head back toward the door.

"I might actually need a half hour to wrap." He turned back toward me. "If you don't mind."

An open expression settled over his face, like he asked for more than the time.

He did, though. Terrible things had happened, were happening, would continue to happen in that office. And in his life. In this moment, when he wasn't touching me or giving me any heated smiles to cloud my judgement. Right then, when things were laid bare, he asked if I could handle this. If I could handle him.

All of him.

It was a bad idea for me. He knew it as well as I did. But the fangs, from a lizard creature that I'd killed after teleporting with it from some alley onto Spencer's desk, weighed heavy in my hand. He wasn't balking at my...complications.

"Just don't take too much longer. Idle hands..." I shrugged.

"Is a terrible movie. Here." Spencer reached into his back pocket. "Take your book back before I forget."

The book with the names that had sparked this little adventure in house cleaning. I snatched it from him. "Hey, that is a great movie. And you know this is missing a few names." I wagged the book at him, then toward his office.

"Where there's a bee, there's a hive."

That was true. Unfortunately, in this case.

"Hey, Boss," the man in the doorway said. "Garren is starting to—"

Both Spencer and I held up hands to forestall whatever else the man was going to say. Spencer followed it up with, "Nate, she doesn't want to hear any of those details."

Damned skippy, I didn't want details. "Well, go finish and hurry it up. I'm hungry."

His lips curved. "When aren't you hungry?"

Valid question. "Right after I've eaten.

Curve evolved to full grin.

"Sure, Spence. Poke the hungry bear like she won't bite you in the ass. Just don't let any of them blab to anyone else about this book or the..." I brandished the fang-laden hand. "If I hear word about either, I will make every single man in there, and these two too, regret it and remember why they do. I swear to gods."

"These are my men, Greer. If they betray me, I will handle it."

"All well and good, but when people betray me, I handle it myself."

Spencer smiled like I'd said something cute and nodded. "Understood."

"Boss?" Nate's voice had tightened a few pitches up. Something he needed to learn to control if he wanted to maintain his position of relative power.

I planted a peck on Spencer's lips then tipped my head toward the office. "Go handle your business."

He walked to the door without any lingering looks or touches. The spring in his step disconcerted me a little. I turned to head for the elevator before I could dwell on it. The scream got louder then cut off completely with the click of the door closing. Sound proofed. At least that meant the two guards outside the room heard nothing about the lizard person.

"You're a hard bitch," one of the guards called out to me. "Aren't you?"

I swiveled around. "Excuse me?"

The guard on the left flapped his hands a bit. "I mean, I like it. Don't get me wrong. It's just an observation." From what I could see of his forearms, dude was ripped the way Bruce Lee was; unassuming, whipcord muscles that could rip a phonebook in half.

"What's your name?" I set my fists on my hips. The right one was bruised from something. Probably a bullet or two.

Dude clammed up like...a clam.

"His name's Tanner, ma'am." The other, bigger, bald dude said. "And I'm Victor."

Gotta love people selling other people out. Except when that kind of reaction got other people killed.

"What the fuck, Victor?" Tanner reached across the doorway to punch his comrade in the arm.

He'd used real names. Another not so good response.

"I'm not having her ask Boss and him thinking I'm the one who fucked up."

That was something. Not much, but something.

"Well, Victor. As I told your boss, I handle my own shit. And Tanner." I held back the urge to move closer to them and poke sharp things in their faces. Mostly, I needed some time to go chillax by myself.

Tanner looked wound too tightly to deal with more than a few words of wisdom, so I gave him some.

"Every woman is always exactly as hard as she needs to be."

31 – WICKED MEN

I FELL HALFWAY out the truck when Spencer popped open the driver's side door. The seatbelt saved me.

He blinked at me. I straightened and tipped my head toward the passenger side. "Hop in, hot stuff."

I expected an argument or something. What I got was the car door closing on me without a word. He walked around the front of the truck, eyes toward his feet with a bemused little smile on his face.

He climbed in and pulled me into a long, slow kiss. "Where are we going?"

Wasn't that the question to end all questions?

"That depends." The truck rumbled to life at the press of a button.

New-fangled, fancy truck. I focused on that and other concrete things instead of the larger possibilities. "Do you want to stop by your place to grab some things?"

"Where are you taking me?" No fear in his voice as he buckled in. Simple curiosity. "I thought your apartment building died."

Was murdered by someone trying to murder me. "Yep." I turned to back out of the space.

"And your friend Lex threatened me."

I wanted to tuck my head to hide a smile. Driving through the garage made it much harder to do. "Do you want to stay with me tonight, or not?"

"Yes, ma'am."

"Then, we should stop by your place for you to grab some things." I stopped the truck before turning onto the road. Left or right depended on him.

He shook his head. "I have a bag in the back."

My eyes narrowed, though I kept my gaze forward. "You just expected me to invite you over tonight?"

"I didn't expect you in my life at all, Darling. You can't anticipate the earth shaking beneath you or a lightning bolt to the chest."

There went my ribcage tightening again. I couldn't breathe and had too much oxygen at the same time. Spencer peeled one of my hands off the wheel and threaded our fingers, making things better and worse for me. I pulled out onto the road just to give myself something concrete to focus on.

"The bag is for...unexpected adventures."

A lot of possibilities hid in Spencer's pause. Probably a lot of emergencies when everyone was trying to kill him. Something I needed to consider.

When I got a new car to put it in.

When I had money again to get the car. And the bag.

Spencer pulled our hands to him and kissed our knuckles. My skin warmed.

"So," he settled our hands on his leg, "what happened between you leaving and you popping in again?"

Mood killer right there, but whatever. Driving was more important. "I had some food, then there were things, then I was in an alley and that weird thing happened. You know. The one that practically dropped me in your lap last time." There. That covered things nicely.

"You are skipping over a lot."

Truth. "I am."

"Why?"

"I can't tell you one thing because of a promise, and I won't tell you the other thing to protect you."

A sigh escaped him. "You don't need to protect me."

"Do you know what that lizard-man-creature thing was?"

"No."

I nodded. "Neither do I, and I got the impression that knowing about their existence is bad." Impression bolstered by people trying to kill me.

"Their existence?" Spencer's eyes burned into my peripheral vision. "There's more than one?"

Oedipus Rex.

This was how people got in trouble. And I had no way to convincingly backtrack. Best to be out with it. "Dude I killed was told to take me to the alley. Pretty sure he was supposed to kill me, but I struggled enough that the other lizard-man-creature thing got annoyed and used a stun gun on my ankle. My skin flared, exploded him one direction and the two of us the other. There was weird light and dark and neither swirliness, then I landed in your office. There. You happy?"

Spencer said nothing for a while. Long enough that, were I inclined to, I could have relaxed into the silence. But, I'd asked a question and said a bunch of weird ass shit. I needed him to just write me off as crazy and we could move on from there.

"Sounds..." he drew out the S and the pause thereafter much longer than necessary, "complicated."

I pulled my hand away from him. Tried to. He clamped down with both hands and pulled the lot against his chest, laughing at my mutters as I tugged. The ass.

When I parked the car, Spencer grabbed my bag before reaching back to grab his. So, I hopped out of the truck and met him on the other side. I slipped my hand under his elbow for the short walk up to the door.

"Not that I'm complaining, Darling, but where are we?"

I pulled away from him to get the keys for the door, self-conscious suddenly. Cautious. "This was Gabe's house."

The door opened smooth as butter. I could have used the distraction of a fussy lock or a horror-movie creak. Anything to pull me out of the vulnerability that had welled up over my feet, making my footfalls on the redwood-entry feel louder than they should.

As I closed the door behind us, I watched Spencer's quick, visual survey of the house. Seeing his face would have been better, but I seemed to be locked in place behind him.

Almost as if he'd heard the desire, Spencer turned back to me. He studied me in that way he had, intensely and without judgement. "You've never brought another man here, have you?"

I shook my head as if speaking the words might hurt or make him turn on me.

He approached me, slowly. Like I was a feral cat. When he moved in range, he tipped his head up pressed his lips against the center of my forehead. "Thank you."

I tipped my head down. Let it rest against the crook of his neck. Breathed in his cologne and his spice beneath. He wrapped his arms around me, bags and all, and just held on to me. Held on until I straightened and pulled away. Not a retreat this time, though. An invitation. "I'll give you the tour later. Right now, let's go get some grub."

The deep freezer held a treasure trove of meat and pre-chopped veggies, if I felt inclined to cook. Today did not feel like one of those days. The freezer-to-oven meals would take longer than I was willing to wait. But Gabe hadn't made it through all the spaghetti sauce we'd made the last time we cooked together. Bittersweet freezer victory.

"Get ready for the best spaghetti you've ever had in your life," I said as I came back into the main kitchen. Mostly speaking to shake off the weight of my sadness.

Spencer pinched his lips and gave the red block in the freezer bag a dubious look. "Remind me to take you to Italy, so you can eat those words."

"I'll take that challenge."

"Yes, you will."

Cooking in that kitchen, even something as simple as boiling some noodles and defrosting sauce that had taken hours to cook, settled me in a way that nothing else had. Having Spencer there making conversation didn't change the feeling like my feet finally hit the ground after treading water for weeks. He might have made it better. Cooking again for the first time in the house alone might of broke me a little. Like everything else had.

Almost everything else.

I didn't hide my interest in Spencer's reaction to the food. My fork stayed on my plate while I watched him like a hawk. Halfway through his first bite, he closed his eyes.

Victory. "That's what I thought." I twirled my own forkful and shoved it in my mouth.

When he opened his eyes on me, he smiled. "I'm still taking you to Italy."

"Yes, you will."

We blazed though eating without much conversation. Companionable silence and happy eye contact. He helped me clean up despite my protests, mostly because he splashed me until I submitted.

He didn't want a tour of the house. I took him up to my room.

"If you want to take my bathroom, I'm going to take a shower in the hall." I kept my bag with my dresses in my hand, to keep him from peeking in while I was gone. I wanted to surprise him with the dress he liked.

"Do you mind if I turn the lights on?"

Whoops. I flicked the overhead light on and hustled over to turn on the desk light, too. "Sorry about that. It's all the same to me."

"You have the layout memorized, so you don't need the light." He nodded. "I get it."

"No, actually. It doesn't matter how dark it is. I can see."

He tilted his head. "You're a cat."

Several things ran through my head, about petting and purring. None of it would help me since I didn't have the time to continue that conversation. So, I just kissed him quickly and shook my head. "Cats would be so lucky." Before I left the room, I grabbed my pajamas.

I hung the dresses up before I showered to give them the steam treatment. Between that and hanging around until tomorrow, they should be ready. I took a longer than normal shower to ensure any wrinkles fell out.

When I came back into the room, Spencer had one towel around his waist and was using another to scrub at his hair. I stopped short in the doorway to watch the muscles in his arms and chest move under is skin. Very nice.

He smiled before turning his head toward me. "You're glowing again, Miss Flannel USA."

I pushed off from the doorway but forced myself to the side of the bed farthest from Spencer. "I'm always glowing."

"Not as much as you were just now spying on me."

He flicked the towel in his hands over his shoulder, sending a wave of him straight at my nose. Freshly showered he smelled even better. Good enough to eat. Between that and his beautifully shirtless state, I didn't even try to argue his effect on me. My skin had already given me away, so I shrugged. "You look good."

"What's with the get up?" He gestured up and down my figure.

"Practicing to be a nun?"

"No, I just..." Too many things I didn't want to explain.

He dipped his chin down and lifted an eyebrow. "Is that what you usually sleep in?"

"No, I usually sleep naked."

He smiled as if he'd already known how I would answer. "Then get naked and let's go to bed."

"Not going to happen."

"I know," he lifted his hands. "You told me why we can't have sex and the way you glow when I kiss you proves it."

"Still no."

He frowned. "Why not?"

"I don't trust me with our pants off."

"Greer, I already told you—" He stopped and blinked at me a couple of times. "You don't trust *you* with our pants off."

I nodded. "Correct."

A grin ripped across his face. "That, I can live with." He started around the bed toward me.

Shaking my outstretched hands, I stepped back. "No, no. You need to get some pants on too. Lickity-now."

He threw his head back in a laugh, but stopped his approach and turned around. I watched the terry cloth sway its way back into the bathroom. Which was a damned shame.

The bigger shame came when Spencer walked back out in pants similar to mine. That he hadn't added a shirt helped, though it frustrated me. If I accepted my weakness, I would head to one of the guest bedrooms. I didn't want to be alone, though, and he looked so good heading toward my bed.

He turned on my nightstand lamp without taking his eyes off me. "Lose the shirt."

The soft order rolled across my skin, pulling a smile from me. I didn't refuse, but rather moved away from the bed. Spencer frowned until I turned off the overhead light. He pulled the sheets back and sat on the bed while I got the desk light.

Spencer watched my face as I unbuttoned the top which made me feel like I was already completely naked. Holding my shirt closed, I sat down on the bed.

Spencer joined me, still watching my face.

"You want to get the light?"

"I want to see you, Greer."

I shrugged a shoulder. "You will, but you'll only remember if you're touching me and you'll have to break contact to reach the light after."

He got the light then turned back around toward me and cradled my face in his hand.

Moment of truth time.

Instead of ducking his gaze, I forced myself to watch him while I pulled the shirt off. He kissed me without looking down. He cupped my right breast, which dropped my head back. His lips trailed down my neck and lower. The man dragged his teeth against me, forcing a hiss from me, which made him chuckle.

Wicked man.

When his teeth closed around my nipple, the shadow of his head danced on the walls. I set a hand on his chest. "You have to stop."

His eyes flashed rebellion when he looked up at me. "Greer."

The open need in his voice sent a shudder down my spine. Every inch of me wanted to continue. Every inch except the two that could see and the one that remembered what that meant for me now. "Spence, I'm bright enough to make shadow animals on the walls. You have to stop before I can't tell you no anymore."

He heard the loophole. I know he did. It twisted his lips down. He swallowed. His nostrils flared. "I hate this, you know."

I was kind of with him. "One day, Spence. Can you wait one day?"

He set his chin on me. "I don't want to. I really don't."

"Neither do I, Spence. But—"

"We have shit to do. I know." He kissed the top of my breast without moving his chin. "If we can't fuck, we should probably get some sleep, then."

Big letdown. Even if I knew from the get-go that we wouldn't be having any.

The both of us wriggled down in the sheets. I rolled over to press my back against his chest. My eyes closed. I'd been right. This felt so much better without the shirts. If we could just get rid of the pants as well, it would be completely perfect.

"Hey, look at that?"

I twisted my head back toward Spencer. "What?"

"You *can* make shadow animals in the glow from your boobs." He had a massive shadow dog howling on the wall across the room.

I waved my hand between my chest and his hands. No change on the wall. I hadn't really expected one, since I was the light source. "*You* can make shadow animals." I could see through them, though. That was something.

Before he got more inventive, I grabbed a hold of his hand and set it on my chest. He didn't complain. I let my eyes close again.

"What are your thoughts on kids?"

I whipped my head back around toward him. "You're talking about kids now?"

He lifted a shoulder. "I'm too horny to sleep."

I had a similar situation, but that didn't mean I needed this conversation. "You could always go take care of yourself, somewhere I can't see or hear you, then come back to bed."

"I already did that in the shower, but..." He rocked his pelvis against mine.

As if I hadn't felt his erection pressed against me before. Being able to rebound that quickly wasn't as common in men as it was in women. I wished I could do something about it. Even without the time constraints, I couldn't go more than the one time. Damn. Perhaps we could think of other things to do with his resilience.

"Shit. Spence, you've gotta give me something else to think about."

He chuckled. "So, about you having kids."

That was more of a buzz kill than he knew. "I can't have children."

"Can't?"

"Can't," I confirmed, in no uncertain tone.

"Well, there's adoption or surrogacy. I bet you would be a good mother."

I was, for about an hour, but I didn't want to talk about that. I needed to steer this conversation very carefully. "Do you think you would be a good dad?"

"I couldn't be any worse than my father."

As I'd met his father, I could understand the sentiment, but Spencer didn't know bad parent like I knew bad parent. But, hey. At least thinking about my mother killed any kind of buzz I had. Despite the warmth and promise of Spencer at my back.

Odd thing to be grateful for.

Now I just needed the anger to subside enough for me to get a decent night's sleep.

My phone vibrated its message notification. Less than a minute later, it rang in the tune I'd downloaded specifically for Magus, the Carnival of Animals finale. Text followed by a call from Magus didn't bode well.

Spencer tightened his grip around me. "Let it go to voicemail."

"I can't ignore that ringtone."

"Magus?"

"You got it."

He released me. I scooped up my phone from the desk and answered it on my way to the bathroom. Rather than duck all the way into the room, I leaned my shoulder against the doorway. "Hello, Magus."

"Greer."

If I hadn't put the brakes on Spencer, this conversation would have felt a lot more awkward. "What's going on?"

"I wanted to call to ensure your safety."

"I am fine." We both knew he wouldn't call to check on me out of the goodness of his heart. "What happened now?"

"After your apartment building went down we've been trying, and failing, to predict where Gale Force might strike. We assumed he would use everything he knows of you to stalk you at your favorite haunts."

Made sense. "Except he doesn't know that much about me."

"Right. We figured that was why we hadn't heard much since the apartment. He planned to wait for you to come out into a public enough place for him to track you down."

That also made a lot of sense, but Gale Force hadn't spotted me and Magus had still placed the call. "Where was he seen?"

"He tried to kill Senator Marcus at a campaign event this evening."

Not what I expected. Probably nothing the Gold 4 expected either, or they would have sent someone to warn or protect him. Granted, I didn't know that they hadn't. "You said tried. So, he's still alive?"

"Critical condition at an undisclosed location, but he is expected to make a full recovery."

That was good. Conniving little shit that he was, he didn't deserve to die. As far as I knew.

I could have been wrong.

For a split second I wondered if Magus had called to tell me this because he knew who was in my bed.

If he knew, Kai probably would shortly thereafter. I'd have to tell him soon anyway. This didn't feel like a fling.

Even if Magus did know about Spencer and I, he would not have called to pass along the information. Knowing the culprit was a superhero probably needed to remain a secret.

"I hope he recovers," I told Magus and meant it.

"Men like him usually do. The reason I called, was two-fold. First, to let you know to be extra cautious. For Gale Force to lash out at the senator, he might be losing his grip on whatever level of sanity he had. You need to be careful."

I was, mostly. Other than the sexy criminal in my bed, I hadn't made too many questionable choices. Still, forewarned put me a few steps ahead. "The other reason?"

"We have reason to suspect that Gale Force was hiding the strength of his powers from the Gold Committee."

On the one hand, I could understand someone doing so. Since inclusion in the union system was mandatory for all men with superpowers, finding some way to stick it to the man could give a person a spot of pride. Something to get themselves out of bed in the morning. Make them feel normal. I certainly didn't give many people most of my secrets. Even those I cared about.

This much sharing of information rarely worked out too well for me. "How much power are we talking about, Magus?"

"That is unclear at this time."

Of course it was. Balls. "And you still won't give me his name to do some searches of my own?"

"It's against policy 303 dot 911 point 52 to tell you that."

He could have told me without rattling off the policy number. It stank of the kind of throwing hands up in the air that happened when the Nazis took power. Just following orders was not an excuse.

I didn't point out that giving me the information he already had probably violated other regulations. I was safe for the night and had more information than I did before. I said, "Thank you, Magus," because I knew yelling at him again would not win the kind of change I needed.

"If I find more I can give you, I will let you know."

Sure he would.

Okay, okay, he had. He'd just held back the one I could really use in that moment. I needed to calm myself down. Spencer and I would handle the thing tomorrow and move on from there.

"Good night, Magus." I said, but he'd already disconnected.

Perhaps the timing of the other text had been a coincidence, but I had to check. The number had no name my phone recognized. The phone number was unfamiliar too. 303-911-5211. Wait. I closed my eyes to run though the policy number Magus had thrown at me. Missing two numbers from this phone number.

That Magus. A sly devil. More than likely, his phone had quite a bit of tracking technology attached to it. Giving me that kind of information over the phone would have probably gotten him in big trouble. I didn't know what big trouble constituted in the superhero world, but sharing governmental secrets that could get people killed usually came with a hefty price tag, or pain and jail time.

I opened the text. It was short, like most communication with Magus. Just the name Michael d'Angelo and an admission that they could never verify the name. He'd come in as a runaway. I remembered seeing several Michael's in the book, but I didn't remember last names.

Google was a magical thing, so I started the search as I walked back to the bedroom. "Hey Spence, could you bring me that book with the calendar and names in it? It's on the desk."

Spencer didn't say anything, but the sheets shifted. It wasn't until I looked up at his dull expression that I realized my mistake. I lunged forward and slapped my hand on the center of his chest. "Gods, Spencer. I'm sorry. I'm so, so sorry. Magus called, and my mind was elsewhere. I didn't mean to."

He pulled my hand from his chest and kissed my knuckles. "Didn't mean to what?"

Spencer didn't remember. He couldn't. "I'm still topless and I ordered you around like I did the men earlier today, but I didn't mean to do it. I just wanted the book."

Spencer cupped my cheek in his hand. "Calm down, Darling. It was just a mistake."

"But I—"

"Shhh," He set a finger on my mouth, then kissed it to boot. "What did you need the book for?"

I stared at Spencer, trying to figure out what was wrong with him. I'd taken control over him and he didn't even bat an eye. Did he not get the magnitude? "Spencer."

"Darling, I would happily be a deer in your headlights any day." He grinned at me, but the intense eye contact spoke volumes.

The fool wasn't afraid of me or what I could do to him.

I couldn't believe it. And I didn't deserve it. Not from him. He didn't know me well enough to trust me this much, but there it was. Written all over his face.

"What did you want this for?" He wagged the book at me like he hadn't just blown my mind.

I shook my head and wrapped my arms around him.

He hugged me to him, but whispered into my ear, "Don't think you can distract me from finding out what you wanted with it."

I probably could, but we didn't have the time for that. Well, he did. I didn't. I answered him anyway. "Gale Force is on some kind of a rampage so Magus found a way to give me his name."

"Gale Force?" Spencer stiffened against me.

"Yeah, he's the one who's trying to kill me. Already tried couple times that I know about. So far." The most recent, non-lizard person who'd tried. I needed to get a ticketing system so people could wait their turn. "And, I'm sorry to be the one to tell you this, but he also attacked your father. They expect him to recover, but he's in critical condition."

Spencer had an odd mix of sadness and anger quivering on his face when I leaned back to look at him. He probably needed his privacy to deal with his feelings on the subject, but I would steal his complexities from him if I walked away. I did the best I could manage and rotated away from him. We remained in contact, but he could have a moment for his face to decide what kind of emotion needed to happen.

He tightened his arms around me once I'd spun halfway around, making me feel guilty. I didn't want him to think I'd planned to leave him.

I tipped my head against him and took the book from him in the same moment. He didn't fight either. "Do you remember seeing a Michael d'Angelo in the book?"

"Third page in after the calendar."

I flipped there, then past it a couple pages before coming back to it. "This says Michael Brooks."

He nodded against my head, almost a nuzzle. "Michael Brooks Marcus. Gale Force is my brother."

32 – THE CALM BEFORE

WE WERE TOO close for me to whip my head around at Spencer. Instead, I slow-motion twisted and rocked my head back far enough to look him in the eye. That anger-sadness battle bit at the corners of his mouth, while worry dragged his eyebrows down and in.

"I've gotta say, Spence. I don't care much about most of the men in your family."

He kissed my temple. "Neither do I, Darling. Neither do I. Come to bed."

Spencer didn't sound riled up any more. Blessing and curse as he duck-walked me to the bed.

"You should probably make sure your phone's close." I took one of his hands, so I could kneel on the bed. "Someone's probably going to call you soon about your father."

"I can miss the call tonight and rush out in the morning."

I turned to face him. "Spencer."

He pulled my forehead against his and shook his head gently. "Greer, I want to sleep with you before the world takes you away from me in the morning."

Gods. He meant it. And he was asking for something more intimate than sex. The peace of laying down next to another person who would stand by you in the morning.

So, I sat down on my heels and pulled him toward me. "Come here, Deer in My Headlights."

We shuffled a bit, finding the best position for our limbs beneath the covers. Curled around each other we talked and poked and tickled. He asked me ridiculous things and made fun of my answers. He told me about his past relationships, and how his side businesses had ruined them. He asked me about mine.

I didn't have much to tell. I didn't want to bring my first love into our safe, happy conversation.

He dosed off somewhere around the time the sky started to lighten. I forced myself to stay awake, to listen to the occasional soft rumbles that came out of him and to let the warmth of him sink into me. This felt too perfect for it to last too long. So, I took in as much of it as I could.

Morning looked good on his face even before his eyes opened and he hugged me tighter to him. "How long have you been watching me?" He smiled.

"Probably not as long as you watch me on any given day."

"I like looking at you."

He wasn't so bad himself. Whatever expression showed on my face pleased him. He kissed me long and slow.

Spencer's phone vibrated on the nightstand for the umpteenth time.

"You should probably get that."

He sighed and rolled away from me. I pulled the sheet and blanket up far enough to keep my shine off him. Just because he didn't seem to care about my hypnoboobs didn't mean I didn't. I also fought the urge to curl up against him as he moved to the side of the bed. He needed to focus now.

"Yes. This is he. Uh-huh. What? Okay. Yes. Yes. Send me the address and I'll be right there. Text is better for me. Okay. Bye." He rolled back over to me and swung an arm around me, though he didn't tangle our legs.

I got the picture. "Was that about your dad?"

He nodded. "Second and third degree burns over seventy percent of his body. A couple of broken bones. Dislocated joint or two. He started to regain consciousness at some point last night, but they've put him back under for his own safety and comfort."

That was terrible. I didn't like the man, but I wanted him publicly ridiculed. That sounded like someone with a vendetta. And for it to be his own son? Spencer's brother? I could imagine, because I'd been to a similar place, except I was the one in the hospital bed. "I am sorry." I couldn't think of another thing to say and I knew how ineffectual it was. I'd hated it so much when people had peddled me with that bullshit. Yet, here I was.

"Thank you."

He didn't sound like he choked out the words. I would have. I would have snarled my thank you and fought my way to the closest exit. Spencer, though, looked happy. How was that even possible? "Spencer, I..." had nothing.

He shook his head and kissed my forehead. "Last night was exactly what I needed."

"Really?" I turned him down, or postponed him, several times. And here he was thanking me.

"I'm not sure if you noticed, but my life doesn't leave room for a lot of down time."

I could relate. Lately, my down time consisted of being passed out for one reason or another. Last night had been good for me, too. Something I would have missed out on if we'd had sex.

Spencer stayed there another five minutes, just lying next to me with our sides touching. When he finally hopped out of bed, he scrambled his way through dressing. He'd probably given the person on the phone some sort of time frame. I watched him without leaving the bed, mostly sad that he was putting clothes on rather than the other way around.

Fully dressed, and smelling delicious, he finally crawled back toward me over the bed. "What are you planning for the rest of the day?"

"Probably a nap. Some handsome thing kept me up all night."

"Lucky thing." He kissed me. "Do you want to walk me out or would you rather stay in bed."

Staying in bed had its appeal, but I could do so when he was no longer the menu. "Can you help me find my shirt?"

He searched with me without a word. It had tangled itself in the bedsheet. He handed it over and waited for me to get up before moving. Since he waited on me, I didn't dawdle. Spencer's hand slipped under my top and warmed the small of my back.

At the front door, Spencer dropped chin to his chest and looked up at me from that vulnerable posture. I didn't believe it for a second. "What now?" I had nothing else to give him for the moment.

"Go ahead and get you some beauty sleep." He kissed me, "Not that you need it."

"Smooth talker." I turned him toward the door. "What time should I expect you here to pick me up?"

"Two."

That sounded fishy. "Two a.m., because that seems a little early for a party."

"This afternoon. It's planned to be finished by seven so the performers and staff have the time to reset their space for their upcoming performances."

"Oh." That made sense. I wanted to feel angry for the early call time—regular people wouldn't be able to easily take off work, but this performance wasn't for them.

Spencer kissed my temple. "See you then."

I stood in the doorway while he walked to his car. My hands wanted to reach out to him, as dramatic as that sounded. As soon as his car hit the grate at the end of the street, I closed the door. I would see him soon enough. No need to get all chick flick on the situation. I probably just needed some sleep.

His spice and musk clung to the sheets when I lay down in them. Already, the bed felt empty without him. I hated myself for feeling so lonely after one night.

At least I woke well rested and with plenty of time to get ready. After polishing off some more spaghetti, I started in on prep. Shower with the leg shave. Hair. Make-up without lipstick, for the moment. All of that and I just got to sliding on the bright red dress when the doorbell echoed through the house.

I grabbed my tiny purse already filled with phone, ID, and a bright red lipstick.

When I opened the front door, Spencer's mouth opened to say something, but he froze in place. His eyes darted all over me. I wanted to make fun of him, but I could relate. His tux hugged him in all the right places. Cream-colored shirt and tie that could have been made to match this dress.

"You look good, Greer."

"As do you."

He pulled me to him and kissed me hard like I wanted him to. I smiled when he pulled away. "I take it you like the dress?"

"I'd like to peel it off you."

Good. "Let's hurry up and get to du Luna, so we can come back and do that."

33 – ATTACK ME WITH YOUR LOVE

A HYBRID OF praying mantis and human greeted me as Spencer stopped the truck in front of the huge, blue and grey-striped tent. The tent spread from two tall points in its centerline, each topped with flags the shape of gibbous moons.

People dressed just as formally as the two of us streamed in the flaps held open on either side by Hercules-beetle body builders. The women were beautiful and off-putting in the same moment. Similar to the praying mantis woman.

The make-up alone probably took three hours, let alone the apparatuses moving around on the mantis' head. Some of the people walking in didn't take a moment to notice that show had already begun.

Senator Marcus' kind of people.

"Oh, Gods, Spence, I didn't even ask you how your father is." I turned from the circus to him.

"He's hooked up to tubes and wires. Most of his body is wrapped up like a mummy, skin grafts and ointments and dressings." He shook his head, profile a marble statue. "I don't want to talk about it anymore."

I nodded. "I'm here if and when you want to, though."

He pulled me to him, but held back from kissing me. "I know, Darling." Spencer stared at me from kissing distance, gaze stabbing through me.

Waves of heat rolled over my skin and down my spine.

He climbed out of the truck without another word. I used the time he took walking sedately around the car to paint my lips bright, cherry red.

When he opened my door, his eyes dropped to my lips and flicked back up. No words or smile. Just the intense focus that was his characteristic, letting me know that he noticed. He noticed and wanted me to feel it. He would let me know his reaction later. When he had the freedom to smear the color all over our faces.

Right then, he took my hand, and led me into the wonderland.

Someone crawled around on four stilts while their giant claws threatened every new comer. Inside the tent, a woman flew through the air, suspended from above. Another man rode a bicycle behind her, swinging a butterfly net of sparkle and gold.

Every direction I looked, the performers danced and leaped around us. Other than a few areas marked off with mosquito nets, there was no space between the performers and us. Thrilling and terrifying. I couldn't see how they could continue perform without incident in the growing crowd of people. Of course, with their talent, they knew their boundaries better than I knew mine.

Spencer let me drag him around the whole tent while I took it all in. We had a job here. We needed to be focused so we could protect Spencer's women from people who did not appreciate their way of living. Knowing didn't stop me from taking the few minutes of freedom to pretend this was a normal date.

"Spencer Marcus," some woman's voice cut into my focus on the ribbon dancers spinning above me. Time to go to work.

The woman who came up to us had impeccable make-up that did nothing to hide her middle-age status. She didn't need to. Women like her could live another thirty years and still make men quiver.

Women, too.

"Two events out in public in the same week with the same woman?" she smiled almost pleasantly. A little bit of frost gilded the edges of it, like she hunted for the moment to strike. "Is it possible Denver's most eligible bachelor is off the market?"

He was mighty quiet next to me. I sure as hell wouldn't answer for him. But I did want to know.

When I cast a glance at him out of the corner of my eye, I found him watching me again. Either considering what to answer or whether to. I couldn't tell. Not a twitch on his face betrayed his thoughts. His hand in mine didn't move. I didn't want to pressure him, but I lifted a shoulder and the eyebrow closest to him.

"You damned-well better be off the market," he said it with his face still.

I dipped my head not even trying to hide my smile. He squeezed my hand. There it was.

"My nieces will be just broken up to hear that. Not to mention the auction circuit." She wagged a finger at him. "You fetch quite the hefty price."

"Sounds like a pea under a princess kind of a problem." I didn't mutter it quietly enough. I didn't care.

Spencer kissed the back of my hand with a, "Now, now, Greer. Let me introduce you to Tricia Harwood. She put together this afternoon's event."

Which meant I probably needed to be nice to her. I reached my free hand out to shake hers. "Nice to meet you, Tricia."

"Same to you." She gave me a firm shake I could appreciate. "Is that 'Greer' like Pam Greer?"

That, I didn't like so much. "Like Greer Garson, actually."

"Hmm," she pressed her lips together.

Yep. She had no clue. Why did no one watch the classics anymore?

Spencer blinked like he got it. I'd ask him about it later.

"Yes, well," Tricia nodded to the both of us. "I believe the bartender just finished setting up, if you want to get there before the rush. Appetizers should be floating out now. Plenty of food, so eat lots. Do get around and mingle. And try not to rub it in Charley and Ashley's faces that you're seeing someone." She gestured in several directions as she talked, almost like a flight attendant pointing out the exits.

In the front, over the wings, and in the rear of the vehicle.

"I'll try, Trish."

She went in for the double kiss on Spencer, and me, and bustled off to talk to some other people she saw. "Busy lady."

Spencer nodded vaguely. "Would you like something to drink?"

A cocktail would hit the spot, but I needed to focus. "Probably a ginger ale or something."

"I'm going to get you drunk, one day." Spencer said it conversationally as he started us toward the bar.

"Ditto, Spence, but I need you sober and ready today."

He glanced at me from the corner of his left eye. "Tonight, as well." His voice dropped a couple notes when he did.

Wicked man.

I wagged my finger in his face. "You stop that right now. I have a hard-enough time focusing when you don't say a word."

He bit at my finger. Almost caught it too.

He'd pay for that later.

A tiny body ran into Spencer's other side, followed shortly by a slightly larger one. Both clung around his legs so he could only stop or trip over them. "Uncle Spencie!" rang out in near perfect unison.

I let him go so he could bend over the two and properly hug-shake them.

It loosened their arms enough that he could squat in front of them. He narrowed his eyes, though amusement danced in the honey-brown. "What did I tell you girls about sneak attacks, huh?"

The two looked at each other like they knew they were in big trouble.

He didn't let them answer. Just started tickling both at the same time. They giggled and fought, but didn't run away. Instead, they worked as a team, attacking his unprotected side while he focused on the other girl. Back and forth. The three of them laughing and taunting each other.

Fucking adorable.

The two regrouped and attacked at the same time again. He tipped over in controlled slow motion. Foe down, they pounced. Yelling in victory, until he wrapped an arm around each of them and rolled to standing.

They kicked their patent leather shoes, but he had their arms pinned. I set my palms against my thighs, fighting the urge to attack him from the back. If I knew the girls at all or whose they were, I might have gone in for it. The two had called him Uncle. The couple standing close by watching and smiling like me had to be the parents, but Spencer had only the one brother. As far as he'd told me.

"Sarah," Spencer said, breathing hard. "I don't know what I'm going to do when the other two are this big."

"Lose." I offered.

The parents laughed.

He cut me a wry look, before looking back at his two captors. "Can I set you down now?"

"Yeees." They managed to speak that word in perfect unison.

"Are you going to be good when I do?"

"Nooo." That one too.

At least they were honest. Spencer shrugged as if he were powerless to them and set the two on their feet. They started in a figure-8 around us.

Spencer stepped toward the girls' parents and the girls switched from 8s to circles in the opposite direction with hand slapping each time they passed the other. With all the ruckus and music going on under the tent, they didn't add much noise.

"How are you doing, Sarah?" Spencer hugged the mother.

I watched the other man, but he didn't seem to have a problem with this. He'd dropped his gaze and was watching his girls circle like sharks. Sarah had to be Spencer's sister, then, because I doubted the Indian man was related to him. Perhaps by adoption, but I felt like he would have mentioned this.

"First trimester was worse this time." She set her hands on her bump. "But I can eat solid foods again, so things are looking up."

"That's good. And Hari, always nice to see you." The two did the men handshake-hug thing.

"Indeed. And who is this?" Hari nodded to me.

"This is my girlfriend, Greer." The man practically beamed incandescent introducing me.

My face hurt enough that my smile probably matched his.

Both Sarah's and Hari's eyes shot open and they pulled their necks back. Hari's mouth dropped half open. The two girls stopped dead in their tracks and glared demon-fire anger at me.

"Nuh-uh." The taller girl said with more attitude and anger than her little frame should have been able to hold. She would be a force to be reckoned with when she grew into that personality. "He's *my* boyfriend."

"No, Charley. I'm the oldest. He's *my* boyfriend."

"But I'm taller, Ashley. He needs a tall girl."

I refrained from mentioning that I was tall. Taller than most women, but just the right height for Spencer. No kind of reason would calm their fight down. I couldn't get angry with them. They had good taste. I'd certainly fight someone for—my brain clicked. Charley and Ashley. Got it.

My two rivals were certainly cuter than I expected. Diffusing this would take a little ingenuity.

I squatted down into the tackle and tickle zone. "How about for today, he's Charley's boyfriend and I'm Ashley's girlfriend? Then, next time we'll switch. Does that work?"

They narrowed their eyes and looked at each other, faces twitching while they spoke their secret language. When they turned back to me, Ashley penned me with a fiery glare. "Only if we get to ride on your shoulders."

"Ashley," Sarah chided.

I looked up at Spencer, who, from the grin on his face, was enjoying the hell out of this. "You game?"

He dipped his chin.

"All right, girlfriend." I set one knee on the ground for stability as I offered Ashley my back. "Hop on."

"You don't have to do that." Sarah's embarrassment flowered thick in her voice.

I ignored her while I helped Ashley find the least wobbly position. When we found our balance, I asked, "Are you ready?"

Her nod vibrated all the way through her grip around my neck and forehead. I stood as smooth as I could manage.

"Whoa!" she whispered when she made it to the top.

Sarah had covered her face. Her head shook too. Hari watched Spencer and I become vehicles for their little ones with an odd expression on his face.

I didn't know him well enough to ask.

"We were going to get something to drink, if you wanted to join us?" Spencer spoke like this situation with the girls was normal.

Perhaps it was. Being tackled hadn't surprised him. What an odd contrast of man, he was.

He led the charge, with Hari not too far behind. I set a hand lightly between Sarah's shoulders, giving her a moment to protest. She only walked where I guided, which seemed consent enough. "I can't believe she talked you into that."

"It's the height, Sarah. All kids want to know how it feels to be tall. I've got that in spades." I shrugged carefully. "My niece is the same, but she climbs up without asking, sometimes."

Mentioning my own mountain climber relaxed the muscles under my hand. I couldn't understand why she thought I would take offense after I agreed to Ashley's terms without protest. I hadn't even tried to negotiate.

Sarah relaxed in just enough time for me to soak up all her tension and add to it. Because my luck always seemed to bob in the sewers.

Kai stood behind the bar, waiting for us to come order.

This was not the way I wanted to talk to Kai about us, or rather the lack of us. Why was he even here in this place that I happened to be? Were there no other bartenders in Denver? Could they not have bussed some in from Vegas? What the hell, Murphy?

34 – WHEN THE FUNK HITS THE FAN

THE LEAD IN my chest weighed more than the girl on my shoulders. There was no escape.

"Hey, Greer. The usual?" Kai managed to say it with a smile that reached his eyes.

How did he do that? "Cranberry and ginger ale is all for me today. Can't drink and be a ride."

He nodded and got to making the drinks in the pop-up bar.

I didn't need to know, but I wanted to know, so I had to adult up and ask. "What are you doing here?" See? I could be a grown-up with the best of them.

"With all the things, M thought it best to spread the love a little." He set my drink down like this was any other day. "If he'd known you planned to be here, he would have sent more back-up."

I took a sip. "Rude."

"Things follow you, Greer, like bugs and fire."

"That's why I called you rude and not a liar." Were we okay? Perhaps he hadn't seen Spencer and I together. The kids had thrown the dynamic between us a bit. Which meant I still had a chance to talk to him in a private place with the right words.

"Oh, we're name calling, are we?"

That sounded a little different. Almost biting. He knew. He'd seen. He just wouldn't air the laundry right now. I nodded to him, acknowledging the awkward space, then turned to find something less painful.

Like a red-hot poker to jab in my eye.

Instead, I nearly ran Tanaka over. She recovered with grace I wished I had and smiled to boot. The man next to her didn't seem so keen on what happened, but I doubted much pleased him beyond waxing his handlebar mustache.

"Pardon me, Greer," Tanaka said. "I didn't mean to surprise you, but I wanted to tell you how lovely the dress looks on you."

"It really does." Spencer came to stand at my right shoulder. The girls' parents followed, closing the circle of people.

Spencer continued with a nod to Tanaka. "And may I ask, who this is?"

We were playing that game. Except it wasn't a game. He needed to not be attached to the women he employed or his house of cards could collapse. In this, at least, I had some recent practice.

"Spencer, this is the woman who made this dress, Tanaka."

He blinked his surprise, then bowed without unseating Charley. "Then I am deeply in your debt."

Gods. Even playing the game he found a way to make blood rush to places. I needed a distraction and I just so happened to have a monkey on my back. "And this is Ashley, my new girlfriend."

I squatted so she could shake hands of the two new people. Before the crazy, cross-hand rounds of introductions could get underway, Spencer stepped in front of me. His controlled expression stopped me from chiding his rudeness.

He leaned his mouth next to my ear. "My brother's here."

"Shit, where?"

"Oooo, you shouldn't say that." Ashley wagged her finger a couple of inches from my eye. "That's a bad word."

I darted my glance all around me, trying not to move too much and draw attention. "It's not a bad word, Ashley. It is an adult word that is fine when used outside school, not in front of grandparents or parents, and only when it is absolutely correct. Spencer, where?"

"Behind me, dressed in a tux. Not the…um…other suit."

The other being his superhero costume, I guessed. "How close?"

"Just coming into the tent."

The other side of the tent was more than half the tent away. I had to ask, "Are you sure?"

"He is my brother."

Right. "Okay. I need to talk to my friend, and you need to usher."

"Greer?" Tanaka asked. Her earlier smoothness had ruffled a bit.

She needed to know what was going on. So did everyone else. But not in such a way that it put people in danger. Thin wire to walk. Tanaka, though. She'd already dealt with more shit this week than most.

Here went nothing. "Tanaka, now would be a good time to leave. I can't tell you more than that. If you can take people, do, but don't cause a panic. Okay?"

Tanaka swallowed, blinked, and nodded.

Next thing was next.

Gods, I needed to take my own advice. Don't panic, maybe grab a towel, and focus.

I turned to the girls' mother. She'd already narrowed her eyes at me. I shook my head before she started. "You should probably follow them to the nearest exit."

Hari asked. "Why us?"

"Because Spencer likes you and Ashley's my main squeeze." I reached up with both hands to take hold of Ashley before I kneeled.

She let out a disappointed, "Aww," which her sister echoed. Neither argued, though.

I understood. I'd make it up to them when I could. "Okay, Spencer. I need you to make sure they get out."

That earned me the anger glare from Spencer. He barely kept it at half-mast. Despite everything else, he had his public face on lock. Impressive.

"Seriously, Spence. Go with them."

Grumbly eyes narrowed at me, he waved the family away. Maddening. Sarah and Hari hustled their girls away while Spencer planted himself in front of me. "Are you trying to get me out of the way before the shit falls down?"

"Yes. I need to keep you safe."

"What about you? Who keeps you safe, Greer."

Most of the people who should have protected me, betrayed me. My heart didn't want Spencer to be one of those people, but I didn't know. How could I ever know? "I do."

"Not good enough. Come with me." Spencer slipped his arm around me and tried to usher us toward the door.

Tried.

Because I couldn't leave. Not until the whole tent had been evacuated. I had no idea how to do that without tipping off Gale Force and letting him escape again, or worse.

I started toward the bar, only to have both of Spencer's arms wrap around me.

"Damn it, Spence, if you pick me up, neither of us will like what happens."

He did not. Frustration reigned his expression. "But we need to go."

"I need to get to the bar and confer with someone. Someone who knows the people who handle this kind of thing."

Understanding dawned and Spencer loosened his grip on me. Didn't let me completely go. When I took a step that direction, he matched it. "Spencer."

"My brother doesn't like you and you'd be hard to miss even if you weren't wearing that dress. I'll cover you."

He had a point. Bright red did stick out.

I sighed. We moved in smooth motion. Trusting him to keep the lookout, I slid behind the man Kai waited on. The man in a very fine suit nearly barreled into me when he whipped around. He looked up and our eyes met. His round pupils snapped to unhappy-lizard slits.

Just what I needed.

"It was Aldin Davis, wasn't it?" I offered my hand again, because why not? He couldn't order anyone to kill me here. Probably.

"Greer Ianto, what did you do to—"

"Oooo, not the place, buddy, and really not the time."

His jaw did a weird thing that solid jaws didn't do. "You will tell me what you did with my man."

Would I? Maybe to keep him off my back. "We'll have words at a later date about everything, but right now you should leave and take some people with you."

"You cannot force me to leave."

"It's not a threat; it's a warning." No time. "Whatever. Die mad about it."

I hip-checked him out of the way, nearly knocking myself over in the process. Spencer steadied me and set himself between us, which meant I could focus on Kai.

A frown flickered on Kai's face before he covered it with an almost blank smile. The almost, cut into my squishy parts. Gods, but now was not the time.

"What do you want?" Not quite as courteous as the last time.

We both needed me to overlook the aggression. "G.F. is here."

The tension in Kai's face shifted to his shoulders. Mixed blessing that we had something larger than us to deal with.

"You saw him?"

I pinched my lips. "Spencer did. He's his brother."

"Of course, they're brothers."

As I'd reacted the same way, I waited for Kai to tell me our next move.

"Keep him in your sights. I'll make the phone call."

I also could have called. It might have saved us some discomfort.

Alas.

Kai came back with a face I did not like. Something not great had happened. "What? What's that face?"

He paused long enough to open two beers for the man getting angry to my left. "There are other concerns, but he's sending people."

"Other concerns?" What the fuck other concerns could be more important than finally spotting the man, the superhero, who'd killed multiple people and tried to kill a state senator. If we played this right, we could catch him before he tried anything else.

Kai's hands few mindlessly, pulling glasses and mixing drinks with most of his focus on me. He had skilled hands, that was for certain. "The finishing touch on the top of Mike's specialty shot."

Code speak in front of the lay people. I got it, though. Fire. "Lots of topper?"

"Enough with the weather."

"What about the weather?"

Kai gave me a significant blink, blew at me, then spun a finger in the air before setting back in to his drink mixing.

Blowing and twirling. Tornados. Shit. "This isn't the season."

"It isn't," he confirmed.

Of all the rotten fucking luck. It *had* been warm. Warm enough to breed violent storms when the moisture came in, apparently. "Sirens?"

"Disabled."

That couldn't be luck. They tested tornado sirens in Colorado like the sun wouldn't rise without them. "Both G.F.?"

"Locations?" Kai shrugged. "Power?" He shrugged again.

All things considered, I knew what I'd bet on. Not that it mattered. Tornados and a tent, even a well-constructed one, meant more danger than I'd bargained for.

I gave him a questioning expression and said, "Nearby," without raising my pitch at the end. If people listening in didn't know I asked a question, perhaps it would keep them from freaking out that something wicked came this way.

Kai shook his head. "Not yet. He'll text." He tipped his chin toward my chest.

I usually tucked the phone there, so I would feel it when it rang. I'd opted for the tiny purse today, but I reached inside as I ushered Spencer away.

"Between the noise and the code, I only caught half of that." His face pinched in concern.

My purse lost the fight to keep the phone inside it. I grabbed Spencer's hand and set it on my cheek. He frowned more when I stepped in closer to him. I didn't want to talk loud but I also needed him to shield me from any passersby as I tucked the phone in securely.

"Not that I don't appreciate the view from up close." The amused curve on his lips left his eyes bare.

"There are fires, not sure how many, but the danger is being multiplied by the weather. Tornados. Sirens have been disabled so no one will know to take cover when one comes. How does a person even figure out how to disable them or where they are? Is there a central—"

Spencer took hold of the sides of my face. "Greer. Calm. Focus."

Right. "We've gotta get people out of here. I don't want to start a panic, but—"

A woman screamed behind me.

Woman and not two girls with it. Greedy as it was, I hoped Sarah and her family made it out already. Because I'd met them, they were more important to me than the others. I knew faces and names.

My heart twisted when I turned around and saw the ribbon dancer fly across the tent. She clung tight to the ribbon she'd performed on until it snapped her off like a whip.

Something I couldn't see smacked her down. No graceful parabola of flight. A force straight down from where the ribbon had abandoned her. Paper and smaller debris blew out from the place she hit in a powerful wave that smacked against my shins.

Screams. People running away. Some people running to help the woman and getting knocked down. The people running out the door flew up and back toward the center of the floor with the performer. The men seemed to land a little lighter than the women. I saw one or two of the men stand afterward. Not so much with the women, though I did catch some movement.

Spencer and I shuffled toward the bar and ducked down against the temporary wall. Though the wind at this level rose, the false security of the wall settled me a bit. Even if it didn't hide us from view. Too many people ran in frenetic horror.

We'd run out of whatever time Gale Force's sanity allowed. Not that I knew he had slipped into clinical insanity, but he had to be off his rocker to attack people. People not hurting anyone. And now he wouldn't let anyone out through the doors he could see. There had to be another way out of the tent.

"Do you have a knife or something?" I asked Spencer as I dialed the Gold 4 hotline.

He shook his head, pulling his right pant leg up. A gun smaller than I would have taken him for, came out of a holster. "I have this."

"How is that supposed to help?"

"Only one way to stop Michael."

His calm expression as he checked over the gun over. The unhurried, steady movements of his hands. No hesitation or anger in him. He'd really kill his brother. Someone else might have questioned how he'd come to that point.

There were always reasons.

"But that doesn't solve my problem." I needed a way to get people out. Storming the master of storms sounded like a bad idea.

"Greer," Magus picked up, though I could barely hear him.

"When is someone coming?"

"As soon as we can figure out what's going on. All the lights in the city are frozen on green. It's a mess."

A mess? Some cars on the streets with the drivers getting angry was a mess?

We didn't have time for traffic. "Your boy is swinging people into the air and slamming them down. There are injuries. If people haven't died yet, they will."

"Understood."

He hung up. He hung up on me after I told him people could be dying. Either that meant I'd pissed him off or he had too many other catastrophes to deal with. Whichever it was didn't matter. We had our work cut out for us.

I scanned the room in the hopes of finding a new way out from this angle. "This is a nightmare. We have to get people out of here."

"There's probably a service entrance Michael doesn't know about." Spencer wrapped the fingers of his empty hand around my wrist. "We can probably make it before he realizes."

"Good idea."

He pulled me and I duck-walked around the bar behind him. He checked to see if Gale Force was looking our way. Spencer invited me with crooked fingers and pointed toward the swaths of fabric draping down from the sloping ceiling. I guessed the superhero was focused elsewhere. Elsewhere like killing or maiming everyone in sight.

I darted for the flap of fabric, through more overlapping, plastic tarp, and into a hallway. The light gleaming in the seams at the end of the hallway smelled of sunshine and freedom. Good. We had a way out. I turned around to head back in.

Spencer's hand held me back. "What are you doing?" His eyes danced when he asked me. Not quite panic, but anxiety I hadn't seen in him before.

What did he mean, what was I doing? "We've got to let the other people know how to get out."

"Greer, with the Hargroves and Tanaka gone, I don't give a shit about anyone here but you." He leaned his face close to mine, so I could read the truth of it in burning his honey-brown gaze.

I pushed my lips against his, swinging my hand around the back of his head to tilt him the best angle. A woman in a bright yellow spider costume nearly bowled us over. She didn't apologize as she ran toward the light of freedom.

Spencer took a step to follow her. I grabbed his shoulder. He looked back. Fear-fueled anger ran rampant in his posture. "What?"

"I'm not going anywhere until all of those people inside are safe or there is no possible way for me to save them, so you can either come with me and help or get the fuck out my way."

He scowled at me, fathomless fury. The look could start a fire if he wasn't careful with it. But it wouldn't change my mind. I reached my hand into the space between us. He took my hand without the scowl lessening any.

35 – HIGH STAKES

THE MAN WOULD not leave my side even when I told him to go help someone out. Maddening, but he didn't fight me about leaving any more.

We snagged people running by and pointed them in the right direction. The people with big injuries, we guided out or set up with lesser injured people to help each other. Gale Force knocked down more people running for the door than Spencer and I sent out the back.

People who thought they might make it past him unscathed.

Gale Force hovered above it all, slightly manic smile on his face. The shape of it reminded me of Spencer's, if a little soft. And creepy. His eyes preened over the sea of moaning and still shapes collecting beneath him.

We didn't have a chance to save everyone on our own. Too many.

A figure moved on the other side of him, with teeth-grinding caution. I recognized that butt and long braid anywhere. Kai. Kai climbing up one of the two main masts of the tent. The trapeze platform brought him closer to the floating man.

We'd saved all the mobile people on this side of the tent. The rest had piled up well within Gale Force's line of sight. We'd have to risk being seen to get them out.

Light flashed in a line. Bolt knocked into Gale Force and the two fell to the ground, shaking with thunder. Reinforcements. About damned time. I stood from my crouch to check the damages and see how I could help.

Too soon.

A blast of wind knocked me ass over tea kettle. I must have hit hard. It looked like the world had brightened under the tent.

Pushing to my hands and knees showed me my error.

The tent was gone. Ripped away by the blast that had send me on a magic carpet ride. One of the main masts had snapped in two, while the other, the one Kai had been on, remained whole and leaned more than the bell tower in Pisa. I didn't see Kai. Didn't see Bolt, but thunder rumbled somewhere close enough that I figured he would be back.

Some of the people who had been pinned down by the lack of exits scurried away like spiders leaving the egg. Good. More people would be safe. If they made it to sufficient shelter.

Spencer lay on his back next to me, eyes opened and focused on me. Mouth pressed into a thin angry line. He could have been angry with me because we hadn't left when he said, which was fine. As long as he was alive to be angry.

"I'm going to have to kill him, aren't I?" His question sounded more rhetorical than anything.

He tried to tighten his fingers around the gun still in his hand. The odd bend in the middle of his forearm made him hiss. He hadn't noticed it. Neither had I. Now that I had, it pissed me off.

I took the gun from Spencer's limp hand. He tried to sit up, but I pushed him back down. "Stay."

If he hadn't been in pain, the fire in his eyes would already have bolstered him to standing. "Greer, I will not. Not if you're going."

"Only one of us will be able to easily avoid jail time for this, even given the circumstances. When I get his attention, leave." I planted a quick kiss on him but darted away before he could grab me with his good hand.

Gale Force's eyes homed in on me as soon as I stood up.

Note to self: Bright cherry-fucking-red not the color to wear when trying to sneak up on bad guys.

No matter.

I wasn't in a sneaking kind of mood.

An ugly kind of grin lit up his face, like Christmas had come early and I was the wrapping paper to rip into. "Dressed up like a whore of Satan."

I lifted the gun and got one shot off before a squall scooped me up from the ground. A few more as I crested the height of the parking lot lamp posts.

His shoulder jerked back and the air lifting me stopped.

I pin-wheeled, trying to remember anything about how to break a fall without breaking everything in me.

My feet hit first and I let my knees bend, my hips. Everything limp except my hand around the gun. I tried to roll when the bulk of me hit; it didn't work like it did in the movies. I rolled, a bit. But my body still hit the ground after falling twenty or so feet. It still hurt.

Shit.

I should have gone for the boobs.

Why didn't I go for the boobs?

Breathing hurt in several places I didn't want to think about. I had no time to think about anything. His shoulder had gone back, but it didn't look like he had gone down.

Pushing toward my knees hurt. This would take a while. Too long. I flipped over to my back without letting the pain stop me and reached up to the stretchy piece of fabric Tanaka had attached to the front of the dress.

Something glopped on top of me. I covered my mouth and nose before the stuff drowned me, but it was only one splash of cold, thick goop. It smelled like the underside of a kitchen sink with all the cleaning supplies open. With all the strong chemical funk, the goop should have burned. Perhaps it would once my skin warmed it.

I pushed to sitting to keep it from oozing any further up toward my face and put my nose over the fumes. My eyes watered. Nose did too. The black goo oozed down toward my waist, soaking into the dress as it went.

Swiping at it and won me a handful of sticky goop without removing much from my chest. The dress stuck to me uncomfortably. When I peeled the added panel back, my skin was covered in black.

The one thing I had going for me, and it was out of commission.

Oedipus Rex and my goop covered pecs.

Gale Force grinned at me from across the way, "Not this time, SparkleTits."

I aimed the gun at him again and shot. Nothing. I shot nothing. The goo jammed up the gun too. Worthless piece of crap, though not entirely worthless. A stream of red dribbled down Gale Force's shirt from his right shoulder.

Too bad I'd not hit the left, but a little lower and further in. Then I wouldn't need the gun anymore.

I tossed the gun at him, for all the good it would do. He flicked his fingers and blew the thing down and away.

When he flicked his whole wrist, I went airborne again. Not as high, this time and not straight up. I sailed in a pretty arc over him and into a pile of broken wood and a few of the sapling trees that had been in the medians of the parking lot. The landing would have been a lot nicer if the wind hadn't slammed me into the bottom third of the broken metal mast.

I heaved in air against the pains in my back and chest. Breathing shouldn't take this much effort.

Another couple of trees piled on top of me, pinning me in place. Not that they needed to be there. I couldn't breathe enough to move.

Several buckets of the black goo blew in from somewhere and spewed all over the wood pile pinning me.

My lungs burned. I struggled to move.

"Keep struggling, Satan's Whore," he said as he came to stand in front of the funeral pyre he'd made of me. "You will burn this time. Burn like the witches burned before you."

I needed to stall him until help arrived. "Dude, you are seriously whacked. There's no such thing as real witches with magic and the pagans who call themselves witches don't believe in the existence of Satan."

"Keep talking, Whore."

"You say whore like that's a bad thing." I wriggled my feet around, trying to find purchase on one of the pieces of wood. If I could climb out of this before he lit me up, I might be able to tackle him and hold him down. "Maybe if you found a woman or man who would accept your bullshit attitude in exchange for your money, you might be a little more sensible."

He pulled a long skinny box out of his back pocket with the utmost in delight on his face. When he pushed his finger into one of the small sides, the other end popped out an inch or so. Black-tipped matches. The fancy long kind I'd only seen in movies where people cut them to different lengths to pick partners. Miss Scarlet with Colonel Mustard.

This box looked like he'd used quite a few. The five remaining after he took this one out would be more than enough to light my fire. "Keep talking, Whore of Lucifer. It will not save you from your punishment."

He really needed a new name to call me. "Punishment. For what? You're the one killing innocent people because—"

"No one I've executed is innocent. Their sins are an abomination to God."

Oh, here we went with this bullshit again. He sounded as bad as the adulterous, grabby-hands preacher. "Hey. Pot. Kettle. Black. You killed people in an apartment building, including a girl less than five-years-old, trying to kill me. Pretty sure killing is numero uno bad on the lists of sinning."

"That's just like a witch." He struck the match and tilted it so the wood caught fire and not just the phosphorous head. His eyes watched the flame while his voice sank down into intimate volumes. I expected him to regale me with how much of a pleasure it was to burn. Instead, he said, "The edict against worshipping a god other than Him is the first commandment. The sixth commandment prohibits murder. Witches are not human."

He dropped the match. The black goo lit up in whoosh, climbing up the frosted branches toward me. I covered my face as best I could with my arm.

The fire splashed up at me like warm bath water. I waited for my flesh to sear away and crackle.

Aaaaaand nothing. Just pleasant warmth. Huh. Perhaps the car exploding in my face thing should have prepared me for this.

My name rose above the loud crackling of the fire in my ears.

Gods damn Spencer. I told him to leave.

Pulling my arm from my face brought a wave of hot air up into my nostrils. The heat flooded in my lungs and stabbed into the places where it already hurt to breath. Apparently, while my skin was fire resistant, my insides were not. Good. Great.

I needed the fuck out of there.

My left foot stuck on several somethings when I tried to jerk it up. I set it back down where it had been and tried the other foot. It pulled free far enough for me to bend my knee half way, but a branch over the knee kept me from moving any more.

"Spencer" and "Babylon" in Gale's weasel voice rose over the popping fire.

Arms jerked angrily as Spencer yelled at his brother.

I took a breath to yell at him to shut the fuck up and get the fuck out of here.

The heat burned the inside of my chest.

The wood shifted under me. Pulled me down.

I spread my arms and legs akimbo, but it was my chest that stopped me. The loss of the foot and a half of height put my face at the same height of the flames. The heat increased. Burning the back of my throat.

Moving my feet didn't work. I gripped at the branches, but only got twigs crumbling in my hands. The lack of good air played havoc with my vision. I couldn't quite make out the branches with enough structural integrity for me to pull myself out. Not that climbing out would be easy. Pull-ups were not my strength.

When I got out of there, I would work out more, so I could handle all the heroics. I could start now, except that the world spun about my head more than healthy. And the edges of my vision had gone all magoo. The center had only gone half wonky. I could feel the center of my sight trying to slip away from me all together. I clung to it tighter than the branches held me.

The struggle to breathe, the struggle to keep from sinking, the struggle to retain my vision. They all took their toll.

Figures stepped out of the air, walked from person on the ground to person. They got more distinct as my head slipped more into the spinning zone. All of them tall, with frayed robes billowing in wind that didn't exist.

One of them, a woman with a spiked, blonde Mohawk, bent over a person. She reached both hands into the man's belly. Her hands sank down into him with no resistance or displacement in his skin. Muscles in her arms tensed and she pulled.

When she pulled, a watercolor mist in the shape of the body came out with her. She set the bodiless person on his feet and released the two fist-sized beans of light she'd used to pull him out.

The mist shivered, almost fearfully.

The woman set her hand against the center of the misted man's chest. He stilled. His colors brightened. Then, like the light dimming on a scrim, he faded away. The woman moved on to the next person.

The same thing happened several times. As the wandering people cleared in my vision, I recognized one in the distance. Auburn hair and green, glowing eyes set over broad shoulders. I helped him find his dog.

"Death."

My word came out barely louder than the sizzle of the fire on the branches. But he heard me. Heard and walked to me. Three normal-sized steps and he crossed twenty yards. It made as much sense as the wind that blew his hair back.

"Yes, Greer Ianto." He dipped his head to me in greeting.

"Am I going to die?" It took two breaths to speak the sentence.

His head tipped to the side like a bird. "Not if you don't want to. He will, though." He turned his head to the struggle between the two brothers.

I didn't ask him which brother he meant. If there was any chance that it could be Spencer, I couldn't allow it. And there was more than a chance.

Gale Force had Spencer up in the air. Floating him on a stream of air shooting out from is hands. The air buffeted him on is upper chest and face. And neck. Mostly on the neck. He was hanging him. Hanging him without a rope.

I would die before I let that happen.

36 – TUG OF WAR

FOR SPENCER, I pushed. Not just against the burning branches that held me. Through them. Somehow. It didn't matter how. Didn't matter that my skin had changed to a shifting, glimmering black sheath over me. Only two things mattered: I was free from the pyre and Gale Force stood in front of me choking Spencer.

Gale Force, who's watercolor mist was veined with a metallic glow. The mist quivered as the brassy glow vibrated. More cracks appeared, splitting the mist into smaller and smaller sections. Metal bisecting the mist of him. The metal veins shot out his skin and undulated in the air. The undulations directed the air, formed the fluid noose around Spencer's neck.

My eyes traced the branching of the brassy vines. His head glowed almost solid metal.

I reached my fingers into the nest. Hooked my fingers into the unkempt knot and pulled. I pulled back in one smooth motion, not allowing for the possibility of their resisting.

And they didn't. Spencer sank to the ground, limp, as the pressure of air holding him decreased.

Gale Force shook his hands. He yelled and tightened his hands into claws. The veins of brass stopped coming easily at my pull. I stepped back and yanked with my weight shift. He tipped toward me, but not far enough to fall. His hands balled into fists and he leaned, straining against my grip. But he could not move me. I had slow burning anger fueling me and superior body weight grounding me.

He turned away from Spencer to see what he was fighting against. I smiled at his shock.

"Demon?"

He should be so lucky.

"No, Michael, but I am here to punish you for your sins."

In the breath between his confused shock and his recognizing my voice, I yanked. I yanked back and out, whipping my hands out into a "Y" a cheerleader would be proud of.

The veins snapped. Light traced the breaking points, burning up the lines of brass in both directions, like fire consuming lines of gun powder.

Gale Force tipped forward as the light burned through his head and arms. Through the tips of his fingers and toes. When the lights converged in my hands they exploded in blue and purple fireworks. The force knocked me to my knees, hard, but I climbed back to vertical. Couldn't be down and vulnerable near him.

He'd dropped to the ground, half on his side, eyes half-lidded. He looked out of it. I kicked him in the balls to be sure. No reaction. He was either out of it, or dead.

Either way worked.

Still, I stepped around him in a wide enough circle that he could not reach out and grab me. Just in case. Walked all the way around him to Spencer. There, I let my knees kiss the pavement again.

I set my hand on his chest. It moved. He breathed. Deep enough for me to feel it. A good sign. I had to be certain, though. Leaning forward hurt in too many places around my midsection. My head swam, but I managed to get my hand on his forehead and my face somewhere in line of sight.

"Spencer, Deer in my Headlights. Please wake up for me, Deer. Please."

His eyes fluttered and half opened. "Darling?"

I ignored the stabbing in my torso and dropped low enough to kiss his lips. He kissed back. Weakly, but he kissed me back.

Thunder shook the ground near us.

"Good." I tried to straighten back to kneeling and the broken pieces of me rioted. Now that I knew Spencer was safe, I could admit serious things were wrong with me.

I moved to stretch out alongside him.

"Bolt is here." Setting my head on Spencer's chest made the things stabbing into my squishy parts worth it. "He can handle the rest."

Spencer curled his good arm around me. I hissed at the pain increase.

He eased up. "Darling, are you okay?"

"Tired."

"Don't go to sleep, Greer." He moved the hand to cradle my head and turn my face up toward him. "You know you can't do that. If you have a concussion, you need to stay awake."

If he could lecture me, he really was fine. I could relax with that knowledge. My eyes slipped closed.

Climbing the light and shadow stairs took more time than usual. I walked the whole way down the fog, taking time to appreciate the cool moist air as I passed through the tunnel. At least the mud had stayed moist. Rather than wish for it to be different, I stepped into the warm stickiness.

The mud squished between my toes, sucking me down to my ankles. I kept walking. Strolling, as much as I could with the mug sucking at my feet. It felt glorious. I bent down and picked up some. I squeezed it into a ball and tossed it from hand to hand. Until I couldn't take the burning itch biting at the inside of my elbow for as long as I could remember.

I moved to scratch and a band across my wrist stopped the movement. Metal clanked on metal. I opened my eyes to a drop ceiling and the very distinctive scent of disinfectant and sorrow.

Hospital smell.

37 – UN-PRIVATE PARTS

I PULLED AT my arm again and got nowhere. The second tug made me look down. Handcuffs. On both wrists. I.V. in my right elbow, the source of the burning itch that had woken me. Spencer in a chair next to my bed, with his chin in his palm and soft, rumbling snores rolling out of him.

It might have been the cool-white hospital lights, but he looked pale. More than a little scruff adorned his square jaw. The beard didn't hide the bruising all over his chin and neck. The bright red splint on his right hand stood in stark contrast to the dark jeans and black t-shirt.

He was beautiful.

Letting him sleep would have been the nice thing to do. But I needed to pee and some asshat had cuffed me to the bed.

I wormed my way down, sliding the cuff down the bed rail and up my arm until I could reach the top of his head. I grazed my fingers over his hair.

"Spencer."

He jerked his head sleepily, then resettled himself out of reach. Just a half inch out of reach, but it might as well have been a mile.

"Oedipus Rex, Spence. Wake up."

His head fell off his hand. The rest of him tipped forward, but he caught himself before pitching out of the chair completely. His honey-brown eyes lit on mine.

"Hi." I wiggled my fingers at him.

He hopped up out of the chair and snatched a hold of my hand with both of his. "You're alive."

Yeah. "Was I not at some point?" It seemed like I might remember dying. A visit from Death should have left another impression.

He gave me a short shake of his head. "You're awake."

Because he'd stated the obvious and I had a pressing issue, I didn't respond to that. Instead, I asked, "Can you get these things off me?" I rattled both cuffs against the rails.

"I don't have the keys."

That would have been too easy. "If you wouldn't mind, you could point a boob at the cuffs."

Spencer frowned. "Seriously?"

"They're very talented." I shrugged.

"What if I want you cuffed to the bed?" His eyes narrowed.

I couldn't tell if he was flirting or joking. My answer didn't change either way. "You can cuff me right back up, but I really need to pee first."

That got him moving. He folded down my blanket gently, like either it or I might break. His shimmying my hospital gown up didn't work until I sat up to help him. He kept the back of his fingers against me as the gown came over the crest of my chest.

I twisted to the right and pulled. The cuff came open. Turning to the left gave me the same result.

"That's..." Spencer pulled the gown back down. No extra touches or looks. He could have given me at least little extra something.

Perhaps when I came back from the bathroom, he would act a little more like himself. I swung my legs around to the right.

Spencer came around and offered a hand up. I didn't need the aid, but I took it.

"What about all the other things attached to you?"

I took hold of the I.V. pole. "If I take them off, it will bring a slew of people in here and I like the company I have right now." And I felt good. Maybe a little low in the blood sugar, but fantastic other than that.

"Your hands are covered in red mud again."

He was right again. I nodded.

"You don't want to tell me about what that's all about?"

I gave him a quick look out of the corner of my eye. "Still trying to figure that out. Though I kind of have some suspicions." Nothing that could be considered normal or sensible.

Like anything in my life was.

Spencer walked me the three steps to the threshold of the bathroom, then disengaged.

I scrubbed the mud from my hands and feet while I was in there. I needed to find a way to keep the mud from clinging to me. I never woke up soaked when I was younger. Something to focus on later. Now, was for spending time with Spencer and figuring out his weird mood.

If he hadn't jumped in to help me back to the bed, I would have worried more.

I sat down and eased the bed up to a comfortable angle to speak. Spencer reclaimed his chair to my right. My stomach rumbled. A small smile curled on his lips. The first I'd seen on him since waking up.

"I have the last half of a dinner I couldn't finish." He reached over to the table behind him and set down a familiar paper bag in my lap.

Even better. Some of the fattiest, greasiest food available. I looked up at Spencer. "My beautiful man."

That won me a full grin that almost made it up to his eyes.

I didn't even taste the food. My grateful stomach cried out in triumph, though. The meal wouldn't cover me for too long, but the edge of hunger calmed. Best I could do without inviting the world in.

"Okay. First thing's first." I set my hands on my belly. "How is your arm?"

Spencer's eyes widened. He leaned far enough forward on the chair to tip the back two legs off the ground. "God damn it, Greer. You've been in some kind of a coma no one understands for five days—five days, Greer, where your body shut down except your heart, lungs, and healing. All of that after my brother burned you at the stake, unsuccessfully, and you came at me with night-black skin. My brother woke up three days ago. Whatever you did to him, he has no power. None at all. He's not a superhero any more. He can't breathe without a ventilator but still curses your name with all the strength in him."

Shit. How was that even possible?

"And you." He practically clawed at the armrests of his chair. "You had six broken ribs. Six, with half of them perforating your lungs and things bleeding out in your gut, but they couldn't do surgery because of your skin, or anything else even mildly invasive, for risk of doing more damage. And the first thing you want to know when you wake up is how my arm is?" His breaths heaved when he finished talking. Either anger or frustration or something else.

"Well..." What could I say that wouldn't set him off again? "I didn't know any of the rest of that and I feel fantastic. So, thank you for the update. How are you?"

He dropped his head into his hand. "This woman is going to be the death of me."

I wanted to roll out of bed and hug him to me, but I didn't know. He hadn't touched me since he sat me back down on the bed. And I didn't want to force myself on him.

"I'm sorry. I'm sorry I made you stay when you wanted to go. I'm sorry you got hurt because of me. But this." I shook my hands at my chest, though he only caught the end of it, peering at me over top of his hand. "This is taking me in some directions I hadn't planned on. I don't want to drag you along and get you hurt again and again if you're not willing."

His eyes bore into mine. "What are you saying?"

"If this is too much for you, you should leave now before you break my heart farther down the line."

The back legs of the chair slammed on the floor as he stood. He didn't even stop to think about it before he started for the door. I covered my face and rolled my back to the door as if that would block out the reality of him leaving. I didn't want to watch him walk out of my life so abruptly. Without remorse.

Gods. I'd lied to him. Telling him that him leaving now wouldn't break my heart. The door closed behind him. It hurt more than the six ribs had.

A hand on my back and I whipped around.

Spencer stood over me, confusion drawing his eyebrows down. "What's wrong?"

"I thought you left."

He smiled and jerked his thumb behind him. "I closed the door."

Despite still feeling the echo of the slam in my chest, I leaned to the side to confirm. Yep. It was closed.

"Darling," he cradled the side of my face with his unsplinted hand. "Do you think anyone else could hold a candle to you?"

I pulled his head down to mine, kissing his forehead first before moving to his mouth. He leaned into me, deepening the kiss a moment before he pulled back with a hiss. I opened my mouth to ask, but he cradled his splint against his chest. He must have set his hand down.

"You need to be more careful, Deer. Here." I scooched to the other side of the bed and pulled the blankets back.

He took a long blink, his eyes shifting from first to fourth gear in the quick motion. "In the hospital?"

I hadn't meant—but the look on his face set my skin to simmer. "We've waited long enough."

"Won't you go back to sleep for a day?" Even asking the question, he folded his leg in a figure four and untied his shoes.

My breath hitched at each loop his belt cleared. All the while his eyes feasted on my face. Still, he stopped himself from climbing in next to me, his hand whiting from his death grip on the bed rail.

"No one else needs to know that I woke up. Come here, Deer."

That got him up over the rail and where he belonged. His weight pressed into me. The spicy musk of him flooded my nose and mouth. He let me strip his shirt from him. We couldn't get my gown completely off without disconnecting me from all the things on my right arm. We left the gown hanging just on my right sleeve.

"What the hell do you think you're doing? Get off her." The voice started at the door, but stomped over.

I wrapped my arms around Spencer before whoever it was tried pulling him from me. Spencer buried his face in the pillow next to mine. "God damn it."

I glared at Mike's masked face over Spencer's shoulder. "What the fuck, Phoenyx?"

He froze, eyes wide. "You're awake."

"And busy. What do you want?"

He held his hands up. "I thought he was—"

"He was." How fucking dare he come in here and tell me who I could and couldn't have sex with? It didn't matter if he was Kai's friend and he wanted to look out for his brother in arms. The decision was mine and mine alone.

"No, Greer." He shook a pointed finger at me. "I thought he was taking advantage of you because you were still unconscious. I wasn't about to let that happen."

"Oh." That calmed a lot of my anger, though it did nothing for my frustration.

"Yes. You could thank me."

"You could leave."

He gave me a mock glare. Mine was not so mocking.

"Alexander will be pleased you're better." He scrubbed at his face beneath the mask and forced a breath out. "And he can stop calling me for updates every hour."

What the hell? "When did Lex get Phoenyx's number?"

"When Phoenyx thought SparkleTits would want her friend to know she was okay." He crossed his arms. "Not everyone had the clout or connections to know where your room is, let alone force their way in."

I rocked my cheek against the side of Spencer's head. "What did you do?"

"My father's in the next room over." He didn't move his head out of my pillow to answer.

I hadn't thought about his father since I woke up. Hadn't thought about Lex either. Selfish of me. "Thank you, Phoenyx."

"You're welcome, SparkleTits."

Awkward pause. Awkward pause. Another tacked on for good measure. Like Phoenyx was waiting for me to fill the space. Perhaps he was. So, I took the opportunity. "Would you tell Lex that a crème brulee will hit the spot when I get out. It's the only way he'll believe you."

He nodded. "Will do."

"Thank you, again. Can you leave now?" Because I appreciated what he'd done for me, and all, but I had plans pressing up against me.

Phoenyx chuckled. "I'll go but you need to know some things while we have a private moment."

I'd been having a private moment. Now, it was a party, except one of us hadn't been invited and we all had on too many clothes on. "What is it?"

"The Gold Committee is aware of you. What you did—stealing Gale Force's power away—could not be kept quiet." He turned his palms up, empty and helpless. "As far as I know, they haven't shared it with the other union regions or the overseers. But you need to be careful. You're not flying under the radar anymore. People are watching you. And they're watching us because of you."

I bit my lip a moment while I assimilated everything he told me. "Am I supposed to apologize for the last?"

He stepped over toward my head and squatted down, bringing his eyes to my level. "Don't you ever fucking think that. You stopped Gale Force. Alone. Without thought or being forced to. Without being paid and without any of the safeguards the rest of us have. You saved lives. You saved Bolt and Kai."

"Kai's alive?"

"Yes. Him and all but seventeen people."

Seventeen was a lot. Too many. But much less than the number of people who had been under the tent. It would take me a while to accept the seventeen, though. "Can I get their names?"

"Officially, no."

Loopholes danced in his answer. I nodded my understanding, but didn't push him to elaborate. Not right then. I had another question. "Is the interest of the Gold Committee the reason I was cuffed to the bed."

He smiled the same way he had the first time he called me SparkleTits.

This would not be good.

"You were cuffed because you kept punching and scratching at all of the people who came in to help you."

"Oh." That wasn't as bad as I'd assumed.

"Punched and scratched everyone except this one right here." He pointed at the back of Spencer's head.

Until this point, Spencer had laid quiescent on top of me. Phoenyx calling Spencer out made him unbury his face and turn toward the masked man. Spencer's beard scrapped against my lips as he moved. If Phoenyx hadn't been so close, I would have done something about it. Would already have been doing something about it.

Gods, he smelled good.

"Spencer Marcus." The nearly-constant smile left Phoenyx's face when he spoke the name.

"Yes?"

"If you hurt her, I will burn you to ashes. Slowly. Inch by inch." Not a bit of humor in his voice.

Gods. This was worse than the protective dad at prom scenario. I needed out of this, quickly. I'd walked through the burning wood that had held me. I could probably find a way to sink through the bed and escape. I just needed to figure out what the hell I'd done and how.

Spencer handled it better than I might have. He reached his right hand out to Phoenyx, who raised an eyebrow and took it. Spencer shook and held on.

"With all due respect, Phoenyx. If I hurt her, you're the last of my worries."

"You've got that right." Phoenyx's smile returned. He took his hand back. "You might just make it."

Phoenyx might not. I could reach his throat from here. But he stood from his squat and headed for the door. He probably sensed my urge to kill rising. At the doorway, he turned back toward the two of us. Toward me, mostly.

"He knows this, Greer, but nurse checks at midnight, three, and six." He darted his eyes to the wall clock and back at me. "You've got about a half hour, but I could probably stall him for another fifteen."

Spencer's eyes cut to mine, then dropped to my lips.

Warmth flushed my face. "Phoenyx?"

"Yes, girl?" He drew the last word out, teasing me like I might rise to the bait.

Maybe another time. "Stall for thirty."

*Keep abreast of Greer's adventures
in the next SparkleTits Chronicle:*

CAKE
AND
DEATH

About the Author:

VERONICA R. CALISTO is the author of many books, some of which she is willing to let others read. When she isn't writing she is thinking about writing, aka: plugging away at her day jobs whose mundanities make her name plants things like Cleoplantra and force her mind squeak out words like mundanities. Most of the time she can be found in Colorado lavishing on a nest built of her books while she listens and sings (loudly) to music which may or may not be playing outside her own head.

If someone's singing while walking down the hall, it's probably her.

Please visit her at her website:

www.veronicarcalisto.com